BITTER WATERS

BY

NEIL THOMAS

Any similarity with anyone living or dead
is entirely coincidental

ISBN 978-0-9865914-2-6

In Memoriam

William Thomas, (-1915) RAMC, torpedoed aboard the SS Royal Edward, on his way to Gallipoli.

Charles Hinde, (-1916) Petty Officer, aboard HMS Warrior, Battle of Jutland.

"What is called 'foreknowledge' cannot be elicited from the spirits, nor from gods, nor by analogy with past events, nor from calculations. It must be obtained from men who know the enemy situation."

Sun Tzu
From *The Art of War*
Translated by Samuel B. Griffith
Oxford University Press, 1963

Military Ranks:

The Indonesian navy uses army ranks for positions from Sub-Lieutenant to Captain. The equivalent of Lieutenant-Commander is Mayor (pronounced my-or) deriving from the same latin root as Major, and not to be confused with the western use of the term in civil administration.

AUSTRALIA	INDONESIA	
Navy	Navy	Army equivalent
Admiral	Laksamana	Jenderal
Vice-Admiral	L. Madya	Letnan Jenderal
Rear-Admiral	L. Muda	Mayor Jenderal
Commodore	L. Pertama	Brigadir Jenderal
Captain	Kolonel	Kolonel
Commander	Letnan Kolonel	Letnan Kolonel
Lt-Commander	Mayor	Mayor
Sr-Lieutenant	Kapten	Kapten
Lieutenant	Letnan Satu	Letnan Satu
Sub-Lieutenant	Letnan Dua	Letnan Dua

In this story, the term ABRI is used to denote the Indonesian Armed Forces. Today, TNI is more accurate, as the Police has been separated from the other armed branches. ABRI is retained – and is still commonly used in Indonesia – for its phonetic qualities.

The then Minister for Science and Techology, Habibie, bought, on unilateral
whim, the whole of the East German Navy
when it was offered for sale

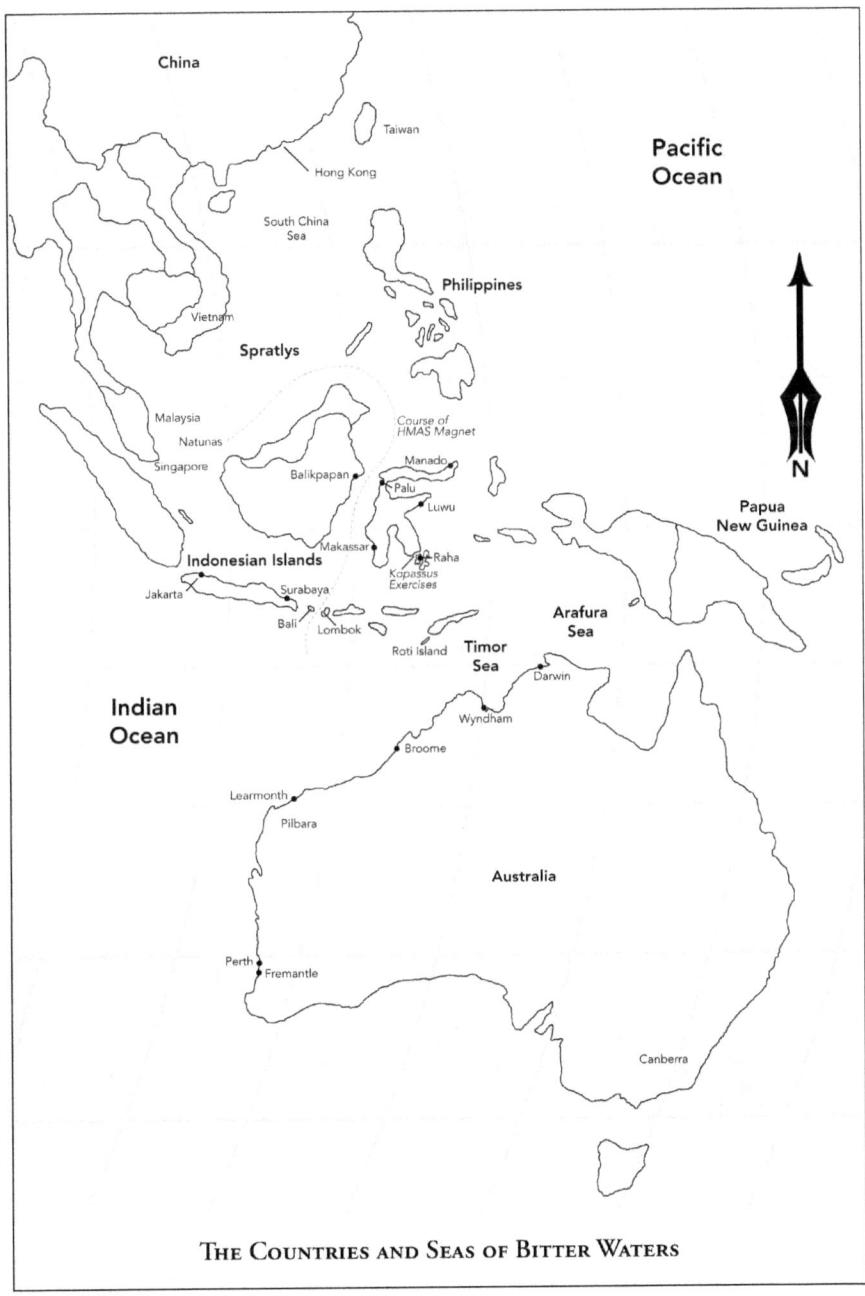

The Countries and Seas of Bitter Waters

Neil Thomas

Part I

EDDIES

Neil Thomas

One

Under the Javan sky the sun sat shortly beyond arm's length, an impossibly hot orb, relentless. As he turned, it sought and found that unprotected spot between his shoulder blades. Nevertheless, he shivered.

'Excited?' asked his wife.

He thought for a moment. 'Oh yes. All that water just went under the bridge again,' he said. 'Funny how you can squeeze years into seconds.'

She smiled, but said nothing. Like him she was looking up the slightly dishevelled pathway that led to a small house, similar to many that dotted the narrow, steep valley which was a seasonal kaleidoscope of rice in all its many stages of maturity, from emerald greens to burnished golds. Whitewashed walls supported the wide overhang of a terracotta roof. He knew perfectly well that, again, like him, she was thinking of the man within, and how he, both directly and indirectly, had had the most effect of anyone on their lives. A surprise telegram had brought them here, to the south of Bandung, delivered to the Embassy by almost archaic means, a motorcycle messenger, though he had not expected anyone to know they were in the country, and this man above all. As they stood there by the gate, he was sure that just as the occupant within had known of their presence in the capital, he knew of it at the entrance to his sanctuary. The visitors pushed open the gate.

A small Javanese woman appeared instantly from the side of the house, the sound of a screen door slapping shut behind her the only mark of her silent approach. Her face was smooth and round, and her hair was formally dressed in a bun at the back of her head. Her feet were bare, showing just below the hem of her batik sarong, and as she drew closer they whispered over the stones of the pathway. A glorious smile spread over her ageless features. *'Selamat datang, tuan; selamat datang, ibu,'* welcome, she said. *'Silahkan,'* please, and proffered with a hand the rest of the path to the front of the house.

As they reached what turned out to be a broad verandah, the front door appeared to the right. It opened, and a slightly-built man, still looking as though he were of early middle age, came out as if to inspect them in the full light of day. This was no more than the Australian's imagination, in response to the Javan's slight squinting at them in the sun, for not only would it have been impossibly rude manners in an educated Javanese, but it was also inaccurate, for he stretched his hands forward in his own way of welcome and, like the woman on the path, smiled broadly.

'*Jend'ral*,' said the Australian, in a way he hadn't said to anyone for many years. And while he had never formally met this General, really a Lieutenant-General, he recognized him instantly.

'And I,' said the Javan, in clear English, 'should I not also say *Laksamana*? And,' with a slight bow to his female visitor, '*Ibu*, of course.'

Both visitors took momentary stock of these greetings. The Australian had made Rear-Admiral, in Indonesian Laksamana Muda, some years before, shortly before leaving the Navy. So he rarely now ever heard the English title, and to hear it in *bahasa* made it even more unusual. The American woman had never forgotten how much respect that simple *ibu*, mother, implied.

'*Laksamana*,' said the Australian. 'Yes, I like that. *Laksamana muda*, though.'

His host laughed. 'Well, then, I must just be *Letnan Jenderal*.'

The woman saw that this subtle adjustment in ranks was not a clarification of authority by which all military men lived. Here, she knew, it was a breaking of ice.

'But, please,' said the Javan, 'come in to the cool. *Duduk sebentar* - please, sit down'

The parlour was as in most Indonesian houses: several small armchairs and a long settee grouped around a glass-topped low table. The flat arms of the furniture were a dark wood; the upholstery a mustard yellow plush with intricately crocheted antimacassars across the tops of the chairbacks. A tall glass-fronted cabinet stood against one wall, a sentinel in deeper shadow. Small porcelain items and some Islamic texts inscribed on wood were visible within it. The walls were light green and bare, except for a few old photographs. A single light fixture dangled from the ceiling, one of the electrical adaptations of the old colonial-epoch oil lamps. One wall was given entirely up to louvred windows, which overlooked the rice paddy directly below the house, and the valley beyond. It appeared that one could slip off the edge of the rice paddy and fall an interminable distance into verdant depths.

As they sat, the woman who had greeted them on the path brought in a tray. She sank to her knees at the table, and, without speaking, placed on it cups of clear tea, a bowl of sugar, and a plate of small cakes. She raised herself and backed away.

The Australian had the look of a man who had lived a life outdoors. His frame was still strong, arms corded, and his hands were rough. Yet his was a lithe strength, maintained by exercise, not meat. The roughness of his hands was a consequence of daily attention to certain chores which a new agricultural occupation required. But his hair was greying, and his skin was beginning to lose the tones of youthful middle-age. His eyes were also grey, direct, with the crows-feet of a man who has spent hours on watch at sea.

His wife was of his generation but would have posed more of a problem to anyone wishing to guess her age. She had managed to keep the length of her hardly-tinted hair, had a matching though less-corded firmness of muscle. It was most evident in movement, but also in the turn of her ankles, just visible below the hem of a long skirt. Her eyes were greenish, and radiated humour and intelligence.

The Javan was small, almost frail, but the frailness that is the mark of an academic, not illness. But there was an enormous intellect behind the calm face, and this man was full, or had been, of a fearful strength.

The Australian had a small package in his hands, which he placed on the table. Both he and his wife were on the settee; their host sat opposite them, in a chair almost exactly at their mid-point. The Australian wondered if that arrangement had been thought out beforehand - it seemed an almost constructed way of avoiding either of them being relegated to subordinate status.

'Please understand that my invitation was entirely informal,' said the Javan. 'I was informed of your presence in Jakarta - it seemed a wonderful opportunity.'

'Do you still teach?' asked the Australian. 'In the school where I first saw you?'

'Ah yes. I keep busy. And I try to repay the opportunity given to me. But one grows reflective with age.' His eyes, a dark brown, reflected an inwardness, giving a hint of distances sought. 'And I am always searching for guest speakers.' The Javan smiled.

The Australian sat back in surprise. 'Me?'

'Actually more than just a guest speaker. But, I am going too fast. Please,' and he gestured to the table, 'you will be thirsty. *Ibu,* please.'

Their host waited till both guests had sipped their tea before he tasted his, and before he continued. Though he changed the subject: 'Do you enjoy your new life?'

The Australian was still mulling over the implications of his surprise, but, as he listened to the Javan's question, it became clearer that the man knew much more about them than he'd even considered. The invitation was only the first sign of this. But he thought he'd test him a little, and cocked his head in question.

The Javan chuckled. 'You are vintners, no, *Laksamana?* But you are right to wonder. How do I know so much? *Why* do I know so much? Please, don't be offended. I am being most un-Javanese. But you see, what I am is very largely due to you. And, if I may be so forward, what *you* are is in no small part due to me.' And he clearly implied *you* as a couple.

The Australian saw no reason to take offence. This man was of considerable interest to him, and offence would serve neither of them. He glanced at his wife, and saw only amusement in her eyes. 'Yes,' he said. 'We are vintners. I promised my wife a vineyard to match the area of an aircraft-carrier's deck. Let's just say we're now going for the fleet.'

'Wonderful,' the Javan laughed. 'I'd expect no less.'

The Australian leaned forward and lifted the small package, a book in a paper bag. 'I'd have brought my own copy,' he said, 'but it's at home, and I had no expectation of seeing you. So I bought this in Jakarta. Would you do me the honour of signing it?'

The Javan expressed his own surprise at the sight of the familiar cover. 'My memoirs?' It was evident that he was very touched, for he fell silent for a moment, but then he said: 'He died recently, you know.'

Not for a second did either visitor misunderstand the reference. 'Not many of my countrymen would call him a 'good man',' said the Australian, 'but he was one hell of an adversary.'

'Beyond my parents he was everything to me,' said the Javan. He got up and found a pen in the depths of the cabinet. He also brought a small book and laid it on the table. 'He gave me this at my graduation.'

The Australian picked it up and saw: *Axia of Sun Tzu*, translation to *bahasa Indonesia* by *Jenderal* Ars Bulyanto. On the flyleaf he saw the signature of the recently deceased author. 'He read Chinese?' he said in surprise.

The Javan understood the deeper question. 'He knew how much knowledge had accrued to the Chinese. But he felt that only a direct translation would put it into proper terms for an Indonesian. Retranslation from English would have compounded the idiosyncrasies of the original translator. Even then he was worried about the effects of time on thought.'

The Australian could imagine this. 'That is why I would like to ask you if you would sanction *my* translating *your* own work.'

The Javan remained silent for a moment, and then looked at the woman. 'I would sanction no-one else,' he said.

This honour felt was all that mattered, she thought.

Two

War games', said *Jenderal* Ars Bulyanto, 'are the way modern commanders develop the understanding of how to use the resources at their disposal.'

No, I wasn't back at military college. Or not quite. I had a surprise invitation, or an *undangan* as they call it. An *undangan* for *Bapak* Commander Trevor Gregory, Australian Naval Attaché, Jakarta, to attend the graduating class at the *KOPASSUS* training school in Bandung. *KOPASSUS* churns out tough bastards, for they're the special forces. Hard as nails and likely to come at you out of nothing at all, or nothing you thought of as cover. Like our own blokes, though smaller and made of steel wire to look at them. And this bunch, perhaps a bit plumper and shinier than most of their mates, officer cadets after all, but no less sharp for it. They'd made the grade, cadets for only another half-hour, then Sub-Lieutenants and ready to kill.

Bulyanto looked as though he had no trouble killing. Late forties, maybe early fifties, a bleak danger in those eyes that roamed over his lads, giving a sort of graduation speech about something new that ABRI was getting into. ABRI, the Indonesian Armed Forces, ten times the size of ours -- and the rumour was that they had doubled the size of *KOPASSUS*. I only hoped the purpose was internal.

There were other attachés present besides myself, also polished up in their best, trying to make the locals think their own uniforms were dull. But I work on the premise that the less glitter you have on your chest and head, the more likely you are to give me trouble. It was types like Bulyanto that made me shiver. And I'd heard he was unorthodox in an army not known for individuality.

'War games also allow neighbouring states a look at each others' capability either to attack or defend, assessing what it will cost them if they become embroiled in armed conflict. War games are also a tool in the diplomatic arsenal, outcomes suggesting explicit alliances of mutual benefit.'

It sounded like an introductory lecture to a course he probably taught, but it was more for the parents than for the class itself. For quite a small man he had a tigerlike presence, no ounce of fat on him, and in his camouflage would be the worst threat imaginable. He brought the jungle to the dais.

'Here at the school, war games have been a strategic planning tool. The curriculum ranged from the analysis of wars and smaller battles actually fought, to the development of ideas for games that are relevant to our country in the modern-day political arena. You are the commanders of tomorrow. Some of you may achieve high command, some of you may be tested on some battlefield, and one or two of you may be doing what I am doing today.'

His credentials suggested he'd done all of it. I'd had the dossier out before I came and had gleaned what little I could. About Bulyanto it said little more than he had just told us, but I thought there was no accident in that. More like a deliberate omission of any of his achievements from ABRI's *Who's Who*.

'In our armed forces we recognize it is here in this school that our most able officers will stand out. Where you are today reflects that potential. In my class, above all, I asked you to put aside any tendency you had to let others make your decisions for you -- it was the individual I was looking for.

That made me uncomfortable. For long I'd thought that most ABRI training was ideological, designed to get you to do things by mass brainwashing. Looking and listening to Bulyanto I was worried about my own prejudices.

'It is an unfortunate fact of life that Man is deceitful. Remember that. It is why we are here. You have been trained in the arts of deception. War is constructed from them. If you can't master them, you fail. The greatest battles of the world tended to be the greatest battles because of some amazingly simple trick played by one general on another. Of course, hundreds of other battles were fought at a more basic level, perhaps a bitter contest toe to toe. But if one side was good at deception, and used it to his advantage, he generally won.'

I wondered if he wasn't actually putting this on for us, his peers in other armies, sort of niggling us a little about what might be going on under that vast carapace that hid most of ABRI most of the time.

'But remember this. War is about victory and defeat. It is not about annihilation, or long, brilliant campaigns. It is about economy of effort, knowing your enemy, continually second-guessing his intent and frustrating his efforts. You don't win by throwing everything at him and hoping for the best. That will surely result in your defeat. You plan, you use all the resources at your disposal to your best ability, and you use subterfuge. If you lose, you carry the responsibility. If you win, you have done your duty.'

Bulyanto picked up a slim package wrapped in a dark material. 'This year we have decided to award a special prize. One of your number has astonished the board of selection. He not only achieved the highest possible mark overall, but, more specifically, he dominated war games activities. Few of you could have known that he was also working on a separate project throughout his final year, one he brought to me himself. This cadet has brought our school into the 21st

16

century almost single-handed, and I believe you will hear a great deal of him in the future. *Kadet* Rusman Soekendro, please come forward.'

There was quite a stir as one of the cadets stood up. Bulyanto had obviously broken some news, and if chagrin were something I could recognize on young Indonesian faces, I thought I was probably seeing it on the remainder of the class. Soekendro marched solemnly to the front and snapped to attention before Bulyanto.

It was unusual this, the singling out of someone on whom to bestow accolades in this secretive culture. ABRI's culture, I mean, not Java's. I wondered what the hell it was he'd done.

The award was presented, if that was what it was, and Soekendro whipped a crisp salute into the folds of a very new red beret. 'And,' said Bulyanto, apparently addressing the crowd once again 'Sub-Lieutenant Soekendro will be joining me on my personal staff as of tomorrow morning.'

And that was the real award, the one road to sure success in this very nepotistic of Services. His career path was made. Now I really wondered what he'd done. What war game had he come up with that made him a star?

The thought stayed with me as I took the road out of Bandung towards Cianjur, Jakarta a few more slow hours drive beyond. What could a cadet have done which would have marked him as a rising star in the eyes of someone like Bulyanto? Soekendro didn't have the killer's eyes which would have marked a youthful Bulyanto. Instead, I'd very briefly seen a confident, intelligent young academic. Whilst he'd been made to stand out from the crowd, if these were the cadets in which ABRI was now putting its future trust, there had been a shift of major proportion away from the old-style army officer. We weren't bad at war games ourselves, but I wondered what an Indonesian one looked like?

The road wound through fertile rice-land, volcanic peaks not far away through the clouds. The clouds were like my own mind, the peaks like the occasional sight I had of something firm in a region where invisible relations between states seemed natural, and a final, fixed result abhorred. The peaks danced in the haze. Sundanese gamelan music came from the local radio station, the cadence of the brass instruments' each rolling phrase like waves breaking on a beach, leaving me thinking of spirits returning under the volcanoes, ghosts of the ancient gods that decided the size of the rice harvest.

Then clouds opened and turned the road into a black, churning river. Suddenly I saw other faces, laughing through the misted, splattered side-windows, faces of small boys who made a game of jumping into the spray sent up by my tyres.

In spite of the downpour, Soekendro stayed in my mind all the way to Jakarta. He was now the symbol of something I didn't understand, a smaller peak in the mountain range of ABRI. At one point, the gamelan became more strident, and I heard the echoes of laughter floating through the rhythm.

Later, when I told Boltroni, Head of Security at the Embassy, about my thoughts, he laughed, and said: 'Too long on Java.'

Three

If anywhere, it had all started when the Jenderal's aide-de-camp slipped back through the door. 'He will see you now.'

I went in to find him again at the window, where he'd been when first I saw him. I saluted.

'Did someone put you up to this?' The question was definitely hostile.

'Sir?' I said, a little surprised.

The Jenderal indicated the material on his desk. I could see that it had been thoroughly studied, comments in red ink covering the papers.

'Where did the idea come from?'

'It was my own, sir.'

'It couldn't have been. Something must have put you on this path?' The question was slightly condescending.

'Well sir, my father was posted there at one time, and I've been reading some of the material on his bookshelf.'

'You've discussed this idea with your father? It was his?'

'Oh no, sir. This is all my own work. I'm not at all sure what my father would think of it.'

'Did you share it with the group?'

'At first I wasn't sure that it was valid, Jenderal. But as I thought about it more, I wanted the challenge of completing it myself, rather than having it watered down by others.

'You don't think much of your peers?'

'With respect, sir, I find them slow.'

'You find them slow? They just don't understand you, Soekendro.' He looked again out the window, his thoughts perhaps where I had taken them. 'You have your wish. This is just the germ of the idea. I want you to take it on from there. I want to see what you can do with it. Take it as far as operational planning if you can, though you may not have the necessary resources without certain opened

doors. But until I open them, you will not discuss your idea or this assignment with anyone. Is that clear?'

And my heart began to sing. I nodded. 'Yes, sir.'

'Have you thought of a name for the main offensive position?'

'Yes, sir. The Soekarno Line.'

The Jenderal blinked. 'Very Javanese, Soekendro.'

'Precisely, sir.' President Soekarno was long dead, but still a hero. I had no intention of so honouring any of his successors.

But it was when the Jenderal gave me the Tionghoa's own axia of war in front of my classmates that I knew I'd been right in not turning back

Excerpted from Rusman Soekendro, LetJen (ret'd),
No Game At All: Memoirs of a Strategist

T he world became a dingo's breakfast in very short order. And no sooner had it done so than that same world's major intelligence agencies turned their focus on Indonesia. For, while the trouble started elsewhere, and early attention was on rooting the terrorists out of Afghanistan's mountainous geography, it soon became clear that the real threat could easily go to ground in Indonesia's mountainous population. And not only go to ground, but actually fester to the point where it could spread at lightning speed through the synapses of a massive, in fact the world's largest, Islamic neural network which currently was only intent on jihad *within* Indonesian borders. When the bomb went off in Bali, it became generally known in Australia that Indonesian militants intended to incorporate northern Australia into some sort of Islamic super-state. Only then did Canberra raise its head from the sands of East Timor and wake to a reality that it had been dodging since it watched the decline and fall of the old Suharto regime. I remembered one of those draft interdepartmental memos which make the rounds so that everyone can give his or her ten cents worth before the Minister puts his thumb to them and sends them to Cabinet. It was meant to address strategic policy and intelligence.

Colleagues,

On occasion we provide a detailed brief on specific bilateral relations. I should like to set the scene for the one you will find attached.

Indonesia is still on a jagged path towards democracy. Political parties proliferate, but policies emerge slowly from the old Suharto swamp of centrist governance and favour-mongering. While the taste of democratic freedoms has brought populist revolts (some barely controlled, as you will have seen, by an increasingly-aware though not increasingly-trained national police force), many of these have imploded under ragged leadership and lack of vision. Perhaps only during Wahid's tenure in the Presidency was there a glimpse of true liberal thinking, but he was one man, and was subsequently unable to translate his vision into strategic policy. He was labelled weak, and political ferment continued. Megawati, the daughter of the President who brought Indonesia her independence, ruled briefly as a figurehead, but was subsequently toppled by power-hungry politicians with firmer control of the key factions. No one yet has the measure of the new President.

As far as I could see, Indonesian politics meant constructing pyramidic coalitions, though volcanic might have been a better word.

Australia should remain attentive to, although not alarmed by, this ongoing change. It is an expected consequence of reversion to civilian rule after more than three decades of de facto military fiat. The country's energies are turned inward, especially as it tries to cope with outer-island restlessness under a Javanese bureaucracy.

It was easy to forget that Indonesia was more than just Java. All the other islands seemed the rim to Java's hub, something that Jakarta apparently had been happy to remind them about now and again. But now the wheel was spinning a little faster, and it seemed that centrifugal forces were stretching Jakarta's control to a point where new and independent orbits might be created.

Were Indonesia even to be in a position to pursue further annexation at the eastern end of the archipelago, Australia's commitment to East Timor and Papua New Guinea can be seen as the necessary brake. Australia believes that the Indonesian military has accepted its new, subordinate role. While it would be prudent to have a policy in place in the event that confrontation on the border between West Papua (formally Irian Jaya but retaking its original name in early 2000) and Papua New Guinea escalated beyond its present level, Australia believes there is neither the will nor the capacity for such an undertaking in Indonesia, and that any such move would be no more than political window-dressing. In light of our extensive commitment to both of these two emerging nations, Cabinet may wish Australia to advise both Indonesia and Papua New Guinea that it will not be drawn into minor border conflicts between the two countries.

A bit late, I thought. They seemed to be happening daily.

Similarly, Cabinet may wish to consider that we suggest to Indonesia that we view our restraint as a quid pro quo for continued right-of-passage through the major sea-lanes that run through the Indonesian archipelago. I believe I need not remind my colleagues that access through those sea-lanes to the South China Seas and West Pacific, especially for resource exports to Japan, is of utmost importance to Australian trade.

In the medium term, there appears to be no new threat from our immediate neighbour. East Timor can remain our priority in this sub-regional sphere of influence, and indeed the signals from all our Western and regional partners, as well as other key UN members, are that they wish our leading role in the UN mission on East Timor to continue for as long as needed. From our analysis, I believe that it may be as many as ten years before democratic institutions are strong enough for us to consider partial withdrawal, though I believe my colleague from Defence will be employed there considerably longer.

Someone called Gareth had stapled a note to it:

Not many secrets there. No worries, I'd say, though you might want to mention ANZUS as still the backbone of our broader regional security mechanism. Cabinet probably won't even look at the attached brief. Not on their radar screen.

I thought it could be put better in terms every mariner understands. Fog for the foreseeable future. Until the bomb went off.

Four

'*Forget about the reasons for now. I want you to tell me how to do it.*' The Jenderal was insistent. '*These are rich lands. There is potential for resettlement. Taken together these are reason enough. When you first came to me had you not this in mind? Hasn't that sustained you through your final year? Hasn't this been the war game to end them all?*'

He was right, of course. But I'd had to work out an approach which would allow an analysis of the resources required and the probability of success. Then I'd become fascinated with the obstacles that existed. '*But Jenderal, there is the whole issue of commitment. The commitment is tied to the reason. If I cannot judge that commitment, I have no means of taking the exercise through to its logical conclusion.*'

'*You are worried about the possibility of retreat?*'

'*If there is the chance that a withdrawal might happen, sir, then I have to apply that factor. Are there partial objectives? Is it all or nothing? Can it be done in stages?*'

The Jenderal looked at me without speaking for a moment. What was he thinking? Had I pushed too much? Was there something still unknown to me? But finally he seemed to have made up his mind.

'*There is a single objective. You set it yourself. The Soekarno Line. Draw it so that it encompasses the principal resources as we defined them. See it as being where the other's defences will be held. But you tell me whether we need to do it in stages. You tell me the resources we need. Set the line where it is logical that it be set. But one thing. The troops will land. They will have what they need at their backs. They will not retreat. When this happens, there will be no pulling back.*'

And then I knew. No longer was it an abstraction. '*We are going to war, Jenderal.*'

'*Yes.*'

Excerpted from Rusman Soekendro, LetJen (ret'd),
No Game At All: *Memoirs of a Strategist*

The Australian continued to ponder the translation. He turned to his wife: 'I still worry about the formality of Indonesian composition'

You must put as much as possible into plain thought and speech, with a minimum of forced structure,' she said.

'But the sayings, the axia, the concepts?'

The Javan inclined his head. 'They were essential to everything I wrote. They are as much steps in trains of thought as they are insights to success. Everything I did flowed directly from them. I would hope they could be there. All I did was to provide an example of their validity three thousand years after they were written down.'

Later, when the Australian was alone with his wife, he said. 'It sort of reminds me of the bible and the lost scrolls.'

'You are both disciples,' she said, straightfaced.

'Bloody hell, woman.'

***

In the end I came to think of Harry Grant as a copper-plated bastard. But I suppose I don't mean that as strongly as it sounds, for I like the man. One of the better Scots I've met and not stingy with his whisky. And it's not for anything he did to me, either, for he's only been on the periphery of my life, one professional open to candid discussions with another. But he definitely got me into it, what came along after I saw him for the last time. Java had already brought me onto the primrose path, but he was like a garden bench beside it waiting to entice you into looking at a certain view, knowing that if you pause for a few moments you will acquire a perspective different from any you knew existed. So your bum gets glued there for a little longer than you'd planned and nothing is ever the same again.

'Your first visit to Hong Kong, Commander.'

It wasn't a question, but neither was it an accurate statement. If it was the new diplomatic passport that was stuffing up the immigration officer's records he couldn't blame me, but I saw no point in a lie. It could be one of those little tests loved by those who had the whole weight of an elephantine bureaucracy behind them.

'No.'

The eyes lingered a moment, then the passport was handed back. 'Welcome.' I gave a brief nod to the unsmiling eyes.

I'd flown into Hong Kong on the tail end of a typhoon. Visibility was poor, and the runway shedding water in sheets as we landed. The high-speed rail link to Hong Kong island flashed past clusters of tall apartment buildings, mini-cities suggesting several years of post-handover prosperity, and I was knocking on Grant's door within an hour of landing.

Harry Grant was a lowland Scot, with a warm, easy manner that belied the neat, slightly starched appearance. 'Come in, Trevor. Journey not too rough, I hope?'

'Bit of a worry during the descent, but otherwise fine.' I said.

Grant grinned. 'Do you remember the old airport -- Kai Tak? Wind shear among the lampposts was every pilot's nightmare, laddie. But even with that last right-hand turn, no-one ever landed in anyone's rooftop laundry.' He chuckled. 'How's Jakarta?'

'The Embassy never was the grey-funnel line.'

'Horizontal rather than vertical command structure?' Then he showed he'd done some homework. 'But you're on your way back. Aren't you getting a frigate?'

'How did you know that?'

'Laddie, it's not so much the ships you sail, it's who you sail in them. I make it my job to know who commands every vessel from here to Tierra del Fuego.'

I'd known Harry ever since the old days of Royal Navy presence in Hong Kong waters, when he'd been a senior naval intelligence officer, but that was long past and Harry had moved over into a private security position with a large Hong Kong shipping firm. Hung Lines. And Hung Lines had recently lost a ship.

'Even Indonesian Navy?'

'Well, top-raters, at least.'

I laughed at him. Sometimes my image of him was of one of those sandy-haired kilted figures you see in whisky ads, member of some regimental mess, and hard on the glassware. He had the sandy hair, even if I'd never seen the kilt. 'That's because I tell you.'

'Aye, you do at that.' Then, '*Ord*?'

'It's not clear yet. There will be some other shuffling. One of the *Mount* Class, anyway. East Ocean Fleet, based at Sydney.' The *Mount* class were our newest frigates, the last of half a dozen only just coming off the slips. They were big, powerful, and every naval officer's dream of command. Their naming after significant Australian peaks was reputed to have been the suggestion of the Prime Minister's wife. This matched most naval officers' opinion of Canberra's methods of important decision-making.

'Congratulations. When?'

25

'A month. This will probably be the last time you see me.' But if he'd already done the other homework, he'd also know this. I remembered the first time I'd met him, when I'd come in as the new attaché, fresh off the deck of an older frigate, then a first-officer Lieutenant-Commander wanting to step sideways for a while and sail the region from a desk.

'Useful to know your allies?' he'd asked.

'More than that. I want to know if they are my allies. It's hard to see beyond my Service's xenophobia if you don't step away from it.' There hadn't been much doubt about that xenophobia. And Canberra's hacking of military budgets had shrunk the navy very quickly --there were few ships left. The shrinkage had further entrenched those conservative views among the remaining senior sailors.

He hadn't said it but that was why, when he was still in British Naval Intelligence, he'd asked my predecessor up to Hong Kong, and his predecessor, too. Trying to gauge what was left of the navy. The Royal Australian Navy, offshoot of that Imperial fleet with which Britannia had ruled the seas for so many years. I'd known about this, about Harry's interest, but my predecessor hadn't given it much thought, came more for the beer at Ned Kelly's in Kowloon, setting aside just enough time to say g'day to Harry on his way back to Kai Tak. For all I knew his predecessor had been the same. Mine had certainly hated Jakarta, and regularly used Hong Kong as a watering hole. Then, I was the new Attaché, one of the Ambassador's several right or left-hand men and women; and, until things started to go wrong, just another backroom body at a busy embassy and at a spot on the globe where I'd thought political tension ebbed and flowed as one with slow tropical tides. The difference between that and the thirty-six hundred tons of warship that I'd recently departed had been night and day. I'd wanted that departure, perhaps for more reasons than even I knew, but I'd left principally because Asia beckoned.

Now, Harry looked at his watch. 'For the few minutes till lunch it's just you and me. A lot going on that we need to talk about.'

And as RAN's man in Jakarta, even though a career sailor without a ship, it was my job to know what was going on. As I'd said to Harry way back then, it had been my decision. Swanning around the Great Australian Bight with grey steel underfoot was not conducive to understanding the region. It would take months, even years, of contact with men such as he, and with the Asians themselves. Eventually, that investment of effort brought the promotion to Commander. But that had been a while ago.

'*Alumina Queen* disappeared on the twelfth of December,' Harry said. 'She'd left Weipa in northern Queensland laden with aluminium ingots a few days before. She'd made a course that took her through the Indonesian archipelago by the way of the Lombok Narrows, the Flores Sea and the Makassar Strait, and was still being tracked by transponder through the southern fringe of the Sulu Archipelago. Because of a severe tropical depression building to the east of the Philippines, rather than thread his way north through the Sulu Sea, the captain decided to head northwest and enter the South China Sea leaving Palawan to starboard. Again, we know her course until she intercepted the typhoon just to the north of the Spratly Islands. Then we lost her.'

'No sign at all? Lifeboats? Wreckage?'

'No. Because of this we began to speculate that this was not a sinking during a typhoon, but a different event altogether.'

'A hijacking?'

'At the time she disappeared there was a Chinese naval manoeuvre in progress around the Spratlys, apparently an attempt to improve its self-image after some face-losing games with the Vietnamese. This naval group subsequently established a rather elaborate screen during its return to Guangzhou. In what we believe was an effort to avoid being seen, it plotted a very ragged course home, keeping itself generally hull down over the horizon from any other major vessels. Course changes were frequent, and radio traffic was cryptic. There were probably three frigates involved, or a destroyer and two frigates. That is what we know of the force that went out.'

'You're saying that the Chinese Navy hijacked her?' I asked. 'Is this known to any of the region's other navies?'

'I wouldn't be surprised if the Vietnamese knew, but we don't hear much from them. And ASEAN's intelligence gathering tends to be held quite close to the chest. Until they have one of those Spratlys meetings, anyway.' ASEAN, the Association of South-East Asian Nations, was the means by which Indonesia, Malaysia, Thailand and their other neighbours addressed regional concerns. Only when there was a common concern did such a disparate group of countries collaborate on affairs rather than obfuscate them. The Spratlys Islands were an affair of common concern.

Harry continued reflectively. 'The navy has a dry dock at Guangzhou. It's effectively screened from satellite observation, but ground reports are that a major commercial vessel was taken on about ten days after *Alumina Queen*'s disappearance. This vessel appeared to have suffered some damage, and to have undergone some repairs. In the dry-dock, she has undergone a major superstructural facelift. It would take a detailed below-deck inspection to determine her provenance.'

'Can you arrange that?' I asked.

'We would have to do it covertly and none of our current contacts has the necessary access.' He leaned back in his chair. 'My hypothesis is this. This ship was snatched at the tail of the typhoon when the watch was groggy or even asleep. It would not have been difficult to overpower the crew. She was then sailed on a reciprocal course back towards the Spratlys. This would have put the maximum distance between her expected position at the time she was lost, and, of course, the area that received the maximum attention during the search. The purpose of the screen was to prevent anyone from seeing what was going on aboard during the return to Guangzhou. I believe that the damage was faked. Probably more important was a colour and name change. I hold little hope that the original crew came through this alive. I should imagine she came in under a naval prize-cre

He made an open handed gesture of frustration. 'There is a period of about a week that we cannot account for. This may have something to do with her cargo. Being valuable to the Chinese, we should be able to find a windfall arrival of ingots at one of the rolling mills. We are currently checking this, but it will take some time. If we find it, we will try and obtain a wee sample of the metal. That would tell us where it came from.'

'But wait a minute, Harry. I thought that the Chinese Navy had cleared up its act? Were this ten, even five, years ago, I might agree that your hypothesis is sound. Piracy was big business to their Navy then. But that had to change. They'd know that nothing this big could go unnoticed, madeover or not. There might still be some rogue captains, but rogue captains don't get dry-dock space in Guangzhou.'

Harry shrugged. 'What else makes sense?'

I didn't have much to go on, but there was the inkling of an idea. 'What if,' I said, 'what if she was meant to go to the bottom, and did go to the bottom?'

'Are you suggesting Hung Lines is indulging in insurance fraud?' Even for Harry I could see that he was considerably put out.

'No, no. Perhaps made to give that impression. Your underwriters may certainly think that for a while. No, I'm thinking of the USS Cole, and that French supertanker. What if there's an Asian cell intent on similar business?'

'Al-Qaeda? Middle-easterners in the South China Seas. Come on, Trevor. This ship wasn't attacked right on the coast. She was in the middle of nowhere, and coming out of a typhoon.'

'Yes, I know. Different means, different people. Same purpose, though. Disruption of trade, fear, all elements of economic warfare.'

'Bloody hell, laddie. I know I give you credit for your imagination, but don't you think you're going a bit wild?'

'If it *were* the Chinese, what would the Navy do with such a large ship once she came out of dry dock?' I asked.

Harry shrugged. 'We can be sure that if this ship is the *Alumina Queen*, she will not reappear on any of the routes she sailed in the past. The best bet is that she will be sub-contracted to a South America run, probably out of Chile or Colombia. That would create the maximum difficulty in establishing her identity. It would keep her out of our reach for quite a while.'

'Then either way you've got your work cut out for you proving you know where she is.'

'Aye, I know.' Harry paused. 'And it's going to be a growing problem. If it gets out of hand, which means that the Chinese see that they can continue to act with impunity, then regional trade is going to take a major knock. Something has to be done *now*. And,' he added, 'probably by a certain regional navy.'

I left alone his continuing assertion that this was the Chinese. 'If it were only just a case of signalling Canberra.'

'Just get their heads out of the beer, Trevor.' Then he said, 'Well, I think we've done what we can for the moment. Let's go to lunch.'

The taxi threaded its way into the streets of Kowloon. Once away from the main shopping areas, the store fronts became smaller and commercial signs less cast in neon. There were still some street vendors trying to get rid of the day's fruit and vegetables. The vehicle eventually drew to a stop in front of an open doorway flanked by herbal medicine shops. Harry led me inside.

We took the lift to a carpeted third floor landing, where an elderly Chinese in a simple uniform sat in a chair beside an ornate doorway. He bowed as we approached and opened the door for us.

Inside, a foyer opened into a large room with several tables. Two were occupied by groups of businessmen. Harry approached someone sitting at a third. 'Cheun. Thank you for suggesting we meet you here.'

A middle-aged Chinese man, dressed in a suit that put Harry's to shame, bowed slightly and smiled. 'You allow yourself too few opportunities for good food, Harry. Far better than fish and chips somewhere around the corner.'

Harry nodded. 'That's why I stayed – returning to Britain would have been an awful fate.' Then, 'Cheun, this is Trevor Gregory. Trevor, Hung Cheun.'

'A pleasure to meet you Commander Gregory.'

It took a moment to click, but then I realized who he must be. I shook his hand. 'For me, also, Mr Hung.' Looking more closely at him, I saw both ease and wealth sitting comfortably on him. For someone who owned a shipping line, he'd effaced whatever temptation he might have had to show superiority. His grip was light, but the hand was strong.

'Please sit down. May I order you a drink?'

'A Tiger. Thank you.'

Hung nodded and fired an order to a young woman waiting quietly at his side. 'Harry, I took the liberty earlier of ordering lunch for us. Mr Gregory, I hope you enjoy Sichuan food?'

'I doubt that I've had the real thing.'

'Ahh.... Well, we'll have a few minutes to talk first, and then we'll eat.'

My beer came quickly, and was served in an iced glass. Both Harry and Hung took a small whisky. 'Your health, Mr Gregory.'

'Thank you. And yours.'

After only a brief look at Harry, Hung said 'You are Australian.'

I nodded.

'So, you are another Asian.' He smiled as he said it, with complete lack of malice. If he looked for a reaction, he didn't find it. 'But not many of your countrymen would enjoy being called Asians, Mr Gregory.'

'Very true, Mr Hung,' I responded. 'Perhaps our isolation makes us cling to the past rather than move with the present. But I think we should move into the *modern* criminal world rather than be taken as relics of a past one.'

'Ah,' said Hung, laughing. 'It's only the criminals that get ahead these days.' Then: 'Perhaps you've heard of the Hung Line? I operate intercontinental container ships and freighters between mainland Asia and Australia, and I have several smaller traders on the Chinese east-coast run.'

'Forgive me, but I know little about your business -- I'm only marginally in touch with mercantile marine affairs. Do you have any commerce with Indonesia?'

'My container ships call there of course, and occasionally one of the smaller traders, but all my freighters are involved in the high-value metals trade between Australia and Japan.'

'Has the change in the relationship between Hong Kong and China altered any of that? You operate from Hong Kong.'

'No, Mr Gregory. I can make my trade where I find it.' Then, 'My earlier remark about your being an Asian was quite pertinent. I know that you are in the same line of business as was my friend Harry. However, you have a continuing stake in this region. Don't you think there are perhaps some not-so-subtle shifts taking place in the regional balance of power?'

'Increasingly obvious Chinese dominance?'

He didn't answer directly. 'There has always been piracy in these waters. Several of my smaller ships have been accosted on the open seas by craft purporting to be Chinese naval vessels on anti-smuggling patrols. I have no clear proof that any but a few rogue elements of the Chinese Navy are involved in this, though my sources used to tell me it went all the way up. Under threat of confiscation of their ships, my captains are forced to open their holds. These people take what they want. They are armed. So, yes, increasingly obvious Chinese *greed*, at the very least.'

He paused again.

'Rapid economic development in China has created major shortages of some important commodities. I am afraid that aluminium is one of them. In this case, a ship has been made to disappear, the cargo, I presume, unloaded, and the crew disposed of. Perhaps you'd expect the ship then to have been scuttled in deep water, but we' and he included Harry, 'believe that she wasn't.

'No-one else but China is patrolling these coasts.' He'd jumped in a different direction. 'Each of the countries of this region has a small navy, but most cannot do much but patrol their own waters. Individually they have no blue-water capability. The Japanese are only just pulling their heads from the sand. Unless there is a recognition of the dangers that are appearing, and some joining of forces to prevent the situation getting out of hand, I am afraid that the sea will be lawless – more lawless than it already is -- and ships and their crews will disappear. Yours *is* an Asian country, Mr Gregory. You depend on the export of natural resources to your regional neighbours to keep your economy afloat. You have a stake in this. But beyond this, of course, China cannot be allowed to flaunt every rule that exists for its own ends.'

'Trevor believes there could be an alternative explanation,' Harry said. 'Remember the problems in Yemen?'

'Terrorism?' said Hung. 'But the ship disappeared completely.'

'So,' I said, 'did the twin towers of the World Trade Centre.'

'But by accident. No-one expected them to collapse.'

'But do you think they expected the Cole to stay afloat? Or that tanker? Wouldn't you expect a severely crippled ship to sink?'

The idea seized Hung and kept him silent. I decided to test his. 'If that is your ship in the Guangzhou dry dock, what action can you take to recover the vessel?'

'Nothing direct in any sense. However, the underwriters would soon find out where she was. While I might not recover my losses, I would at least not be suspected of fraud.' It was quite clear to him that any other alternative would keep him under suspicion for the much longer time it would take him to disprove it. He was silent for a moment. 'I have five other ships on that run. And several others

31

employed in the container trade. While I can absorb the loss of one, I cannot afford any further disappearances. But this will not stop here, I am certain of it.'

'Can you take measures to prevent it from happening again?'

'No one in shipping can afford to make major detours. Our margins are thin enough that extra transportation costs will push us into the red. We'd be talking perhaps two hundred thousand dollars each time if we were to try to bypass the high-risk area. We have to combat the threat, whatever it is, where it presents itself. Within the China Seas.' Hung paused. 'I have to tell you, Mr Gregory, that we are slipping back into the days when it was necessary for merchantmen to be armed. They used to carry cannon. We will have to do the same.'

I knew that if I were in Hung's shoes I'd be thinking along the same lines. 'But that is also a cost for you, quite apart from other implications for safety and international maritime law.'

'Maritime law may have rules but it has no teeth to prevent this. As far as Beijing at least is concerned there is no law. Safety? Well, safety is a relative thing. If you must do something dangerous to save your life, your livelihood, then that is safer than doing nothing. Don't you agree?'

I shrugged non-committally. 'Personally, I suppose I would say yes. But I'm in a position officially where I should have to say no. You're talking about anarchy on the high seas.'

'Then do something about it, Mr Gregory. Sooner or later no one will carry your aluminium, your coal, or whatever else you plan to export. What will you do then? Suppliers are in a more precarious position than buyers, don't you think?'

Plates started appearing on the table in front of us, perhaps in response to a signal that the main business had been dealt with. 'Well, let us not spoil our meal. Good digestion requires harmony between the mind and body. Enough of this until later. Please, try some of this,' and Hung began to offer me one of the dishes. 'We say: *Eat in China, savour in Sichuan.* You may think these dishes hot. But try to pick up the textures beneath.'

While we ate, Hung and Harry sparred over local political affairs, something about which I had nothing to offer. So, for a while, I lost myself in the flavour and texture absent from Chinese food found at home. The meal became something to think about, and I challenged myself to understand Hung's choice of dishes, examining the textures, and trying to separate the flavours.

But I knew that the introduction to Hung was too important to drop the conversation where we'd taken it. Once the last plate had been cleared away, my understanding of the chosen menu, to use Harry's favourite adjective, only a *wee* bit better than when we'd started, I returned us to our discussion. 'What security measures have you considered for your ships?' I asked.

Hung looked pensive for a moment. 'I want a detachment on each. I think a small group of from six to twelve men, well-armed, would be a significant deterrent at the start. I don't want to create a situation where its defence results in a ship being sunk. What I need is a means of preventing surprise boarding parties.'

As if ticking off a list, he went on. 'My ships are all fitted with satellite transponders, permitting me to track a ship's progress independent of its reports. Harry plans to increase the sophistication of our security systems, even to the point of having wide-angle video cameras mounted on the flying bridge. The digitized images will be continuously transmitted to my headquarters. If anything happens in future, I'll have a record of it.'

'You have the men to form the security detachments? Trained men, with adequate arms?'

'Unfortunately not, Mr Gregory.' Hung was shaking his head. 'The arms would not be a problem, but disciplined men would be. However, the arms should fit the men and their task.'

I nodded, saying nothing, but the germ of an idea was drifting into my mind.

Hung's eyes passed over my face and , for a moment, I wondered if he'd read my thoughts. But he remained impeccably polite. 'You travel back to Jakarta tomorrow, Trevor? May I call you Trevor? Good. And I am Cheun.'

'Yes,' I'd said, responding to both questions, but understanding the compliment in the second.

'Now I will leave you to Harry.' Hung signalled to the waitress, who brought us a final round of hand towels.

As we reached the street, a Rolls Royce whispered to the curb, forewarned of our descent. 'Goodbye, Trevor. Perhaps you'll have some news for us the next time we meet.'

I hid my surprise, having the distinct impression that I was being hustled. 'Whatever news I have I shall be sure to pass on,' I said. I wasn't sure that it sounded indefinite enough. 'Goodbye, Cheun. And thank you for a lunch I shall long remember.'

`Hung nodded as the chauffeur shut the door. Harry raised a finger to the passing taxis as the Rolls purred away.

Harry was equally quiet on the return journey, content to let me chew over Hung's story. Once we got back to his office, he shuffled papers for a couple of seconds. 'Coffee?'

On my nod he poured two cups from a thermos flask on the filing cabinet behind. 'Well, what did you think of Hung?'

33

'A very worried man.' But I knew he meant something else: 'You know as well as I do that Australia is in less of a position than Britain was to do anything.'

'I introduced you to Cheun because you're going to be around here a lot longer than I am. And by you I mean Australia. Not,' Harry shook his head, 'that I'm planning on going anywhere soon. Of course, there are other Hungs, but Cheun is the best entry point and I work for him. He's open and pragmatic. He maintains an extensive network of agents in China, and so is an extremely good source of information. If you cultivate him, it will pay off handsomely. But there is also the strategic element to this. You can't afford to have your economy under someone else's control, or threat, even. You need those channels operating without constraint. And obviously you don't want large freighters going to the bottom. Or anything else, for that matter. You're going to have to show your noses up here.'

I nodded. 'I get the message, Harry, but my masters in Canberra are little different than were yours in Whitehall. Your blokes couldn't wait to get away from here. Mine don't really know it exists. Putting a ship into these waters has a lower priority than completing the railway to Darwin. Australia stops at Alice. The Top End's somewhere up beyond the Arctic Circle.'

Harry knew I wasn't being funny. 'Good luck to you, Trevor. Keep in touch. Stop by when you bring your new ship to town.'

But before I was to be able to accede to this invitation, I had to complete my last month of duty. That included addressing what Canberra was waking up to: the possibility of a regional expansion in terrorism, fuelled by local hatreds, themselves fanned by the invisible hands of Al-Qaeda and others. I thought Harry's focus on the Chinese misplaced, though understood how Hong Kong's new relationship with China, and his presence there, was probably influencing his thinking. And I had no proof that my idea was any more sound, though I thought it an idea that demanded more urgent disproval.

I still had some of the afternoon free, and spent the time in a taxi scouring commercial chandlers for charts of the seas between Hong Kong and Australia. Back in my hotel, I spread them out on the floor. An eagle's eye view from the bed confirmed what I already knew: that the north-south sea-lanes upon which Australia depended were clearly in Indonesian hands. Only Indonesia had the jurisdiction to police those lanes. But if it did not – or could not – and those lanes remained insecure, unrestricted shipping northwards from Australia would mean a significant detour to the east around Papua New Guinea, which would result in large increases in shipping costs.

Threat on a grand scale could only be combatted by a significant policing of international waters. The routes under my eye were stretches of sea too dispersed and too large for any single Asian maritime nation to patrol effectively. None of them individually had the capacity anyway, and the length of time it was taking them to deal with regional security issues suggested that a combined effort would take years more to put in place.

I laid back on my bed, hands behind my head and stared at the ceiling. The mental image of the charts seemed to spread itself across the plaster, and a red stain in the upper left quadrant of my vision suggested itself to be the Chinese threat. I tried to think things through, but tiredness was taking over. All I was sure of was that the closer the shipping kept to the window and away from that stain, the less vulnerable it would be. It all seemed rather inane. But there wasn't much doubt about the most important sea-lane that crossed the Indonesian archipelago, the Makassar Strait. I thought I'd have to go and see Jack Krantz after all.

Five

My mind leapt ahead. Somehow the challenge of the assignment had unleashed a mental acuity I didn't realize I had. From the material I'd shown the Jenderal, I focussed on one component, creating a modular concept that I thought was replicable to other sites. Once I had the concept complete, I'd look at the way it would be necessary to adapt it to the different conditions at each site.

Each module had several components of its own. The module began with the objective for the landing. Second was the action necessary to secure a bridgehead with the greatest surprise and least damage possible. Third was the defence necessary to hold the bridgehead during any initial attempt to repulse the force. Fourth was the establishment of longer-term supply lines to allow the broader invasion to work.

Excerpted from Rusman Soekendro, LetJen (ret'd),
No Game At All: Memoirs of a Strategist

S o,' said the Javan, 'you must stay a couple of days. With your permission I will call a guesthouse in the next street.'

The Australian seemed slightly stunned by this. He turned to his wife.

'We're not expected anywhere before the weekend,' she said. 'Even then I'd say nothing is as important as this.'

***

Quite unlike the 21st-century arrival at Hong Kong, the airport at Makassar took me into a 19th-century world of wooden houses on stilts, and the *becak*, the ubiquitous bicycle taxi. The welcome also made Harry's Hong Kong version pale into insignificance. Jack almost wrung my hand off the end of my arm, and gave me a stinging slap on the back. 'Bloody good to see you, mate.'

'You, too, sunshine,' I said, trying as hard to dislocate his own arm. Old memories of shared Aussie football games came flooding in. 'You don't look any different. Still ugly.'

This delighted him. 'Not as bloody ugly as you, you bastard.' He grabbed my pack from me and strode towards a line of cars parked close to the terminal building. I remembered how one always had to walk fast to keep up with Jack.

He was an old school friend, one who had been promised a visit if circumstances permitted, and I'd not seen him for years. He was tall and lean, very little different from how I remembered him, and was someone who spent a lot of time tramping remote fields. He worked for an Australian agribusiness firm involved in marketing cocoa. I thought his leanness bordered on gaunt, but he didn't look unwell, just ugly, so I hoped that a constant diet of rice, with only a little protein, was the main reason.

He was talking almost as soon as we left the terminal. 'There is still a lot of the Makassar of old. It's been an *entrepôt* probably for a thousand years. It was certainly on the old Chinese trade routes, perhaps before the Sung dynasty.'

Apart from my recently acquired coastal knowledge, and the existence of a minor naval base, almost all I knew of Makassar was some vague link with hair oil and antimacassars. 'Home to the Bugis and the Makassarese, isn't it?'

'And one or two other ethnic groups,' Jack said. 'but the Bugis are the most famous. Many are probably still pirates. If you go down to the harbour you'll still see the traditional craft they use.'

'Is there much traditional ship-building still going on?' I asked.

Jack nodded. 'There are small boatyards still doing it as it was always done all up and down the coast. It's harder to find the big trees now, but there are still a few around. The University here has a department of naval architecture which has taken some interest in recording the old methods, but this isn't a culture that transcribes that knowledge very well. People often can't tell you how they do such a thing -- they just tell you to watch. You looking at boats on this trip?'

'Not seriously. I'm more interested in the navigable waters. I thought I'd spend a day here, and then go north. After that, I want to get over to the other coast and work my way south. Then I thought I'd take a sea passage back to Jakarta.' In fact, I couldn't really tell him why I was here, but there was no reason to create mystery where there needed to be none.

'You'll enjoy the overland travel. I'd go with you if I weren't so busy.'

Sulawesi stands out from other Indonesian islands. Often compared to an orchid, it also looks a little like an octopus, in contrast to the solid mass of Kalimantan to the west. My reference charts told me everything I could want to know about the waters between them but nothing about the infrastructure dispersed at different points on the waving arms of the octopus. I needed to take a look. Jack's presence was a bonus.

'I'm starved.' I said. 'Anywhere you know for some good seafood?'

'No Bintang first?' Bintang was Indonesia's pilsner-like brew, as ubiquitous as the *becak*.

'Why not?'

'Yeah,' said Jack. 'After all these years, why not?'

The descending sun shone right onto the first-floor balcony of the Kios Semarang, by the look of it a well-known watering hole. It was doing a fine trade. Below, on the seafront, street food vendors were setting up their carts for the nightly ritual of *mie goreng*, fried noodles, or *udang bakar*, grilled prawns. The roar of propane burners under the industrial-sized woks started to compete with the two-stroke motorcycles and mopeds of the evening crowd.

We propped up the balcony wall for more than a couple of hours, able to dangle our elbows into the street, and I finally lost count of the bottles consumed. The sea was the colour of the ore in a blast furnace, and the palm trees lining the front stood as silhouettes against it. ' I really am bloody hungry,' I said. 'If we don't do something about it, I'm going to pass out right here.'

Jack looked slightly cross-eyed. 'Still the same. Always wanting food.' It was perhaps the final observation of a thorough investigation of the years passed, and memories rekindled. We'd had a good yarn.

'Seafood, remember? And I'm not eating down there.' I gestured at the stalls.

'No worries. Know where to take you. Let me just settle up.'

'I'll get it.'

'Like bloody hell you will.'

'Still the same,' I said. 'Ugly and belligerent.'

Jack grinned. 'Yeah. Good-oh.'

The temperature in the restaurant was cold, and light reflected off the mirrored walls. These effectively doubled the visual space, showing virtual diners no less hungry than the real ones. The place was packed, and the numbers of waitresses almost equalled the number of diners. We were in, seated, order taken and more beer on the table within five minutes. '*Selamat malam, pak* Jack,' cooed one of the waitresses.

I laughed out loud. 'Know you here, do they?'

Jack shook his head. 'Not what you think. Just a good feed once a week, sometimes with someone from head office. Helps with the job evaluation.'

I pointed a finger at him. 'Prime mating material,' I said, our yarn having confirmed his continuing bachelorhood.

He pointed one back at me. 'Primate, yourself,' adding, 'makes sense to eat at the best place in town.'

The food came very quickly, the tiger prawns the ones we'd seen, almost done, on the grill in front of the restaurant. By the time we'd cracked their shells off, and worked our way through a couple apiece, the sweet-and-sour fish was on the table, a whole red snapper dressed in a wild red sauce. While we devoured that, Jack had a quiet word with our waitress. I raised my eyebrows at him. 'No worries,' he said. 'Just a local delicacy to finish with.'

Within minutes she was back with a covered hotpot, and removed the lid with a slight flourish as she left. 'Principally sea-cucumber, but there's shrimp, squid, crab and one or two other things in it,' Jack said with a grin. 'Dig in. Nothing on earth better than this.'

I leaned forward, sticking my nose over a disgusting looking, steaming mixture. However, it smelt far better than it looked, and I overcame my fears. It turned out I still had enough space to do it reasonable justice.

I finally had to push my plate away, feeling more than vaguely unwell. I put that down to fresh air and an excessive appetite, though some minutes later it occurred to me that we hadn't held back on the extra beer. Jack had leant back, and was also showing the signs of someone who had also consumed more than his fair share.

'Bloody hell,' I said. 'You do this once a week?'

He laughed. 'Not all this, no. You had that peaky Jakarta look about you. So this was just for you.'

We'd walked to the sea-front from Jack's house, and then to the restaurant, so we went back out into the town's night sights and smells. After the air-conditioning of the restaurant, it was like walking into a sauna, but I was glad to have the opportunity to help the dinner settle. The shops were still open, and looked as though they were doing the main business of the day. The roads were jammed, though the becaks seemed to be in currents of their own, flowing around and through the traffic with the ease of schools of fish on a reef.

We crossed a main avenue, and the wide open space of the town's parade field. Then we were in the quieter streets of Jack's neighbourhood, houses hidden behind high walls and spiked gates. Jack's house was a surrounded by the shadows of a large garden, but by that time a wonderful lassitude had come over me, the only thing I was interested in was sleep, and I was out within seconds of dropping onto Jack's spare bed.

The slight buzz in my head when I awoke confirmed a vague memory of the excesses of the previous evening, but it wasn't too bad, and the morning *mandi*, cold water scooped out of the tank and poured over my head, cleared some of it. I found that Jack had already gone to work, leaving a light breakfast on the kitchen table, so slaked my thirst with fresh juice, and worked my way through toast and jam. By the end of the second coffee, I felt completely restored.

I went down to the harbour, retracing some of our steps of the day before, but heading further north. The commercial shipping was a patchwork of ancient and modern, many small coastal tramp steamers competing with a dozen *pinisi* for dock space, while container ships occupied a separate modern wharf. I knew that any naval vessel would be anchored at the dockyard a little further up the coast, but there was no immediate means to give me access there.

So, for a while, I concentrated on the *pinisi*, wandering along the dockside and looking at the lines of these historic sailing craft. While they varied in size, their overall appearance was remarkably similar. Bow and stern were joined in a long, graceful curve, giving them the look of an enormous Aladdin's lamp. Each had a long protruding bowsprit, with several lines of standing rigging to the tall, wooden masts. A single set of ratlines ran from each gunwale amidships to each of the cross-trees. The cabin roof aft followed a line parallel to the deck, giving it a strange, cocked look. Fully two-thirds of the main deck opened into a capacious hold. The similarity among the vessels spoke of a long ship-building tradition based on a proven design. Somewhere in the pedigree was Arabian blood.

Most of the vessels were carrying rice sacks and logs, evidence of the trade in these goods between islands, and the lack of roads within them. Some were loading or unloading consumer goods, from soap powder to televisions.

As I stood there, I noticed a different vessel crossing the harbour towards the outer bar. This bore all the trademarks of a landing craft, with a bow loading-door, an open well or centre hold, and an aft wheelhouse-cum-bridge which stood higher than the rest. It had no tell-tale signs of age. My professional eye watched the strong wake, the steady throb of a diesel suggesting that the vessel was heavily powered. I also noticed that its lines were subtly curved – none of the hard planes of traditional steel-built craft. It carried no military markings, but the Indonesian flag fluttered at the stern. It made the bar quickly, and, apart from the top of the wheelhouse, was rapidly lost to sight beyond.

The sun sat directly overhead, and the sweat was pouring off me. I caught a *becak* back into town, and browsed in the gold and handicraft shops lining Jalan Somba Opu, the town's traditional commercial centre. The hissing roar of blowtorches and clink of hammer on anvil spoke of a thriving industry. The gold rings and necklaces on display had a rich, heavy yellow not seen in the lower-carat jewellery worn by western women.

The occasional antique shop displayed porcelain and stoneware. The blue and white of later Chinese dynasties tended to predominate, overpowering the earth tones of other mainland potteries. A Makassarese woman clothed in a batik dress, barefoot, with her hair pulled severely back into a bun, moved some wares in a shop window. She displayed a simple elegance, an economy of movement emphasizing long hours spent waiting for clients. I bought a small earthenware bowl from her, in the bottom of which two small, incised fish shimmered though a transparent emerald celadon glaze. Suddenly hungry, I stopped at a small roadside restaurant. While I ate some noodles, I reviewed my travel plans. Two days travel by bus would take me to Palu, the next major harbour, and further north, and then I'd work my way down the island's east coast. Finished eating, I stretched back in my chair, some of the previous day's lassitude still present, and I felt more relaxed than I had for a long time. Perhaps the riper, clean humidity of Sulawesi was working its way into my system, eliminating the effects of Jakarta's exhaust-laden air. I went back to Jack's for my pack.

It was clear from my earlier research in Jakarta that the Makassar Strait would continue to be the main shipping channel of interest to Australian trade. This had been confirmed with phone calls to both Asian and Australian shipping houses. I also had it in mind that it was not in Indonesia's best interest to lose the passage of that trade, because if the big ships went elsewhere, the smaller ones upon which the islands themselves depended would feel similarly threatened. There were really only two major ports of interest on the Strait, Makassar and Palu, but there was another aspect also: Sulawesi had seen some of the most vicious anti-Christian jihad in the past years. I needed a sense of the whole island. My *what ifs* to Harry had come back to mind: What if Sulawesi was where some of the international terrorist network had gone to earth? Far from Java meant well out of the spotlight. The Makassar Strait and Sulawesi were one and the same. I couldn't make any plans for the first without understanding much more about the second.

Yet I could not cover all this. I needed to understand the extent to which the Indonesian Navy had operational infrastructure along all coasts, and while I needed an ear to the ground to find out whether there were rumours of coastal terrorism, I couldn't do it myself. To capture some of that type of information, I'd have to plug into some local mechanism. What, I wondered, were the characteristics of a society which would abhor Islamic terrorism? Probably those very same people who felt the brunt of jihad. Where could I find them? Not far from Palu. But the main Christian centre was Minahasa, further to the northeast, so Manado, Minahasa's main city, also required a visit.

The ten days I'd allocated for the trip were gruelling. Two solid overland trips, first from Makassar to Palu, and then from Palu to Manado. From Manado I caught a ride in a boxy little freighter flying anything it could scrape together down to Luwu. I was a quite unofficial passenger, and raised the eyebrows of the airport staff at Luwu when they saw me emerge from the hold. But I learned three valuable facts.

The first was that while Palu, unlike Makassar, was not a deep water port, it had a resident provincial *komando*, and often moved troops on shallow-draughted vessels in and out of the bay.

The second, through a variety of quiet visits to churches on the way, sprinkled among the predominant presence of mosques, was of a network of missionary priests who maintained an informal link between them, but had agreed to exchange worrying information at a time when anyone of them might fall victim to a parang wielded by a scarved holy warrior. None I met in the north had anything specific, though more than one hinted at news I might learn south of Kendari. Try Raha, they said.

The third was when approaching Manado, continuing the eye-opening culinary experience shared with Jack, a roadside café offered a meal I could never have dreamt up myself. Between the dishes of chicken and pork, three others sat eyeing me. A hurried conversation with the Minahasan waitress confirmed that I'd correctly identified one. Dog, bat and rat, I learned, were favoured local dishes.

I came down from Luwu in time to catch the two o'clock ferry from Kendari. Kendari, while not of direct interest, for it was not a navigable bay and was too far from the Strait to be relevant, gave me a chance to see an Indonesia with which I was I was only marginally familiar – – small coastal hamlets whose occupants derived their living from both the land and the sea. And I wanted to take a sea passage back to Jakarta. From here I could take the ferry to Raha, and from there another to Buton, where a ship would be leaving for Jakarta in three days time.

The sun was searing, the humidity in the harbour stifling, and I was given a small cabin on the upper deck to be shared with several Indonesians. As the afternoon wore on the cabin became temporary home to more passengers as people came and went, taking turns to rest, or sitting together to talk while eating fruits or confections brought out of many baskets. I'd put my bag on an upper bunk, which gave me some measure of privacy, but the heat radiating down from the ceiling forced me out onto the deck.

The ferry was locally built. It was really a squat, motorized *pinisi* with a wooden hull somewhere between eighty to ninety feet long. It had two decks, with only the upper divided into cabins. The lower deck was open, and crammed into it were about a hundred and fifty people, most lying down on mats, again sleeping or eating. The mixed odours of humanity and spicy food were strong, and the cloying smell of *durian* , a mace-like tropical fruit loved by all Indonesians, rode above it all. The ferry's foredeck carried some cargo, on top of which was perched a single van. This had been manhandled aboard in Kendari.

From the upper foredeck, which doubled as the bridge, I watched for a while as the ferry hugged the coastline, rugged and broken, small bays with sand beaches opening and closing as we rumbled by. Small communities of wooden houses on stilts, some with mosques that sported sheet-metal cupolas, gave the coast a magical air, spirits alive in the graceful coconut palms that cloaked the shore. On retreating finally to my cabin, I found that a plate of rice with a single small fish and some red-hot sambal had been delivered. My cabin mates had already dealt with theirs, and watched me eat a late lunch.

'*Ke mana, tuan*?' asked the portly man across from me.

'I'm getting off in Raha', I said.

'Where do you come from?' asked the man. 'Are you from Holland?' Because of the country's colonial past, most westerners were still thought to be Dutch, at least by persons of middle age and up.

'From Australia.'

'*Dari Australi*', said the man to his neighbours, though it was clear that they had all understood. His unofficial role as questioner seemed to give him some importance among them. 'Why you come here? Tourist?'

'I work in Jakarta.'

'He works in Jakarta' said the man to the others. 'Why you not work in Australi? No work in Australi?'

The discussion blossomed, others gradually finding the courage to ask their own questions and not upset when I responded in kind. I was travelling with a schoolmaster, a village official, someone's wife, and several hangers-on, and they each had to have their turn. In the end I fell prostrate, exhausted, on my bunk to put an end to it. Not that I really minded, but in the end all I wanted to do was sleep. I felt their glances on me as they watched to see if I'd actually be able to fit into the bunk.

The slow deceleration of the diesels brought me around as the ferry pulled into Raha, at about nine in the evening. It took another half-hour to complete the approach and moor to the jetty, whereupon there was a rush to disembark. I waited with my bag on the upper foredeck, watching the lower-deck passengers scramble ashore and the vendors come aboard with food to sell to those carrying on to the next port. In the midst of the movement, the van that had perched on the cargo was eased ashore across a couple of narrow gangplanks. In a couple of minutes, it was started up and driven away.

My eye was caught by a group of men in uniform descending from the upper deck by the opposite companionway. I had been unaware of their presence, so they must have occupied cabins on the other side from mine. Their insignia marked them as naval officers, and some deference shown also indicated that one of them was significantly more senior. As they were pushing their way through the crowd, a Land Rover pulled up out of the gloom. The ranking officer climbed into the front, and when the rest had boarded, it blared its way back towards land.

I made my own way onto the jetty. It was several hundred metres to land, and I took a few moments to look at the other ships moored nearby before setting off. Most were Bugis *pinisi*, lit by low-wattage lights under the coach-roofing, and whose masts inscribed small arcs in the night sky as they moved to the slight chop in the bay. They appeared infinitely graceful, free of the blemishes of peeling paint and caulked seams that the early morning sun would once again reveal. A bucket being emptied from one prompted me to start off for town.

The earlier rice and fish seemed to have been a dream, and by the time I reached the town I was starving. There was only one restaurant sign on the street, and as I headed towards it, I noticed the navy Land Rover parked outside. Inside, all the tables were occupied, but, as I hesitated, the woman behind the cash register motioned me through to a back room. 'More tables,' she said, 'quieter.'

I nodded my thanks and went through. There were half a dozen tables on an enclosed patio, and I took one in a corner. A small girl brought the menu and I ordered a beer, waiting for it to come before thinking about food.

Once again I'd missed the naval officers, suddenly noticing them at a table partially hidden by a screen of vegetation. They were already halfway through their meal, which must have been ordered ahead of time. I tried not to stare, but they were fellow professionals, so I gave my order to the girl and sat to listen.

They were quite convivial. Two of their number were obviously good at telling jokes, and seemed to be vying with each other in impressing the senior officer. He occasionally told a joke of his own, drawing more than his fair share of laughter. A good half of the jokes employed a colloquial language I couldn't follow. But it didn't take a linguist to understand the sexually-explicit gestures that accompanied some of them. It seemed that the only real difference between this and an equivalent gathering in my own service was the drink on the table: no alcohol here.

After a while I forgot about them. The girl bought me some steamed shrimp, rice and a local vegetable, and I ate at a leisurely pace, enjoying the coolness of the evening. There was the occasional sound of someone drawing water from a well.

As I paid for my meal, I realized that I'd not put much thought into where to spend the night.

'Try *Penginapan Muna*', said the pretty young girl at the register, skin the smoothness and lustre of pearl. 'They have good rooms for foreigners.'

Guesthouse Muna was apparently only three blocks away, so I strolled down the street, passing shophouses locked for the night, but with the gleam of light escaping beneath and between the door-boards. An occasional tricycle *becak* passed, the rider clicking a tin can to indicate his presence. I preferred to walk, and said so, enjoying stars visible amongst the light night clouds.

I woke as dawn painted the shadows of the day on my bedroom wall. I found a steaming black coffee on the table outside my door, and sat listening to the movements of the staff in the depths of the guesthouse as I drank it. A boy approached requesting a breakfast order. While I waited for the food to be delivered, my mind drifted and I thought about the course of events that had brought me here. I wasn't thinking of how I came to be in Raha, but how I'd ended up in Jakarta. It had all begun one day on the deck of a frigate.

I think it was some of the shipboard routine that did it, the daily cycle of activities and procedures that keep a ship's crew in top form. I saw that there was a limit to personal initiative. In fact, initiative on a warship could be dangerous, if it upset routine. But I had a year in front of me before I made Commander, and then more years before making Captain. There was nothing in that cycle of routine that I did not now fully understand. So I requested a shore posting, wanting to keep the sense that the Navy was giving me all I wanted. And not wanting, at some moment, to come up against a peace-time wall of boredom. I knew Jakarta was open, and I asked for it.

But perhaps the Navy had been a surprising choice. On Dad's side, I was the fourth in a line of graziers, the Outback cattlemen; on Mum's, more, because her ancestors had been deported earlier than Dad's. Both families were members of that small band which kept moving out with the frontier. Over a generation ago, we landed in the Kimberley. Dad was a man at peace with his hostile environment. When one morning we'd ridden out and stopped at one of the holes with still enough water to keep the stock alive, and I'd expected a vociferous objection, I was surprised at his reaction to what I planned to do.

'Why do you want to do it?'

'Because the world is changing fast, and I must see some of it. I'd like to do it in the Navy.'

'Water, hm?' he'd said. Then, 'I'm glad you've found something else, Trev. I don't think the land will see another generation here.' But he'd spoken more to economics than rainfall, and as the old briar came alight between his palms, smoke curling up under the brim of his hat, his eyes had seemed light-years away, lost somewhere in contemplation of the generations past.

The breakfast boy seemed happy that I'd requested fruit as well as the habitual fried rice. As I ate, my mind drifted towards the idea I'd had during lunch with Cheun and Harry. It was still germinating and not yet in the form to be presented to Canberra formally, but I knew I'd have to put final shape to it soon. I had the lay of the waters through the Makassar Strait, but there were still strands that needed identifying and sorting, and I thought this was a process best undertaken in the area where I believed action would have to be taken. While I'd not come across the seething fire of openly aggressive militancy, fanned by known agents of Al Qaeda, there was an undercurrent of deeper concern flowing round the ripples of holy war being waged across the island.

I finished my breakfast, and subjected myself to the second ritual of the morning,, the *mandi* water quite frigid as I scooped it out of the tank and poured it over my head.

While Raha itself and the immediately neighbouring waters were of little importance to my broader plan, as they were off the main navigable Strait, I had a day and a half before needing to leave for the larger ferry back to Jakarta. I wanted to see the *pater*, and if he had something specific to tell me, I thought I could best use the remaining time here, so I decided to stay a further night before continuing south. I could still look at waters I might not get the chance to see again. I spent fifteen minutes examining my map, then, through the guesthouse owner rented a motorcycle fit for off-road travel. There were roads heading west and south from Raha that would get me to different sections of the coast.

Until I'd run across one or two like him around Palu, I hadn't thought that people like the *pater* still existed. No, that's not completely true - I hadn't comprehended that people like him existed at all. A lost generation of missionary priests doing whatever God and theology school had instructed them to do at least forty years before, and still, perhaps more through luck than good living and adequate health care, generally alive and ministering to small Christian enclaves in what was a predominantly Muslim Sulawesi. Minahasa was so fervently Christian it must seem an affront to the Muslim occupants of the island as a whole. But was the region so different from what one would find anywhere else? Certainly there were other religious wars. But I wondered whether jihad could be just an exercise which, sometimes, in certain contexts, did not require death of the infidel as an end result.

I could not forget the moment, years before, and in another Indonesian city, when I was walking past the main Army mosque, and the bells of Westminster had come flowing from the building. I looked up to the minaret, expecting to see some cleric beating his head for having put the wrong tape in the public address system. It took me some moments to realize that the whole of the city was, at that moment, transfixed by Diana's funeral service; that the music was coming collectively through open windows from every television in the city, and that the guardian of the mosque was watching it, no different from anyone else. What, I'd wondered, did they think of the ceremony? Heresy? Pageantry? I hadn't yet had the nerve to ask. Perhaps the *pater* could tell me.

The *pater* was only slightly different from my mental image of how he would look, after meeting several in the north - a small, almost wizened, man in a black robe. If he'd ever sported a tonsure, age had made complete work of it. His smooth dome was as good as polished. As we talked, seated on one of the bench-pews of his tin-roofed *gereja*, I saw a man wholly at peace with a life that had almost run its full course within the boundaries of a small coastal town, serving the needs of its Christian population in front of the unadorned cross screwed to the wall. There was apparently still local religious tolerance, because no-one had tried to burn him out, but he was frank about broader currents. 'The younger people will not come to services.' Remnants of a European accent of some sort clung to slowly spoken English. 'Fear affects the young in more insidious ways. There are not enough anyway to stand up to the mass of a Laskar Jihad.' These Java-based youth movements had sent thousands of its young warriors on cleansing missions throughout the archipelago. 'It only takes a teenage Muslim neighbour to put the wrong idea into a crusader's head and a whole village ends in ashes.'

'Are there any new movements anywhere on the coast? Patterns of action which suggest outside influences?'

'This is, and always was, a region of inter-island trade. People are used to all manner of comings and goings.'

'But nothing disturbing those regular patterns, or adding new eddies?'

'They have always managed to make a living no matter how much the military interfere, or do not, as the case may be.'

I didn't immediately understand this allusion. 'The military has always had a presence,' I said.

'*ABRI masuk desa*,' he said with a wry grimace, referring to one of the long-standing programs of military infiltration and control of each and every village in the nation. It took a long time for Jakarta to understand the costs of fear stemming from army-led development, but there had never been much of an effort to undo what the army still did. Military salaries were gathered by markedly feudal methods; Jakarta just gave pocket-money.

'Just that, though? Or something else?'

He looked at me through still sparkling old eyes, searching my face for something. Was I a threat to his peace, his parish? Would I somehow bring the wolf that would tear into his flock? Then he looked down at his clasped hands, which he opened as if in supplication. 'Perhaps you'll find something to the west,' he said. 'There is movement that no-one understands.' Then he stood and faced the cross, perhaps asking for forgiveness.

Muna Island, of which Raha was the main town, was quite small, and a couple of hours at a touring pace would see me at the opposite coast. I stopped at the one small petrol station in Raha to buy *benzin*. The sight of a foreigner on a motorcycle soon brought a crowd of young boys. They chattered and laughed at a stranger's appearance, and some ran after me as I started the bike up and left.

I was very quickly out of the main urban area. On the potholed road, I passed mile after mile of small wooden houses almost identical in their architecture, fringed by tropical fruit and coconut trees. I kept my speed down to avoid children, cattle and goats, all oblivious to my passing and intent on crossing the road rather than using it. Chickens squawked with fright at close encounters with my front wheel.

With a continuous blaring of its horn, a Land Rover sped past, clearly less concerned about the other users of the road. A couple of faces peered curiously through the windows at me, and I recognized the naval officers of the night before. As the vehicle sped away, its military plate glinted in the mid-morning sun.

After a couple of hours I reached the other side of the island, I was thirsty. I bought some small oranges from a small girl in a roadside stand and took them down to the beach. I sat and watched moored fishing craft bobbing in the slight motion of the shallow bay as I peeled an orange. Most were canoes with single or twin outriggers, some with masts for a lateen sail.

A fisherman who had been mending nets behind a bamboo shed came over. He stood looking at me, not speaking.

I offered him my peeled orange. He accepted with alacrity, and squatted beside me in the easy manner of one unused to chairs. He was a gummy old soul, but chewed his way through the fruit, segment by segment, talking through his full mouth as he did so.

'It's a busy day here today, many foreigners.'

'Other tourists?' I asked, surprised, as I hadn't seen any.

'Not tourists, foreigners.' said the old man, and gestured in the direction of the sea.

There was nothing visible on the water that gave me any clue as to the old man's meaning.

'Does this road go all the way to the south?' I asked, pointing to the road that had now become an unpaved coastal track.

'One can go that way,' said the man.

'Where does it go?' I persisted.

'It goes to ...,' but I didn't catch the word, the name of a village I assumed. 'But it is hard to get there today. I would stay at home.'

Nothing in the weather suggested any physical constraint to travel. 'Is it far?' I asked. I pulled my map out to work out where the village was.

'About three hours. But on your machine less time.' He was obviously referring to walking speeds. 'Today you may not get there.'

I was still not sure which village the old man meant, and showing him the map confused him. I was puzzled, but I stowed the rest of the water in my pack, and gave him the last of the fruit. As I mounted the bike, he was still squatting on the beach, looking out to sea and masticating the fruit with his few remaining teeth.

The track south followed endless rows of coconut palms, and the beach was littered with debris from the trees. Small rocky headlands became more numerous, until, for a while, the track veered inland and skirted a fairly large bluff. As it came back to the shore, a large bay opened in front of me. As I travelled, I thought about the old man, and the millions like him, who made a daily living from the land and sea in any way they could. They depended on rice, but any supplement of fish or vegetable was the true index of quality of life. It was a precarious balance, only the more wealthy ever approached being well-fed, but there was a high degree of contentment with the age-old ways. Discontent came from the things that disturbed their equilibrium.

My focus came back to the road, and immediately I saw, halfway down the bay, a group of men standing on the shore looking out to sea. Mindful of the old man's remarks, I pulled the bike to a stop beneath a palm, safe from their view. They were studying the sea through binoculars. At first glance I could see nothing to keep their attention, but then noticed a brownish smudge on the horizon. It was not large enough for me to distinguish anything clearly.

I was still close to the bluff, so decided to look for a higher vantage point. What was apparently a goat path disappeared into the rocks, so I left the bike fairly well hidden in the vegetation, and followed the path through the rocks and into the trees. As I reached the crest a hundred feet or so above the water, I had a view of the sea beyond. I pushed my way through a few small bushes to get a better view of the whole bay.

The knot of men was still on the beach. Beyond them, , at the far end of the bay, there was a large limestone cliff, mostly bare of any vegetation. Between the men and the cliff, other groups of men were gathered. Everyone's attention seemed to be focussed on the sea.

What had been a brown smudge had hardened into several shapes. I counted a dozen, and recognized them as landing craft. A larger patrol craft followed astern. As I watched, the landing craft approached the beach in three columns of four, then fanning out to arrive simultaneously. The patrol craft reduced speed, remaining out to sea.

Until that moment, I had not paid much attention to the nature of what I was seeing, surprised more by fact of the concentration of military hardware. Suddenly realizing that I was witnessing a military manoeuvre, I ducked down in the bushes, a reflex stemming from an immediate wish not to be seen. Where was the security that allowed me to get so close, unobserved? The shore party was so busy watching seawards that it had failed to notice my less than surreptitious arrival. But I was now in a quandary – I wanted to see what was happening in the bay, but, if I did continue to watch, it might become more difficult to get away unobserved. The old man's comments were beginning to make sense.

The landing craft slammed onto the beach, front doors thudding onto the sand. Groups of heavily armed men in battledress jumped off and fell into defensive postures on the beach. The sound of gunfire was quite clear. As I watched, some of the landing parties ran forward in loose formation, overrunning some defenders and making their way to the base of the cliff. I could see that there were also defenders at cliff-top.

The clattering sound of a helicopter turned my attention seawards. I was just in time to see it lifting off from a deck at the stern of the patrol craft standing offshore. Once airborne, it began a rapid run toward shore, and, building speed and lift, gained altitude. It started to menace the defensive positions on the cliff-top.

A dozen men began ascending the cliff-face. It was a rough surface offering plenty of footholds so the ascent was rapid. But the defence put up a fight and only nine attackers were successful at the top in attaching their ropes. Shouts reached the beach, and the full-scale ascent began.

Within minutes almost several hundred men had scaled the cliff. I could see them milling around, subduing the remaining defenders, and then forming defensive positions of their own. At a signal, the remaining parties on the beach ran forward and joined the ascent. The helicopter disappeared beyond the cliff.

51

The knot of men below my bluff began to walk away. Judging by the instant revival of the many corpses scattered along the beach, I assumed the landing exercise to be over. The ropes disappeared from the cliff, and gradually groups of attackers arrived back to join the others on the beach. A bundle was quickly assembled into a sizeable tent and my knot of men disappeared into it, followed by one or two others from among the exercise group.

Their disappearance also made it prudent for me to leave, so I made my way back to the bike. I wheeled it back along the track until part of the bluff shielded me from the beach, then kicked the starter. It felt like an eternity before the bay disappeared completely behind me.

The old man was still behind the shed slowly threading new line into a ragged net. I picked up some more fruit at the little kiosk on the roadside, and walked over to where he was working. After a while the old man put his wooden needle down. He took another proffered orange, and again assumed the squatting posture.

'The ships came,' he said.

'I saw some,' I said.

'Many foreigners.'

'Many soldiers.'

'From far away, *jauh*, far.'

'Do you know where they come from?' I asked.

'From *Jawa*,' said the old man. 'For weeks now they have been coming. Sometimes more, sometimes less.'

I wondered why Javanese troops would be brought to Sulawesi for exercises that seemed rather mundane. There wasn't really any shortage of usable beaches on Java, though I wasn't sure about the cliffs. But I also thought that they would not have come all the way from Java in the landing craft.

'Where are the ships from?' I asked.

'There have been many of those built here,' said the old man.

'Here? Not in this village.'

'*Bukan*, no. In Kendari, in Kolaka, and over the water there,' and he nodded in the direction of the south-west peninsula. 'They say that they are for the people to use, for the *rakyat*, but when they need them, they just take them back.'

'Those ships were being used somewhere else?'

'*Ya*, some of them were. They are popular up there,' and he indicated north up the coast. 'They can move cattle and trees and many other large things more easily.' He spat out a large wad of fibre from which he had sucked all the juice. 'I don't like them. Here they bring fire.'

That appeared to be the end of the conversation, for the old man went back to his net-mending. After a moment, I decided that I'd make my way back to Raha, as there was no other track that I could use to go further south. Again I left the remainder of the oranges for the old man and rode away.

That night I went back to where I'd eaten the night before, the owner of the guesthouse indicating that it was the only reasonable choice. The same woman welcomed me, and ushered me back to the rear of the restaurant and to the same table. It had apparently become mine while I was in town.

I nodded to the question '*Bir?*', and sat back to ponder the menu while the drink was brought. I ordered steamed crab, vegetables and rice when it came. The beer tasted rich and satisfying after a day in the hot sun, even if warm and served over ice.

It was just after I'd started a second helping of crab, and was pulling the shreds of meat from the claws, when the noise of a group of men arriving filtered through from the front of the restaurant. It grew in volume, and the same naval officers of the night before, the ones I'd seen pass in the Land Rover earlier in the day, were shown to the table that had become theirs. They inspected me as they passed by.

I was sure this group must have been the knot of men on the beach. I'd not made the connection before, as I'd been too surprised by the whole event to think about it. The number was about right, and the way that they deferred to the senior officer had also been evident from a distance on the beach. As they sat down, he said something to one of the others. Clearly it was an order, for the man glanced at me and nodded. After a couple of seconds he got up and came over.

'*Selamat malam.*'

'Good evening.'

He was slightly overweight for his age, stretching his collar. 'I see you are enjoying some of our good Indonesian crab.'

'It's the best I've had for a long time.'

'*Dari mana?* Where are you from?'

'From Jakarta. I'm taking some holiday.'

'Ah, from Jakarta. You work there?'

'Yes.'

'May I ask what you do?'

The questioning was becoming discourteous and I had a sense of an open trap, because I was what he was, a naval officer, and had been doing something, watching a military exercise, that he and his associates might instantly classify as illegal. While I thought a lie was not necessarily the best way out, one came instantly to mind and was out of my mouth almost before I knew it. 'I'm a travel agent. I work with one of the larger agencies in Jakarta.'

'Scouting out some new places to go? Not many tourists come here.'

I nodded, cursing myself, my heart in my mouth for a moment in case he asked me for harder evidence, perhaps a brochure. 'Yes. Overland travel in this part of your country has quite good potential. We are thinking of some small tours for adventure groups.' Not, I thought, actually so very far from the truth, but certainly not *civilian* groups.

He nodded back. 'Very exciting. Well, enjoy your meal,' and returned to his own table.

The comments that were passed back to the senior officer were too quiet for me to hear, but I was the subject of some more cursory inspection. Then, curiosity apparently satisfied, they concentrated on their meal, ignoring me completely.

I sank my own concerns in another iced Bintang. Almost by accident, though guided by the unspecific comments of an old priest, I had stumbled on some manoeuvres. Certainly interesting, but not necessarily important, though other priests in the north had indirectly pointed me in this direction.. But anything of this nature required a report for Canberra. Anything useful meant that I'd have to dig a little further. Security seemed lax, so it was unlikely that I'd be risking more than I had today.

It was still quite early when I got back to the guesthouse, so I stopped to talk to the owner, who seemed to spend twenty-four hours of the day behind the desk. A few minutes elicited the information I wanted, and then I thanked him and went to my room. A half-page of reading put me straight to sleep.

The next morning coffee and breakfast came together and were waiting for me outside my door when I awoke. I had a view of the strait just off Raha, and watched the movements of small fishing canoes while I ate. A couple of larger *perahu* were drifting south on the tide, large lateen rigs trying to catch the wisps of early morning breeze. None was evident in the flattened profile of the sail.

I left Raha half an hour later by the southerly road. It was a better surface than the westerly road of the previous day, and I was soon well away from the town. I passed through some cashew plantations, but then entered a region clearly less prosperous. Rich soils were replaced by limestone outcroppings. Household gardens became smaller, little plots of green among the rocks. At a fork in the road I veered off to the west, and started to climb onto a broad plateau, unbroken by the normal, rich tropical vegetation. There were large expanses of grey limestone, extensions of the type of cliff I'd seen yesterday, with sparse cover burnt black by the fires of wretchedly poor farmers. An occasional figure could be seen bent double, scrabbling in a small soil pocket. Long rows of stone walls divided this moonscape into small rock-fields. Existence here seemed to be so critical that each and every plant warranted superhuman effort to help it reach harvest.

On the far side, the road again descended towards a sandy bay, but there were also more stretches of cliff jutting into the sea. The cliffs showed marks of the various geological uplifts that had occurred in the past, parallel ledges running horizontally as far as the eye could see, smooth overhangs carved in the shape of the curl of surf that had not broken beneath it for thousands of years. Along the coast were broad swathes of mangrove.

The road ended at the beach, tracks heading north and south, and I went north. The questions from yesterday came back: what had the beach landing been for? Was there some of the military still on the beach?

The track was very much like the one of the day before, except that I had no view of the sea. After a while the mangrove swamps to seaward brought the stale smell of hot brackish water and decaying vegetation. Occasionally a small water channel ran towards the mangroves, and I had to steer carefully across small bridges made of coconut logs.

I was enjoying the warm dappled light that fell through the trees above me, winding my way along a road that followed the lie of the land, convinced that I was alone in the world. I hit a straight stretch that almost disappeared into the shade quite far ahead, and opened the throttle up. As I hit the shade I realized that three vehicles were parked there, and that a group of soldiers was lounging around. Some were smoking.

They heard me before I saw them, two soldiers with semi-automatic rifles at the port already moving into the roadway. I skidded to a halt a couple of yards away, and an immediate sense of having been very foolish went right through me. This appeared quite a different group from the night before.

'What are you doing here? Where were you going?' The questions were rattled off by what appeared to be the platoon commander, a young but heavily-built man wearing the chevrons of a sergeant. He was as ugly as sin, with an attitude to match. By this time, most of the platoon had surrounded me. I switched off the motorcycle.

'I was just motoring along this track to see where it went,' I said, not pretending I didn't understand. Then, 'Just touring.' The platoon commander listened in stony silence. Then he beckoned me over to the side of one of the vehicles. 'Stay here. We'll see,' he said.

A field radio sat on the vehicle's canvas roof, and the sergeant picked up a telephone headset, speaking a call-sign into it. My presence was described. The man signed off and replaced the headset.

'You two come with me. Put him in the back of the truck.'

55

The two indicated soldiers pushed me to the back of the vehicle, and pulled back the canvas tarp that covered it. I was pushed up onto one of the benches, and my guards took up flanking positions. My motorcycle was undergoing a thorough inspection by the rest of the platoon, and I wondered whether it would still be in one piece when – I tried not to think about 'if' – I came back.

The truck bumped on up the track for almost thirty minutes. I had only a partial view out through the front windscreen, the tarp having been tied down again and the soldiers blocking some of my view. The vegetation continued uninterrupted.

Then the vehicle slammed to a halt and the platoon commander jumped out of the front passenger seat, motioning to my guard to bring me. I was shoved out of the back, and marched over to a large tent pitched under a stand of cashew trees. Its sides were tied up to allow ventilation; through them I caught a glimpse of sea and sand beyond a fringe of palms. I was clearly toward the southern end of the bay I had observed yesterday, though the cliffs were not immediately visible.

In the tent was a group of men in battledress. They were enjoying some coffee, and appeared relaxed, but a couple of maps were spread out on the table in front of them, and small models of landing craft and gun emplacements were distributed across the maps.

As I was pushed in one of the men rose from his chair and came over. His insignia made him a full colonel, and *KOPASSUS* was emblazoned in clear lettering on an arm patch. As I digested the latter, and recalled Bulyanto, I saw something similar in this man's face that was just as good as any badge. He looked at me carefully. 'We don't see many foreigners around here,' he said.

I fell back on my lie of the night before. But I was now getting into deeper waters. Did it really sound reasonable, that my presence here was quite coincidental?

The colonel nodded. 'Ah, these crazy tourists. Not satisfied with Bali. Always wanting a new thrill. You're Australian?'

'Yes.'

'Well, Mr ....?'

'Gregory.' I allowed him my real name, for the contents of my wallet would soon give the lie to a false one. Thankfully I'd carefully stowed all official identification of diplomatic status in my backpack in the guesthouse. I hoped he wouldn't look for a business card.

'Well, Mr Gregory, I suppose that we must let progress take its course. After all, you all have money to spend.' He was about to add something else, when a young officer jumped into the tent '*Datang sekarang, Kolonel.*' The information that something or someone finally was coming galvanized the officers in the tent. The colonel glanced briefly at me, then snapped at his young messenger. 'Guard him.'

While I couldn't move without causing trouble, my eyes followed the colonel out of the tent as the group moved toward the shore. As they cleared the trees, I saw groups of soldiers on the beach in similar defensive postures to the ones I'd seen yesterday. When I looked out to sea, there was the same brownish haze.

Whether it was the same force being trained, I couldn't tell. Obviously I couldn't ask. My better vantage point gave me a close-up view of what were well-trained troops. And they carried the steel-wire image I had in my mind of *KOPASSUS*.

As the first assault on the cliffs was underway and the helicopter clattered overhead in a repeat of the exercise of the day before, a Land Rover came racing down the beach from the north and stopped under trees well short of the battlefield. A group of men climbed out. As they approached my stomach sank. They were my naval-officer restaurant neighbours of the night before. Would my story hold? Had I dug myself a pit too deep to get out of? A picture of the shame of being shipped home, *persona non grata*, flashed before my eyes - caught in simple espionage.

Their attention held by the activities on the beach and the cliff, they did not immediately see me. The senior officer came over to greet the army colonel, and offer an excuse for their late arrival.

Then he noticed me.

'What in *Allah*'s name is he doing here?'

'An unexpected visitor. An Australian travel agent who happened to arrive at the wrong time.'

'I know *what* he is, but what's he doing here? *Why* is he watching this?'

'You know him?' the colonel looked at me in surprise. 'He was stopped by my men on the southern track. They brought him up here about an hour ago. He was brought in just as the landing started.' He looked at me more closely. He saw short hair and a shaven face, but I had no idea whether I fitted any other mental picture. Perhaps I was too clean cut for tourism.

'With all due respect, *Kolonel*, you should get him out of here.' The naval officer was trying to control his anger. His features were a little different from the colonel's, perhaps dominated by what I saw as a harder black in his eyes. His *bahasa* was not the *bahasa* of Java. I saw in him something I had not picked in the restaurant, something that I was having difficulty in defining, but which seemed to speak more strongly of the sea than did the attributes of any of his subordinate officers.

'Yes, I probably should, Aminuddin' said the colonel, turning from me, but giving no idea what he was thinking.. 'But this is just a training exercise. He's probably seen this a hundred times at the cinema. All those old World War II films.'

Why was the naval officer so upset when his counterpart apparently saw my presence as only a minor, unworrying, breach in security?

'With respect again, *Kolonel*, I think you should send him away.'

'Mr Gregory, my colleague suggests that you shouldn't be watching this. He's quite right. My men will take you back to your motorcycle. Don't think of bringing tourists here. *Selamat jalan.*'

'Colonel, thank you for your hospitality. You've added a different dimension to my holiday. But I won't try and sell this to my clients,' and I motioned towards the cliff.

'Go, Mr Gregory.'

I recognized an order when I heard it, and saw a spark of flint in his eye. I turned back, catching sight of the naval officer. He was watching me intently, clearly not believing who I said I was.

I was once again unceremoniously loaded into the Land Rover. The loutish platoon commander dumped me at the bike.

'Get out of here. Don't come back.' The order was reinforced by rifles pointed threateningly.

The motorcycle seemed not to have been tampered with, and started without any difficulty, so I went south as ordered. Until I rounded the first bend, my back felt naked. Once down the coast, at the point where I'd descended from the plateau, I stopped, pushed the bike up on its stand, and wandered down onto the beach, where I sat on a piece of driftwood and watched the waves lapping at the shore.

It was a fix I was lucky to have left behind – careless did not begin to describe it. They had treated me with respect, but the military would have needed only a little more suspicion to have put me through quite a nasty wringer. Human rights of detainees was not exactly their specialty.

What I'd seen, a simple training exercise, had not been remarkable. Yet, if it were being repeated regularly, and for different batches of troops? There hadn't been any sophisticated hardware evident, though that could have been under wraps, and the only vessels had been the landing craft, nothing out of the ordinary at all. It all impinged only marginally on my own duties, though *KOPASSUS* made me think of war games and I remembered young Soekendro at the cadet graduation ceremony. What was he doing now?

I sifted through what the old man had said about the landing craft being used for civilian cargo. I remembered seeing one identical crossing the bar at Makassar. And another one just south of Palu. He was undoubtedly right that there were quite a few around. They were eminently practical for this island nation, and a tool not to be wasted until requisitioned by a navy that had something to do.

'Ah, *pak* Trevor. You're back.' The owner of the guesthouse, a man of late middle age, slightly paunchy and with reading glasses perched on the end of his nose, looked up from his newspaper. 'Your key. Oh, the police called around a little earlier. They want to see you.'

Perhaps I wasn't out of the woods after all. 'Did they say why they wanted to see me?'

'No, but they asked that you go around to the station as soon as you get back.'

I thought for a moment. It could be just a routine request but the events of the day suggested something else. The naval commander – what was his name?... Aminuddin – perhaps had not let the matter drop with his army compatriot. *You did check his identification?* I could imagine him demanding to know. A prickle of worry began to form in my mind. Perhaps more than a prickle.

'*Pak* Nahib, I wonder if you could do something for me. Could you get me a ticket on the night ferry back to Kendari? It's possible that I've overstayed my welcome. Nothing serious, but perhaps I should move on.'

'Very wise, *pak* Trevor. With these men in uniform you never know. I can send one of my boys to the ferry office. Once you're gone, perhaps they'll forget about you. Very often they just want a foreign visitor to be in their register.'

It took the boy half an hour to come back to the guesthouse with a ticket for a berth similar to the one I'd had two days before. 'Departs nine o'clock, *tuan*,' he said. 'But it's best to be there by eight-thirty.'

At eight-fifteen, I said my thanks and paid my bill, adding a tip. 'Perhaps you could say that you think I've gone south to take a ferry across to Buton if the police come back. It's only a small untruth.'

'Perhaps, *pak* Trevor. But it's best not to tell untruths to these people. They can make life very difficult. It is already a risk to have sent my boy to get you a ferry ticket, but he knows to say – if the police ask – that you approached him directly to buy the ticket – he does it all the time for our guests – and that I was unaware. He will make himself scarce until after the time the ferry docks in Kendari in the morning – I have told him to go visit his aunt and stay the night there.' I nodded. I'd been fortunate that he'd not reported my immediate return at the end of the afternoon. I expressed my gratitude for his help

He shrugged in self-deprecation. 'All I've done is make your stay a little more pleasant. Travel safely, *pak* Trevor.'

It was fully dark when I left for the ferry. The wharf was only half a kilometre from the guesthouse, so I walked, taking a couple of back streets through town to avoid the police station.

The nightly departure of the ferry to Kendari was an important event. Passengers, touts and spectators milled along the jetty. I looked for an increased police presence, but didn't see anything to suggest surveillance. I stepped through the gate as part of a larger party, my ticket was inspected without comment and I was waved onto the quayside.

I stayed back from the ferry, standing in the loom of a couple of larger *pinisi* that were moored across from it. Only when the last boarding call came at eight-forty five did I walk over to the gangway and up the companionway to the upper deck and the crammed cabin. Eyes of my cabin-mates sparkled out of the gloom as I looked for my berth. Voices crackling over a tannoy and shouts from the wharf announced the cast-off, and the ship trembled as the diesel built up revolutions. At a signal from the bridge the screw bit, and the ferry started to move astern. She swung in a long, sweeping arc to starboard, and then slowed. As the way came off, the thrust was reversed and she began to move ahead. The distance between the lights on the jetty decreased and they sank slowly towards the water as the ferry picked up speed. Within fifteen minutes the town had almost completely disappeared.

I came out of the mists of a final doze that had capped a good night's sleep and looked out of the cabin window just as dawn was breaking. The ferry had entered the narrows into Kendari bay, and was about fifteen minutes from mooring at the dock.

Most of the passengers were on deck and I threaded my way through them, looking for the head. Small children still lay asleep among the bundles of personal goods. Several men were just completing their prayers at the small *musholla* on the stern deck.

I had my pack ready, and was standing at the rail looking at the waterside habitations, when the dock came into view as the ferry swung towards it.

Unlike three days before, when I'd left Kendari, the crowds were not milling along the edge but were held back by a cordon of police. The prickle of worry that I'd managed to shed the night before now reasserted itself as a much larger thorn. I wasn't aware of any VIP aboard.

If the welcome party were for me, I was in trouble. Perhaps Nahib had been questioned further by the police. Perhaps there *had* been surveillance, and it had been thought better to pick me up under provincial rather than local authority. I knew that I didn't want to find out whether I was the intended recipient of their welcome. I ran back towards the stern and onto the side away from the wharf. Small motorized canoes were picking up passengers from the lower deck already, ferrying them to the opposite side of the bay.

I beckoned to one. The man held up three fingers. Three thousand rupiah. Daylight robbery, but there was little choice. I nodded and climbed over the rail, scrambling down the side. Open windows cut into the lower deck gave easy footholds. I stepped into the canoe, careful not to capsize it.

'Five thousand if you go now.' The man nodded with delight.

I sat down and pulled a piece of old sail cloth around my shoulders in attempt to shield some of my features from anyone who might be watching from the dock. At the roar of the outboard I grabbed the gunwales, the canoe lurching to port as it turned. For a moment I thought that I'd end up in the water, to be ignominiously pulled ashore by the police, but the canoe righted as it straightened out into the bay. No shouts came from behind.

It took ten minutes to cross to the far side. Up the bay, large bamboo fishing platforms stood like monstrous black-widow spiders in the shallow waters, the area beneath them in dark shadow.

At the small landing dock, which seemed to open directly into a water-side market, the boatman bobbed his thanks, knowing he'd made a day's wages. I grabbed my pack, and threaded my way into the market, searching for a telephone.

The market stank. The overnight catch had already been landed, and the concrete slabs of the stalls were covered with a rainbow arc of fish. Stall owners called to me jokingly as I passed, clearly hoping that I might just buy something. Then I was into the turmoil of the street beyond.

At a small store with a phone kiosk, the woman demanded a down payment before letting me dial.

'Jack.'

'Trev? You're up early. Where are you?'

'I'm back in Kendari. I'm calling because I may be in a spot of trouble.'

Jack laughed. 'You? In a spot of trouble? What've you done? Hit a copper?'

'Not quite, and I can't explain it now. But I need to get out of here, and I don't think I can use the local airport.'

'Jesus, that sounds serious. Let me think a minute.'

My quandary was that to be able to leave Sulawesi quickly, I had to go to Makassar. However, the southern half of Sulawesi is like an inverted horseshoe. I was on the east coast of the eastern arm. Makassar lay on the west coast of the western arm.

Jack came back on the line. 'Look, the only way I can think of is by the Kolaka ferry. If you're in Kendari, you'll have to get yourself over to the other coast, and take the car ferry across the bight to Bone.' He pronounced it 'bonay'. 'I can meet

61

you there tomorrow morning. It'll take you until afternoon to get to the ferry. It'll mean another overnighter.'

'You still going to Bali?' I asked.

'Yeah. I was going tomorrow.'

'Get me a ticket, too. I'll pay you back later.'

'There's a midday flight. If you're in Bone at dawn, we can get to Makassar airport in three hours, and be in good time for that one. No need to come into town.'

'Thanks. I can't tell you how much I appreciate the help.'

After a long drive, a weary taxi-driver dropped me at a small coffee shop near the Kolaka dock, once I was sure that there was no repeat of what I'd seen in Kendari. I stayed inside, drinking coffee, until it was almost time for the ferry to leave. Again it was dark when I boarded, and the ferry left on time.

Maybe I'd been wrong in my assumptions. But I didn't think so. More likely, the police must have assumed, when I had not disembarked in Kendari, that I had never got on in the first place, that the ferry ticket purchase by the guest-house boy had been a ruse. If I had not arrived in Kendari by the only immediate means possible, then it was highly unlikely I'd be further on within the space of half a day. Perhaps they thought that watching distant outgoing ferries was a waste of effort. Whatever they did think, it seemed my luck was holding. I was ahead of the pack, imaginary or not.

The ferry was flat-bottomed, built of steel, and overbearingly hot inside. I found a corner of the upper deck where no bodies were sprawled, put my pack down, and sat against it. Eventually I dropped off into a fitful sleep. My broken dreams had me being chased through the outback by something without shape, all the more terrifying for being unknown.

Jack was waiting for me when the ferry docked next morning, his landcruiser parked in a waiting area near the end of the jetty built out over the mudflats.

'You alright?'

'Didn't sleep quite as well last night as the night before. Haven't shaved for two days.' I rubbed my chin.

'Well, climb in. From what you implied the sooner we get you out of here the better.'

As we made our way from the coast, and climbed up into the limestone hills of South Sulawesi, I recounted what had happened. Jack listened without comment. When I'd finished, he thought for a moment.

'It's hard to say whether you're in the shit or not. I agree with you that they've probably lost your tracks. Getting off the ferry the way you did in Kendari was a smart move. If it *was* you they were after, and they'd caught you, they could've held you for days. What branch of the army was it? Did you catch the insignia on the uniforms?'

'I ran into a *KOPASSUS* unit. That's what the colonel sported.'

'They're Special Forces! Hard as nails. Throw fear into everybody.'

'I know. That's what makes it interesting. There was also a naval officer there, who seemed to have considerable authority. If the police were after me, I'd bet he instigated the whole thing. The army type forgot me the minute I left.' *Aminuddin*, I said to myself, the name engraving itself in my mind.

Jack shook his head. He knew the undesirability of getting mixed up with the military, largely a law unto itself. When ABRI was around, disappearances were common. The added complication of my official position occurred to him a few minutes later.

'You'd better spend a couple of nights in Bali. Establish your presence there as quickly as possible. You may need some witnesses to your having been elsewhere – in Bali itself -- at approximately the same time. People here are notorious for not knowing exactly what day of the week it is.'

'I'm not sure. I'll think that one through as we go.'

The countryside became more precipitously hilly as we went. The last few ranges before the west coast were perpendicular cliffs, thrust skywards at some distant period. Luxuriant foliage closed in on the road, making it tunnel-like in places. Small basins of tightly-packed rice terraces opened in verdant blazes of sunshine. I found myself beginning to relax as I paid more attention to the landscape and less to the road behind.

We hit the coastal plain almost three hours after leaving Bone. We reached Makassar airport quickly, the main road forming the western boundary to the single runway. At the departure hall yellow-suited porters clustered around the landcruiser, but Jack waved them away.

'Merpati, Trev. The flight should leave in thirty minutes. I hope the plane has arrived.'

I followed him through check-in and security. Our boarding passes were examined cursorily and we were waved through without comment. There was nothing to suggest that extra security had been set up. When Jack gave me my boarding pass in the waiting room, I saw that it was made out in the name of G. Trevor. Jack saw my amusement. 'It's a common mistake here. I thought it might add just enough confusion if anyone decided to look at the manifest. You did say you only gave that *KOPASSUS* type your last name, right?'

'Smart bastard.

'Just brightening life up a little.'

'Again, many thanks.'

'You said that before. Always ready to help a friend.'

As he turned away to buy a newspaper at a kiosk against the wall, the thunder of a jet made me look out of the window. A single-engined fighter was passing the gate area, and I followed its progress to the in-bound end of the taxiway, where a large green hangar with *Skadron Udara 5* in large letters painted over the door stood separate from the domestic civil operations. A couple of military helicopters were anchored nearby. Makassar was the strategic command for Eastern Indonesia, and here the airforce was the most visible presence of the military. What, I wondered, were the less visible elements doing now? Did they want to know who and where I was?

Six

I met him, my collaborator in the other Service, when he returned from Sulawesi. The Jenderal called me to an inter-Service meeting. 'The other elements, Soekendro. This is not only my thinking. Time now to understand the navy.'

So I listened to the Laksamana sing his favourite tune. 'A disposable fleet! A real windfall for us. I still marvel at the idea. Not many navies have ever had that luxury.'

Apparently he had been laughing about this for a long time. and still brought up the same comments on frequent occasions. His associates put up with it; as Laksamana Madya, he was the senior officer of this navy group. However, once the mirth disappeared he was a shrewd planner and a hard driver. He cultivated some of the ingenuousness as a screen. And the East German fleet had been disposable, to the West Germans. They'd put it on the block almost the minute the wall came down. But we'd done little with it to that point, keeping the vessels mothballed for future use.

'Now, the rearmament plan. Our contacts in the Persian Gulf are ready to deliver whatever we want. All of the corvettes are to be readied for a rapid refit. I want it done away from prying Javanese eyes. It will be the general understanding that these ships are in such bad shape that each one will take a long time to bring back to operational condition. Understood, Aminuddin?'

My new collaborator nodded. 'Yes, Laksamana. I believe that is the understanding anyway.'

'Let me make clear the nature of the rearmament work. Nothing heavy. Anti-aircraft guns, sea-to-sea and sea-to-air missiles. We may be able to get some Exocets. If so, we will prepare a couple of the corvettes especially for those. None of this demands complicated engineering.'

And then he came back to the old program, the one which even I knew was, until the Germans answered our prayers, the only one we had. 'Now, the landing craft. Where are we since we saw that first one launched? How many are operational?'

Excerpted from Rusman Soekendro, LetJen (ret'd),
No Game At All: Memoirs of a Strategist

Plans settled, and accommodation arranged at a nearby guesthouse, the small gathering around the coffee table took on a different aspect. It was no longer a formal meeting of ex-officers of different militaries. The understanding that deeper confidences were to be shared, ones that would take time, brought a sense of ease to the three persons there. The Javan still maintained his upright posture, spine straight, arms on the wooden armrests of his chair. But the Australian visibly relaxed, sank into the plush and crossed one leg over another. His wife, as she had been, sat close to him, right hand resting on his left.

'Of all the factors that allowed us freedom in what we did,' said the Javan, picking up the thread of the conversation from where they'd left it almost half an hour before, 'it was the earlier acquisition of the East German fleet which was the key.'

'But how did you, as KOPASSUS staff, manage to integrate the naval issues with what must have begun as an Army scenario?' asked the Australian. 'Or,' he said, on reflection, 'did it?'

'We'll get to that,' said the Javan. 'But as a general answer, no it did not begin just as an Army idea. It had different roots, in a period of discontent with New Order policy. Though if I reduce it to personalities, two persons were key to my involvement in the naval role: Laksamana Subagio, who had the ability to run two naval planning institutions in parallel, one completely clandestine. And a young Buginese Officer who trained me in what I did not know, but had to know, about the sea.'

The Australian, who had had his own experiences with Buginese seamanship, said: 'I don't think I'd be hard-pressed to say who that was.'

'No,' said the Javan, 'I don't think you would.'

***

I wrote my report and filed it to Canberra. A mixture of half thoughts and actual facts, but no hard sightings of anything of major interest. The manoeuvres I put in as standard exercises, and perhaps less rigorous than we'd put our own blokes through. No worries.

I was at my desk, with a chart of the South China Seas in front of me, trying to learn more about the waters around the Spratlys, when I looked up to find a pert blonde head peering around my office door. 'Trev, we're using the Embassy cottage in the hills for a dinner tomorrow night. We'd love it if you would come up and join us. Stay over if you can.'

Celia Marshall, a career diplomat at the Embassy, was one of my main colleagues. We shared all our information, trying to cross that divide between military and civilian approaches to government service which so often seems to grow larger rather than smaller. I had little time for prima donna positions on territory, and early on had told her so. She took a long time getting over the surprise. Or so the ambassador had said.

'Morning, Celia. Well, that's kind of you. I was planning on spending a quiet weekend at home, reading. But I suppose I can do that just as well in the hills. As long as your kids let me.' Like their mother, Celia's two pre-teen daughters were fairly precocious, and tended to demand visitors' attention. Celia's lushness of both body and mind had been known to cause male attention to wander during meetings she attended. I was very fond of Dunc, her husband, and had kept a reasonable propriety in my dealings with her. Eventually I came to liking her professional manner so much that my thoughts almost never entered any red zone.

The hill station was about an hour south of Jakarta, the favourite overnight or weekend retreat away from the heat and pollution of Jakarta for expatriate and national alike.

'Will you come up with us, or shall we see you there?'

'I think I'll come up in my own car,' I said. 'I may just take an extra day and go on towards Bandung on the weekend.'

'Good. Come when you like, but dinner at eight sound alright?'

'Fine. Tell Dunc I'll bring the wine.'

'That'll cheer him up. He's a bit morose these days.' She left without providing enlightenment.

The Friday traffic to the hills is always bad, so I left at three hoping to escape the worst. I'd brought my bag to the office, so there was no need to return home, and at that reasonably early hour took my Landcruiser south on Sudirman, and then headed east towards the toll road that would take me on towards Bogor.

At the toll I took the card proffered by the young attendant, then closed the window. Not in a hurry, I pushed the car up to about eighty and settled there. I started to reflect on other threads that might go into a future report to Canberra, as I had some up-coming work on ASEAN which would require a change of focus from terrorism. Deep in thought, I paid only minor attention to the road.

About twenty minutes south of the toll, I vaguely noticed a car pulling out to overtake. But then I saw, about a hundred metres behind it , a large truck heavily laden with construction materials, approaching fast. As I slowly pulled myself back into the present, I saw that the car did not immediately pass, its front fender only slowly drawing parallel to my door. I put on my own brakes.

The massive explosion just by my left ear brought an instant reaction and I braked harder, automatically veering away from the sound. Simultaneously something punched the windscreen. Microseconds later the centre rearview mirror disintegrated as a second punch hit the windscreen. The landcruiser slewed under me as I fought for correction but overcompensated.

The passing car accelerated, but as it pulled away, my front fender clipped the car's rear wing. Broken steel from the wing cut into the car's tyre. As the tyre exploded, a sudden pull to the left caused the passing car to fishtail and the driver braked, trying to regain some control. I thought myself better off ahead of him, and pushed the Landcruiser's accelerator to the floor, asking for its reserve power. But I clipped the car's front end as I passed, and pushed it towards the median. The car hit the guard rail, started to slide sideways, and came back into the fast lane. The first flip developed slowly, but then it was cartwheeling side-over-side.

In the few seconds since the explosion, the truck had continued at its relentless speed. It slammed into the cartwheeling car, and consumed it. The car disappeared completely. A thunderous belch of flame flashed from under the truck as the shock of the impact started to ripple along it. Its load slowly began to climb towards the sky, and then burst into metallic and concrete fragments that flew across the highway, their momentum keeping them bouncing southwards for hundreds of metres. This catalyzed a second accident involving two cars and a bus in the northbound lane. The truck came to rest on its back halfway up the right shoulder.

I was shaking, wondering how I had caused such a serious accident. But as this went through my mind, my eyes focussed, and I saw the two exit holes left by bullets in my windscreen. Only then did I understand what had made the concussive blow to the side window.

The landcruiser seemed unaffected by the contact with the other car, though I could not tell what cosmetic damage it had suffered, apart from the smashed side window and the holes in the windscreen. These were near the top, through a darkened area meant to shield eyes from the sun, and perhaps not too visible from the outside.

As some semblance of rational thought took hold, I saw that if I stopped and put myself into the hands of the local police in an attempt to explain the accident, it would start a train of action that could last days, possibly with me in custody until diplomatic efforts prevailed. *So get to Marshall's, fast*, said my subconscious. *Get the car under cover and call the Embassy*. I thought there was no sounder advice, and kept going.

The remaining thirty minutes into the hills and to the cottage brought my shivers down to a quiet morning-after quake. A tea estate nestled in the mountain pass was visible above me, and the twin volcanic cones of Panggrango and Gede were partially obscured by the late afternoon cloud. It did not look as if rain were imminent.

The house boy opened the gates for me, a young man in sarong from a local village. '*Selamat datang, tuan.*'

I nodded back in response, drove the Landcruiser to the far end of the drive, and parked it sufficiently hard against the wall that no-one could walk in front of or along the driver's side. I climbed out through the passenger's door. Crystals of tempered glass from my side window were all over the floor.

The house boy grabbed my bag out of my hands and ushered me into the house. He showed me to the smaller guestroom where I immediately examined my face and hands. There was a slight shock of pain in my right cheek, and I saw some cuts made by the glass splinters, though none appeared to have embedded itself. The cuts had already sealed, and were hardly visible once I washed and patted my face dry.

I heard the rattling of teacups on the verandah and went out to find tea poured, and a plate of freshly fried banana beside my cup. I sat and thought while I drank my tea. Had the bullets really been for me? What was certain was that had I not been watching the mirror, seen the truck, and eventually slowed for the other car, I'd be dead by now, the bullets having passed, I thought, fractionally ahead of my forehead.

I'd not seen what sort of car it was, nor the people in it. I assumed that there had been two, given that the shots must have come from the passenger's side. However, it had happened so fast, and the car had disappeared under the truck so quickly, that I could not even be sure what colour it was.

It was almost dark, the dregs of the tea cold, most of the banana eaten, and a phone call made, by the time the Marshalls arrived. The girls climbed shouting out of the car, and ran over to give me hugs and kisses. Celia came over smiling. Dunc followed behind looking a little worn. Another woman climbed slowly out of the seat she'd shared with the girls.

'We're later than we expected. Major pileup on the Jagorawi, with a traffic jam kilometres long,' Celia said.

'Don't worry. I've been sitting here enjoying the sunset in the hills. Quite relaxed. Looks as if you could have done with the same.'

'Don't I know it, mate' said Dunc. 'First the job, now the traffic.' He definitely looked careworn, and tiredness was etched into his face. His stocky frame showed more than a hint of slump. 'Don't know how anyone can be sane around here. Oh, meet Anne, a friend of ours.'

The woman came forward. 'Hello.' Medium height, dark brown hair pulled into a ponytail though some wisps loose and falling forward to shadow her face. She'd adopted Indonesian dress, a plain blouse over a batik sarong, and sandals on her feet.

Belatedly I hoped my inspection was unobtrusive. 'Hello, Anne. I'm Trevor.'

Celia laughed. 'Sorry. I should have said that. He's Trevor.' She poked me. 'A gnome at the Embassy.'

Anne must have thought the introduction a little cruel. 'Not even a troll. Just someone who seems to have something on his mind.' She had a slight freckling in her skin, which suggested younger years lived under sunshine but not on heartless beaches. There was a hint of colour on her lips, but no other signs of cosmetics. Her comment suggested an unobtrusive inspection of her own, because I hadn't sensed it.

Celia turned to me. 'Do you, Trev? I hadn't noticed.'

'No,' I said. 'Quite happy to be here.' But I found Anne still looking, so I said: 'Nothing that a quiet weekend won't cure.' She nodded, smiled a little and turned away to follow the girls. I found myself watching a slight swaying walk across the lawn, almost oriental in its flow, and thought that the only true purpose of fabric was to clothe the female form.

'Mmm.' I turned at the sound to see Celia watching me. 'Nice package.'

I winked. 'Almost as nice as you. Different curves, though.' And watched how graciously she blushed.

By the time the Marshalls had their bags unpacked, the welcome tea had been repeated. Dunc sat down with me while Celia followed the girls, cup in hand, who were showing Anne the pool in the gardens to the side of the house.

'Well, how's your day been?' Dunc munched a piece of fried banana. 'Better than mine I hope. Lost samples, mislaid analyses. I don't think I'll ever get this crew up to scratch. They don't even like going to the field!' This last was anathema to Dunc, an engineering consultant to a mining and metallurgical company, who was first and foremost a hands-on practitioner of his craft. We were kindred spirits, and not only in our regard for Celia.

I had to make a decision. 'I want to show you something,' I stood up and motioned towards the landcruiser. Dunc followed with a puzzled look on his face. I brought him to the front passenger's side of the car, and stood against the wall and pointed across to the other side of the windscreen. He didn't see the bullet holes at first, as there was only the glow of the front-porch lamps to light the vehicle, but as his eyes accustomed themselves to the dusk he picked them out. He climbed onto the front fender to get a closer look.

'Bloody hell! Are those what I think they are?' Even in the dusk I could see that he was shaken. I nodded.

'Where did that happen. Up here?' Dunc tried to grapple with the thought of someone letting loose with a gun in the surrounding hills. Then the realization came that there were two holes, less the sign of accident, more of intent. 'Someone shot at *you*?' he said.

I nodded. 'On the Jagorawi. Right at the pileup. I caused it. Well, not strictly, but partially.' And I explained briefly what had happened.

'But why would someone take a pot at you?'

'I don't know. Perhaps it was a mistake.'

Dunc showed a little scepticism. 'You probably wouldn't say even if you bloody well knew.'

'I've got no idea. I've thought about it a bit, but there's nothing I've thought of yet that might account for it.'

'Whatever you do, don't say a word to Celia,' Dunc said. 'She'll worry herself absolutely sick over this. God, that was a horrible sight. I don't think anyone could have survived. There was a car burnt almost beyond recognition, and a twisted wreck of a truck. It's amazing that you weren't hurt. Thank God you weren't.' Then he added 'Does the Embassy know?'

'Yes.' Standing orders required it. 'But I'm OK, that's the main thing.'

'Yes, but for how long? If this was intentional perhaps they'll try again. Though they'll have to send someone else,' he added, with a macabre laugh. He was immediately contrite. 'Sorry. That was a stupid thing to say.'

'I'm way ahead of you. Don't worry. I'll tape these over with something that matches the tinted window, and drive the landcruiser back to Jakarta tomorrow early. I'll go into the Embassy and talk to the duty officer directly. He's alerted the security blokes, but we've agreed not to draw attention to you up here.'

Celia walked over to us as we were talking. We steered her away from the car, linking arms with her and joking as we did it. 'Two men all to yourselves. You don't know how lucky you ladies are,' said Dunc.

'Yes we do,' she responded and gave him a kiss on the cheek. She then smiled at me and gave me a similar peck. 'There.'

Dunc raised an eyebrow. 'We're both blessed,' he said. 'Bring on the wine and let the ceremony begin.'

'Tonight's dinner is partly for Anne. It's her birthday. And she's been staying with us while she changes houses, so we couldn't really leave her behind.'

71

I took my first proper look at the woman who followed Celia through the door, earlier observation of a swaying walk aside. She was now dressed in a flowing skirt and plain silk blouse. She was fresh from her *mandi*, dark hair darker, and she wore serenity like a wrap. Celia took her hand. 'We call him Trev. Trevor, I suppose I should say, but we've known him too long for that.'

'Actually Celia has never introduced me to any of her friends before,' I said. 'I'm honoured.' And it was true.

'Perhaps from what Celia's told me about you it should be the other way round.' Her gaze was open and frank, one person looking without guile at another.

I was curious. I'd never thought of Celia talking about me to anyone, and I wondered what she'd said. 'Has she said anything I'd be ashamed of?' I asked.

Anne laughed and turned to Celia. 'What was that really awful thing you said the other day?'

'I didn't say anything awful at all,' protested Celia. Then, slyly, 'What thing, specifically?'

'I think I'm being wound up,' I said. 'Dunc, help me out.'

'Anne, what would you like to drink?' Dunc called from across the room, pretending he'd heard nothing. He made a show of finally finding some music to his taste for the evening.

'Some cold white wine, if you have it, Duncan.' She gave me a kind smile. 'He wasn't much use, was he?'

Her accent had already said she wasn't Australian, but I hadn't known that Celia had any American friends. Even then she didn't immediately answer the puzzle of the softer accent.

'Anne does for her Embassy largely what I do for ours,' Celia said.

'Well, better, I hope,' I said, and received a dirty look. 'Have you lived here long?'

Anne laughed. 'I lived here when I was small, and sometimes think I never left. But in the months I've been back I see many differences.'

Celia came over and put her arm through mine, her body touching me like a feather. 'I met Anne many years ago before I knew Duncan. She's a special friend. And I'm very happy that we've crossed paths again. I missed her.'

Anne smiled at her. 'I missed you, too. Though it was too easy to get into trouble when you were around. You had a sure way of attracting it.'

'It or them?' asked Dunc. He made a show of wanting to know more of this past history, though there was no suggestion of an insecure relationship. I knew it to be quite the opposite.

'Oh no.' Celia laughed. 'Girls' secrets!'

Anne nodded straightfaced.

Dunc looked rueful, but then brightened. 'Well, she fell for me in the end. A fairytale ending.'

'My prince.' Celia kissed him on the lips. She looked at me. 'Anne is very bright. Made me look like a dunce.' It almost seemed an apology for Anne's svelteness against her own full figure, but I knew her too well for that. Celia always marked intelligence top. 'She has her whole staff wrapped around her little finger.'

Anne laughed. 'We work well together.'

'They're in awe of you,' said Celia. 'Your *bahasa* blows theirs away.'

I groaned. 'Well, I'm just a poor sailor stuck at a desk. You're losing me already.'

'You, *Commander* Gregory, are also far smarter than you let on. For that reason you can sit next to me at dinner.' Celia grabbed my arm and pulled me towards the table. 'Come on, you two!'

'You and I will have to sit below the salt, Anne. Perhaps they'll throw us a bone.' Dunc assumed a put-upon air, and Anne took his arm.

The dinner table, set for four, was already laden with several dishes, and Celia took the covers off. There was no sign of the girls.

'The other ladies aren't joining us this evening?' I asked.

'The girls are watching a video we rented this afternoon. They may join us later when they get hungry. But you'll get your kisses. Both my daughters have a major crush on this man,' Celia said to Anne. 'It's disgraceful the way they behave.'

Dunc hadn't yet fully come out of his moroseness, so it came round to me to talk, and I recounted some of my recent trip to Hong Kong, including lunch with Hung. The others were amused at this contact.

'Looking for a different job, Trev?' asked Dunc. 'Tired of the Navy and want a merchant command? Does Hung have an opening for you?'

'He didn't offer me one. But he as good as gave me an order. Wants me to sort out the piracy problem all on my own.' I limited all references to known Chinese naval practice.

'And have you? Did you persuade your Admiral to come steaming north, guns ablazing, ensign streaming? What a sight that would be!' Dunc took a deep breath, and shook his head.

I smiled at Dunc's imagery. The dinner settled into a quiet discussion of Anne's process of finding a new house, the girls' progress at swimming lessons, and

Celia's latest letters from home. The food had a simpler rural style to it, compared to the more cosmopolitan influences found in Jakarta – unadorned steamed vegetables, a chicken stew, fragrant white rice, food that would have been common in the maid's village not far from the gate.

We went out onto the verandah for coffee. Lights in the valley below matched the sparkling phosphorescence I'd often seen in night waters. Dunc, inside, put on some quiet jazz saxophone, and, unasked, brought me a cognac. 'For the shock,' he said, quietly. Celia and Anne were in separate conversation about the girls.

'Which one,' I asked. 'The car, or the introduction?'

I left early the next morning, having explained to Celia after dinner that I'd had to change my plans. I made the excuse that a call had come through from the Embassy before they arrived, and that I'd been requested to join the Ambassador for an official function the following noon.

'Poor you,' said Celia, knowing that I could not refuse. Yet there was a puzzled look in her eye as she waved goodbye early next morning, still half asleep. 'Why can't you go mid-morning?' she asked.

'I had a slight argument with a lamppost yesterday,' I said, trying to explain away the minor damage visible on the driver's side. Some black plastic insulating tape that Dunc had dug out of his own toolbox seemed successfully to have hidden the bullet holes. 'I want to get the car in to town for repairs.' It sounded a weak excuse. 'Please say goodbye to Anne for me.' No-one else had yet surfaced.

It took me an hour to get back into the centre of Jakarta. No-one took any notice of the scratches on my car, and there was no trouble on the way down, probably a relief to the two-man security detail which had picked me up just before Bogor and kept watch from a few car lengths ahead. I drove straight to the Embassy, left the car in the garage, and went to the security gate. An exasperated duty officer let me in. 'How could you get into trouble up in the hills?'

'I don't know. Is Head of Security in yet?'

'You're a little early. He'll be here by 0930.'

I spent the fifteen minutes before Boltroni's arrival dictating a summary of the preceding afternoon's events on my dictaphone, and I had the tape ready in hand when Boltroni appeared at my door.

Boltroni was a serious but warm man, and though we weren't immediate colleagues, we were as good friends as was possible. 'So, what've you been up to?' He'd had a long history in the police force, before taking early retirement. Then seeing nothing but boredom ahead, he'd managed to leap into diplomatic security as a means to satisfy whatever urge he had to travel. The urge really was to keep working, but he disguised it well, always talking about where he was off to next. This morning, though, he was all business, dressed, as had been his habit during all those years, in something very close to a copper's white shirt and black slacks.

I repeated the story, gave him the tape, and he gave me a receipt for it. 'Duly recorded. In both senses of the word. I don't like this much. Who've you been upsetting?' He was angry. Listed diplomats were not supposed to be used for target practice. My vehicle had diplomatic plates and it was unlikely that the attackers had made a mistake.

I didn't immediately answer, but took him down to show him the damage to the car, and as with Dunc, the bullet holes brought the whole thing to life for him. 'God in Heaven! Well you've had a night to sleep on it. What do you think it is?

'I've dismissed the accident or mistake. This was intended for me and it was professional. It was my luck that it didn't work. But I've only the faintest idea why. That someone should want to do it, I mean.'

Boltroni looked surprised. 'You have an idea why? Something you need to keep quiet? Locally, I mean?'

I nodded.

'Then we can't request a copy of the police report, because that will immediately alert them to something that they may not know. You're absolutely sure that no-one could tie you in to the crash?'

'There's no reason to believe that there's a witness beyond whoever survived from those two vehicles. It wouldn't have been clear enough for anyone travelling in the opposite direction to have seen. Besides, they were caught up in their own trouble.'

Boltroni nodded. 'We'll see. Leave your vehicle here. We'll get a new windshield and side window brought in through the diplomatic bag. Once they're fixed, we'll send the car out to the workshop for the paint job. Take the other landcruiser for now. It may be useful for you to be seen in a similar vehicle even if the plates are different. I'm going to call the Ambassador. Wait for me.'

I stared at the ceiling for a while. My senses were still a little numb, delayed or extended shock I supposed. It was almost as if it hadn't happened. But I had the memory of the fireball firmly fixed in my mind, and it wouldn't go away. Definitely not my imagination.

Boltroni came back, and it turned out that I hadn't completely lied to Celia. 'Well, that woke him up. I think he spilt his coffee. He wants to see you, but not right now. Suggests you join him later this afternoon. He has a reception to go to, and wants you with him. Feels that it will cover for any sense that you've been up to no good in case anyone thinks you have. Full rig at five. So, what no good have you been up to?'

I told him about the only thing I thought it could be - a *KOPASSUS* Kolonel who might have lost face to an angry naval officer.

Boltroni showed his doubt. 'No, makes no sense. You said it yourself - standard training maneouvres. Nothing there to get anybody hot about.' He was silent a moment. Then: 'Stay close to home. From now on I want someone stationed at your house full-time. No, no,' he said to my look of protest. 'Even though I think you're wrong we're still going to treat this seriously. It would be my head as well as yours if we didn't.'

'Tell me what happened.'

Ambassador Brian Kessler was also formally dressed, with his salt and pepper hair almost as severely arranged as the rest of him. He stood up and walked around the desk in his study as I was ushered in. He extended a long arm and gave me a warm handshake. Gold sparkled at snow-white cuffs.

I went over the previous afternoon's events once again, and the explanation I'd given Boltroni. Kessler remained silent until I finished.

'Do the Marshalls know about it?'

'Only Duncan, sir. The physical damage to the car was slight. He helped me mask it. Celia was too involved with her kids to pinpoint what was going on. However, she may not take long to piece it together.'

Kessler nodded. 'Well, we're going to keep it completely under wraps. No comment to the Indonesians. Your car stays at the Embassy out of sight until it's completely repaired. Boltroni has mentioned the extra security?'

'Yes, sir. But I hope that it's not really a necessity.'

'So do I, Gregory. But we'll take no chances. Canberra would have a fit.' He went on. 'Today's just for show, really. Foreign Ministry reception. Something you can turn up at without comment. If anyone is looking, they'll see you unharmed and unconcerned. Play that part.'

'Yes, sir.' Unharmed maybe, but beginning just to be a little concerned.

'Right. Help yourself to a sherry from the tray over there. I'll just check on Mrs Kessler. Her rig's even more elaborate than yours.'

Seven

So I divided my modules into two. Those where the objective was solely one of overcoming the defence infrastructure, and those where there was intent to take longer-term possession of the target. The critical time to mount the offensive would be just before the monsoon rains. It would make repulse that much harder.

I had no illusion that what I was proposing, what I had proposed, would be easy to bring to fruition. I was still mastering the computer skills necessary to create the algorithms that would be the culmination of my work. I had started on those, but wasn't yet sure how to structure the aspects of my plan governed by the laws of probability. I thought that the modular approach would simplify that greatly, but recognized that the modules were not independent of each other. The final outcome of the whole scheme depended on the combination of success from each module. But it was essential that each module contained the appropriate probability factors. Without those, I'd have absolutely no power of prediction.

Excerpted from Rusman Soekendro, LetJen (ret'd),
No Game At All: *Memoirs of a Strategist*

'A nd *Laksamana* Subagio - did you have direct access?' asked the Australian. 'Or was it always through the *Jenderal*?'

'From your own experience you know how we work,' said the Javan. 'Almost always decisions are made at the very top. Horizontal liaison, while important for information-sharing, produces few results. However, *Laksamana* Subagio seems to have understood quite quickly that the team of Amin and myself had some unique qualities. Perhaps because Amin showed little Javanese deference, he was given more rope than most. Much of it he dangled with me. We took full advantage of it.'

'The *Jenderal* wasn't worried?'

'At some point the *Jenderal* said to me: "Continue to cast your design in the frame of the Tionghoa. Keep me informed. When I believe you have overlooked something, or when I have a question, I will tell you. There is too much to do for you to depend continually on me"'

'Then in fact,' said the Australian, 'you did not work how I might have expected.'

The Javan smiled. 'No. We did not.'

***

It wasn't so much that Kessler or Canberra thought I should dance under Indonesian noses until they tried again. I still had a job to do, and this aspect of it had been in the works for months. So a week later I climbed out of the Embassy car in front of an imposing five-storey building set well back from the main road. The diplomatic plates had elicited severely correct salutes from the guards at the gate. I went up the steps and through the tall front doors. An aide whose name was Mathius was waiting inside.

'*Selamat pagi*, Commander Gregory. Welcome back to Navy Headquarters. Please follow me.' Mathius turned, and walked towards the back of the building.

We went across a large central patio around which the whole complex had been built, and the offices of the senior staff appeared in the block ahead, larger suites with aides stationed at intervals outside the doors. Their desks were sheltered from the sun by the large overhanging veranda.

My friend Mathius stopped at a door marked *Letnan Kolonel S. Hendamin, Liaison ASEAN.* A second aide sitting at the desk by the door rose and slipped through the door. He reappeared a moment later. '*Silahkan*, Commander Gregory. Please enter. *Kolonel* Hendamin is waiting for you.'

The incumbent was a tall, smiling Naval officer. 'Commander Gregory. A pleasure to see you again. Please come in. Sit down. The drive from the Embassy was not too bad, I hope?'

A group of chairs had been arranged at one end of the office, and I relaxed back into one. 'Official car, *Kolonel,*' I said. 'Courtesy of the Ambassador. However, Jakarta's traffic does get worse by the day.'

'Unfortunately, Commander Gregory, it will get worse yet. More car factories are built daily. We soon will not be able to move. Why do we do it?'

The question did not require an answer. An orderly appeared with two steaming cups of clear tea. These were placed on the low table between us and Hendamin waved a hand in their direction. 'Please, Commander Gregory. The refreshment may make some amends for the traffic.'

We'd hardly touched the tea before other officers began to file into the room. Three, who I'd met before, were junior to Hendamin, and subsequently did little more than record the meeting and carry out Hendamin's requests. Slightly different from the RAN, where, if I were the host, I'd be recording everything myself and running my own errands.

The fourth officer, who had not attended our previous sessions, wore a weary arrogance, an attitude which made me think he was Naval Intelligence. Though the same rank, he behaved as if he were a bit higher in the Navy List than poor Hendamin.

'It was a pleasant surprise to find that our Foreign Minister finally invited your country to observe our upcoming ASEAN manoeuvres,' Hendamin started. 'I think I can safely say that this will probably be the most comprehensive exercise we have ever mounted. The reasons for the degree of collaboration are fairly obvious. Most of our members are becoming quite concerned about our separate and joint abilities to create something like a regional security mechanism. The manoeuvres have been set for thrree months hence. While there may still be some changes in location, we have advised our partners that the waters around the Natuna Islands offer the best opportunity for the range of manoeuvres we expect to undertake.' Hendamin was always businesslike and forthcoming, and I never had to dig the information out of him. 'May I ask you, Commander Gregory, now that you have the invitation, what ship your country will send as observer?

'Australia has decided that this visit would provide an excellent opportunity to mount a broader training exercise. The frigate *Magnet* will come as the observing vessel, under the command of Captain Leach, West Ocean Fleet. However, we should like to request that she be accompanied by two other vessels. This will allow our own ships to undertake a series of exercises of their own in the voyages to and from your own manoeuvres.'

Hendamin showed a little surprise. 'I am unable to comment on this, of course,' he said. He was jotting a note on a slip of paper as he spoke. He passed it to one of the junior officers, who got up from the table and left. 'It will have to be dealt with by my superiors. We will let you know as soon as we can.' I doubted the errand boy was going to bring the decision back right then.

Hendamin went on. 'In consultation with the other ASEAN members we are completing the initial list of manoeuvres. These will be drafted into sailing orders at a later date. However, I can give you the list as it currently stands.' He passed me a stapled document which I scanned rapidly. The manoeuvres were divided into strategic and tactical operations. Over the next half hour we went through the manoeuvres as initially defined, and I thought that the whole affair was taking on the look of something with a definite message for the large neighbour to the north.

Out of the corner of my eye I'd been watching the Intelligence officer. He'd been frowning continuously, though I didn't think Hendamin had gone any further than his position allowed. Perhaps it was a personal thing. But then he decided to throw his bone in. 'And what would these ships be doing during the ASEAN manoeuvres, Commander Gregory? They would be in Indonesian waters.'

As we'd been off the topic for a while I thought he was a bit slow. 'The bilateral agreement would have the senior ship participating as an observer during the actual exercise. We would suggest that the other ships be allowed to visit other ports on courtesy visits.'

'They could *not* be included in the observation party', he stated. 'One observer is indeed enough.'

'We will be guided by your advice,' I said, refusing to be drawn into some sort of argument. These were decisions that could take some time, and all issues would have to be reviewed and approved by staff significantly higher than this man. 'Our ships will be going on to other ports in Asia once your own exercises are over.'

Hendamin nodded. 'Then we will advise you once a decision is made.'

There was no more business, so I stood up. 'Thank you, *Kolonel.*'

As I left, I passed a knot of mid-ranking officers in the corridor that led to the large courtyard. *Aminuddin!* The name flashed from my subconscious, and I looked at individual faces, wondering if by some terrible chance I'd bump into him here. Thankfully he wasn't present. Then I was telling the master-at-arms at the door that I was ready for my car, and in two minutes was heading back into the traffic.

Eight

But Amin was not Javanese, and I was interested in how this out-islander had managed to climb the ladder as fast as he had. The Jenderal had warned me about him, had told me I'd need his technical knowledge if I were to complete the sea-based component in time, and, as I'd learnt, in his hands was the refurbishment of these ships thought so critical.

'Thirty-seven,' he said. 'Sixteen corvettes, twelve landing ships, nine minesweepers. The critical difference, Rus.' And he ran through his ideas on their strategic value, how they should be used. Then he told me more about the landing-craft program, already underway on this island of his.

None of it set me back, for I'd allowed the time. But Amin gave me insights I'd not thought of, made it clear to me that there were variables about the sea to which I'd not given sufficient weight. It became my custom to call him daily, to ask questions to which only he had the answers. And so we became a team, subordinate to the Jenderal and the Laksamana, clearly, but really the heart of the matter. And Amin, looking at numbers, total displacement one could put to sea, put it simply, adding to the sayings of the Tionghoa. 'A lot of ships makes a navy.'

Excerpted from Rusman Soekendro, LetJen (ret'd),
No Game At All: Memoirs of a Strategist

The Australian and his wife took their leave shortly before six, she believing that the developing relationship within the Javan was still tenuous, and that while both men still had a tremendous amount of ground they wished to cover, they should do so at a pace neither tiring nor in any other way pressured. In fact, she saw that both men needed some time to accommodate what they had already learned of each other, and that future friendship would only come if anything adversarial disappeared very early in the conversation. A break was important, and the Australian had interpreted her nudge correctly. Perhaps surprisingly, he almost always did.

Later, he said. 'I wanted to ask at what point I actually became a piece on his gameboard.'

'You can ask him tomorrow. But ask carefully. It will embarass him.'

***

The yeoman-at-arms sent me straight to the Deputy Chief-of-Staff's office when I arrived, an unexpected appointment. Vice-Admiral James Dixon was alone in his office when I was shown in.

'Come in, Commander. Sit down. A good journey?'

'The usual, sir. Managed to sleep most of it.'

Dixon had only crossed my path once before, for a final briefing before I'd left to take up my Jakarta posting. I knew a lot about him, it being common knowledge throughout the Service that he'd been on a stellar trajectory until Canberra sold the *Melbourne* out from under him. It was our only aircraft carrier at the time, figurehead of our naval might, but Canberra was more interested in the scrap value the Chinese were willing to pay than any strategic value the ship might have to Australian defence. Dixon was scathing about the move, and that had landed him in hot water. But he was too good to be shunted from the Service, and when it became known that the Chinese had disassembled her rivet by rivet and drawn up a set of construction plans for a similar but improved ship, Canberra decided that it might after all profit from his insights. He'd held several senior posts since and was now the most important officer in the Navy under its top man. What I remembered most about him was the cobalt-blue stare he gave you, a colour I'd only ever seen in high-latitude skies once the gale had blown its course. If the stare persisted a different gale was imminent. He was, of all our senior Navy staff, the one who looked as though he'd just come off the bridge of WWI battleship, closely-trimmed beard, solid body, Edwardian mien. I always expected the slight smell of cordite when I saw him.

'Good for you,' he said. Then, without pause, though with no real sign of the higher Beaufort-scale values in the cobalt blue, 'I want to know what's going on in Jakarta. Have you made any sense of what happened?'

The wires had been hot all week, though with little result. 'Not yet, sir. The intelligence report still was not in when I left yesterday. The papers have not reported anything other than that neither the car nor its occupants could be identified. The car must have been a worse wreck than I thought.'

He threw a file across the desk to me. 'Came in this morning. Read it.'

I opened the file to find a three-page document, coded top-secret. And I was only partly prepared for its contents. 'It *was* a military sedan.'

'You thought it was? That wasn't in your report.'

'No sir. But during the past week I've been considering all possibilities. It was almost inevitable that my imagination would put army plates on that car.' I went on reading, and very shortly found that hypothesis wrong. 'Navy?!

'Yes, Commander. Navy. So please tell me why.'

I thought rapidly. 'Well, sir. I'd say either hate or necessity. But I hadn't thought the hate to have reached extermination point, and I can think of nothing in what I saw to suggest necessity.' I amplified on what I had seen on the beach, and the two encounters with naval officers. 'I don't understand it.'

'D'you think the senior officer knew who you were the first time he saw you?'

'No sir. I'd never met him before.'

'I didn't ask that. Could he have known who you were?' The blue picked up a touch of frost.

I was having to rethink certain things very rapidly. 'I think it very unlikely, sir. They have a very large navy, and I'm almost certain he'd have no reason ever to have thought about the Australian attaché.'

'Perhaps.' Dixon did not sound convinced. 'Then if it was just pure hate, this man must be a little unbalanced.'

'Or, for some reason, desperate, sir.'

'And why desperate? Didn't you say it all looked like a normal exercise?'

'Yes, sir. But perhaps I *have* seen something of wider significance.'

'You'll have to think very hard about that. But for now the question is whether anything got back on the shooting,' Dixon said. 'Do you think that *whoever* masterminded this knows that they got the shots off?'

'I doubt it, sir. The crash and explosion happened so quickly that even if they had radio in hand, it's unlikely that anything got through.'

Dixon nodded. 'Good. The last thing we want to do is pull you out and communicate to them that we know what happened. Until we know why it was done, it's business as usual. However, you'll be briefed on improved security'

'Some changes because of this?'

'I've told Intelligence to take another look. Check in with them before you go back.'

'Yes sir.'

'Now, brief me on ASEAN. There'll be a full meeting of the Department tomorrow, but I'd like a run through.'

I recounted my meeting at Indonesian Navy HQ in Jakarta. Dixon listened without comment until I mentioned the Australian observers.

'They didn't like the idea of three ships?'

'I don't think it's a problem, sir. It was more for form than anything else. I think we should continue to plan on the basis of three. By the time we get the official word it could be the day before the manoeuvres.'

Dixon nodded. 'We can keep them in international waters until the last minute.' He paused. 'Anything else, Commander?'

'Yes, sir. Alumina Queen.'

'Anything new?'

'Grant says that the ship in drydock is not her.'

'Isn't she, by God! Then where is she?'

'I think she's on the bottom, sir.'

'Yes, I know you do. That's not enough, unfortunately. We've had absolutely no intelligence to suggest that Al-Qaeda has any marine capability. And aluminium doesn't float. No cargo to come to the surface.' He shook his head. 'But if it can't be proven to be a consequence of the typhoon, what or whoever it was will eventually kill trade through those sealanes.'

'It may become serious sooner than that, sir. Underwriters will refuse coverage. We'll find that nobody will carry our cargoes.'

I went on to describe Hung's thoughts on shipboard security in greater detail than my report had done, including the electronic measures. 'The basic problem is the one of properly trained men. Assuming, of course, that to be the final recourse. And I have an idea there, sir.' I spent half an hour going over my ideas, the threads finally having settled into a full cloth.

When I'd finished, Dixon sat looking at me for a few seconds, a half-smile on his face. 'Well, that's nothing if not original, Commander. Where did the idea come from?'

I explained how I'd thought the problem out.

'But you're not worried about this other thing?'

'Not immediately, sir. And if *you're* not, as you said, it's business as usual until we know any different. This would be an ideal way of indicating that we suspect nothing.'

'Yes. I can see that. Very well. Let me sleep on it tonight. Include it in your presentation tomorrow. What else?'

'Well......, I was wondering about my ship, sir.'

Dixon smiled. 'Yes, I expect you were. However, given all this, that is also something I shall have to sleep on. You'll have an answer before you return to Jakarta.'

'Thank you, sir.'

The Departmental meeting lasted all morning, and I was the last of three speakers. By that time the acerbity of the comments and questions had dulled. It seemed to be known that I'd been in some sort of scrape, though no-one actually knew the details, so I detected acute listening to see whether anything would come out about it. I disappointed them by focussing entirely on the hijacking.

'Commander Gregory's assessment of the actions of this unknown group leaves us all stunned, of course,' said a Captain in Naval Intelligence at the end, 'but perhaps we should have already guessed that it would come.'

'Perhaps you should have, Edmonds,' repeated Vice-Admiral Dixon, who was chairing the meeting. The rebuke hung on the air.

'Well, of course, if our people were only kept properly posted, there'd be no difficulty.' The Intelligence Officer was clearly wishing he'd kept quiet, but he continued to dig a hole. 'We can only analyse what we're sent.' He made intelligence gathering sound a passive enterprise, in other people's hands.

'I sincerely hope so,' said Dixon, issuing a cobalt-blue gale warning, 'but I haven't checked. Perhaps I will.'

Edmonds coloured, and finally shut up.

Dixon went on. 'It's a further facet of our defence strategy that we must be able to protect those parts of the trade environment that are vital to our economic interests. It's not news to anyone at this table, at least I hope it's not,' a glance at the Intelligence Officer, 'that defence is no longer a matter of keeping undesirables out. That is, out of this continent. As a country and an economic power, one dependent on exports, our defence interests stretch well to the north of the Equator. This is the first direct threat to those interests relevant to this Service since World War II.'

'Commander Gregory's strategy, which he outlined this morning, is designed to harness resources which, in a sense, are not available to us. The politicians are unlikely to give us the money, and an equivalent force sitting idly by, let's say, could do the job at a fraction of the cost.'

'I'd like critical reviews of the proposed operation by the end of the week. Intelligence will look at possible reactions on the other side of the fence. Who we are hitting. Special Operations will provide a blueprint for the operational unit. Men and equipment. The operation will fall under Navy Command, Canberra, but it makes no sense to run it from here. An operational office will be established in the field closer to the expected site of action. Until such time as I decide otherwise, the development of the plan will be the responsibility of Commander Gregory.'

The meeting broke up shortly afterwards. 'Come up to my office after lunch, Gregory. I want to go over this once more.'

I saluted. 'Yes, sir. Thank you.'

'You may not thank me yet,' said Dixon as he left.

'The Vice-Admiral's not back yet. He said to wait.'

I sat down. One wall of the office was a huge chart of the southern oceans, extending from the Southern Australian Basin, north through the Coral Seas and the West Coast into the Pacific and Indian Oceans. Part of it was what I had studied on the ceiling of my Hong Kong hotel room. My senses suddenly expanded, and I could almost feel myself the continent and the seas. It made me shiver.

The door opened and Dixon came in, followed by the only naval officer senior to himself. I'd not met him before, but knew the Chief of Naval Staff from photos and by reputation. Real life made him slighter though no less tall, but he carried his authority differently from Dixon. Perhaps the extra height gave him his ease, though his movements were more fluid.

'Admiral Dixon has been bringing me up to date on some of your thoughts, Commander,' said Admiral Bluing. 'You seem to be doing your best to get us involved throughout the hemisphere.'

'Well, sir, events themselves seem to have created the need.'

Bluing nodded. 'That wasn't a rebuke, Commander. It's good to know that we occasionally post someone who looks and listens. With regard to the piracy, d'you think this idea of yours will really work?' And though he said *piracy*, there was no hint that he was resurrecting the buried concept of the Chinese PLA. Nothing I'd heard in Canberra's halls suggested that Al-Qaeda was far from anyone's attention. Edmonds apart, perhaps.

I felt sure that Bluing and Dixon had their own opinions firmly decided. 'I think it depends on how it is presented to the Indonesians, sir. It may take some careful diplomatic wording to present it as a joint concern. And perhaps even more careful approaches to suggesting how to stage it operationally.'

'You know how to approach the latter?'

'I have some ideas, sir. But I wouldn't put them on the table at the start. To work, a combined operation requires that the other side commit itself through its own ideas. We'd have to look at those before we tried to put the whole thing into shape.'

Bluing nodded again. 'Well, it's your job for the moment, Commander.' He might have seen a hint of disappointment in my face. 'Yes, I know, your ship. But I don't want any old sailor meddling in something he doesn't understand. This must be yours for a little while yet. You keep Admiral Dixon fully informed as you go. He'll let you know if and when we get the green light from the politicians. If they make it difficult for us, we'll work it through other channels. It's time to be assertive.'

Bluing headed for the door. 'You can give him the other news, Jim.'

When Bluing had gone, Dixon told me what the news was. 'We can't have a mere Commander running this operation. You've been promoted. Congratulations, Captain Gregory.'

I grinned in amazement 'Thank you, sir. That's very generous.'

'It would have come with your command. Just think of it as an interim consolation prize. But it increases the load on your shoulders, Gregory. I hope you can carry it. I think you can.'

'I think I know where to steer it, sir.'

'Then do so.'

Neil Thomas

Nine

Amin is angry. 'My colleagues failed in their simple task.' The Buginese show their anger in a way the Javanese do not, and I can see the history of his people written on his face.

'It was always possible,' I say. 'Now the question is whether that failure brings divergence from the pathway from that event.'

'You cannot predict this?'

'Not with full certainty. And there is one possible pathway that bothers me the most of all.'

'Discovery?'

'No. Discovery I have not yet had to rate at more than moderate certainty. No, it is the outcome of a possible association that I cannot foresee. The imponderables around synergies of thought between two intelligent people are too many to address.'

'Should we try again?'

I see that he is not serious about this option. 'Can you not think of something better?'

He considers. 'Full attention at a point one hundred and eighty degrees from where discovery lies.'

Yes! So it was clear that he was the man for the job in hand. One did not give a clerk a plough and tell him to be a farmer. In a quiet moment he told me something of his past, said that he felt something of it, but had no words for it even in his own tongue. His father and grandfather had both drowned at sea, different pinisis, but in the end his common heritage. He'd sailed with uncles who'd managed to survive the occasional disaster that struck all seamen. They told him of his family, became his family. He'd absorbed it all. His entry to the naval academy had been a proud moment for them, someone who was maintaining a tradition but in a different way and in a different world. Few from Makassar had ever done it. None had reached where he now was. Daughters from the best families had been offered to him in marriage, but he'd politely refused. For him it was not yet time for that. He didn't want sons who might not know a drowned father. There was too much pain.

Excerpted from Rusman Soekendro, LetJen (ret'd),
No Game At All: *Memoirs of a Strategist*

They made slow love that night, not just because age brought that sort of leisureliness, but because they were both committed to a mutual peace that required intimacy as a major element of communication. Once she had said to him, in a younger moment, when the male urge had overtaken him and he evinced a certain hurry: 'I hope you're enjoying this. You seem to be on a different bus.' He'd collapsed beside her, roaring with laughter. 'No,' he'd said, when he could speak again. 'Same bus, different driver.'

***

Laksamana Madya Subagio was named by Canberra as my contact, and I ran him to earth in the Strategic Planning Group's HQ, not far from where Hendamin hung his shingle. As a Vice Admiral he was part of the same navy.

'Welcome, Captain Gregory. I get to meet you at last.'

'It is an equal pleasure for me, sir.' I shook the proferred hand.

'I know how it is,' continued Subagio. 'One's tours of duty sometimes prevent one from meeting those whom one would like immediately to meet. You lead a busy life, I expect?'

'As busy as my superiors can make it, Admiral.'

Subagio nodded. 'Please, sit down.'

I took the proferred chair. As I did so, I had a chance to study him. Unlike most Indonesian naval officers I'd met, Subagio gave the impression of a throwback to earlier times. Short and well-fed, he had the oily warmth of an outer-island sultan, one who'd give you his most beautiful servant girl in welcome as your first night's companion, then bring you to a slow boil so that you'd live through the next day in absolute agony before gracing his dinner menu as ragout of long pig. Despite his words I was sure that meeting me had not been high on his list of priorities.

'Do you enjoy your duty in Indonesia, Captain?'

'I can't think of anywhere else in Asia that I'd rather be, sir. Our proximity as neighbours suggests that ours is a more important bilateral relationship than any we have with other countries of the region.'

'Sound sentiment, Captain. For Australia. Of course, it is only recently that your country has been thinking this way. I don't have to think too far back to recall an entirely different philosophy. And your press did nothing to hide it. Nor,' he added, in some reflection, 'did your military during that recent East Timor debacle.'

This was very unsafe ground, and I had no authority to make any comment about implied Australian lack of regard for Indonesia's position on the Timorese.

'My Government works from a position of ongoing *rapprochement*. I certainly work by that understanding.'

'Good, Captain. Good. And now, have I been honoured with a reason for your visit today?'

'I came because of a common security interest, Admiral. Your Foreign Ministry has recently received a visit from Ambassador Kessler, and there may have been some communication with your own ambassador in Canberra. They will have been talking policy.' I paused. It was essential that I put my thoughts into the clearest words possible. 'What I would like to examine are the more practical aspects of our defence mechanisms. My Government believes that a threat has surfaced which is of concern to us both. I hope I may talk freely about it.'

Subagio suddenly looked cautious, worried even.

'You must forgive me, Captain. It is not at all clear to me what you mean. I regret that there has been no communication about any meeting in Canberra or Jakarta.'

I would not have been surprised by the lack of a Canberra meeting. A telex from Dixon had told me to start exploratory discussions without being specific about Canberra's position. However, Kessler had certainly seen the Indonesian Foreign Minister, and that would not have happened without Canberra's go ahead. That the Indonesian Foreign Ministry had not yet passed on to Defence the gist of Kessler's message was interesting, but not necessarily significant.

'Then let me put it into simple terms, sir. Trade in the region is being disrupted. Lawlessness is erupting in the China Seas, and this can only bring ancillary effects to the positions of you and your ASEAN neighbours. Perhaps it has only just reached the point where it is of international concern. But we wish to nip it directly in the bud.' I gave him a bald account of the Alumina Queen.

And then it seemed as though Subagio began to laugh inside. He sat back in his chair, the slight tension in his face slackening, and his eyes opening wider in some sense of delight. As that almost quintessential oiliness came back I wondered what I'd said to bring this change. I went on. 'It's the opinion of my Government that, in consultation with yours, we should find a solution. It's my belief that the only mechanism which would work will be one we decide on and design jointly.'

'Why do you think so, Captain?

'This may be a focussed campaign rather than the work of some opportunistic few. Allowing it to succeed will cause severe economic damage to our trade and may bring financial ruin to some shipping companies. The difficulty for Australia is that this .. *piracy* .. is operating beyond your sea lanes. We cannot maintain the level of security necessary to prevent this from escalating.'

'You think we can?'

'Not in any direct sense. Not yourselves nor your ASEAN partners. With respect, Admiral, you have not managed to achieve unity in security or defence objectives to date. And your own capacity is quite limited. You would not be able to provide any blue-water protection.'

'Then I don't understand why you have come, Captain.'

'Because I believe that a simpler mechanism by far would stop this business cold. Our problem is that we would cause alarm bells to ring here in Jakarta were we to go ahead unilaterally.'

'I still don't understand.'

'We would like to place armed units on all ships over 40,000 tonnes on the north-south route through the China Seas. It is our intent that these be units trained specifically for the purpose of preventing further hijacking. But would your Government want Australian servicemen patrolling your sealanes? With our men on board, through the Lombok Strait and other passages, that is, in essence, what they would be doing.'

Subagio sat back in surprise. 'Most definitely not.'

I smiled. 'You see my problem, sir.'

'Your problem, Captain?'

'I have to find an alternative. That is why I'm here.'

'You still have me mystified. But I am intrigued, so please go on.'

'My proposal to you is that the units be Indonesian military. We would provide overall coordination and on-board command through a single officer seconded from the Australian Navy. Your men would bring their own unit commander, who would have co-responsibility with his Australian counterpart during any action. We would pick up and drop off your men in Indonesian waters. Obviously they would not be needed on board south of the equator. It is to the north of the line that the problem lies.'

Subagio gave me an intent look. 'This is quite ingenious, Captain. But why did you come to me with it?'

'Strategic planning, Admiral. I believe that's your responsibility?'

And again I had the sense that I'd hit something deeper. Subagio barely nodded.

'Canberra believes your Group to be our immediate counterpart, Admiral, even though this is work more suited to Special Forces. Admiral Bluing thought that this would be an excellent opportunity for us to establish some different ties.'

Subagio thought for a moment. 'It is work for Special Forces, Captain, but we have capable Marines who might do just as well. I will think about it. Do you have a schedule in mind?'

'The threat increases by the day, Admiral. The sooner the better.'

'Yes, yes.' Subagio consulted his diary. 'Let us meet again in two weeks, Captain. By then the necessary corroboration between Defence and Foreign Affairs may be complete and we can make firmer plans. This is not a light undertaking.'

'Thank you, Admiral. I'll pass your comments on to Admiral Bluing.'

'And my compliments, Captain.'

Then, as I stood to leave, he became suddenly thoughtful, even distant. But his eyes bored right through me, almost as if he was seeking the real reason for my coming. Just ragout, I thought, not even the servant girl.

Ten

Most of the East German ships were moored offshore from the naval base at Surabaya, at buoys specially laid for their significant number. Before Amin could move them he had to complete the basic inspection. Not the armaments, for we were going to change them all, but the most fundamental, the engines. Would they get us there? Amin took in his engineering team.

'And are they reliable?' I asked Amin when he returned.

'Do you mean will they go on running? The answer is, yes. You might say they were showpieces.'

'We don't need showpieces.' I said. 'But if you are wrong, you may be running more on Allah's will than anything else.'

'I think,' Amin said with a slight smile. 'with regard to the engines, His will was done.'

Excerpted from Rusman Soekendro, LetJen (ret'd),
No Game At All: *Memoirs of a Strategist*

At breakfast the next morning, the Australian felt an accuity of mind that had not occurred for as long as he could remember. That there was a physiological contradiction in this did not escape him. 'I think I was going senile,' he said.

His wife, who had devoured the papaya, and was working her way through the toast with the appetite of an athlete, said: 'Don't think so.'

'No? Why do I suddenly feel invigorated today, after so long?'

'Oh. I thought you were always saying something about how much our love life kept you young.'

He wagged a finger at her. 'You do keep me young and you bloody know it. I'm not talking about that. It's Soekendro. Something to do with talking to him.'

'Clearing a logjam of stagnant thought?

'Mental constipation through and through. I needed this years ago.' He drained his coffee.

'You've hardly started yet.'

'Don't I know it, love.'

***

I perused the list of dishes. 'Any preferences?'

'It's been a while since I had good dim sum. I'll go for everything they have.'

'Well, that's easy. But I'm not sure that we'd have room.' I ticked half a dozen of the combinations listed and gave the paper to the waiter. Around us was the steady hum of conversation from Chinese families on a Sunday morning outing.

I had phoned Dunc the night before, intending to invite them all. Celia answered, but she said, 'We're tied up with a swimming competition for the girls. Anne was going to come too, but it may just be that dim sum would appeal more.' I'd heard the laughter in her voice.

'Have you been here before?' Anne asked. The restaurant looked popular, the clientele perhaps now regulars. But it was no hole in the wall. The polished red granite pillars shone, in contrast to the matte finish of the painted walls. Anne shone too, I thought, in a sleeveless silk blouse and simple skirt. She'd put her hair into an intricate tress, which opened up the whole structure of her head to view, left her ears totally exposed and reached well below her shoulders. Her forehead was rounded, her face oval but not long, and I thought I couldn't have put the ears anywhere better myself.

I shook my head. 'I've tried a couple of other places. This one is quite new. The building only went up last year. Part of the city's rapid change.'

'When I lived here before, we had a house in Bogor. My father is a New Englander, and liked to live away from the lowland heat. Bogor was a paradise. I used to play among the trees of the botanical gardens with my small Indonesian friends.'

'What did your father do?'

'That's not too easy to answer. He was a Harvard scholar who built a lot of high-level relationships in his early days, and continued to invest in them through the series of appointments he held. While he never worked for the government, he still saw himself working in the foreign service. While he was never an official diplomat, when we lived in Bogor the Indonesians saw him as the senior US Ambassador. It didn't go down too well with the real, junior one.'

I thought a bit. 'Would that have put him here in the 60s?'

Anne laughed. 'How old are you implying I am?'

'No, sorry. You're right. Later than that. But in the earlier days of the Suharto's New Order.'

'I'll accept that. Dad came out at a time when US fears of communism in the region were still rife. There was still full engagement in Vietnam, and Sukarno was a too-recent memory for comfort. Dad was the brake on official policy. He was highly critical of US acceptance of the Indonesian Generals as bedfellows. He saw no likelihood of any ease into democracy, which, as a democrat, bothered him.'

'The Generals tolerated him?'

'More than that. They loved him. No formality, you see. So they could cultivate him all they wished. When they wanted to know what the real US Ambassador was saying in his stilted communiqués, they went to him.'

'Where are your parents now?'

'Dad still has an Emeritus Professorship at Harvard, though he's not been seen much recently. My mother died last year.'

'I'm sorry.'

'Thank you. Very mundane, I'm afraid. She fell down some stairs and died some hours later. Dad was away at the time. It affected him terribly - both what happened, and the fact that he was not there to help her when she needed him.'

'I'm sure it did.'

Anne tried to shed the reflective look that had clouded her face. 'And yours? Are they in Australia?'

'Oh yes. Right on the family station in the Kimberley where they've always been. What you'd call a ranch. Can't get Dad away from it. But Mum's happy. Lots of friends around. Even if they are miles distant.'

'Brothers and sisters?'

'Just a sister. Married to a farmer, but further south than the Kimberley - in Western Australia. More prosperous. And producing the grandchildren that keep Mum happy.'

Anne laughed. 'You're lucky. Always wanted a sister. Or a brother.'

'How did you and Celia really meet?'

'At the hotel we had both chosen for a skiing holiday. We became friends very quickly. I was adjusting to a normal life, and had few friends. We saw each other continuously through our college years.'

'Where did you study?'

Anne smiled. 'Yale. Oh, nothing to do with offending Dad - in fact, he thought it was a good idea. Glad that people wouldn't have to think he'd got me in to Harvard. Though now I think secretly he'd rather I'd followed him.'

Just as I was contemplating the fact that I was in the company of an extremely intelligent woman from an unusual family, the first dishes started to arrive, enclosed in small bamboo steamers. Several sauces were placed on the table. The waiter took the lids off the baskets, revealing small cakes, dumplings and thinly wrapped fillings. He left without identifying what they were.

'This is where we experiment. Try and match the sauces to the food.'

'Mainly shrimp and pork,' said Anne. She dipped something in a light soy sauce. 'Mmm. That's good. It's shrimp.'

We were quiet for a few moments. The click of chopsticks was audible around us, evidence of others fumbling less than me. Anne turned out to be an expert, and as I realized that, I wondered what else she was expert in. 'Tell me what you do.'

'You mean Celia hasn't told you?'

'All she has said is that you work at the US Embassy, doing more or less what she does, but implied that you file a lot of papers.'

This made Anne laugh. 'Yes, that's Celia. Always scared that she'd drive men away from me if she implied anything more useful.'

'Oh. And has it?'

'No, no, Trevor. That's not fair.' She was still laughing. 'Every man unto himself. Talk about past relationships, or lack of, comes later.'

I raised my eyebrows. 'Good. Just let me know when.'

'I think, Trevor Gregory, that you do more than just file reports to Canberra.'

I recognized this as a way of changing ground. 'You mean that really I'm a sailor? Should be standing on the bridge, guns blazing, as Dunc implied?'

'What I mean is that you are sincere and serious about a very interesting job, which gives you excellent scope to make something out of it. Not just a file pusher.'

'I think I'm in the right place at the right time, though, apart from the many new contacts, I'm not yet sure what makes that so. However, I do know that when I eventually get that bridge beneath my feet, it'll be a fundamental part of what will make me a good skipper.'

'Will that be soon?'

'It should come after this posting. I'm next in line for a frigate.' I hesitated to say my posting was rapidly coming to a close. It seemed that doing so might just close a door I wanted to open some more.

'Does Australia have many?'

I laughed. 'We can't match any one of the US battlefleets with all the ships in our Navy. If you want numbers, we have little more than half a dozen serious surface warships. It makes a command hard to come by. You might think that this means we put a lot of emphasis on diplomacy and friendship. Really it's just a consequence of a lack of defence spending.'

'As an insider, so to speak, what do you think of the Indonesian Armed Forces?'

'ABRI? Big, in the main lacking training, but a very cohesive institution which looks after itself. Every President since Suharto has made it a priority to tame them. If you remember, there was an open revolt by the Commander-in-Chief in Wahid's early years, all tied up with involvement in the East Timor massacres, and the sense that Wahid might immediately grant independence to Aceh. That was perhaps a defining moment in loss of face, especially for the army, which was fully committed to hardline oppression. The next C-in-C was an admiral.'

'And the Navy itself?'

'Many more ships than Australia, even, but low on technology. Canberra isn't worried about it.'

'Are you?'

I thought that an interesting question. 'Does it sound as though I am? No, I don't think so. But I've learnt that the Indonesian Navy is as serious about its function and reputation as the other Services. Indonesia is not a naval power in the traditional sense, and its geographic extension makes for difficulties in policing of its own national waters. The Services are not generally very modern, though there has been a major and very quiet push to change this. I've tracked the changes in the Navy. I have come to respect it more than I did as a salt-water First Officer.'

Anne made a small face at me. 'You got rid of some of your crust?'

I laughed. 'Yes. But it took a while. Caked right on.'

Anne had finished eating, and was replenishing our tea cups. 'And you get promoted for it,' she said with a smile. 'How does a sudden promotion come out of something you imply is so humdrum?'

'Things have been going on here that required an attaché with a little more seniority. Not much to it, really. It would have come with my ship.'

'Not going to tell, eh? Official secrets?'

I laughed. 'Oh, alright.' And I proceeded to outline the Alumina Queen affair in detail, my belief that it was not piracy but terrorism, and my suggestions on how Australia might deal with the problem. I enjoyed talking to Anne about it. 'So I've been given the job of working out the details with my counterparts. It needed an extra ring on the sleeve to do it.'

'Of course. Nothing to do with a pat on the back, job well done, etcetera.'

I rolled my serviette into a ball, and pretended to throw it at her.

'No, no. Just teasing. But why did you make the Al-Qaeda link?

99

'Will you think me really simple if I say that I didn't like the coincidence of the initials in the ship's name? AQ.'

She sat back in surprise and thought a moment. 'Yes, it's either very far-fetched and completely wrong, or it's the message itself.'

'As a message, it's extremely compelling. I want to know who might have sent it.'

'What do you mean?'

'I doubt that Al-Qaeda itself made any such link. Perhaps someone else is intent on the West just believing so.'

Again she thought. 'So you don't think Al-Qaeda did it?'

'As I said, I think we're meant to believe so. I just want to disprove any other possible reason.'

'Do you have others?'

'Absolutely none,' I said.

'You don't think Jemaah Islamiyah could be behind it?'

I thought of the press given to Abu Bakar Bashir, the muslim cleric said to have founded this group. The coincidence of *bakar* being a root *bahasa* word of anything implying fire and burning made it a good name for anyone wishing to incite religious hatred 'Well, if they exist, which, in spite of the mad cleric's denials, I tend to believe, I'm not sure that I'd consider them local proxy for Al-Qaeda.'

Anne was silent for a moment. 'Don't you think this country has a class of people who might fit a classification of not-very-well-educated-and-easily-led, and who might very quickly pick up on the Palestinian model of martyrdom for their cause?'

'The model maybe, but you know as I do that an Indonesian generally doesn't carry his hate on his sleeeve. So such a movement would require remarkable leaders. That cleric may provide the religious grounds, but it's highly unlikely that he runs an efficient terrorist organization.'

'No, I don't think *he* does. I think someone else does.' Anne said.

'Well, the Bali bombers are behind bars.'

'And therefore not a threat?' She said, sceptically.

'The safest and most unsuspicious place from which to lead?'

'The prison system in this country is like a sponge. Anything can be done if you know how.'

'And if anyone in authority wanted to sidetrack attention, they'd mount a search for other, non-existent leaders?'

Anne gave a slight smile. 'Devious mind you have. But it's one possibility, right?'

I thought a little about the conversation we were having. It was no secret from Anne that I was Naval Attaché, and, anyway, blokes like me tended to wear *that* quite openly on their sleeve, even when not in uniform. But Anne was showing an interest in terrorism quite beyond what I'd expect from any ordinary Embassy staffer. Most would refer to it in disgust; she was seeing it as some form of intellectual challenge - understanding its elements, working out its operational sleight-of-hand, and drawing out of me things I'd never considered. My earlier attempt to find out what she did at the US Embassy had gone nowhere - had, in fact, received a very simple brush-off.

'I think you think about this quite often. At work, perhaps?'

But that didn't work either. 'Don't we all?'

I hadn't minded the earlier moments when she teased me. 'Do you feel like a walk?' I asked.

'I love walking. Where?'

'We could go back into the city. Jalan Surabaya will be alive today.'

'Yes, let's do that. I love browsing the antique stalls.'

' Mainly a lot of junk, but the fun is in preventing the vendors from making a fool of you.'

'Have they ever?' asked Anne.

'Have they ever what?' I replied innocently.

'Made a fool of you, Captain Gregory.'

'Demotion imminent? Once or twice. I bought a lovely old dish there, quite small, a few weeks ago. Once I got it home and looked at it under a better light I saw a great bite-sized chunk of painted plaster-of-paris where some thirteenth-century Sung stoneware was supposed to be. Fortunately I hadn't paid too much for it. And it is still quite lovely to look at. If you don't get too close.'

'Take me there. Maybe it'll happen again.'

I found a parking spot halfway between Taman Suropati and Jalan Surabaya. Large, mainly modern houses hid behind high concrete and steel fences. As we rounded the corner, Jalan Surabaya stretched off into the distance. The stalls were on one side of the road only, the rest of the street being given over to pedestrians. It was quite crowded. Anne put the strap of her purse over her neck so that she could hold it well forward. 'Preventive measures,' she said, and tucked her free arm through mine. 'Lead on.'

We spent almost two hours wandering the length of the street, browsing among brassware, porcelain, stoneware, wood carvings and even fossils. 'This was where I bought that dish,' I said, at one point. The vendor didn't recognize me.

Anne looked at the stoneware on offer. It was a more fundamental, serene pottery than the stark blue and whites of the later periods. She picked up a small dish similar to the one I'd bought in Sulawesi, two fish incised in the bottom, seemingly following each other. The glaze was a rich, lustrous green.

The vendor had been eying us like a hawk. When he saw that there was possible purchase in the air, he circled for the kill. 'You like, mister? Five hundred, only!'

'If he wants five hundred thousand rupiah for this, it's either stolen or repaired. You can't get them now for under a million.' I took it from Anne and looked at it closely. Visually there was nothing wrong, but I could feel a different texture to the surface at one point on the rim. 'Repaired. Here. Feel this.'

I turned to the vendor, who looked at me innocently. 'This good plate, Sung dynasty,' he said. 'Very old. Very rare. You buy. Five hundred only.'

I gave it back to him. 'I wouldn't give you one hundred for it'. I turned and led Anne away.

The vendor decided that this was a bargaining gambit, and followed us onto the street.' Four-fifty, mister. I give you very good price. Four-fifty, no, four-twenty-five. You buy? Why not tell me your best price.'

The tirade followed us down the street. By the time he gave up, he'd come down by almost half without any prompting from me. 'Buy for the lady. I give you best price. Three hundred.'

Anne looked at me seriously. 'Well done, Captain. Boarders repulsed.' and then broke into giggles.

I bowed my head solemnly. 'Thank you, Admiral. But it was close. Took water in over the bows.' Then I tucked her arm back in mine and headed back into the fray.

I dropped her off at the Marshalls' a little before five. Dunc pressed me to stay to dinner, but I declined. 'No, honestly, Dunc, I have to set some things up tonight. Thanks anyway.'

'Thank you, Trevor, for a lovely day.' Anne was smiling at the door as I turned away. I waved out of the car window as I pulled away. 'Call you next time I'm in port, Admiral.'

When I got home, I pulled a Tiger out of the fridge and put my feet up on the back patio, working slowly through it and the cold meal my cook had prepared. The mosques in the neighbourhood were sending out the call to prayer, and the interlapping of the Arabic chants was slightly stifled by the humid early evening air.

I had recognized for a long time that there was a part of my life that was quite empty. After a while this had become my choice, not so much that I preferred my solitude, rather that the message seemed to be to wait. Romances in my earlier professional years had not gone far, mainly because of time spent away from home and the pressure sailors' girlfriends put on themselves to get married. Many such marriages fell apart in short order.

Anne had fitted herself to me this afternoon, but with a confidence in herself that was different from Celia's, a calm completeness. It also seemed to be the product of having dealt successfully with solitude, of coming out the other side with the foreknowledge of a contented future.

But there was something else. For that split second, as we were talking about the Alumina Queen, and she had sat back in surprise at my mention of a simplistic coincidence in initials, I'd seen a set of mental gears shift into high. And then we'd gone into things more deeply. She was no Embassy clerk, I knew that - her evasiveness had proved it. And she had a local staff that adored her. Whether there were some particular initials that fitted the agency she worked for, I did not yet know, but what I suspected was that she was her father's daughter, and that the Americans were calling on her strengths in a moment when they were specifically needed. At this very moment, in Indonesia, if one said Al Qaeda, one certainly implied Jemaah Islamiyah and all of the other invisible synaptic tendrils, even if I wasn't convinced. But Indonesia needed no Al Qaeda to loose the dogs of terrorism; a few others had long waited for jihad, and the smallest excuse brought it. Al Qaeda just brought slightly more focus -- and, as Bali proved, death to foreigners.

But it was not Al Qaeda the organization, or any Indonesian linkage, which was my immediate worry. I was concerned about their actions. I still had to prove that Alumina Queen had been a casualty of terrorism. The hardware on the seabed, if it were there, might never do that. Only catching the perpetrators in the act would. *Operasi Lautan Lepas* - Operation Open Seas - finally negotiated with Subagio, was my main focus until Canberra gave me my ship.

On that other front I thought that, at some point, I would have to mount my own operation. *Uncover Anne*, I thought I might call it.

Eleven

I went to Jakarta with Amin for the presentation. The tactical purpose of each ship had required careful consideration of deckplans, including sea-to-air and sea-to-sea missile launchers. Four had helipads on the stern deck. The Laksamana ordered Siswanto to his office immediately.

'You have calculated our disposable assets?'

No civilian banker likes to be asked how much money is on hand when it is clear the military has plans to spend. But ABRI owned the bank, even if it had no-one on staff. It was clearly the question Siswanto dreaded.

'Our total asset base is over fifteen trillion rupiah. That includes all pension funds and miscellaneous deposits.'

'And if you convert that to dollars?'

'About two and a half billion, Laksamana.'

'Good. I want three letters of credit deposited with banks in the Gulf. The first two should go out this week. They should each be for the maximum. Next week you'll send the third.'

'But that's completely impossible! We'd never cover them. It's illegal.'

'My friend, I can replace you at any moment. If you don't do what I say, you're of no use to me.'

Siswanto shuddered visibly. He made a half-hearted protest.

'Enough,' the Laksamana snapped. 'Do it. We'll pay afterwards. You'll get your reward.'

Excerpted from Rusman Soekendro, LetJen (ret'd),
No Game At All: Memoirs of a Strategist

The Javan looked refreshed, and his welcome had an eagerness different from the day before. 'Did they look after you well?'

'No worries,' said the Australian. 'Good bed, good breakfast.'

'Wonderfully peaceful,' said his wife, laughing. 'The sound of the wind down the valley and through the bamboo was the sound of a different planet.'

'I prefer your description to your husband's,' said the Javan. 'It is why I'm here. There is a magic to Sunda which is not quite found today elsewhere on Java.'

The Australian suddenly recalled a moment in the distant past when the Sundanese gamelan had evoked visions of untold spirits. 'Someone once said to me that awareness of that magic meant I'd been here too long.'

'Did you agree?' asked the Javan, in not-so-mock seriousness.

'I think I was afraid to answer. I didn't want anyone writing 'gone bush' on a performance report. Things were already too serious for that.'

***

So completely laden was the freighter that as she came into sight she looked almost submerged, and it had taken her a full half hour to reduce speed to five knots. 'We will take station five hundred metres from her starboard side, *Laksamana,* and transfer the men by launch.' The frigate's captain was stiffly formal, clearly nervous at Subagio's presence.

I had joined Subagio on the last leg of the commercial flight into Palu. Only an hour north of Makassar by jet, Palu had finally been chosen as the logistical centre for *Operasi Lautan Lepas.* Kalimantan sat not far to the west, and the resulting narrowness of that part of the Strait meant that large ships would come relatively close to land, making the transhipment of the men who would protect them an easy task. Ship-owners wanting to avail themselves of this Special Forces service were instructed to use the Makassar Strait as their transit route through Indonesian waters. Palu Bay was shallow, so normal transfer from land would be by a small coastal patrol craft. A frigate had been sent from Surabaya for the opening transfer, but even she had had to receive the unit of men, and ourselves, from a patrol craft.

I left them all on the bridge as I made my way to the companionway down to the frigate's launch. As I made the jump into the tossing craft, a dozen sets of careful eyes in faces otherwise expressionless watched me join them. The unit leader nodded to the launch crew, and we crossed the two hundred metres of water between the two ships.

The transfer was completed quickly, though the gear came across on a second trip. I swung up onto the freighter ahead of the Indonesian troops, and found a young Australian officer standing with the ship's deckhands, watching the launch sitting at the foot of the companionway.

'Lieutenant Falsom, sir. Welcome aboard.'

'Thank you, Lieutenant. Is the captain on the bridge?'

'Yes, sir. He said to bring you up when he saw you in the launch.'

'Lead on. Ready for the next few days?'

'Yes, sir. Looking forward to it. Worried a bit about the language, though. It's not Strine, is it.'

'Certainly not that, Falsom. But you'll manage.'

'Hope so, sir.'

'Who's the captain?'

'Beggle, sir. Australian.'

The captain was a middle-aged man, quite smartly dressed in light shirt and dark trousers. Company insignia combined with his badges of rank to give him the air of someone happier with more tin rather than less.

'Gregory, captain.'

'Happy to have you on board, Gregory. Wasn't expecting an Aussie with this lot.'

'Came to get a feel for the men and the operation. I can't run something like this just from a desk.'

'You're running it?'

'I'll be overseeing it all from Jakarta, yes. All the links are up?'

Beggle indicated to Falsom. 'He was checking them all yesterday with your blokes. No worries. Right?'

Falsom nodded affirmatively. 'Working fine, sir. Run from this little unit here.' He indicated a computer tower and monitor set to one side of the bridge. 'Of course, there's the standard radio hookup, too.'

'Good. No problems with quarters for the men, captain?'

'Not really. It's more than we normally carry, of course. But we had the chippies in before we left to set up some more bunks. The ship's big enough to take them.' It was a bit of an understatement.

'Right. Thank you, captain. Good luck. Come on, Lieutenant, I want you to meet your opposite number.' I led Falsom back to the deck. 'You're up on your operating procedures?'

Falsom looked a little pained. 'Off by heart, sir. No reason to worry.'

I grinned at his youthful expression of hurt. 'I'm not, Lieutenant. I told you you'll manage.'

Falsom and the Indonesian unit commander greeted each other cautiously, the first time that either had come face-to-face with an unknown quantity. 'Get to know each other well,' I said and they both cracked salutes as I made for the ladder. '*Selamat jalan.* Safe journey.'

'Well, Captain Gregory?' asked Subagio, once I was back aboard the frigate. 'How does *Koperasi Lautan Lepas* look?' He seemed to enjoy the play on words, the *Koperasi* saying that this was more than a mere *operasi*.

'It has the potential to frighten the hell out of any unsuspecting hijacker,' I said.

'Let us hope that it does,' said Subagio, his lips glistening as if in anticipation of the evening meal. 'Back to Palu, *Kolonel.*'

Six ships cleared the Makassar Strait into a harmless South China Sea. It was the seventh ship after the joint creation of *Open Seas* that found itself the bait in twenty-four hours of maritime cat and mouse. Warrant Officer Notman and *Letnan Dua* Hassan were the Unit Commanders.

Notman's radio message was picked up by three receiving centres. One, in Darwin, monitoring the frequency constantly. All messages received were immediately forwarded by radio link to Canberra, where they were logged in at Naval HQ. This was for the record.

The second centre was a radio room on the top floor of the Australian Embassy in Jakarta. My staff had increased by two: another radio officer to increase the Embassy's coverage to an around-the-clock watch, and a navigation and communications specialist to run a computer tracking system established specifically to keep an eye on the ships under the protection of *Open Seas*. When an alert was called, both officers were on continuous standby at the Embassy. Bunk quarters had been set up close to the radio room.

The radio officer phoned me. 'Alert from Dolphin, sir. Friend maintaining a close course.'

'Right, Tom. I'll be there in twenty minutes. Advise on the cellular link in the meantime if there's anything further.'

'Yes, sir.'

It was just past nine, and I'd been thinking about a small drink before heading to bed, but was glad that I'd not succumbed to the temptation. My security detail was watching television in the spare room. 'Time to go.' The driver nodded.

The third centre was at the Surabaya Naval Base. Canberra knew of its existence, because of the protocols that had been put in place to start the joint operation. It had been agreed that all shipboard patrols should have a link to their own HQ. However, it had also been agreed that while any action was underway, the Australian patrol leader was the superior officer, and that only he would manage the live command link. The Indonesian patrol leader could establish radio contact with his own HQ at any other time. *KOPASSUS* maintained an Eastern Regional command in Surabaya, and it was there that they set up the radio post.

Traffic was light, and I was at the Embassy in fifteen minutes. I went straight to the top floor. 'Tom, Mike.' I nodded to the two men there.

Mike was already bringing up auxiliary information screens on secondary windows on his large flat-screen monitor. He broke the screen into six windows in tile formation, and transferred two of the three video channels to the two leftmost tiles. The top centre tile showed the ship's codename, and speed and position data from the on-board transponder, including summary details on local weather. The bottom centre tile mimicked the on-board radar. The shadow was clearly visible as a green icon in the bottom left corner of the tile. The top right tile functioned as a real-time electronic notepad, allowing instantaneous transmission of any message written at either end. The bottom right tile had a set of pull-down menus that allowed me or the navigation officer to access the other ships currently under *Open Seas*. By using the mouse, any one of the tiles could be expanded to fill the whole screen for better viewing.

The system was designed as a running log, with all screens being captured in memory. A stand-alone tape machine hissed regularly, as the system downloaded the previous segment of time onto a short section of tape.

'All systems OK, sir,' said Mike, once he had run some software checks. 'Radio link is strength ten.'

'Good.' I sat at a separate desk. A second monitor carrying the same information had been set up for my sole use on a small LAN. I watched the screen for a few minutes noting the features displayed on each tile. The view of the ship was good. There didn't seem to be anything that the boffins in Canberra had missed.

I clicked on the top right tile. 'Evening Dolphin,' I wrote. 'Standing by.'

'Good on yer, Alice,' came back shortly afterwards, pecked in with one finger. Mike coughed discreetly.

The next couple of hours brought no change. The shadow stayed where it was, and the video screens showed only normal on-deck activities. I saw a routine round by the deckhands checking that all cargo hatches were properly closed.

At eleven thirty-five the notepad blinked. 'Suspicious shapes off port stern quarter.'

'Wake up, lads,' I said. 'I think we've caught a fish.'

Language was the big issue, not many Aussie sailors being fluent in anything beyond the mother tongue, but I'd spent some time putting together a manual in both languages, basically an essential guidebook to a combined operation. Using it, Notman, during familiarization exercises with his opposite number, would point at the English part, and Hassan would know immediately which Indonesian part to refer to. The two men, as other pairs on other ships, had to establish a simple working relationship, there not being time for anything else. Notman would not have more than a few simple words of Indonesian, and Hassan's English was probably rudimentary. I thought it more likely that sign language would end up being the universal tongue.

It turned completely dark, and still no lights were visible from the southwest. Yet the other vessel kept its course, neither passing nor dropping back. The scope showed it there, but it was unlikely that any boarding party sent out under the cover of darkness would show on its screen. The attackers would be low in the water, probably in one or more inflatables. Notman would be on the port wingbridge, glued to his nightglasses scanning deceptively quiet waters. Then the screen flickered and a message came over the satellite downlink. 'Alice, this is Dolphin.' I put on my headset to follow the command sequence.

Notman would have been watching the southwest quadrant continuously, the ship still invisible, but his nightglasses must have picked up a flicker in the background shadows of the sea, like a blip in the wave on an oscilloscope.

'Bang on, Hassan, bang on,' bleated in my ear, spoken quietly into Notman's sound-activated shouldermike. It was the standard *Open Seas* code for the final alert, '*Bangun*' the imperative Indonesian command to 'wake up'. It had seemed appropriate.

'Three inflatables, several men in each, five hundred metres from the ship.'

Then came the one hundred metre confirmation, the point at which action was authorized, the rules of engagement finally activated. 'Alice, this is Dolphin. Three zodiacs, six men apiece, one hundred metres, bearing 220.'

'Roger, Dolphin. Standing by.' I expanded the port video image to fullscreen, giving me a view as good as Notman had on the flying bridge.

'One zodiac passing astern, one port side, one standing off.' I saw the zodiac headed straight for the port side, running parallel to the ship until it was just aft of amidships. Its crew was clearly visible. A rope sailed up, and there would have been the soft clunk of a rubber-coated grappling hook catching the rail. One of the shapes began an immediate ascent, running up the ship's side.

Notman gave the mandatory double-click on his shoulder-mike, alerting Hassan to the imminent arrival of the boarding party. Hassan did not respond immediately, but a single click came through about ten seconds later, indicating that he had seen the shadow now coming over the rail. Two more men were on the ascent. All were dressed in dark clothing, and carried semi-automatics on slings.

Once three men were over the rail, one stayed by the hook, and the other two ran across the deck to the opposite rail. I did a quick switch to the central video feed, a wide-angle view of the near foredeck where any initial action had to be fought. One man crouched, keeping a watch towards the bridge, while the other made a signal towards the second zodiac with a shielded flashlight. Within three minutes there were ten men on deck.

Hassan had his men hidden in the strategic shadows, pinpointed through careful study the first night aboard. Each man knew his relative position, planned to take out opponents in an immediate arc of fire. While it wasn't possible to ensure that every man had a separate target, nor that each boarder was covered, the first fire was expected to reduce the attacking force by more than half, leaving only a small mopping up job to be done.

It was clear that the sudden shouts of pain and collapse of half their own number caused instant panic in the boarding party. There would not have been more than the quiet cough of unexpected shots. I saw random movement and gunflashes. But as if instantly realizing the uselessness of such a reaction, they stopped firing and made a diving jump towards the little on-deck cover that existed, huddling in the small shadows of the central main hatches of the ship's hold.

I counted six attackers down, leaving four still as combatants. I felt a little sorry for them, waiting for the next step. It came almost instantly as Notman flicked a switch and wide swaths of light from floodlights recessed in the deck cut horizontally towards the main hatches, eliminating all shadow. The remaining attackers were blinded and attempted to shoot out the lights, but only hit one before they were themselves shot.

Hassan gave the signal to break, and his men in the cover of the deep shadow forward of the main hatches came aft at a crouch, hidden from the men guarding the two zodiacs now frantically looking for non-existent cover. Both were taken down with leg shots. Then Hassan's men kicked the rifles of the attackers away. A double click indicated Hassan's confirmation that the deck was secure.

'Zodiac three, two hundred metres astern, six men.' They were in for a wet night. Back on the port side video I saw Hassan signal to the sniper in the superstructure with a raised finger, drawing it across his neck in a cutting motion before pointing in the direction of the remaining zodiac. He emphasized the action with a single raised finger again. The sniper took fifteen seconds to sight towards the zodiac's bulk. If the craft were side on, there was a chance he'd hit both the nearside and farside chambers. If not, one punctured chamber should be enough to cripple the craft. If the bullet hit anything else on the way that was too bad. The whipcrack of the single shot bounced from the steel bridge plating.

The lone occupant of the port-side zodiac could have been aware of little more than a shadow folding over him as a corpse was slung over the side directly over his head, and it must have broken his neck instantly as it drove downwards, the zodiac almost leaping out of the water on the rebound. The line was cast off, a second corpse securely fixed to the grapple, an effective sea-anchor. The pattern was repeated on the starboard side.

I could hear Notman humming. He'd had no direct control of the deck action but it had gone well. He spoke to the captain. 'Give me five minutes to check the deck, then your men can come up. I'll give you the word. But watch the radar. I want to know what our friend does.'

On the deck, Hassan had the three captives that were conscious and able to sit grouped into a bunch on the edge of the main hatch cover. Three others were lying on the deck at their feet. One lay a little apart.

'*Mati*.' Hassan pointed to the single figure, dead. A broad stain spoke to a major haemorrhage from the leg. He'd probably pumped his life out in thirty seconds.

'*Bagus*, Hassan, well bloody done, mate.' It was a deserved approbation, a short sharp action with the intended result. And there were captives to whom to put questions.

Though Notman knew I'd been looking over his shoulder the whole time, rather like a perched parrot, he still had a report to make. 'Dolphin to Alice.'

'Go ahead Dolphin.'

'Party broken up successfully, Alice. Sardines on ice. Will advise numbers shortly.'

'Roger, Dolphin. Well done. Alice out.'

I pushed my chair back from the screen with a satisfied release of breath. It had worked well. I had no idea what the fallout from the pursuing vessel would be, but hoped it would take its crew long enough to find out what had happened that they would not push the incident further.

I decided to have a coffee. While the action was over, there were still some decisions to be made, and this was where the fun was going to start. I was pondering on when to send the first communiqué when some letters started to spread across the top-right tile of the monitor.

'No casualties. Ten barracuda from eighteen. Three sharkbait, one on ice, three flounders, three sprats. Nice night, Alice.'

I shook my head at Notman's imagery, but didn't have much difficulty deciphering his cryptic choice of codewords. I'd seen most of the action. Ten boarders from eighteen (what finally happened to the others?), three went overboard, one dead on board, three seriously wounded, three fit (or reasonably so).

'Good work. Who are they? Report as soon as you can.'

It was past two in the morning before another signal came through. Mike prodded me awake. Again the message slowly spelt itself across the screen. 'Captured hijackers won't talk. No identification. Chinese features. Out.'

'Damn.' I could imagine that their interrogation at the hands of the *KOPASSUS* team had not been particularly gentle. And I thought about the trouble brought by the issue of nationality. Though they appeared to be Chinese, therefore perhaps PLA, we hadn't seen their ship. . But I didn't think Al Qaeda had made any pact with China. It looked as though Harry was right and I was wrong.

I made up a summary report of the night's events, and left a copy for the Ambassador. 'Fax that to Canberra and Hong Kong, Tom. It looks as though the fun's over for the night. I'm going home to catch a few hours sleep. I'll be back in by nine.'

Sleep took a while in coming, my mind continually rerunning the video tape of the deck action. It was my operation. I was directly responsible for the first time in my life for mens' deaths. Perhaps I had not recognized that in its brutal reality when I first put the idea together. Assigning the blame to them for having put themselves in front of my bullets did not assuage any of the guilt. The torment of all soldiers, I thought, dragging it down into my dreams.

'Well, Captain Gregory. I should say we gave them something to think about, wouldn't you?' Subagio was clearly in good spirits, less oil, more warmth. Perhaps I'd graduated off the menu.

I nodded. 'It was a success, sir. Your men did a fine job'.

'Yes, I think they did. Apparently none of them was hurt. But the six we took wouldn't talk. While we think we know who they are, we cannot yet be sure.'

I wondered whether they'd used the whole *KOPASSUS* bag of tricks. 'I think, Admiral, that it will still be business as usual for a while.' A single event was not enough proof of any theory, and even though I might be hanging onto the torn threads of my own, there was still the need for the perpetrators to understand that the waters were being policed.

'Oh, I agree, Captain. I wasn't suggesting that we stand down. The question is whether our northern friend works out what happened. Can we assume that he would take the warning?'

'We'll only know by their future actions. I've brought the schedule of sailings over the next few months. Surabaya already has this list, of course, but this is my particular concern.' I pointed to one of the later entries.

Subagio examined it, and his eyebrows raised. 'High stakes indeed. It's the first since the operation began.'

'Yes, but we can't assume that it hasn't been part of the plan since the beginning. I've even wondered about the presence of an agent since the Alumina Queen disappeared. Either in Hong Kong or Northern Australia. This would be a red-letter signal.'

Eyes wide, Subagio was thinking aloud. 'Do we change our approach? New rules of engagement? Slightly more hardware?'

'Both of those I think, sir. But I'll have to confirm with Canberra first. I'll get back to you if I may?'

'Yes, Captain.' Then, 'This will keep you very busy.'

Twelve

So we accepted the full Australian request, three ships for the ASEAN manoeuvres, finding that it made all the difference.

Excerpted from Rusman Soekendro, LetJen (ret'd),
No Game At All: Memoirs of a Strategist

Eventually the Australian did ask: 'When did I actually become a piece on your gameboard?'

The Javan smiled at this. 'Nothing actually became a piece on my gameboard, as you put it, in any fixed moment. Concepts came and went, and the algorithms adjusted themselves according to defining events. However, I understand your question, and I would like to ask you this: When do you believe it happened?'

'That's not fair. I was doing a job, and could never have been more than an intermittent blip on your radar. But there must have been some time when I was seen as a threat. For instance, the first time I went to see *Laksamana* Subagio. I remember him looking as though he'd like to boil me whole.'

The Javan laughed. 'If I were to tell you that I heard about that visit, you'd assume we already considered you a factor. But let me ask something else. How quickly did you consider the Alumina Queen to have been an Al-Qaeda target?'

'Quite quickly. It had to be one of the options. In fact, I thought it was the most likely one.'

'Then let me just say this. The minute you considered it an option, as you put it, was when you became a factor.'

'Because it was a ruse?'

'Did you ever conclude that? No, you couldn't have. No, it was like the Bali bombing - what were conceivably exogenous influences suddenly became endogenous ones, in terms of my strategy, I mean, and had to be factored differently. If I may say this respectfully, you generated so many exogenous influences - Muna, the joint patrols, the Natuna manoeuvres - that you became a full subroutine named Gregory.'

The Australian tried to control his laughter. 'My wife often calls me names, but that one has escaped her.'

His wife had listened to the exchange with some scepticism. 'Actually, I think you became completely *endogenous* when you met me.'

The Javan gave a slight bow. 'There was worry about *you* in certain quarters well before the two of you became a team. But perhaps that was *the* defining moment.'

***

'Tell me precisely what it is that Anne does at the US Embassy.'

I'd caught Celia at her desk, shuffling some of her own papers. 'Well, she does the sort of thing I do. Political analysis, structural change, democratic development, things like that.'

'You mean she gets her hands dirty doing it, or she's just an analyst?'

Celia shrugged. 'Mainly an analyst, I think. Why?'

'Because I think I'm getting the run around from both of you,' I said. 'And I don't believe it.'

'Why not?' she frowned.

'Because she comes from a very high-powered family. And what you are describing could be done by any medium-level foreign service flunky. She's not here earning any spurs. She's doing something serious. What is it?'

'Why don't you ask her?'

'Oh, I have, but have yet to get a clear answer.' In fact, we'd had two dinners out on the town, and had spent some of each one in some minor fencing around her reason for being in Jakarta. Old ties was becoming rapidly thinner as an excuse. But I wasn't about to run the risk of putting her off completely. 'I'm glad to say that she appears to dislike it as much as I do. But seeing how the two of you go so far back, I thought it would be easier to pry it out of you.'

'Trev! That's not very kind.'

'You, my dear, set me up with her. I'm not sure whether your motives were completely altruistic. You knew quite well what I was up to even before that weekend - it's no secret in this embassy. I just wondered if you were trying to find a way for it not to be a secret, in a different one.'

Celia laughed. 'Female conspiracy?' Then she turned serious. 'I've known you for quite some time, and yet I've never seen you with any sort of partner. I can almost say the same for Anne. Can't I be guilty of plain and simple matchmaking?'

'Well, perhaps. But you still haven't answered my question. What does she do? Or perhaps I should say: What is she?'

'What do you think she is?

'I think she's in intelligence. Which might make her CIA. And if I were to put my neck right out on a limb, I'd say she's in charge of the Al-Qaeda file.'

Celia put her hand over her mouth in some surprise. 'You *are* suspicious.' She was quiet for a moment. 'I can't answer you, Anne must. If she and I weren't such old friends, perhaps I'd tell you what I know.' She paused again. 'But go carefully with it. I think this would be good for both of you.' She started rustling papers again, in some confusion. 'Now get out of here, you old sea dog.' And she stuck her tongue out at me.

There was an embassy flap the next day over something thought to be relevant to defence, a low-level report that had taken a long time to reach my desk, which said that the Yanks couldn't make their minds up again about not selling arms to Jakarta. A faceless bureaucrat in Canberra insisted I send my analysis immediately, so that he'd have something to pass on in the morning. By the time I'd got it done, but only because Kessler's pencilled request at the bottom suggested I comply, it was six-thirty. I'd only been superficially aware of the Embassy closing down around me, and when I finally checked my watch I groaned. It was already dark.

I shut everything up quickly, and went to the radio room. 'Anything likely to come up tonight, Tom?'

'Nothing due through for a couple of days, Mr Gregory.'

'That's right. There isn't. G'night.'

I ran down the stairs to the parking lot. My security detail was waiting by the car. 'Sorry, lads. Exciting desk work.'

By the time I'd showered and left the house it was an hour later, and it took another half hour to get to Anne's. I blessed the fact that I'd bought a gift the night before, a few hours after receiving the invitation, and sent out for flowers during the day. I slipped the gift into my pocket.

Anne answered the door.

'I thought that perhaps you weren't going to come.'

'It was a bad day. I'm sorry to be late.' I gave her the flowers.

She smiled. 'You're forgiven. Come in. D'you like my new hole in the wall?'

117

Because neither of our schedules had worked out, I'd not been able before to see what she was moving into. I looked around as we went through the main room to the kitchen. It looked suited to a single person with few belongings, and I knew she'd rented it furnished.

'It's bonzer. Fits you like a glove.'

She laughed at this description. 'Celia said something equally incomprehensible.' She found a vase, added some water from the tap, put the flowers in it, and put the vase on the kitchen table. 'I'll find somewhere else for them later.'

I followed her through to the small back patio where a group of people was gathered. Apart from Celia and Dunc there were several Indonesian couples. Some were introduced as friends from work. An elderly couple, who showed a more personal relationship with Anne, I tentatively identified as friends of her parents. *Their* children were all abroad. 'The pattern, don't you think, these days?' said the husband, indicating the present gathering.

Introductions complete, Celia grabbed my arm. 'I'll take him off to where the drinks are, love. You stay and entertain your guests.' Before Anne could say anything Celia hauled me back to the kitchen.

'You're an oaf, Trevor Gregory. Where've you been? Anne wouldn't have me know it but she's been watching that door all night.'

'I really am sorry, Celia. You know what my job's like right now. I truly lost all track of time.'

'Anne glows when she comes home from seeing you. And when she thinks I won't notice, she'll ask some question about you. It's getting to the point where I can't answer them.'

I was not unflattered by this. 'Well, you could always excuse yourself and call me. We could work out the answers together.'

Celia laughed 'Wouldn't that work well. I thought you were against conspiracy.'

'Not if I'm part of it.'

By the time we rejoined the others, Anne was making motions for them to help themselves to the buffet. 'You can wait a couple of minutes, Trevor, and enjoy your drink. Relax a little, first.' I could see a gleam of humour behind her eyes, which suggested she was well aware that Celia had been chewing me out.

Dunc hung back, too.'I thought the evening was going to be a complete flop. I was planning on moving to a hotel. Celia would have been impossible to live with had you not come.'

I laughed. 'Oh, shut up, Dunc. Not you, too. I should have thought you'd be commiserating with me over what is obviously an imminent breach of my solitude.'

Dunc raised his glass. 'I drink to it.'

'Goddamn it,' I said. But I drank, too.

As the evening went on, new scents from night-flowering plants joined the light breeze flowing across the patio, and the group was relaxed and convivial. While we'd started off by deliberately avoiding talking local politics in deference to Anne's Indonesian guests, the latter had little compunction in launching into the topic and describing the latest scandals to hit the headlines. Once or twice, when the conversation split between groups, I could hear Anne talking fluently to her guests in Indonesian.

My attention wandered. I found myself wondering, as I had many times in the past couple of days, where the hole was in my reasoning on the Alumina Queen. Subagio was increasingly pressing the message that the surviving highjackers had nothing to do with any Islamic group. 'How could they,' he said in one phone call, 'if they're Chinese?' I knew he was thinking Indonesian Chinese, who, if they weren't still worshipping multiple deities, were more than likely to be Christian. I also wondered why it was taking so long to find out.

'Wake up.' Dunc prodded me.

'What did you say?'

'You were lost in thought, dwelling, no doubt on pirates. Has anything happened?'

'We've just foiled an attempted hijacking of a freighter. We managed to take a few captives.' I avoided details on the operation itself.

'Who were they?'

'We don't know. We didn't get a glimpse of their ship.'

It was evident that the Indonesians knew nothing about the subject, and I knew that it had not yet reached the Indonesian press. Subagio had said that there might be a press release later in the week. I explained roughly what was happening.

'And you have managed to get our Government to cooperate with yours on this, Mr Gregory?'

I nodded. 'There has been a better response than we expected. The shipboard units are Indonesian, and the command is jointly shared with Australia. It has worked well. And your special forces are very capable.'

'*KOPASSUS*? Yes, we're all a little afraid of them. They don't show much pity.'

I read the same message in their words as I had put in my report. 'I'm afraid that the people we're up against show little pity, either. We think that they've murdered at least one crew. In those few minutes when they make their attempt, it's hard not to give them back what they hand out. They'd have little compunction in killing your troops.'

'And is Canberra happy?' Anne asked.

'Making political mileage out of it,' I said. 'The message to the populace is that our northern neighbour is now with us in the 21st century, and that Timor is behind us. No more *konfrontasi*. All *koperasi*. Mind you, the press is still suspicious.'

'So would I be,' said Dunc. The Indonesians politely said nothing.

They were the first to leave, excusing themselves for having stayed so late, and Anne saw them to the door. With the elderly couple she showed more affection than the others. When she came back I asked: 'Friends of your parents?'

She nodded: 'He was one of Dad's colleagues.' Then, as if to avoid some lingering sadness: 'More coffee, Duncan?' She went around our cups again. 'I have a little bottle of cognac tucked away in the cabinet if you would like to get it. I don't believe in keeping it for medicinal purposes.'

'My angel,' said Dunc. 'Trev?'

'A small one, please.'

'I think I'll have a little one, too, Duncan,' said Celia. 'I don't often have a real reason to have one.'

Anne raised her eyebrows.

'Your new home, love. I want you to be happy here. I'll seal it with a wish.'

Dunc brought back four brandy glasses on a tray, and passed one to each of us.

'To Anne's new house,' he said, lifting his glass. 'And to all who sail in her.'

Anne broke into fits of giggles. 'Duncan!'

I reached into my pocket. 'I brought you a little gift.'

Anne carefully opened the paper and sat looking at its contents. After a moment she said 'Did he recognize you this time?'

In her hands was the same dish we'd examined that Sunday. 'Oh, yes. Coming back a third time was a real giveaway. Good job it was mid-week. Business was slow. I put half-an-hour of hard bargaining into that.'

'Thank you, Trevor. I shall treasure it.' She gave me a demure kiss on the cheek, then took another sip of her brandy.

Dunc's toast had caused Celia to spill most of hers, and she put down her empty glass. 'And now it's time to go, Duncan.'

Dunc drained his brandy. 'Aye, my love. I'll saddle the nag.'

'And I'm driving. You're a little drunk.'

'Aye, my love.'

'Never mind. Goodnight, Trev, goodnight, Anne.' Celia hauled Dunc to his feet and pushed him towards the door. 'Out!' She gave a little wave to us both as she drove away.

Anne closed the door.

'I should go, too, Anne. It's been a long day for you.' I looked down into her eyes.

'No longer than for you. I'd like a little more cognac. Have another with me.'

I followed her back out to the patio, and sat beside her on a long bench. There was the sound of the crickets in the late evening, and the decreasing hum of the night city. She gave me my glass, and sipped her own. Then she picked up the small dish I'd given her. 'It's a lovely memory, not an antique.' She traced the two small fish swimming after each other in an eternal translucent pursuit, and asked: 'Do you think one ever caught up to the other?'

'I should think it depended on tail currents.'

Anne let out a small laugh. 'Are those something sailors always depend on?'

I was quiet a while before answering, looking for the right words. 'I think I've always had the tide against me. Like those dreams where no matter how hard you try, you stand in quicksand, and the other person is always beyond reach.'

She gestured with the dish. 'Prescient potters.'

I nodded. 'Though I think the question is whether we're on the same path.'

'It would be a good start, wouldn't it.'

'Especially if it were untrodden. I haven't tried walking it properly before.'

'Why haven't you?'

'Probably because I sensed the risk was too great.'

'Are you thinking of risk now?'

'I sense little risk. There may be uncertainty, but that's not the same as risk.'

Her hand slipped into mine. 'For me there's lot's of risk. But absolutely no uncertainty.' She let go, and stood up. 'I don't want you to go right now.'

I shook my head. 'I don't want to be anywhere but here.' Though that in itself was not quite enough. 'But I need to ask you a question.'

Her eyes were as dark as the shadows around us, hunting over my face, perhaps with worry. 'Yes?'

I wondered how to put it gently. 'I need to know what it is that you do. If you can't tell me, how will I know which particular part of me really interests you?'

She gave a slight smile. 'That was a very delicate, un-Australian way of questioning my motives. Which I probably deserve.' She looked down at her hands for a moment. 'The bit that interests me has nothing to do with work. But that doesn't answer your question. So, what do I say?'

I lifted her chin with a finger, so that she was looking directly at me. 'Is it so secret?'

She shook her head. 'Not really.' She was quite troubled. 'Oh, hell. It has nothing to do with breaking some sort of official-secrets-oath. It's just that I'm very highly trained only to talk to certain people about these things.'

'Then if that's all it is, I shan't worry at all. And if, over breakfast, I were to raise the subject again, is it something that we might explore over a second coffee?

There was still some question in her eyes. 'If you're still here for breakfast then it's a deal.'

'Oh I'll be here.'

She relaxed. 'Then finish your cognac. I want to lock the door.'

When she came back I had the night firmly in my gaze. 'What do you see?' she asked.

'A star. You can't often see them here through the haze.'

She slipped her arm through mine. I felt the warmth of the contact through my shirt as I turned. My forefinger lifted itself to her lips, tracing their shape.

Her gaze was very steady. 'Kiss me.'

'I was just anticipating the pleasure.'

'Well, hurry up.'

From there it was a slow progression of touching and quiet talk that took us to the second-floor bedroom. Then there was no sound other than the rustle of clothes slowly being removed from two bodies that ached to be in contact.

She cuddled up to me, soaking up my nakedness against hers, while I did the same. Then it was a slow kiss, eyes open, watching each other in the subdued light of the bedroom. I ran my fingers up and down her back, feeling her shiver.

'It's been a very long time,' she whispered.

I said nothing. Her slight perfume and her warmth combined to create in me a new sense. The feeling of relaxation and urgency was a heady mixture. I moved my whole body over her in slow deliberate strokes.

We became bolder, touching, accumulating a wealth of knowledge. I felt her finger tips come alight, caressing with a flame that felt brilliantly blue. It shone in the back of my brain, warming every extension of my body.

'Don't move yet,' she murmured.

But we had reached the point where there was no distinguishing the individual contact, only a long, lasting note of pleasure.

So we read each other's secrets, through the rhythms of our sounds and thoughts, not easy the first time, but both feeling a wonderment beyond physical. And then a dam opened in my mind, enveloped me in the torrent that tore through it, and I flew into a rainbow Outback. Anne was gone, too, flying with me.

Afterwards, she propped herself on her elbows over me, her breasts warm on my chest. She moved them slightly side to side, a voluptuous demonstration. 'That is something I want again and again.'

I felt a new white peace.

Part II

SPRINGTIDE

Neil Thomas

Thirteen

`There are four main blocks, Jenderal. For simplicity's sake, I've named them East, Central, West and South. As strategic objectives each must be seen to be different. I could put a different block in here,' I had pointed to an area on the map, `but that will resolve itself. At the moment I'm considering only those blocks where we would have to commit resources.'

The map covered the Jenderal's table. Its corners were weighted with pieces of polished petrified wood, and the annual rings in one piece spread as if they were ripples across a pond.

`The East block is strategically important. If we cannot control it, the whole plan is vulnerable. It is from there that a sea defence westward can be mounted. We will have to prevent that.'

`The Central block is a critical area of control. It is closer to the West block. West and South are our ultimate strategic objectives. Those are the ones we want. When we have them, we can abandon East if we need to, but we must retain Central.'

`On further analysis, I've divided the whole exercise into three stages. Stage one sees us establishing our presence in Central and West, and controlling East. Stage two is a brief period of reinforcement in West and movement of men and material to the edge of the block. We have to cross that,' again I pointed to the map, `to begin stage three. That will be complete when we control South.'

`We can't reach South independently of West? From this direction?' asked the Jenderal, indicating a different approach. By water.

`The probability of success of an independent entry is far too low, Jenderal. We can better protect our resources by entry into West, and an overland run to the boundary here for the subsequent push into South.

`But a deception?'

`The value of a diversionary manoeuvre could be very high, Jenderal. A core of panic would serve us well.'

Excerpted from Rusman Soekendro, LetJen (ret'd),
No Game At All: Memoirs of a Strategist

Come,' said the Javan. 'This is the moment when I normally take a walk.'

He led them through a back gate, and they came out onto the side of the valley, rice terraces tumbling away beneath them. It was not yet too hot to work, and there were people dotted about, some weeding, others trimming grass from the earth bunds that separated each terrace. 'They will take that grass and feed it to their sheep,' and he pointed to an old man in shorts, t-shirt and knitted white hat bearing a bamboo yoke with a heavy basket of grass slung at each end, which, as he walked, bounced in rhythm to his stride. The man's calves and thighs were corded with muscle, the veins huge under his skin, and his bare feet slapped the wet soil. 'Tomorrow,' said the Javan, 'we will go and visit him. He has the champion ram. You must see it.'

The path wound along the valley, sometimes wending slightly downwards, sometimes upwards, but always along the edges of the terraces. Other paths intersected it, but it was clear that the Javan was sparing them from too much exertion in the increasing heat. 'Most days, when I'm here, I work at my desk in the early morning, and then take this walk.' he said. 'It clears my mind of all the things crowding it. Then I eat, and sleep. Later in the day I am then able to work again.'

They came to a broad curve in the valley, and here the Javan stopped. He bade them look across to the far side. Before them, and curling away at each side as if they were looking at the view through a fish-eye lens, the patchwork of paddies grew into a thousand fragments of greens and golds. Above, the sky was similarly fragmented in blues and whites. Below, the single dark line of the small river ran right across this canvas.

'Water,' said the Javan, 'starts there,' and he pointed at a cloud, 'falls there,' he dropped his hand in a vertical line to indicate the paddies opposite, 'and drains there.' He indicated the river below. 'This tapestry of life depends on it. I remind myself so every day, and then give thanks to Allah in His immeasurable wisdom. Without Him I am nothing.'

***

A canopy covered the patio, protection from whatever full tropical downpour might decide to invade later in the day. We both had our elbows on the narrow table that rested between two chairs, the others pushed aside, unneeded. Juice and assorted breads sat between us. Coffees, still the first, were off to one side.

Anne had a sarong wrapped around her, covering her from chest to foot, though only the tip thrust lightly into the fold across her breasts kept it in place. To my mind, it was likely to give way at any moment. She'd found another for me, and I'd wrapped it around my waist in Thai style, a half-knot at the side giving it a decidedly more masculine air. Though under attack I thought my knot unlikely to afford as much protection as Anne's elaborate cantilevers. She moved around to my side of the table. I sensed things change, a shedding of past, a shifting into something else. That she'd made this decision I knew before she spoke. 'Second-coffee time.' Only then did she lift her head. It was all one, the emanations, the sounds, the movement.

But I was still slow. 'Second-coffee time?'

'The time when all things are revealed. You stayed, I promised.'

I remembered. 'I think we both promised.'

'Yes. And even though your first coffee is undrunk and cold,' somehow she knew this without even looking, 'I'll do it on principle, not intake.' And with that, she was back into her humorous self. She gave me a last fleeting kiss as she moved, pouring all of herself back into her sarong, before pouring away the cold coffee. She flopped onto her chair, elbows thumping down onto the glass. One arm then reached blindly out for the coffeepot.

'I told you about Pops.' Coffee splashed, mainly into the mugs.

I nodded, assuming that Pops was Dad or Pa, or whatever other diminutive term existed for an American father.

'Really he and I are not so different,' she said. 'I know these people so well, it was natural for me to want to come back here.' She paused, tracing something imaginary in the table glass, eyes down, far away. 'Head hunting is the term we use in the States, when somebody comes looking for you, wanting you for a very specific purpose. I was head-hunted.' She look up, in puzzlement. 'Can you say that? Head-hunted?'

'Well,' I said,' you can in Irian Jaya. But it generally implies painful death and a contribution to someone else's nutrition.' I thought briefly of Subagio.

Anne laughed. 'They like brains, don't they. Not much different, then.' Then she went on. 'A man came knocking on my door, inviting me for interview. No letter, no prior job description. Just a first-class air ticket to Washington, all expenses paid. They even put me in a limo.'

'A phone call wouldn't have done it?'

'I don't know. But perhaps they didn't trust it would.'

I nodded.

'They were very straightforward - what did I think about this, what did I think about that, if this were the situation how would I describe it in ten words or less, stuff like that.'

'And languages?'

'Yes. Could I still talk my way through most of Southeast Asia, etc.'

'Your eyes would give you away.'

Another laugh. 'I don't think I was expected truly to go under cover. No, I got the sense that they considered the best cover was just me, being myself, talking, listening, reading.'

'And talking, amongst others, to Dad's old friends.' Somehow I couldn't bring myself to using the term Pops.

'Yes. His proxy, really.'

'Did you talk to him about it?'

'Not immediately. They didn't exactly say not to, but there was an undercurrent that said it hoped I wouldn't.'

'Secrecy?'

'Mainly. But I think they were also worried he'd talk me out of whatever they were going to offer me.'

'They didn't say?'

'Not then. Just stuck me back in the limo, thank you for coming Ms Webb.' Another pause. 'It came in the mail about three weeks later. South East Asia Policy Analyst, desk at the Embassy, residency in Indonesia assumable immediately, air ticket attached, bank account opened, nice little stipend already deposited.'

I whistled in surprise. "Serious stuff.'

She looked at me in mischief. 'Too true, cobber.'

I made a pretend grab for her knee. 'And your job description?'

She batted my hand away. 'About eight words: Tell us about Islam. Keep your eyes open.'

So I hadn't been far wrong. Insight and intelligence, she had them both. I just didn't know which were the right letters yet. 'And you've thought all this through?'

'I had to. I wasn't going to jump on a plane just because someone sent me an air ticket.'

'No, I didn't mean that. I meant you've thought through purpose, motive and expectations.'

'That's what I *did* mean, honey. The why and the who.'

The softly-said *honey* took me by surprise, an endearment that came out of her so simply and naturally, one I hadn't heard her use in ordinary friendships, that my reaction was evident on my face.

'What's wrong?' Anne asked.

'Nothing at all,' I said. 'No-one's ever called me that before.'

'Ohh.' Then, 'I should hope not. It's not something Ozzie girls say, is it?

I shook my head. 'More likely to be *mate*.'

Anne shook hers. 'Unless she's one of your sailors, mate is what you do, not what you are.' She put a hand over her mouth to cover her laughter. 'But at least I know you've never had an American girlfriend before.'

'No, Admiral,' I said, 'I never have.'

'In the end I called on Pops. Asked him if he had some friends who might find out certain things.'

'Did he approve?'

'Of the appointment? If sitting me down and bringing me up to date on certain things expressed approval, then I think he did. He's always been one for continuity in policy dialogue, and saw his own departure from Indonesia as a break in that continuum. He's right - it was.'

'But didn't the US government go on through official channels?'

She nodded. 'They thought that was enough. I'm still not convinced they don't realize there must always be a parallel, unofficial dialogue with someone in whom the Indonesians will trust.'

'But someone did.'

'Mm-hmm. One of Pops' students, who knew me as a kid.' She paused. 'Now Head of the NSA.' Another pause. 'The National Security Agency.'

'Yes. I know what it is.' So, I wasn't so far off, I thought. Three different letters, that's all. ' And you?'

'I'm an unofficial immediate personal adviser.' She said it as though she was ticking each adjective off on a finger as she went. 'So you won't find that written down anywhere. And I haven't actually had face-to-face contact since this started.'

'Then really this is a covert operation.'

'Yes, it is. Though the Indonesians are not stupid. Perhaps it's as important to them as it is to us.'

Though there was one more question. 'When did it start?'

'The same split second we went after the Taliban.'

The final agreement was that HMAS *Magnet*, the lead ship of the squadron, would put into Tanjung Priok, the base for the Indonesian Western Fleet, but that the accompanying two ships, *Mowbullan* and *Ord*, captains apart, should stay offshore for a night. The following day, captains restored, the same two ships would join *Magnet* in observing the ASEAN manoeuvres, before departing for further visits to Thailand and India.

`Welcome aboard, Captain Gregory, sir. Captain Leach is in the wardroom. Would you follow me?' The young officer looked as though he was as fresh from training as Soekendro.

I'd required no more than a taxi to reach *Magnet* at her berth, but Boltroni had continued to insist that I take my security detail, so it was the landcruiser that pulled up at the gangway in the late afternoon. I'd brought several copies of my briefing file on the ASEAN manoeuvres, and Leach and his fellow captains spent a few minutes examining the contents.

Leach was senior captain of the West Ocean Fleet, Fremantle-based, but an East Coast Navy man like nearly all the rest of them. Canberra had little trust in West Coast sailors, with none currently in command of a ship. We were seen as too independent for a navy which Canberra preferred to adhere to the uniformity implicit in the thousands of gallons of naval grey paint applied annually. So I'd been put through the East Ocean Fleet, slotted into the *Fraser*, forced into the Sydney mould. That, as much as anything, had made me jump for the Jakarta posting. But if Leach was ex-Sydney, he'd left that quirk somewhere in the Bight, no innate superiority in his attitude. `Anything more specific we need to know, Trevor?' He showed as much attention to my notes as he'd give to his pilot's course through the Malacca Strait, an intensity readable in his short, dark frame. Nothing else was in his mind for those few minutes. The other officers present were taller and leaner, but as quick as Leach.

'The manoeuvres have taken firm shape as the defence of an island chain from an invader. Navy HQ Jakarta hasn't tried to hide the political message - it's plainly directed at the Chinese and focused on the Spratlys.'

I pointed to an appendix to my report. `I've included some notes on navigation in and around the Natuna's, where the manoeuvres will take place. Principal hazards are covered, and Jakarta has agreed on where best for our ships to be stationed as observers. It was surprisingly easy to deal with Navy HQ on these points.' And I *had* been surprised by Jakarta not demurring at three frigates - quite a show of force by RAN standards.

The next hour was dominated by Leach's questions about *Magnet*'s lead role as observer. The commanding officers of *Mowbullan* and *Ord* asked more questions about Indonesian Navy capability in general. There were some questions about the apparently still-mothballed East German pig-in-a-poke, but I refused to be drawn into a discussion on the merits of the purchase. I still knew very little about what Indonesia intended to do with the ships.

`You're with us for the manoeuvres, Trevor, and you'll stay for the reception.' Leach took it as given.

`Yes, Norman. Thanks.' I'd already received an invitation, and had made a particular arrangement of my own.

Leach nodded. `Right, gentlemen. Let's leave it there for now. Reception's at 1900 hours. That gives everyone a chance to relax for a while. Lieutenant Block will show you to your cabin, Trevor.'

At 1830, I shut my cabin door behind me, made my way onto the main deck, and found the Officer of the Watch making the last minute preparations for receiving the guests. `Evening, sir. Enjoying your stay?'

It was an artless comment, and I decided to rib him. ` Not a bad ship, Lieutenant. Looks clean.'

`Don't let the Captain hear you say that, sir. He'd have us out with holystones at dawn if he thought anyone doubted it.' But the ship was spotless, ready for showing off to a neighbour.

I leant over the rail, watching the movement of the yard in the early evening lights. The stink of heavily polluted harbour water was quite strong. As a taxi pulled up at the foot of the gangway, a rating made a warning noise to the Officer of the Watch, who came over to investigate. He noticed me straightening up. `A guest of yours, sir?' A single female shape was making its way across the walkway.

I nodded. `Yes, but give her the official welcome, will you? It's her first time anywhere near anything like this.'

`Ahh. Right. Form up, welcoming party.' He put some extra polish into the commands, and had the red carpet walled with men-at-arms in seconds. I walked around to the inboard end of the line. Anne could not see me at first and had to cope with the combination of the salute of the Officer-of-the-Watch and the threatening mien of the gauntlet she had to run. The Officer-of-the-Watch took pity on her. `He's waiting at the other end of the carpet, ma'am.'

She looked down the double rank, and walked rather self-consciously towards me, feeling the silent breath of the motionless men on her back. I took her arm through mine. `You're honoured. First aboard.'

Anne was still in some shock. `I thought I was in trouble. Then, that perhaps I was supposed to inspect them.'

I laughed. `They were probably inspecting you.' I peered at her dress. `I think your buttons are clean.'

133

She shook her head. `Don't have any, sailor. They get in the way.'

I left that one alone. `Would you like to see some of the ship? I don't think Leach would mind.'

Anne nodded, still obviously in some awe of its bulk. The lights added shadows that seemed to increase the ship's menace. I walked her around the main deck, enjoying the touch of her arm on mine.

`I thought these ships were all guns. I haven't seen a single one.' She was puzzled.

`It's missiles these days. That was a launcher platform you saw on the foredeck. We have guns up on the superstructure, but it's a technology that's rapidly ageing compared to what missiles do. Those guns are some up-close insurance.'

Anne shivered. `Death is never far away, is it?'

By the time we returned to the gangway, other guests had started to arrive. A marine band was playing near the stern, under a large marquee set up over the helicopter deck, and I guided Anne towards it. Leach was resplendent in his tropical dress whites, though slightly Blighish, perhaps, in his obvious sense of command. `Miss Webb. A pleasure. I hadn't realized that Trevor was bringing anyone. He looked quite solitary this afternoon.'

`He very kindly invited me to see what a warship from down-under looks like, Captain Leach.'

Leach laughed, and showed that he'd placed her. `Nothing that you wouldn't find tenfold in Charleston, Miss Webb. You've already taken her around, Trevor? Good. Then grab a drink from any passing steward.' He turned back to welcome a new arrival.

Uniforms ruled the night. The formal dress uniforms of the Indonesian Armed Forces mixed with the informal dress batiks worn by senior civil servants. Women wore the semi-obligatory dress bun of hair, some with gold adornments, others with transparent scarves.

Anne mixed with the guests with ease, enjoying the shifting contacts, the eddying conversations, both in English and Indonesian. It was a natural current, and I was myself caught up in it, joining in the open curiosity of another nation's Service examining my own. The secret was in hospitality and graciousness, for the Indonesians liked nothing more. We were good at the first, but tended to blunder around the second.

I felt a touch on my arm and turning found Subagio beside me. `Admiral! I'm glad you were invited. I hope you're enjoying yourself.'

Surprisingly, Subagio had elected to wear batik, perhaps permitted at his rank. He looked very sleek in the swirling patterns of night-enhanced colours, a seal at home in dark, warm waters. `Very much, Captain. We do not see your ships here very often.'

I introduced Anne.

`Miss Webb. *Selamat malam*. I must say you make a charming companion to this young man.' He said it with a slight twist, as if what he thought of the young man would have quite a different connotation.

Anne replied directly in Indonesian. `I admire your uniform, Admiral. I see more peace in it than most of the others.'

Subagio looked at me with eyes opened wide. `Ah, Captain Gregory. Now that was very deft. You must take some lessons from this charming lady. I think there is a great deal of wisdom behind those sparkling eyes.'

I laughed at Subagio's surprise. `Sir, I am just learning to recognize it.'

He nodded. Then, `Might I just have a quiet word with you, Captain? One must take advantage of times like these.'

I looked at Anne, who smiled and took Subagio's wife by the arm leading her towards some canapés. Subagio waited until he considered them well out of hearing, then showed himself more sea-lion than seal.

`Notwithstanding your charming companion, Captain, I prefer to keep most of my work separate from my private life. I find it easier to argue with my superiors.' There was a glint of humour in the eyes, but it faded fast. 'I expect that Canberra put the decision in our hands?' His eyebrows also asked the question.

I nodded.

`Then yes, Captain, new rules of engagement. They don't put a foot on board. It really is time to cut this off in the bud.' The humour had gone, and in its place was a disparaging glare, the bleakest sign of equatorial anger I thought I'd ever seen.

The guests departed within a couple of hours, duty, protocol, hunger and curiosity satisfied. It was quiet at the ship's rail apart from the sounds of other ships carried on the night air.

`A culture that I have never understood,' said Anne.

`The Indonesians?' I asked, innocently.

`No, dolt. The Navy,' said Anne. `What is it about men and the sea that they dress themselves up and run away for years at a time?'

`Excitement, danger, adventure, friendship,' I said, not committing myself by tone of voice to any or all, but I thought of the years past when each had been true. I still missed them to some degree, but now understood that the Navy was just a tool, and that I was capable of playing a different role in the broader geopolitical mesh of which warships were only a small part.

`They're almost all the same thing.' said Anne. `And male values only, perhaps. If you'd said duty, perhaps I would have understood. Oh, I'm not belittling what *you* do. But the people that live on this thing - they're cooped up in monastic glory just waiting for the chance to fire those missiles. They don't live for much else.'

`There's always shore-leave on Bali,' I said. `But perhaps they're glad to help prevent the need to fire those missiles.'

``Australia expects that every man will do his duty'? But leave the women at home while you do it.'

'Some are in the Service now.'

`And you. Would you go back to sea if you were married?'

`I might. It would depend on many things.'

`Could you get to the top of your Service without going back to sea?'

`I don't know. We're the shipless generation. There aren't enough postings for all the officers on the Navy List. But the senior staff were all sailors.'

`Blue-water men.'

`It's not a disease, you know.'

Anne laughed. `I think that's blackleg or blue-tongue or whatever your cattle get.'

`What colour's mine?'

She peered up at me. `A sort of speckled grey. Did you have your mouth open when one of those gulls flew by?'

`Shut it just in time.'

`Keep it that way.' She leaned against me in silence for a moment, fundamental in her warmth. Then, `Walk me to the gangway, Captain. It's time for this landlubber to go home.'

`You have an invitation to visit the wardroom, Admiral. More informal get-together.'

She touched my lips with a finger. `I'd love to, Trevor, but I'm quite tired. And they'll be locking you away in your cell soon. Isn't it time for compline?'

I laughed. `Let's find you a taxi. I don't think I can take any more of this.'

But she held me back for a moment. `It's been a very special evening, Trevor. Another side of you, which I enjoyed seeing. Now, help me back through that alleyway of prime Australian beef.'

Equal rank allowed Norman Leach and me to be on first name terms, and, notwithstanding Anne's definition, mates as far as the Service allowed it. We found ourselves enjoying each other's company. For me, the voyage from Tanjung Priok was a needed break from the routine of my desk, and the renewal of the rise and fall of a deck beneath my feet and the sounds and smell of a ship at sea were a touch of manna from heaven. For Norman, I think it was a slight lessening of the loneliness of the senior rank. Off-duty hours in the wardroom found us talking about practically anything. But Norman specifically wanted to know about Asian approaches to conflict resolution and whether there was naval capacity to achieve it.

It was a signal to me from Canberra on a follow-up to some of the details on *Open Seas* which finally opened him up. He read every official signal that came onto his ship. He'd not made a direct connection between me as attaché and me as commander of the operation. When he did, and sorted out the implications in his mind, he was a little embarrassed. `I owe you an apology, Trevor. I had no idea you'd put this together.'

I shook my head. `I was in the right place at the right time. Not a big thing.'

He pressed on. `What are the troops like?'

`I'd thought that they were going to train some marines, but they chose elite Special Forces units. I suspect they included some amphibious specialists. They looked quite at home on a ship. I'm happy that the whole idea has been taken seriously.'

`They did what was expected of them? And no command worries with our bloke?'

`There have been several patrols, but only one boarding. Our man's report specifically praised their skills, and gave full credit to his opposite number. It went off very well.'

`And China?'

`Never responded.' I went on to tell him the substance of my last meeting with Subagio.

`Christ, Trevor. Perhaps that's what it's all about.'

I shrugged. `I think they're just opportunists. It's just a slightly bigger opportunity.'

Leach shook his head in disgust. Then, `What are we going to see during these manoeuvres?' He was not asking for numbers of ships.

`A heavy emphasis on organization and backslapping. This is more about keeping Services busy and presenting a front. I talked about the political message the other day. That's for external consumption. But there's an internal message that ASEAN wishes to put about. That there *is* potential for them to act together on serious issues. However, what they will call a successful outcome to the manoeuvres will not prove a combined capability. It will only prove to them that they should have fewer suspicions amongst themselves and move towards a self-recognition of strength in unity. So they will slap each other on the back and go home happy.'

`And the individual navies?'

`None is really strong. Only Indonesia and Thailand approach anything greater than coastal police forces. No blue-water capability anywhere. Add up all the hardware and you're still nowhere near China. Indonesia has two submarines. China has more than thirty. They all have a right to be worried.'

The words were running through my head again the next day as I leant over the rail. Several ships were in the water around *Magnet*, grouping for the first day of exercises. It was to be a mock sea battle using pre-assigned weapons levels and some random air attacks. I took a close look at the single Singaporean corvette as it passed, and, had it been a real fight, I suspected that one or two of the larger frigates from other nations would have fared badly had they engaged it. The hardware it carried had little to do with my analysis.

I went up to the bridge, where Leach was keeping his own staff busy on regular duty activities. `The Indonesian sub is just sitting there. We picked her up half an hour ago. Doesn't seem to be trying to hide.'

I looked at the sailing orders. `She ought to be well away by now.'

The day passed in some high-speed ship-manoeuvring and various gunnery and missile exercises. There was the constant boom of blank shells. We listened in to targeting talk and missile locks described over a pair of radio channels restricted for the purpose, and *Magnet* herself kept her receiving systems active, intent on gauging radar technology and strength of each of the ships present. The occasional aircraft made dummy attacks before heading for some distant airfield to refuel. The submarine didn't move.

The following day, the fleet stood closer to a couple of the principal islands in the chain. Several vessels not evident the previous day were lying further offshore. Leach had his glasses trained on them. `Tank landing ships, three Indonesian, one Thai by the look of it.'

`Scan for their frequency, can you?'

`You want to listen in?'

I nodded. `One of the Indonesian LSTs has to be the command vessel. She's adorned with aerials.'

After a couple of minutes a radio officer passed me a headset. `I think this is it, sir. Direction and signal strength are right. Afraid I can't tell you what they're saying.'

I slipped the headset on. My eyes were still on the vessels but my mind focussed inward to the radio traffic. It seemed to be just a discussion of sailing order. Who would hit the beaches first. When the tanks should disembark.

A different voice came on the air. `First two vessels keep station one hundred metres apart. Course 050, speed five knots. Engage engines in thirty seconds.'

Aminuddin! Not a voice I would forget. `*What in Allah's name is he doing here?*' His question shot back into my mind, and I asked it in return. I kept my glasses trained on the LSTs, and saw the churning water at the stern of the forward two as their screws bit. They began to crab forward through the water.

`Second group station three hundred metres. Same course and speed. Engage in thirty seconds.'

It sent a chill up my spine. *Aminuddin!*

The second pair of LSTs settled their sterns down and followed the first. I could see that the second pair would end up bracketing the first once they hit shore. The beach was in clear view about a mile away, a pristine stretch of sand flanked by vegetation that almost came down to the shore. The island was big enough to have some higher ground stretching into the distance.

A pair of helicopters lifted off from the first two LSTs before the ships hit the shore. They swooped low in over the beach and made fast passes along its length. I heard them send an `all clear', then they shot up and over the trees and disappeared inland. The LSTs slammed their forward doors down into the sand and troops erupted from them.

The landing exercise near Raha. Aminuddin, the senior naval officer. The man's anger at finding me calmly drinking coffee with Army officers. All these pictures came back into my mind. But these were LSTs, bigger and older ships of a completely different design to the ones I'd seen in Sulawesi.

`What is it, Trevor? You look as though you've seen a ghost'

`Heard one, Norman. Heard one, quite by chance. Why, I wonder?'

`Why what?'

I gave him a *précis* of what I'd stumbled on in Sulawesi. `The officer commanding here was there that day.'

`You recognize his voice?'

`There is a distinctive quality to it beyond the accent. I know he's not Javanese.

139

It sticks in my mind.'

`Coincidence. It's the same type of exercise. Probably the same troops.'

I looked more closely through my glasses at the beach. Some of the berets were distinctive. But there were other regiments present. `Yes, some of them may be. They were also *KOPASSUS*. Their best. The ones we have with *Open Seas*. They're getting a lot of practice.'

I heard him again, on and off, throughout the day. He'd been on one of the second group of LSTs, and I identified it as the one I'd thought earlier was the command ship. At some point he had gone ashore, liaising very closely with an Army ground command. His orders back to the ships reflected his movements. He was an effective officer, his orders crisp and focussed.

`Captain, sir! The sub is moving.'

`Ah, at last. What is she doing?'

`Coming to the surface, sir, about two miles to the south west.'

We were watching when the conning tower became visible, but there was hardly any forward motion.

`Engine problems,' said Leach.

`Could be. May have been the ballast tanks. It's the *Cakra*. She's only just come out of refit.'

`Back she goes.'

But whatever the problem, it seemed they had it solved, and the sailing orders were quickly revised to make up for the lost time. The third day was given over entirely to submarine detection and minelaying. *Cakra* played hare to the surface greyhounds, which filled the water with sonar signals, and *Magnet*'s sonar officer complained of a headache by midday. Torpedo craft doubled as minelayers, dropping their lethal charges along courses intended to close the sea to the unwary. The boom of anti-submarine mortars came across the water. By mid-afternoon the exercises were all but over, and the smaller ships were busy in mine and torpedo recovery.

Shortly after five Norman received a signal. `Compliments of the captain of the *Slamet Riyadi*, sir. Would you join him on board for a debriefing and dinner at 2000 hrs? Captain Gregory is invited also.'

Norman raised his eyebrows. `Safety in numbers. Have a drink with me at 1900. Then let's go and see what they have to say.'

Magnet's launch took us across to the senior Indonesian vessel shortly before 2000, and as we approached I saw she was of the same class as the frigate I'd visited in Palu. We were welcomed aboard with considerable ceremony.

As on *Magnet,* several days before, dinner was served on deck, under a large canvas awning. Officers of seven other navies were present. I encouraged Norman to gravitate towards three Vietnamese officers who were standing slightly apart from the crowd. Plates heaped high from a buffet meal that I thought their own Service could not have afforded, they gave slight formal bows as we approached. I introduced Norman and myself, and the senior Vietnamese officer did the same, but names slipped quickly in the language gap.

`You are Australian. Observers ,' said the senior Vietnamese officer.

I nodded. Norman seemed happy for me to carry the conversation. `Enjoying some contact with neighbouring Services.'

`Australia have many ships?'

I laughed. `No. About half as many as Indonesia.'

`But big?'

`No. About the same size.'

This seemed to surprise the Vietnamese officer, who rattled off some comments to his companions. Surprise also showed on their faces.

`Big land but not big Navy. Not like China. Big land, big Navy.'

I nodded. `I'm afraid we can't compare to China. Nobody here tonight could. Even if all the ships were added together.'

`Chinese Navy dangerous. Must make plans to prevent Chinese Navy. Keep them away.'

I felt that this was a fruitless topic. `You have had some contacts with the Chinese Navy? Your ships?'

Crooked and discoloured teeth sprang from a smile. `We play cat mouse with Chinese ships. They lose face with Vietnam. We small Navy but good.'

`Are these good navies like Vietnam?' I gestured around at the other officers.

`Not hungry enough. Still play games. Vietnam not play games.' It was rather a disparaging remark, but the arrow was well shot. Vietnam's late entry into ASEAN might still cause some of its other members some discomfort.

Something on the edge of my vision caught my attention. I took a sharp breath, excused Norman and myself, and was given formal bows of farewell. `Not a great deal of respect there,' said Norman.

I was searching the gathering. `They're forced to sit on the sidelines at the moment. It's a bad time for them. China hangs over them like a sword.'

I knew what it was that I had seen. `Norman, I've got to do something rather difficult. Will you excuse me a moment?'

He looked a little surprised. `Yes. Of course. Anything I can help with?'

`I have to mend a fence. Give me a few minutes alone.'

A small mixed group of Indonesian and Malaysian officers was chatting easily in their joint tongue. One of them stiffened as he saw me approaching. I noted his rank but used the western equivalent. `Commander, I should like to introduce myself.'

`I think we have already met.'

`I regret I pretended to be someone else.' The rest of the group looked puzzled. I introduced myself formally to the group as a whole and introductions came in return.

The other gave a thin smile, but his eyes gave nothing away. `I did eventually discover that. It was perhaps a silly game.'

`I found myself in a situation which was quite embarassing. I think I would have caused you more embarassment had I told you who I really was. I *was* on holiday.'

He nodded. `I am *Letnan Kolonel* Aminuddin.' He turned to the others. `Captain Gregory was recently a travel agent. He appears to be a man of many talents.' The undercurrent in Aminuddin's words catalyzed some curious glances. `However, for this evening, at least, we should be gracious. What did you think of *this* exercise?'

`More interesting as diplomacy than training, if I am honest. Have you asked the same question of your Vietnamese colleagues?'

Aminuddin looked at me in surprise. `You've been talking to them? Unfortunately, we share little language in common. It makes it rather difficult.'

`They're frustrated. They'd rather you were doing this a lot further north.'

`Captain Gregory, we are hardly ready for anything like that. This, even, was an innovation.'

`Then perhaps the message that was intended for northern ears will not carry much weight.'

Aminuddin smiled thinly again. `Don't read so much into it. This was a friendly gathering to test some skills and techniques. Nothing more.'

I thought I'd done as much as I could, and I had a clear vision of hate. Enough to have wanted to have me killed? `I enjoyed meeting you on more common ground. Perhaps we'll meet again.' I shook hands with each of the officers in the group, and I could feel Aminuddin's intense irritation behind the calm face and hard eyes as I walked away.

Norman was swapping stories with two Thai officers. He'd paid a courtesy visit to Bangkok, and was talking about the hazards of navigating the mouth of the Chao Phrya river, most of which were linked to local traffic. There was some mirth over the stubbornness of rice barges to cede way according to navigational norms, which had tested the skills of his junior officers far more than the flood surges from heavy upstream monsoons. `But put the two together and I'd rather face the pack ice of the southern oceans,' he said. I could see that the Thai officers thought he was crazy, that they couldn't imagine anything worse than the terrible cold, but they were polite enough not to say so.

Fourteen

'It has been said,' commented the Jenderal, 'that I do not wish to attack cities because I come from a village.'

An aide entered with two glasses of steaming kopi tubruk, grounds swirling above the layer of sweetened milk lying like a mist of death below the surface of a lake. He put one on front of each of us. A quick stir of my spoon dispersed the milk, but the image in my mind of an oar which would soon be dipped into more lethal waters took longer to clear.

'In fact,' he continued, 'the only reason I wish not to attack any city is because of the cost. Time, men and resources. We could pay heavily in all three.'

'But in Central we must, Jenderal. It is the key to everything. In South, the panic will do the work.'

'Then in Central we will have to have strict limits on sacrifice. I wish to know beforehand what I will lose, not after.'

Excerpted from Rusman Soekendro, LetJen (ret'd),
No Game At All: Memoirs of a Strategist

They discussed war that day. Not any particular war, but wars in general. The whys, the whats and the whos. Both men agreed that wars were inevitable, part of the hundred-years cycles of nations, though insofar as they discussed the whys, they arrived at no fundamental analysis, observing just that, empirically, these cycles were so.

The woman played no more than a minor role in these discussions, observing to herself that it was still no more than a part of the process of familiarization of two military men, each with the other. In certain moments of honesty she said to herself that men were always like this, showing knowledge, defining early positions; under Nature, the stronger would then make off with the female. If either man saw her smile at these moments, they did not remark on it.

There were times when something in a particular argument would catch her attention. And then one or the other of the two men would be the recipient of silent approbation. Surprised, perhaps, at these instants of intellectual attraction, she acknowledged gratefully that the rest of the time their cerebral plumage was fairly drab.

***

A professional's life is a series of steps. Whether they all lead forward and upward depended, I thought, on making the right decisions at the right time. At this instant, I knew neither that I'd come to a path it was essential I take, nor that the outcome would be far-reaching - I thought I'd already made my choice by coming to Jakarta, doing my job and learning what I could along the way. Then *Open Seas* taught me that some doors in life are opened by extra effort.

The manoeuvres left me with a greater sense than ever of wanting to know what had happened to the East German ships. None of them had been evident and I'd not been able to pry the information out of my Indonesian contacts, though there were moments when I felt that the protocol surrounding my position was a useful excuse to tell me nothing. However, there were other ways. One of them brought me to see the Ambassador.

I liked Kessler. In his embassy, rank was irrelevant. And he would always listen if you had something important to tell him. And I'd already penned him a memo on the subject in question, thirty-seven ships, a Red Fleet. `Almost all sources say that the ships were in a sorry state. The conclusion is that Indonesia bought itself a pile of scrap.'

Kessler continued to listen, leaning forward with his elbows on his desk, chin in hands.

`After their arrival, they remained berthed for a long time at Surabaya. Perhaps there was no proper thinking on how to make them operational - they were bought at bargain prices, so perhaps it was a case of jumping in before anyone else could buy them. But it also seems obvious from some of the scrapes their crews got themselves into on the trip from Kiel that good seamanship is a quality still lacking in significant numbers of the Navy's sailors.'

Then I said: `They're not at Surabaya now. I've been looking at some of the material that has come in from Canberra - I've a routine request in for satellite photos and other intelligence analysis, which I depend on for some of my work. I wanted to show you this.' I put two black and white photos in front of him.

`This is Surabaya taken three months ago.' I pointed at the first photo. `This group here is the main concentration of East German vessels at anchor off the naval base. A few are dispersed through the yard, but they're fairly easy to pick out from their distinctive deckplans and armaments.'

`This is Surabaya taken four weeks ago. Almost all the German ships are gone.

146

Given the complete lack of mention of the cost of refitting and manning them in successive Government budgets, I fully expected them to stay at anchor here for years. What seemed strange to me was that all the ships should have been moved. And, of course, the obvious question was, `where have they gone?'.'

Kessler sat back, still silent.

`I surmised that if they had come back west, they would have passed near enough to Jakarta for someone to have spotted them, and we would have read about it in the press. So the obvious answer seemed to be that they had gone east.'

I pulled a third photo out of my briefcase. `There aren't too many places east of Surabaya where ships that are described as non-operational would go. In fact, there's really only one yard with any capacity to effect repairs and that is Makassar. *This* is Makassar.' An urban mass evident on the coastline ran from the photo's top to its bottom. `This is the Makassar yard. That is one of the German ships.' A small shape was evident within the larger infrastructure of a waterfront complex.

Kessler finally spoke. `Where are the others?'

`That's what had me puzzled. Why had only one ship shown up? I sent back to Canberra for a broader scan of the Makassar Strait. It came back yesterday. This is it.'

I slipped another photo out. `The eastern shore of the Strait off Makassar is a maze of small islands. Some are inhabited, some are just sand spits. They stretch well up and down the coast from the city itself, and some distance to sea. Here, towards the north west, there are several isolated sand spits. There's the fleet.'

He looked closely at the area I'd indicated. It showed a concentration of vessels, but the naked eye could not distinguish any detail. `You've examined the images carefully?

`I have the necessary equipment upstairs. There's no doubt.'

`Why are they there?' he asked.

'I've been wondering. It wasn't as if they were in the way at Surabaya - they had an isolated offshore anchorage. There had to be some other reason. So I created a computer composite of the German ships as they were when lying at Surabaya. That's this set of pages. Each has an image of nine ships, bar the last. Thirty-seven in all. I then did the same thing to the images of the ships as they now lie at Makassar. That's this set.' I laid them side by side on Kessler's desk. `I can make twenty-five fit. The others don't.'

Kessler looked puzzled. `They're not the same ships?'

`Yes, they are. But they're not. They've undergone some changes already. There are some amazing transformations coming out of this Makassar yard.'

`But I thought that it would take months to do each one.' He was still puzzled.

`If it were unionized labour, and nine-to-five, that would be the case. And if you wanted to do it from bottom to top. I can only see the top. I then did some calculations, made some calls to Sydney and Fremantle, and found that if I had a team of trained refitters, and all the new armaments to hand, I could put one of those ships through the changes I can see in just five days.'

`But that's impossible!' he exclaimed.

`No, it isn't. It's been done.' I corrected myself. `It's being done. And some of the secret lies in what they've chosen. No heavy guns. It's nearly all missiles. The launchers come ready made. In a sense all you have to do is weld them to the deck and plug them in.'

`But why?' Kessler wondered. He was clearly a little shaken. Several thousands tonnes of scrap had suddenly taken on strategic value.

`I don't know. What *is* clear is that this is something quite different from what is being put about.'

`It's not just Indonesia's continuing fascination with secrecy? That we'll find out eventually that they'll be going into coastal patrols? Or can we link it to any particular irritant facing the Indonesians?'

`There's nothing within the ASEAN sphere that suggests itself as needing rapid response. It's clear that Indonesia sees China as a serious longer-term threat. They may be preparing to posture further against the Chinese, though it's a fairly thin hypothesis.'

He nodded. `It doesn't sound right. None of the other island disputes can be seen as threatening. Yet, if we read this as wanting to tip some scale or other, where else do we look?'

I thought about some border bullying going on. `What about east?'

`East? Papua New Guinea? What the hell for?!'

`There are murmurs of border problems. Maybe we're looking at another Timor. We've been quick to send some significant help to PNG. Is Canberra concerned about another annexation?'

Kessler shrugged. `Concerned about the bullying, yes. Thinking that it's bigger than that, no.'

`I think I'd better get out to Makassar and take a closer look. I need to find out more. This is a riddle that has to be solved, what sort of bunfight they have in mind. It's no good asking questions here - there'd be no answers, just blank stares.'

`What are you suggesting?' He was frowning, not liking the fact that another unknown was presenting itself. Unknowns generally turned into delicate issues for Australia. `What more do you need to know that the satellite can't tell you?'

`Ambassador, I know what's happening to the top. I don't know what's happening to the bottom. Are they putting in new engines? Do they need new engines? If I have the answer to that, I probably have the answer to several other questions.'

`I don't like this at all. I can't officially send you out there to do something clandestine. You'd be totally without support. It's a big risk.'

`There may be bigger risks brewing. In comparison, this would be quite a small one. It's an answer I need as quickly as possible. And *I* have to go. There may be other things that haven't made themselves obvious yet.'

`When would you go?'

`This weekend. This is not something that can wait.'

`You'll be on your own, Gregory. I won't be able to bail you out of trouble. And Canberra's not likely to authorize a fishing expedition without a lot more justification. They're sensitive to anything that could cause the slightest ripple.'

`Understood. As far as I'm concerned, I'm pursuing my normal duties. If the Indonesians ask, they can be told I'm sick in bed. I'll worry about flak from Canberra if and when it happens. I'll keep clear of any trouble, but I think the purpose overshadows the risk.'

`Arrange with Boltroni for any cover you need here.'

`Thank you.'

I gathered up all my photos. As I left his office, Kessler said: 'Gregory. Be careful.'

'Yes.'

From my office I called Boltroni. `I need to arrange a deception.'

`What's the deception?' Boltroni asked.

`That I'm sick at home, when I'm not.'

`Going somewhere?'

`Have to disappear for a few days. But I don't want it known that I'm travelling. I need enough movement around the house to give the impression of my presence.'

`Who can know you're not?'

`Only those that I tell, Chief. Anyone that comes asking gets the storyline.'

`When's ETD?'

`Probably very early Saturday morning. I'll confirm that later. And I'll need two return tickets to Makassar. Mr and Mrs Beach.'

`Mr *and* Mrs? Beach?'

`Cover, Chief. But Mrs Beach doesn't know yet.'

`Hi. I wondered when you'd call.'

`I need to make some plans. I was wondering whether you'd like a little adventure this weekend.'

'Sorry. I'm away. But what did you have in mind?'

`I need to go to Makassar. I thought you might enjoy a change.'

'I could meet you there after. What are you going for?'

I recounted some of the conversation I'd had with Kessler. 'I have to find out whether the refits include engine replacement, things like that. There may be visual signals that could tell me – alterations to the funnel, perhaps.'

But that wasn't what was worrying me now. 'Where do you have to go?'

'I'm going to start in Balikpapan.'

Mike slipped into the house unobserved as a hidden passenger in the landcruiser when I returned from work.

`Make yourself at home, Mike. Beer's in the fridge, and there'll be dinner on the table in an hour. It's just one tonight.'

'No company?'

'Plans have changed.'

I spent the time putting together a lightweight pack, boots, camera, binoculars and a spare change of clothes, and it was well after dark when the driveway gates opened again. They shut behind the landcruiser as it slowly gathered speed down the narrow street, only two people visible in the car. One or more of the parked vehicles well obscured by the night may have held the watchers we always thought were there.

`Right. Blok M.'

The driver nodded. We'd already discussed where to do the switch.

`When we get there, drop me in front of Pasaraya. I'll go into the store. Park the car - Mike, you'll have to stay well hidden. Give me fifteen minutes. Get one of the taxis from the line outside, and move him up the exit road a little. It's dark up there. Tell him that you're waiting for someone and that you'll drop him off from the car. Mention a good tip so that he doesn't decide to take another passenger.'

`I'll make sure his signal light is off,' the driver said.

`Yeah, good. Right. All clear?' Both Mike and the driver grunted.

I dropped out of the vehicle right in front of Pasaraya. The broad glass windows of the department store were alive with lights and mannequins in local and foreign fashions.

Fifteen minutes later, I gave my driver's name to the security guard, who called him on the intercom in the parking area. Within a couple of minutes, the landcruiser nosed its way through the evening crowd. Mike was hiding under a dark blanket on the floor behind my seat, and even in the light of the storefront he was completely invisible. `Right. Let's get on with it.'

`He's up the road, on your left under the trees,' said the driver.

I could feel my pack at my feet. `Ready, Mike?' I heard a muffled reply.

The driver took the landcruiser slowly up the street, and I switched off the interior light so that it wouldn't come on as the door opened. `When I say go, Mike. Three, two, one, go!'

I slipped out right beside the unlit taxi, feeling Mike take the door from my grip. I opened the taxi's rear door, leaned in, pushing my pack across the seat, and climbed in after it. The landcruiser disappeared down the road.

`Selamat malam.'

The taxi driver returned the greeting, showing no awareness of any strange behaviour in his passenger. He listened without comment to the directions to Anne's house and then slipped into the night.

`All packed?'

'All ready to go?'

She pushed the door behind me and then slipped into my arms.

'I really needed to ask 'What's in Balikpapan?"

'Don't know yet. That's why I have to go.'

'No hint?'

'Just this. Then I'll see you in Makassar. Whenever I get there.' And the kiss slowly developed.

A radio-taxi collected me at 0530, and I was at the domestic departure terminal at Cengkareng by 0615. I checked in and went through security to the cafeteria inside, where I bought coffee and croissants. Shortly after, I was called to the plane, but wondered about Balikpapan, which lay west of Makassar. Question unanswered, I thought.

On the way into Makassar, Jack took the toll road, running past plywood factories before reaching the shrimp ponds that edged the city. As we turned left off the highway, he pointed to the right. 'The naval yard's in there, if you're planning a visit.'

'I'm not. I've something else in mind.'

His house had architectural features that dated from Dutch colonial times, with a high-pitched roof of red terracotta tiles. Rooms were high-ceilinged and windows shuttered, floors tiled in hand-made ceramics. Modern additions showed in lighting fixtures and bathrooms, and ceiling fans produced cooling vortices of air. He showed me to the main guest room, where a double bed stood under a mosquito-netted frame. A ceiling fan hung still in the humid morning air. 'Will this do you? You said about company?'

'It's fine, Jack. Thanks. She's now not joining me till after.'

He raised an eyebrow. 'You can tell me about her later. Meanwhile get yourself sorted out and come out onto the verandah. I've got some refreshments on the way.'

I found Jack sipping a fruit juice, his long face full of concern. He put his paper down. 'It's like the end of the school year, Trev. Good marks and bad marks. Care to tell me about what you're going to get up to?'

I proceeded to outline my plan. I explained why I had to do it.

'My oath, Trev. I haul you out of one scrape for you to jump right back into another. I don't like the sound of it. Last time you were lucky.'

He got up and went to a tray of juices on a sideboard. 'Avocado or papaya?'

'Avocado, please.'

'And when are you going to do this?' Jack asked.

'I think it should be tomorrow morning. I could spend days trying to work out how and where, but,' I shook my head, 'in the end I just have to go out there and do it.'

'Well, I've got your kit set up. And I've got you a pilot.'

'A what?!'

'You wanted me to lend you my boat. But I'm not letting you swan off up the coast alone. You'll take Ahmed with you. He's worked for me and takes care of the boat. He'll be no trouble. He's almost seventy-five. But he knows these waters well.'

I recognized the value of that knowledge, but there was the other. 'There is just the possibility that it may not be very simple. I don't want to get him involved.'

Jack shook his head. 'I'll have a little talk with him. He'll enjoy the challenge.

152

But he swims like a fish, even at seventy-five. First sign of trouble he slips over the side. No-one'll know he was there. Now, there are a couple of things I need to do. You behave like a tourist for a while and go out and enjoy the town. Tonight, I'll take you out for dinner. Feed you up for your ordeal.' He was immediately contrite. `Sorry. Hard for me not to pull your leg.'

Face wrinkled by age and the weathering of the tropical sun, Ahmed squatted calmly at the throttle of the outboard, watching wave forms and land masses. Dressed in the uniform of most of the area's fishermen, age-old t-shirt and ragged shorts, gnarled crusted feet splayed across the thwart under him. The dinghy skimmed its way northwest, away from Makassar and the coast. The old walls of Fort Rotterdam were barely visible onshore.

I'd spent half an hour with the old man, once Jack had left us at the dinghy park just opposite the fort, trying to make it clear that we were heading into something unknown. The old man remained inscrutable throughout, politely muttering `Ya, tuan,' at regular intervals. It was evident that he took the care of the dinghy as a personal challenge and would not relinquish it to anyone else. It was Ahmed and the dinghy, or nothing at all. Jack had told me so. So I'd slung my gear into the craft, and helped Ahmed launch it in the shallow waters of the bay.

It had been a simple matter, transcribing the site of the anchorage from the satellite photos onto a coastal chart. Ahmed had looked at the chart, and acknowledged that he knew where Pulau Pasir was. Once seaborne, he shook his head when I offered him the chart again. He knew all the waters, he said. Pulau Pasir was in that direction. He waved in the general direction of the horizon, over the port bow.

I sat on the bow thwart, morning wind whipping my face. Pulau Pasir meant Sand Island. The chart showed several, the photo had too, but the one I wanted was at least two hours up the coast. But we'd have to go well to seaward, and then come back from the northwest, to avoid giving the impression that we'd come directly from Makassar to look at the ships. I wanted some sort of reason for being there. A homeward drift after a half day's snorkelling seemed to be the best approach.

Jack had dumped another bag in the dinghy before disappearing. `Water and food.' I pulled a flask of water out and drank some, then offered it to Ahmed, who shook his head.

The coastline sank slowly behind us, but there was never a lack of islands climbing out of the sea ahead. Most showed degrees of settlement, with rusted galvanised roofs clustered under leaning coconut palms. Small craft, from dugouts to long-tailed canoes, and flat-bottomed ferries lay on the beaches. Occasionally, one would pass us as it headed towards land, and small brown hands lifted above the gunwale in greeting. Fishermen sat crouched in dugouts balanced on a single outrigger, slowly jigging a single line.

After a while the settled islands grew less, and the dinghy seemed to shrink in size against the flat expanse of water. This grew a darker blue as we sped over greater depths. I watched the chart, and, checking the compass heading, signalled to Ahmed that I wanted to go further to port. I intended the sweep to be a large one, and wanted to see the ships no closer than my starboard horizon.

They came into view almost an hour later, their distant combined-bulk hiding individual lines, and I signalled to Ahmed to slow down. The strong optics of my binoculars almost brought the warships into the dinghy, and I examined them slowly, separating the lines of each one, comparing what I could see of their outlines with my mental picture of their original form and armaments. Some fitted and some did not.

I rummaged in my bag and pulled out a clipboard which had an enlarged version of the satellite photo showing just the anchorage. I started to compare the visual images, trying to get a sense of the changes that were occurring.

The ships were anchored in several rafted formations. The Parchim corvettes were apart from the smaller Kondor minesweepers, and the satellite photo showed a cluster of Frosch landing vessels hidden on the landward side. Of the corvettes and minesweepers I could only make out sixteen, though there should have been twenty-five. I signalled to Ahmed to pick up speed slowly again so that I could examine the fleet from a different position.

It took us an hour to make our way slowly northward from the fleet, keeping at least five miles distant. I plotted several different sight lines on my chart, annotating each with figures on the type of ship visible and the aspect at anchor. The northerly drift of the tide minimized the use of the outboard. By the time we'd reached as far north as I wanted to go, I'd made a total of twenty-three ships at anchor. Nearly all the corvettes and minesweepers were there. The Frosch landing vessels were not. As far as I could tell, another corvette and a minesweeper seemed to have undergone a facelift. As this included some new paint, the modified ships stood out from the rest of the fleet.

I took a final look through my glasses. I'd noted earlier that there were crews aboard, but distance and perspective had made it hard to work out how many were in each crew. As we moved north, and the perspective changed, I could now tell that each rafted formation had only a single crew, and this confined to a single ship. These were vessels that had already undergone the facelift, but I could not tell what the crews were doing. The refitted ships were all to the seaward side, the unmodified ships to landward.

Ahmed beached the dinghy on another sandspit several miles north. He rigged a small sail as a shelter against one side of the dinghy, using the emergency oars as poles, and sat down in the shade with an opened rice bowl. I wasn't yet ready to eat, so decided to stretch my muscles. I pulled the other elements of gear out of Jack's bag and waded out into the water, slipping the mask and flippers on when it was chest high. It was easy to slip below into the cool water, and I turned away from the island and began a slow kick. The seabed dropped slowly away, small isolated clumps of coral appearing on the sand ahead. I spent the next hour wandering among the clumps, watching the form and colours of the fish that swam to escape me. Sometimes I lay motionless under the surface hearing no sound other than my magnified heartbeat.

When I came out of the water, Ahmed was squatting at the end of the spit communing silently in the general direction of the warships. They were barely visible. I lay down on a towel under the sail with a pack of Jack's sandwiches, and then almost immediately sank into sleep.

Ahmed woke me when the light was already half gone. We quickly loaded everything back into the dinghy, and Ahmed settled it in the direction of the ships to the south, keeping the throttle low, using the now southerly tide to help carry it to where we wanted to go.

It took well over an hour to reach the vessels farthest to seaward. Night had fallen, but, even so, Ahmed cut the motor several hundred yards away. Using an oar over the stern, he gently sculled the dinghy in the direction of the landward side of the formation. Lights were visible on the outermost ship to starboard, powered by a diesel generator somewhere on board. Its rattle covered the slight scuffle of the oar on the transom and the riffle of water over its blade. I stayed low in the dinghy, pulling on a dark t-shirt and trousers. A flashlight went into my waistband.

The loom of the ship came out of the night over my head and almost instantly a rusted waterline caked with weed and barnacles scratched at the dinghy's fibreglass hull. Ahmed shipped the oar and used the dinghy's way to hand it along the ship's hull. Away from the inhabited vessel it was very dark. The occasional moan of steel on steel marked the very slight movement of the ships against each other.

Ahmed was searching for a mooring point, and he watched the ship's side carefully. A large hemp fender grew out of the gloom above his shoulder, and he grabbed the lower end and looped the dinghy's painter through its weave. He let the dinghy come round so that the bow pointed into the tide. The fender let off a stench of dead weed and droppings.

I pulled myself onto it, trying to balance its slight roll against the hull as I did so. The ship's rail was directly at face height, and I went up and over it and dropped quickly to the deck. There were no lights on the ship.

There were five vessels in the raft formation, all corvettes. The three to landward had not yet been touched. It was the two to seaward that were of interest. These were the ships that had already been through the Makassar yard, two of the several that had been sufficiently changed above deck to draw my attention. Now I wanted to get below deck.

I kept my right shoulder to the slab-like wall of the superstructure and made my way towards the bow. At the forward end the wall cut at a sharp angle across the deck. Out of the gloom I could make the shape of the twin barrels of the 30mm gun that was mounted on the deck above. I slipped around the foredeck to the opposite side, the next ship coming into view, a mirror image of the one I was on. My perspective gave me a view of the form of the anti-submarine mortars mounted aft of the gun.

I crossed the next ship in the same way that I had the first, unable to use the flashlight above deck. On the third vessel I had to take greater care, as some of the light from the work-lamps rigged on the outermost ship was filtering through the night onto the decks under my feet. The armaments stood out clearly in profile.

On this third ship, I climbed up onto the bridge superstructure and slipped into the shadows of the radar tower. The fourth ship was laid out before me, and I recalled details I'd seen in the satellite photo. The main changes to armament were the elimination of the twin 57mm gun from the afterdeck. Smaller 20mm guns had been set up on opposite sides of the upper reardeck. Where the upper foredeck 30mm gun mounting had been there was now the box-like trunk of multiple missile launchers aligned to the ship's longitudinal axis. The anti-submarine mortars of the upper foredeck had also been replaced by missile launchers.

Behind the radar mast another pair of 20mm upperdeck cannons had been fitted. A single multiple missile launcher sat between them. Behind the fire-control mast the maindeck torpedo tubes had completely disappeared. A small helicopter deck had been fitted in the place of the main reardeck gun, and the anti-submarine mortars previously fitted to the upper foredeck had been moved aft. Two racks for depth charges were evident.

In the shadows, I thought about the conformation of weaponry that had been fitted. What, to the East Germans, had been an anti-submarine-warfare craft had now become a lethal sea-to-air and sea-to-sea attack vessel. The increase in missile launchers was a clear indication of the major shift to, and dependence on, electronics that I'd mentioned to Kessler. Removal of the main guns would have brought the ship's displacement down significantly. This weight could be added back in terms of ammunition and missiles without affecting ship-speed, as long as some of the structural steel supporting the guns had also been removed. I felt an added sense of urgency to board the fourth ship and get below deck.

I climbed off the bridge superstructure to the portside main deck, close enough to the worklights to feel as if it were daylight, though I slipped across to the fourth ship without difficulty. The smells of freshly-welded steel and new paint were noticeably stronger. Two steel doors to the rear of the main-deck superstructure were open, and a quick inspection showed that the forward one gave access to main-deck quarters and internal entry to the bridge. The second showed a clear drop towards the ship's engine room. I took the second, and within seconds was well underdeck. The old stink of the bilges added to the newer smells.

I followed the main passageway aft, passing two new doorways cut into it, one on each side, both open. A quick inspection with the flashlight showed access to magazines, where simple electro-mechanical lifts had been fitted to raise ammunition to the main deck. Judging by the size of the lifts, this was where the rear-deck mortar bombs would be housed. Smaller lifts suggested secondary storage for the anti-aircraft ammunition.

At the end of the passageway another hatchway stood open, clips turned inward. Steps led further down, into what the flashlight showed to be the engine room, and, as I descended, a massive space opened ahead. Three engines, three shafts. As I made to step closer to one engine and give it a more detailed examination, a sense of suddenly knowing that there was more to discover took hold of me, and I knew what I would see. It was not that the engine room seemed less cluttered than I expected. It was more that it still held some of the frantic energy that had been expended. New engines, solid marine diesels from a German manufacturer.

Even so, I stood back in surprise, knowing now that I had to consider this extra dimension. There had been no mention of such an order at the time of the ships' purchase, but now I wondered whether the bargain price for the ships had not been sealed with a much larger, secret order, through some other channel. But, however it had been worked, it went hand-in-hand with what I'd seen on deck, and added extra urgency to the rest of my search.

The flashlight revealed some signs of work on the steel over my head, but not the significant changes I was looking for. I worked my way further aft, past the main propeller-shaft bearings.

And there it was. Much of the original structural steel put in to support the massive weight of the reardeck twin 57mm gun had been cut out. So had its magazines. Remains of some of the lower struts were still evident where they had been only roughly cut flush to the ship's main frames. In place of the old steel were lighter frames meant to hold a few torpedoes. As there were no longer any torpedo tubes on deck, this meant that the absent helicopter would have some role in carrying and launching them. The frames showed the same simple electrically-driven lift device to elevate the torpedoes to deck level.

Just as the new deck configuration had made me pause, and the new engines more so, what I saw here spoke to a great deal of planning and design. Strategic planning, I thought, a trickle of something clawing its way in.

Time was worrying me. I'd been on board for more than half an hour, so I took a last quick look around the metal cavern and headed for the companionway. I needed to do a similar check forward.

That took me a further forty minutes, because the forward layout of the ship was more complicated. Some of the doorways were closed, requiring very careful pressures to open them and avoid the screech of a stuck clip. The below-deck search forward gave further confirmation to the firepower theory. This was a ship stripped down to carry as much lethal weight as it could. All unnecessary structural steel had been ripped out, presumably lifted by crane out through the holes under the pedestal rings of the big guns. The steel added back to reinforce new gun pedestals was probably less than twenty percent of what had been removed. The new engines were undoubtedly lighter than the twenty-year-old diesels that had been pulled out, with a power-to-weight ratio perhaps twice that of their forebears. Installing the principal magazines deeper in the vessel had lowered the ship's centre of gravity, resulting in a large overall increase in the munitions she could carry, while maintaining stability. The missile launchers required little underdeck reinforcement.

I climbed slowly to the bridge, seeing a new navy being born in my thoughts. The only aspect of my search that was incomplete was the operations centre for the missile launchers. But I was by now certain of what I'd find.

Behind and below the bridge a large electronics centre had been installed. What would probably have been a single fire-control point at the rear mast for the one old launcher had been replaced by a centralised compact operations room with multiple screens and several operators' positions. A quick survey of the room suggested that several pieces of equipment were yet to be installed, though the wiring was in place. It just remained to plug in all the components. I sat for a moment in one of the chairs, feeling colder and colder.

Then the noises from the next ship filtered through my thoughts. Standing well back from the bridge windows, I looked down onto the next deck.

It was evident that the next corvette was being refitted identically. I could see several teams of steelfitters at work, involved in the final installation of the anti-aircraft guns and missile launchers. The bright flame of oxyacetylene welders sparkled and crackled in the night. Someone was making a final inspection of the helicopter deck. None of it work that needed to be done in port.

The appearance of two lights, a white masthead light and a green starboard navigation light, at some distance from the ship, caught my attention. They approached the lit corvette rapidly and the outline of a fast launch came out of the night. There were shouts, and a line was thrown. The launch disappeared beyond the seaward side of the vessel.

A sudden movement on the opposite bridge made me step back into deeper shadow. A party of officers appeared, most of them standing looking forward at the work in progress on the deck. One stepped back into what would be an identical operations room. Within seconds he reappeared on the port flying bridge, pointing directly at me. He made some comments that I couldn't hear to the officers behind him.

I'd overstayed my welcome, that was evident. Not that I thought he'd seen me - he was probably making some comment about what he'd find still to be done here - but I should have left as soon as I'd completed my search. I'd been mesmerised by the concentration of effort on the next corvette and thought it worth a few minutes of observation. Now, it was clear that the inspection team was headed directly for where I was hidden, probably to look at the electronics work.

I jammed the flashlight into my waistband and jumped for the port bridge door. Outside was the external ladder. Halfway out the door I stretched out a hand to grab the upper rail of the steps and put my palm straight into someone's face. The man let out a startled shout and grabbed my shirt. I put all my weight into forward movement and pushed him over backwards. We fell the eight feet to the next deck, I landed on top of him, and felt a crack through his arm as it broke. But pain crashed through my left ear as he hit out with his own heavy flashlight. He collapsed groaning, nursing his broken arm.

In a dizzy agony, I scrambled up, jumping back out of his reach. But I was still a deck too high for escape onto the next ship and had to leap over the rail, catching it as I did, lowering myself to a full stretch, listening to the thunder that had followed the lightning in my ear. I was still several feet short. As I let go of the rail the man's body crashed against it, his flashlight coming down precisely where my left hand had been, a split second before. I fell to the maindeck, keeping my knees bent and hoping to make a safe landing in the dark.

It was further than I thought. I collapsed, cracking a kneecap on the deck as I landed, and my leg seemed to lose all strength as I got up and hobbled to the rail, scrambling over it onto the next ship. I scuttled forward around the superstructure, but had not disappeared before the light from a wavering flashlight picked me out. There was a another shout that came through the murderous pain in my ear.

But I made the safety of the shadows. I was hobbling a four-minute mile now, reaching for the next vessel, but as I rounded its forward superstructure I tripped and fell again. I heard my flashlight roll away from me in the dark. I fumbled, but was unable to find it. Now angry, I ran for the final pair of rails. Again, I scrambled over them.

There was a chorus of shouts coming from behind. They still seemed to be a couple of vessels away, but the echoes off the superstructure in front of me were deceptive. I lost no time in running around the last ship as fast as my limp would allow. On the far side I shouted a warning to Ahmed.

159

I ran down the port rail, feeling for the fender's rope, skinning my palm on the flaking rust. I heard the harsh cough of the outboard as Ahmed started it, and the coarse fibre of the rope was suddenly there. I swung myself up and over the rail, and slid down the fender's line. Ahmed's hand was guiding my foot as I reached in the dark for the dinghy's gunwale, and I collapsed onto the thwart, yelling `Cepat, cepat!' Quick!

Ahmed needed no urging. But, rather than turn directly away from the ship, he ran down its hull, keeping the dinghy hidden from the deck. Once at the stern, he headed north into the night. We were almost a hundred yards away before we were spotted.

A couple of shots came from the ship to which we had moored, cracking into the night over our heads. Within a few seconds, the roar of the launch gaining speed broke through the subdued noise of our own outboard. Ahmed jammed the throttle open, and the dinghy jumped forward. I fell forward into the bow, to try to keep it down against the surge of the bow-wave, our escape now in Ahmed's hands.

He signalled to starboard, and, turning, I could see a couple of the other rafted anchorages. One was similarly lit, but one was dark, and he changed course to keep the rafts on a slight tangent to the direction in which we were heading. Beyond the dinghy's transom, I could see the navigation lights of the launch. It had not yet managed to make up any ground, but it was clear that we'd not escape it on an extended flight. Somehow, we had to lose it.

Ahmed continued to keep the lit raft of warships to starboard, examining them closely as we sped by. Suddenly he grunted and pushed the outboard control hard to port. The dinghy slewed hard over and ran directly towards the space between two of the ships, the launch no more than a hundred feet behind.

I could not see more than the narrowing cone of darkness that sat between the water and the rising sheer of the ships' hulls. Ahmed throttled back, the dinghy's stern lifting as its wake surged under it, and I heard a shout from the launch, which had taken an oblique course towards where we now lay.

Suddenly, the dinghy shot forward. I prepared myself for a grinding shock as the two hulls closed inwards in a sandwich trap, and took my hands off the gunwales, anticipating the contact with steel. But it didn't come. The dinghy shot out into an adjoining cone that spread before us. I glanced back and saw the hulls move together again. The gap had almost disappeared. Ahmed had read the swells under the ships, and taken a chance on their movements being enough for the small dinghy to pass through. There were shouts behind us, and the crunch of the launch hitting a hull and bouncing into the gap.

Ahmed didn't waste time. He kept the throttle fully open and sent the dinghy in a curving arc towards the unlit raft of ships. Within a minute we were shielded from our pursuers, who were still extricating the launch from its wedged position. The dinghy stayed on a course that kept us well out of sight of any of the crews on the ships we passed, and within a couple of minutes more it was obvious that the launch had lost us. `Pulang,' I said to Ahmed. I wanted to go home. I touched him on the shoulder. He'd done well. But it had been a long night, and we would still have to be very careful on our course back.

It was almost dawn by the time we got there, the dark wall of the fort blacker against the eastern sky. Ahmed switched the outboard off a few yards from the beach and let the dinghy drift in. I took the old man's hand and thanked him quietly. He muttered the traditional response, ` Tidak apa apa, tuan.' It was nothing.

I helped him haul the dinghy up the beach and into its shed. In the predawn light I could see a few scratches from the rust on the corvette's hull, but there was nothing that anyone could really link to the activities of the past twenty-four hours. I picked up my bag and limped out into the street. A bejak driver was fast asleep on the passenger seat of his tricycle just beyond the gate, and I nudged him awake.

Anne was there, asleep on a divan, curled into a ball, a shawl protecting her from the breeze of the ceiling fan. I stood looking at her for a few moments, thinking about what she'd found in Balikpapan, wondering at the defencelessness of her sleep, then picked her up and carried her through to the bedroom. She didn't come to full consciousness, but there was the firm grip around my neck of someone who'd been on watch, and who had wondered if I'd return. Without thinking of the bath I needed, I lay under the mosquito net, not willing to let her go. Sleep came through the residual motion of the sea and the scorch of the sun.

The light clatter of dishes in the depth of the house finally intruded into my dreams. I lay with eyes closed for a while, thinking about the night before, then opened my eyes slowly.

I was alone in the bed. One shutter was laid back to let a beam of light cut through the mosquito net at my feet. The rest of the net seemed on fire with the reflection. The fan flut-flutted through the air overhead. As I moved to peel back the sheet the pain that shot through my knee reminded me that not only my ear was damaged.

I lifted myself over the side of the bed and hobbled into the bathroom. The cool water of the *mandi* soothed some of the superficial aches, and the soap washed away crusted salt and some of the marks of contact with steel. I put on a sarong that had been lying over the back of the chair beside the bed.

Jack and Anne were on the verandah, where we had sipped fruit juices two days earlier. They both watched me hobble over, and, as I leaned over Anne to give her

161

a kiss, I'd have fallen had she not supported me.

`What shall we do with the drunken sailor?' she hummed quietly.

I tried a grin. `Occupational hazard. All sailors are maligned.' But I could see that I'd be making amends for the worry I'd caused.

Then Jack spoke. `And do we get to know if you brought Ahmed back safe and sound?'

I nodded. `Very, old son. And thank you for it all. He was amazing. Actually, I think he enjoyed it.'

`Then spill the beans.'

I'd known I was going to have to tell at least part of the story, so I pulled a chair up close to Anne. I started talking of the day slowly at first, taking sips of my juice to kill the effects of residual dehydration. I took them as far as climbing on board one of the deserted ships to get a closer look at her condition.

`And that kept you out till five in the morning. Good try, Trev. And the crimson ear, the crack on the knee? And some other bruises not too well hidden?'

I'd not really appreciated that the parts of my body that were in pain had some definite discolouration. `Ah. Well. I slipped and fell a couple of times. The decks were covered in oil.'

`Of course,' said Jack. `And what did you find aboard?'

`That I was right, and that there are some major changes being made to armaments, and therefore to purpose.'

`These are the ships that everyone is calling scrap?' asked Jack. `It sounds quite unlikely.'

`I think that's probably the whole point. Disinformation is as effective a weapon as the firepower itself. These ships are going somewhere.'

Anne spoke for the first time. `Do you know where?'

I looked at her. `I'm not sure that I do. And it worries me so much I'm not even sure I want to.' I touched her knee, needing the contact.

She was torn between still being mad at me for disappearing for so long and the professional analyst who had a wealth of knowledge in her head, and perhaps some sort of answer. Finally, she shook her head. ` I can't work it through yet.'

The window shutters were open, and the fan in the kitchen whirled quietly like a giant bat stuck in a slow vortex.

'So,' I whispered to her. 'How did you get here?'

'I went to Kalimantan and spent a day in Balikpapan. I know someone at the University there. I though I might get some ideas on local movements.'

'Did you?'

'Some. Not enough. I'll have to go back.' Then 'You're alright? You understand that I didn't know if I'd ever see you again?' And her arms held me tightly.

'I'm fine,' I said, not really wanting at that moment to tell a harrowing tale. But the knowledge that I would tell her washed with certainty through my mind.

Jack could see that she was unhappy. `Right. C'mon Anne. Let's get Cap'n Bligh here some breakfast.' He'd walked between us and grabbed Anne's hand. He pulled her to her feet, looked her in the eye and said very quietly `He's good at what he does. Always was,' and dragged her towards the kitchen.

I groaned. `How about some decent Torajan coffee first, Jack? Get the appetite going?'

But then I heard Anne mutter under her breath. `I'll get him going. I'll pour it right on that purple kneecap.'

I sprawled on the grass, shaking with laughter, and Anne pulled away from Jack and picked up a magazine. She rolled it in a cylinder and sat astride my quivering body, thumping my shoulder with it. `Idiot. Jerk. Stupid bloody Aussie. What was I supposed to do when you didn't come home? Dream of you down there with the crabs?' I pulled her into my arms and felt the wetness of her tears, but there was nothing I could say. Slowly my laughter subsided, and her tension melted.

Jack went and made breakfast.

Fifteen

`The final decision must be taken quickly. All the indicators are that now is the moment to move. If we leave it any longer, it will be too late.' I had addressed carefully how a Central Government would deal with a rogue province. Level of rhetoric had proven a direct proxy for subsequent action, and we were now seeing the persuasive effects of the former. This was not the first time I'd voiced concern, but it was the first time I'd voiced certainty.

The Jenderal considered, then nodded. `Orders will go out within twenty-four hours.' He turned to the Laksamana. `Can the Sulawesi action be completed in time?'

`We've already withdrawn most of them from service. Assembly will be complete at the departure point between ten to fifteen days from time zero. It will all be as we planned.'

`Then withdraw the rest. This is time zero.'

The Jenderal turned to me with a different question. `The Palace Guard. What have you decided?' He had set me this as a different challenge.

`The komando force must be inside the compound before any alarm is given. There is one way to achieve this.' I proceeded to explain the plan. `They have been trained in the essence of the exercise but none knows its true purpose. They have been told that it is necessary to clean house. That is what they think they will be doing.'

The Jenderal nodded. 'Confined to bed. The press will eventually be issued with a release covering an unsuspected illness with an unknown prognosis. The recovery can be lengthened or shortened according to need.'

Excerpted from Rusman Soekendro, LetJen (ret'd),
No Game At All: *Memoirs of a Strategist*

The humidity built as the day passed, and what had been a relatively sunny day suddenly became moody with thunderheads. The wind built, the tall bamboo stands lashing against each other as if in mock flagellation. The birds were gone.

Inside the house, the old lamp was lit, and swayed occasionally to stray drafts from the louvred windows, now firmly shut. The shadows from its ornate metal stays played on the walls like an abstract version of the Ramayana, the Hindu epic, and the woman remembered the times past when she had gone to the hours-long shadow plays with her small friends. Entertainment had been simpler then, but far more terrifying than the technicolour dramas played out today on television. The old sheet against which the shadows were projected was a flimsy wall against the world where those shadows lived, and where evil definitely did. The open night sky above such a theatre was always full of spirits, called by the shadows.

The rain, when it came, fell in a wall of solid sound, a hard continuous note against the roof. It poured off the eaves in cataracts, directed into drains placed from the experience of rains past. The drains boiled with young rivers, as if born out of mountain caves.

Then, almost instantly, it stopped. The absence of that sound was momentarily deafening because the ears had attuned to one noise and its complete attenuation made all other common noise, and even silence, suddenly strident.

And then, out of the hills, came the tack-tack-tack of the drum of the rural mosque, calling all around to prayer.

It was uniquely Sundanese, she thought, that sequence - wind, rain, silence, drum.

***

`But a perforated eardrum?' Dixon was incredulous.

`Yes, sir. I got into a bit of a scrape.'

I was becoming accustomed to the late night Jakarta-Canberra flight, and in spite of my earache, had managed to sleep a few hours. I was no longer limping, but the bruise across my ear had been perfectly plain for Dixon to see.

I proceeded to outline the preliminary satellite analysis that I'd undertaken, and my suspicions of some secret movements of the fleet. I spread the photos out on Dixon's table. One showed saltwater stains.

`Wait a minute. This was your analysis? Not Navy Intelligence?'

`No, sir. I've a standing arrangement where Intelligence sends me high-level photography. I use it for *Open Seas*. But I've also taken to running comparative analyses of naval ship movements. This stood out like a signal.'

Dixon reached for his phone. `Get Edmonds up here. Immediately.' To me he added. `Hold your story for a moment.' Then into the phone again `Bring in some coffee. For two.' It seemed a rather pointed omission. He waited a few seconds.

`He's on his way? Good.' He hung up and began looking at the photos. He asked a couple of questions about the aerial view of Surabaya.

Edmonds came in a couple of minutes later, the same Intelligence officer who had been the butt of Dixon's sarcasm at my briefing prior to setting up *Open Seas*. Dixon waved him to a chair.

`Gregory's telling us a story, Edmonds. Listen carefully.' He nodded to me.

I gave Edmonds the benefit of a quick summary of what I'd told Dixon and then went on to describe my visit to Makassar and the anchorages. I didn't elaborate on the details until I got to the ships themselves. Then I pulled a couple of sheets of paper out of my briefcase, and laid them side-by-side on the table. I pointed to the first sheet.

`I managed to get close to a corvette. This is the deckplan of the Parchim-class as it was when the corvettes were recommissioned for the Indonesian Navy. Twin 57mm guns aft, twin 30mm forward. Torpedo tubes on the aft deck. One quad launcher behind the fire-control tower. Torpedo mortars behind the forward gun. Not much else. Standard machinery was three diesels generating close to 11000 horsepower. Three prop shafts.'

I pointed to the second sheet. `I sketched this from what I could see of the refit. You'll see that it agrees well with the magnified satellite photo. The heavy guns are gone. The ship has been fitted fore and aft for missiles. Anti-aircraft and anti-missile cannon have been mounted in lateral positions. The torpedo mortars are now aft.'

Edmonds spoke for the first time. `That's all obvious from the photos.'

I ignored him. `All the heavy underdeck reinforcing has gone. Displacement is probably down well over a hundred tons. Missile and gun magazines have been rebuilt. Engines have been replaced. This is a more lethal vessel.'

Dixon put his coffee cup down. `So you went aboard. With our approval, of course. And then banged your ear on a steampipe.'

`Badly cluttered below, sir. Not much room.'

Dixon left it alone. `And the refit time?'

`At the most, seven days for the core changes, sir.'

`Impossible,' muttered Edmonds. `No facilities. No experience.'

I'd had enough. `You should look at your own photos. It's staring you in the face.'

Dixon enjoyed Edmonds' discomfort, and I could see warning signals in the cobalt blue. `Its not about lobbing shells anymore, Captain. It's all about radar and locking onto targets. Missiles don't require a heavy gun to get them there. They do it themselves.'

`Of course, sir. I know that. I'm talking about dockyard facilities for major refits. Trained men. The Indonesians don't know how.'

`Edmonds,' Dixon's tone grew icy, `the Indonesians do know how. As Gregory said, it's staring you in the face. Now, let's suppose *you* knew all that, what would you think they had in mind?'

`I'm not sure, sir. The whole thing's been a bit of a joke. Nobody gave any credence to that purchase. The ships have been sitting in mothballs.'

`Well, Captain. I have an idea. Why don't you go back to that Section of yours and put some intelligence to it. I'd like a full analysis on my desk by nine tomorrow morning.'

`Now, sir?'

`Yes, for God's sake! Now, Edmonds.'

`Yes, sir.' Edmonds almost stumbled out of the room.

`And the new engines, Gregory?' Dixon's mind had been working elsewhere whilst he'd lashed Edmonds.

'It surprised me initially, sir. But it speaks to the same planning - I think we'd find the diesels were what clinched the original purchase. Perhaps they were very quietly installed at Kiel.'

Dixon whistled. Then, `And what do you think Edmonds report will say?'

I wasn't going to let Edmonds off the hook. `Probably not a great deal. ASEAN threat perhaps.'

`Whereas its not ASEAN?'

`I think it's not ASEAN at all, sir.'

Dixon picked up his phone again. `Is the Chief-of-Staff at home? Good. Tell him I'm on my way up.' He looked at me. `Come with me. I'd rather you told the story.'

Half an hour later Bluing asked, `What do you think they've got in that yard?'

`One good crane operator, several skilled teams of steelfitters, and perhaps some good mechanics, sir. They need very little else. Tearing it out is not like putting it in in the first place. And all they had to do was weld the holes closed. The secret is in the weapons systems. But they require little else than good electrical connections. All the tests are inbuilt. If the radar works, they're home dry.'

Then I added `But it's clear that they've been prefabricating a lot of parts, sir. All the magazine lifts looked as though some care had been taken there. The helicopter deck, too. The engines were set to the same mounts - if they were installed at Makassar, I doubt whether they had more than a few technical delays. And practice would have made perfect.'

Bluing nodded. `It's the Uganda all over again.'

`The Uganda?' asked Dixon.

Bluing nodded again. `At the start of the Falklands crisis in 82, the Brits requisitioned her out of the Mediterranean cruise trade. She went into the Gibraltar yard on a Friday afternoon and came out Monday morning completely refitted as a hospital ship. Including a helicopter deck. Some of the Moroccan steelfitters were on the Honours List.'

He spoke again. `Evidence of some serious planning and training. What about the rest of the navy?'

`From what I can tell, sir, it's just the German ships that are being refitted. There are regular departures and arrivals at Surabaya, but they look like normal duty tours. The only ships in drydock have been there a while.'

`What's your interpretation?'

`Sir, it makes no sense at all if we base it on our traditional thinking of their navy. Inter-island patrols to catch smugglers. It's as if there's a complete re-orientation of strategic purpose in their use of hardware. What if that separation in purpose mirrors a separation in intent?'

`A navy within a navy?'

`To some degree yes. Navy facilities are being used to upgrade these vessels. But the level of effort and the outcome point to something quite different. And why do it at Makassar?'

`Yes, that is a puzzle.'

`I think it's because one cannot entertain stealth in anything on Java, sir. Everybody knows what's happening. But if you move something offshore to an outer island, you have a natural break in communications. And the Makassarese have no love for the colonial Javanese.'

`Is there any extra-ASEAN entanglement that requires such urgency?' asked Dixon. `Spratlys? Natuna?' he added. He was prodding me for the same analysis I'd given Kessler.

`On the surface, yes, sir. There's no doubt that Jakarta is extremely worried about the Chinese. If the Chinese gain total control over the Spratlys, Indonesia has to face a common border with her somewhere between the two island groups.'

`Even perhaps an expeditionary force for the Spratlys? Has Indonesia decided to deal herself into that game? Would she gain from taking control of some of the islands?' Dixon was thinking out loud.

`Possibly, sir. It's pretty certain that there's a good deal of oil under those islands. Indonesia's known reserves are declining. The exploration of the Timor Gap is promising but still not completely proven. One could suppose that oil was the imperative. It certainly seems to be so for the Chinese.'

`You have your doubts.'

`The Chinese threat is still embryonic. It would not require such a massive secret undertaking. In fact, it would be to Indonesia's advantage to let the Chinese know what it was doing. And the whole ASEAN position would be stronger, Indonesia being the *de facto* senior partner.'

`It still doesn't sound very likely,' said Bluing.

`No, sir. I agree.'

`Then what else is going on?' asked Dixon. `None of this suggests the need for the secret rearming of a navy.'

`An armada, sir. But perhaps not under the control of the sovereign.'

`A navy within a navy,' repeated Bluing. He was suddenly lost in thought. Then, `Who is behind the President?'

`What?' said Dixon.

Bluing turned to me. `Is he involved?'

'We're in different times now, sir. Were we back in the immediate post-Suharto years I'd have said it could have been C-in-C ABRI himself. Though he lost apparent power when he was kicked out by Wahid. No, from that point on, no President has chosen any Minister or C-in-C with whom such conniving might occur.'

'But ABRI may still resent Wiranto's ouster,' said Dixon.

Bluing nodded. 'And the Vice-President?'

'Difficult to say, sir. I'd have thought there wasn't enough respect from the military. And remember what Wahid said during his time - a President who couldn't see and a Vice-President who couldn't speak. The Vice-Presidency has always been where potential presidential opponents were marooned. It's been a successful strategy.'

`But the Defence Minister?'

`I think the Defence Minister is a stronger candidate. The sense is that ABRI is turning more to him on substantive matters. Unlike his other civilian predecessor, this one has always been close to military issues. I'd put him ahead.'

`Ahead in what?' asked Dixon.

`The next succession, Jim. That's what this is all about. We have somebody thinking ahead. Someone who sees that having his own navy might be a very useful card in dealing the President out. The question is, is the game decided?'

`But there are still a couple of years yet in this presidency, and he'll almost certainly run for another term.' Dixon spoke with certainty. `He won't abide anyone cobbling together his own fishing fleet from the German ships.'

`If he knows. And if he manages to hold on to power. Perhaps he's already losing it and we don't know. Or didn't know.' Bluing was looking at the satellite photos. `Is this the signal?' He paused. `Where are the arms coming from?'

The question was directed at me. `I don't know, sir. I'd suggest that a signal go out to our Embassies to review known arms sales. Perhaps our friends in Washington might help.'

`Any chance that these will have been bought under the counter? That Jakarta has a second arms budget?' Dixon was showing some concern.

`They've been caught in the past understating defence expenditures, Jim. But there's no doubt that Jakarta has been squeezed for cash lately. If these arms were bought on the open market, there has to be some assurance that the cash will be found. How would you do that?'

`Letter of credit against some assets. But I'd have to own my own bank!' Dixon laughed scornfully.

`Yes,' said Bluing. `You'd have to own your own bank.' Then to me. `Do they?'

I nodded. `ABRI has at least one. Bank Intan Cahaya. Untold assets, but mainly military. Pension funds, land.'

`Mortgage the lot,' muttered Bluing.

`Beg your pardon, sir?'

`Commitment in one fell swoop, Gregory. Mortgage the lot. Spend your equity on productive assets. It's like buying into a prize-ship before you've captured her. There's no money left in the bank, so everyone's committed to the course, even if they weren't before. `You want to retire rich? Then get out there and fight."

The room was silent for a moment.

`Then it's a question of identifying the prize-ship,' said Dixon.

Bluing nodded. 'But even more important is the name of our privateer. If we can't work that out we're stumped. But we know where to start to look. Jakarta.'

So I put it into the middle of the room. `PNG, sir. I think they want to add Papua New Guinea to Irian Jaya.' But I didn't say that I thought Subagio might make a good proxy for the one we had to look for. It was the strategic planning that did it. No-one better than he.

I was in the canteen trying to sink a cup of tea when the call came through. `Navy HQ, sir. A dispatch from Jakarta. *Open Seas* is on the go.' I left the tea gladly. I'd been watching the schedule, and if my comments to Subagio had been

171

right it would have to happen now. `Advise Admiral Dixon. He may want to watch this.'

`Yes, sir.'

I was in my chair double-checking the system when Dixon came in. 'What have you got?'

`Lieutenant Imrie has reported a contact a dozen miles astern. Almost certainly a warship. The pattern is almost identical.' I gave him a run-through of the images on-screen.

`The changes to the rules of engagement are understood?'

`Yes, sir. This particular ship cannot be let fall into Chinese hands.' I did my number on the electronic notepad. `Evening, Starfish. Standing by.'

`Message clear, Alice. Starfish wide awake and waiting.' came back within the minute.

It was now a waiting game. Dixon brought some reading files into the operations room, poured himself a coffee and settled down in another chair. I had an updated set of satellite photos and ran through them with a magnifier. It looked as if another refitted ship had returned to the anchorage. I was still waiting for an enhancement of the Makassar yard, though didn't really need it now.

The shadow on the screen was a little closer, the ciphers in the corner of the radar window suggesting about nine nautical miles. I could imagine the tension on the freighter's bridge, palpable fear in the crew over a foreign warship, an alligator with gun-barrel eyes rolling to the slight swell of the sea.

The cargo vessel was running at a steady twenty-two knots and her deck-lights had been cut back to minimum. I could hear Imrie advising the captain to send his men below. `Standing orders, Captain. Sorry.' As with all sailings since the last attack, pre-departure briefings had gone through details of the zodiac approach and at what distance they became visible. But another half hour passed before Imrie picked up movement through his night-glasses. Then it was clear that the other side had also upped the stakes. `Lima, Santoso. Ada lima.' Five zodiacs were visible.

His opposite number, Lieutenant Santoso, did not take the warning of five approaching zodiacs without checking. I could see his shadow spend a further half minute confirming Imrie's observation. `Bagus, ' came across the ether, carrying a happy grin with it. He made a gesture with his hand indicating that he would warn and regroup his men. And before Santoso was off the bridge Imrie was tapping the confirmatory message into the computer. `Five inbound Alice. Action imminent.'

I turned to Dixon. `Signal, sir. Raiders inbound.'

`Can you see them on the screen?'

`Not yet, sir. Craft that small have to be quite close before the cameras can pick them up. And the deck lights are low at the moment.'

Imrie stuck to the rules and gave me the one-hundred metre message. `Five zodiacs splitting into two, two and one, about five men in each.' The radarscope showed the shadow closing fast and now at a distance of some four nautical miles. That was all to the good.

I heard Santoso counting down through the radio to his men. He could not be with all groups at once, and what was to come would depend on split-second timing from his men and a fair degree of agility. They had been warned of the difficulty. Santoso had taken the starboard side, relying on Imrie at port. At `nol', zero, there was a muffled report and then the flash of a stun grenade. Almost instantaneously other grenades exploded around the ship. The sniper would have fired from the superstructure at the same instant.

`Lights, Captain!' Imrie shouted.

Night exploded into startling day. Single searchlight beams from portable lights stabbed the waters at the ship's side, and I could see several shapes plunging over the rail, attached by abseiling lines. Santoso was checking with each section leader on progress. Another voice broke in. Santoso barked an order to his sniper for a second shot.

The explosion of the decklights into the night almost made Dixon jump out of his chair, and he muttered something under his breath. The wide-angled cameras showed the shapes of the zodiacs in the water, though it was not clear what was happening in them. This time all the action was planned for water-level, and I hoped the surprise had worked.

Santoso came onto the bridge and I heard the exchange. `Success, Imrie. We take three. Slow one down with bullet. My men get wet.'

It was apparent that Imrie did not realize for some seconds that Santoso had spoken to him in English. When it sank in, he broke out laughing, and it was clear Santoso had made him struggle hard to communicate in Indonesian. `You crafty bastard, Santoso. Did I say anything before that you didn't like?'

`Asian brother, Imrie. You learn to be careful.'

`Pick up the rocket, Santoso. Light up the night.'

`Distance?'

My eyes paralleled Imrie's in their glance at the radar. `Three miles.'

I could see Santoso make some settings changes and lift the launcher to his shoulder. He stepped out onto the port flying bridge, looked through the sight, and then the missile flashed into the night, its brilliant tail rapidly decreasing in size until it disappeared. For some reason Santoso didn't wait for the flare, but dropped the launcher and headed for the gangway. `I check my men.'

Imrie didn't fire the rocket, but it was now his job to follow it up, and all he had to do was wait, camera in hand. He hardly had to wait at all. It was as if a full moon had instantly pulled itself above the horizon, the missile-mounted flare breaking into a skylifting light over a pointillist sea. Mike made an instant switch at the controls in Jakarta and right in the centre of my picture sat a frigate, the alligator surprised on the surface. Imrie was no less impressed. `Oh God that's lovely.' He kept the camera on the ship for the full life of the flare.

And as he did so, it was as if a horse's hoof kicked me hard in the belly.

But the sound channel still fed me Santoso, and I could hear him with one of his section leaders. `Well?' His concern was the same as mine had been, the action having been at water level and the zodiacs now hardly visible to the naked eye.

`They've rafted them up, *Letnan*. All four that came close.'

`Ah, they got the fourth?'

`Y*a, Letnan*. They'd just stopped in the water. It's just been confirmed.'

Imrie was tapping more data into the electronic link as Santoso came onto the bridge. `All clear?' Santoso nodded. Imrie turned.`Alright Captain. Your men have the ship again. Let them loose.'

Imrie had to ask Santoso the hard question. `All your men came back?'

`Wet but alive.'

`Ah, bloody good, Santoso. That's bloody good news.'

`Too bloody right, Imrie.' The two men broke into howls of laughter.

I wondered whether I'd ever get the signal Imrie was supposed to send. But I could understand Santoso's laughter, and all the reasons why Subagio had not managed to extract any information from the other raiders he'd caught.

Dixon caught my groan just as he was showing his own signs of exultation over the operation's success. 'What's wrong with you, Gregory?'

I almost couldn't tell him, the pain in my belly so strong, and my last meal making a supreme effort to spread itself all over the floor. 'She's Indonesian, sir.' I knew every one of their ships like the back of my hand, and needed to see no number to confirm it. 'Based in Surabaya. She'll have followed the ship up the Makassar Strait. Choreographed all the way.'

He wasn't taking it in. 'What the bloody hell are you talking about?'

'I don't know, sir. But she's not Chinese. She's Indonesian.' And though perhaps there was a moment in which I could dispassionately lay Harry Grant's Chinese theory to rest, and see why certain other answers had not come, the truth, at that very same moment, was more than I could fully understand.

Sixteen

Believing the motorcade to be bringing the most recent Vice-President of the Cameroon, a non-aligned troublemaker, for a late evening dinner, the palace guards came to attention as the convoy entered the grounds. Most of them died on the spot from the silenced pistols of the motorcycle flankers. The remainder were quickly finished by a second bullet.

At a signal, the doors of all the cars opened and masked troops spilled into the drive. The official welcomimg party was submerged in the wave and bundled into two of the cars. Other bodies were hauled out of sight behind the squat but regal forms of the guardhouses. The flankers assumed gate duty. There were few pedestrians in the avenue in front of the palace, and the dark of the night left them with little confidence in the stories of slaughter that they later tried to tell.

The troops formed into three squads. These went into the palace in different directions, briefed on where to find most of their quarry. The surprise was complete, no shouts of alarm. An inner guardpost was dealt with as summarily as the ones outside.

Members of the third squad stood to attention outside the Presidential quarters. The Jenderal opened the door and I went through with him, half of the squad behind. The remainder formed a guard around the quarters. This had been fully rehearsed. They knew the safety of the President was at stake. This had been a cleansing operation. A new Presidential Guard was taking over, untainted by the laxness of the Guard now dead. The success of this operation had shown just how lax they'd been.

The Vice President of the Cameroon was left to enjoy a quiet meal at an unexpectedly different destination, the Bogor Summer Palace.

Excerpted from Rusman Soekendro, LetJen (ret'd),
No Game At All: Memoirs of a Strategist

The Javan was as good as his word, and met them at the gate. 'Come. He's waiting.' He led them off along the valley again, in the direction taken by the man with the baskets the day before. They ascended an offshoot of the main valley, and were soon in a small village of traditional wooden houses, many on stilts. He took them through some gardens, and then they found themselves in a small clearing. Along one side of the clearing stood some sheep, each one tethered separately to a wooden stake. Each halter was decorated with coloured wool. The sheep, all black and white, but with large variations in patterns, had large curling horns. The man they'd seen the day before came forward and spoke rapidly to the Javan. 'Haji Umar, the head man of the village,' said the Javan in presentation, and the man in the white hat held both hands forward, and clasped the visitors' palms in turn. '*Selamat datang, selamat datang.*' he said, his smile showing only a couple of teeth still anchored inside. Welcome, welcome.

No sooner had they been presented to the group at large, than two young men each led an animal to opposite sides of the clearing. They were brought forward as if to touch noses, separated by several feet, and then released. As if by magic, each animal slowly bowed its head, and in a movement so fluid as if it were under the control of unseen forces, sprang forward into the air and crashed precisely and deafeningly into the horns of its opponent. The immediate deceleration brought them back to earth, whereupon they each backed off by a few paces, and then again flew at each other. This pattern was repeated a half a dozen times, and then the handlers ran forward to restrain them. 'Very good,' said the Javan, and pointed to one. 'That one won. Did you see?'

Later, he said: 'Raising and fighting the *domba* Garut, the Garut sheep, is the main pastime of the men in this valley. You will only find it in the highlands of Sunda. Only the rams have those wonderful horns, of course. And only a few rams become champions. Did you see how Haji Umar's ram beat his rival? Wonderful strength, such beauty in the air.'

They had seen several bouts, and Haji Umar's ram had indeed been the victor of his own match, and acclaimed by the audience. In the sudden unleashing of what was a colossal force, and its equally complete absorption in the opposing set of horns, the Australian had seen battle as it had been conducted almost since time primeval. Yet the rams were not allowed to continue combat until one was seen to suffer. There had been no uneven matches. Victory was the outcome of pace and focus, not death. Only humans insisted on the latter, he thought. He wondered whether there was any other message.

***

The afternoon sky in Jakarta was as heavy and menacing as the blow I'd been handed in Canberra. The taxi from the airport was buffeted by hard squalls as we entered the city, and it all seemed apiece with the nosedive I saw my career as just having taken. Dixon had been exasperated though not cruel. 'Find out what this is about. That, now, is the limit to your job.'

178

The taxi dropped me at Anne's door just after five, the maid let me in, and, with big round eyes told me that the *ibu* was busy upstairs. She giggled into her hand as I raised my eyebrows at her and walked past.

I found Anne seated on a balcony, and she gave me a welcome that was both personal and loving.

Her quiet face, beautiful in its serenity, brought up more of the feelings that had lain undisturbed in me since prehistory. `You're a monsoon storm to the desert of my past,.' I said. Her hand was small and warm under mine, fingers curling up like lace. I looked at it and then at her. `I'd like that hand to bathe my children.'

And with that I'd finally silenced her, though as her other hand went to her throat, too late to hide the red tide rising fast, she did manage to say `We *will* have to talk about how many you want.'

'I don't understand it either,' she said later, having read that other side of me, and knowing that something wasn't right. But I'd brought it up without her digging, needing her insights.

'I understand now why many questions weren't answered - why they never got any information out of their prisoners. But I can't understand why they mounted such an elaborate charade.'

'D'you really think they shot those men?'

'Perhaps I could answer that if I knew why they did it.'

'I'd prefer a ketchup theory.'

'Me, too, love. But neither of our two blokes who witnessed the actions picked up on anything that spoke to anything other than a true-blue hijacking.' I was convinced that I'd witnessed true slaughter. 'The complication,' I said, 'was that the ship was carrying uranium ores. Probably enough to do something very nasty with, once enriched. Subagio knew it, and knew that I knew he did. But why mount such an elaborate hoax? A mock-hijacking of a ship and cargo you have no use for?'

'You don't know that, honey. And you won't know until you prove whether or not it was ketchup.'

'Even if it wasn't, that won't supply the answer. I think Subagio would sacrifice any number of men without qualms if he wanted to. If fooling us required it, he'd have done it.' I thought a little. 'As long as neither group was apprized of the other, and mounted their operation from the stance each was ordered to take, any outcome would have appeared natural.'

Anne shivered. 'That's pretty bloodthirsty.'

I nodded. 'I think the ketchup theory's out.' This is pure *sambal*, I thought, that

179

hot Indonesian sauce which could overpower the flavour of everything else and blow the top of your head off if you overdid it.

The morning paper gave me the news before I heard it from any other source. *`All Indonesian archipelagic sea-lanes closed.'* But it was put out as a statement without any explanation beyond the Government apparently exercising what it saw as its right. What it meant was that any shipping would now have to circumnavigate the archipelago rather than cross it at one of the strategic points. Hung's comment came back, about Australian commerce being held to ransom if ships had to go the long way round.

I thought perhaps I might still have an inside track to Subagio, even fearing him as I was beginning to, but phone calls to Naval HQ went no further than the switchboard. No-one was available. So I thought I'd take a chance. `Boltroni, I want the car.' I listened a moment to Boltroni's query. `Naval headquarters. It's an unofficial visit. No warning - I want to surprise them. No, don't worry. Just the driver. This should be safe.'

The sentry at the main entrance was not accommodating. I produced my diplomatic identification, but the unannounced arrival brought an officious response. I explained who I wanted to see.

The name brought the sentry up short. He went back to his post, where several other armed soldiers stood looking equally severe, and muttered something to them. He picked up the phone and in a few seconds began to speak. I wondered whether *he'd* get past the switchboard.

Several short conversations ensued, each time the sentry looking at my identification and reading information from it. The increasing stiffness of the sentry's spine suggested that he was being shunted higher up the ladder each time. Finally he put the phone down and came back to the car. Without looking at me he told the driver to pull forward to the main door. My papers stayed firmly in his hand.

At the step Mathius waiting. He did not look happy.

`What do you want here, Captain Gregory? You should have phoned for an appointment.'

`Lieutenant, I've been phoning all morning. No-one answered. I decided to make an unofficial call. Is Admiral Subagio here?'

`Yes, yes. He's here. But he's very busy. I don't know whether he'll see you.'

`Well, show me to his office. I'll wait.'

Mathius led off with displeasure evident on his face, no other words forthcoming as we walked through the corridors. He showed me into Subagio's antechamber. A junior aide sat at a desk right by the inner door, and a muted conversation ensued between the two. I did the only thing possible and sat down in one of the chairs against a wall.

Mathius went out without saying a word. The aide continued to sit at the desk. Over the following half hour, a procession of officers came and went, passing the aide with little comment. Subagio did not come out. A tray of coffee went in.

When it was evident I was being ignored, I crossed the room to the aide's desk. `Does the Admiral know I'm here?'

The aide had an empty face. `The *Laksamana* cannot see you.'

`Is the Admiral here?'

`The *Laksamana* has visitors.'

`Will you give him my card?' I was angry enough to want to stuff it up his nose.

The aide put it on the desk. `I will give it to the *Laksamana* when he can see you.'

`That is for him to decide.'

The aide shrugged. `When he decides to see you I will give it to him.'

I sat down. I neither knew whether Subagio really was inside or whether he knew that I was outside, but there was only so far I could go and I was already pushing the limits. No conversation was now audible through the wall. The other officers could be drinking coffee alone.

Almost another hour passed before there was any movement. The door handle turned, and the door was held partially ajar for a moment. Voices filtered out. Subagio was there. The aide got up from his desk and went in. The door closed again. I noticed that my card was gone.

Within half a minute the aide came out again and resumed his seat. But nothing was volunteered. `Well?' I asked. `*Tunggu*,' came the reply, wait.

After a further ten minutes a buzzer sounded under the aide's desk. Without getting up he pointed to the inner door. `*Silahkan*.' Please.

While it was a different Subagio to the one I knew, no welcome on his face, no recognition of a professional relationship, it was not a Subagio entirely different to the one I thought sat under the same skin. His `Yes, Mr Gregory?' nailed shut any past warmth.

`Good afternoon, Admiral. I happened to be passing. Given the news, I thought that I should call.' The atmosphere in the office was glacial, and the other officers present ignored me, discussing amongst themselves the contents of some documents. Subagio pretended distraction.

`News, Mr Gregory? What news?'

`Of the sealanes, Admiral. Their closure.'

`An internal Government affair. Nothing to concern you. I expect they'll be opened again soon.'

`May I ask how long you think they'll be closed?'

`You must be deaf, Mr Gregory. I told you I expect they'll be opened again soon. Is there anything else I can help you with?'

`*Lautan Lepas*, Admiral. I think there is something that needs to be explained.'

`Ah. Yes. *Lautan Lepas*. It's cancelled, Mr Gregory. If the ships cannot transit our sealanes. there is no need for any further collaboration. Please tell your Ambassador so when you see him again. Is there anything else?' He made a couple of rapid remarks to the assembled officers on the content of their conversation - he had obviously been listening to them the whole time he'd been talking to me - and I felt the door of indifference finally close.

`I'm sorry, Admiral, but that's not good enough. It was an Indonesian warship that stalked and boarded that last freighter. For all I know, the previous attempted hijacking may have been a similar ploy. It is of considerable concern to my Government that we appear to have been misled. I cannot understand why you should want to create tension when it was all important that we build ties. Perhaps when you are less busy we may talk again.'

`Tension, Mr Gregory? Any tension that exists is entirely yours. And I doubt that we shall need to talk again. Goodbye.' He did not offer his hand.

I could do nothing but nod and walk out of the door. There was nothing further to be gained by courtesy. I stopped only to collect the documents that had been retained by the sentry, and then the car took me directly back to the Embassy. I went straight up to the Ambassador's office. `Is he home?'

My instant admittance to Kessler's office was a raw contrast to the two hours I'd spent in Subagio's antechamber. Kessler pointed to a chair and waved a report from Canberra that I recognized. `I've read this, and Boltroni advised me where you'd gone. What news?'

`I decided that a quick personal call might get me some useful inside information. I miscalculated. I was not wanted. In fact, I clearly have an enemy.'

`You don't know why they closed the sea-lanes?'

`I think I do. Perhaps they weren't expecting us to see their frigate last night, and wanted to keep a fake operation going. I may have blown the whistle too soon.'

`Whistle?'

`That flare we sent up. It may have blown their operation too soon.'

Kessler's eyebrows lifted. `I hadn't thought of that. What are they up to?'

I shook my head. `I don't know.' But then I had an idea. `You know we have a ship directly north of here.'

He looked surprised. `No, I didn't. What of it?'

`If she goes the long way round the issue is all but conceded.'

His surprise grew. `Really got your goat, didn't they?'

`I'm bloody mad. Sorry.'

Kessler put me on the next flight back to Canberra. An extraordinary meeting of the Defence Committee had been called and he'd been asked for some input, so he decided I was better than a few comments in a coded telex. I was getting used to this commuting, and was able almost to walk straight into the meeting.

`This cannot be allowed to continue unchallenged.' The Defence Chief, General Bruce Gall, had prefaced his emphasis on the main issue with very few opening remarks. `While it might be argued that as the waters are international it should be the international community that protests the closure, it doesn't take much knowledge of geography to understand that it is only Australia that is being held to ransom. The sealanes are north-south. They are essential to our economic prosperity and an integral part of our defence interests.' As well as the three Service Chiefs-of-Staff, representatives of the main Government departments were also present.

`Before we draft a resolution to the Minister on dealing with Jakarta I should like each of the Chiefs-of-Staff to review concerns that relate to his field of command. Particularly I should like a summary analysis of the defence positions that address this particular bilateral relationship. They may add weight to whatever actions we decide are necessary. John, would you start?'

Brigadier John Townsworth, tall, dapper, nodded. `Papua New Guinea. The border skirmishes that brought a direct request for field support from Port Moresby resulted in two battalions in the field. One regular infantry, one special forces. Conditions are difficult, and the regular troops are due to be rotated. It's a significant force to be tied up by a minor irritant that looks as though it was carefully planned and skillfully executed.'

`Terror campaign?' asked Gall.

Townsworth nodded. `From what they could tell of the remains. And the few who will still live near the border.'

`And in the Top End?'

`2nd Cavalry Regiment has just returned to Darwin from field exercises in the Pilbara. It's a little under strength, and I'm not convinced that we yet have the hardware we need for those conditions. The rate of wear and tear is extremely high. It costs us as much in operational terms to move the machinery to the practice theatre as it does to conduct the actual exercises. We'll have to increase our spares inventory. And don't forget that PNG is different ground. Worse than the York Peninsula.'

`Cairns?

Townsworth shrugged. `The Rapid Deployment Force is largely tied up in PNG. It keeps it combat ready, but we couldn't redeploy beyond a thousand kilometres without taking up a lot of airlift capacity. We still couldn't redeploy for immediate combat within seventy-two hours. But we've got them where we need them, haven't we?'

`All the indications are that it's PNG, yes. This looks like a smokescreen.'

Townsworth looked relieved.

`Paul?'

Air Marshall Paul Litner laid his notes on the table. Once a noted fighter pilot, he would never fit into a tight cockpit again. `One fighter reconnaisance squadron is on rotational duty through the barebases along the north and northwest coasts. I've made it plain before that these are vulnerable and not sufficiently stocked for anything but a low-level conflict. We're conducting regular coastal sweeps behind the Maritime Patrol Group. Another squadron at least would have to be relocated to Cairns to provide effective backup, using the forward base at Scherger. Principal limitation to round-the-clock air support continues to be air-to-air refuelling. Fuel has to come too far. You know my thoughts on this.'

While the origin was apocryphal, the story had become part of Defence lore. Litner, who was a man of caustic wit, in a moment of frustration over decisions on where to put defence dollars, was scathing about Navy's new barges. Someone, perhaps Litner, recalling that an admiral's barge was what ferried a fleet's commander from shore to ship, and vice versa, immediately christened Bluing 'Admiral Barge'. So *Barge* Bluing was a phrase often heard in Navy's wardrooms.

It didn't stop there. Much of Litner's command revolved around No 1 Squadron, the F-111 aircraft at Amberley, Queensland. Termed 'pigs' by the people that flew them, derived from Aardvark, but also, perhaps, because they were expensive in terms of lives, the appellation 'Boar' was quickly found appropriate for Litner by naval staff who disliked any other service dreaming up a better derogatory label for their admiral than they had ever done.

Gall, at one point, disgusted by the degeneration of respect that the new name-calling seemingly implied, issued an order that it should terminate forthwith. He was unprepared for the news, which reached him almost immediately, that he was now *The Gaul.*

Only Townsworth, because of his height, escaped the fray, for long having been known just as Tiny.

`And the Jindalee radar system?'

'We have over-the-horizon coverage across the full arc of the Indonesian archipelago, and we'll see anything in the air going east to PNG if it's over the Timor or Arafura Seas. But beyond Carpentaria we're still limited, and this still isn't a fighter-control system. We'd have to borrow a plane from the Americans if we thought it was going to get serious, and I'm not convinced we'd do that in seventy-two hours either.' Litner grimaced at Townsworth.

`Ted?'

I thought Bluing had been given the last slot because of the implicit recognition that the closure of the sealanes was *his* problem. In a way, it was.`We're seriously understrength. Three ships from the West Ocean Fleet are away on manoeuvres or visits. Patrol craft operating out of Darwin can cover coastal operations only. We can't get that squadron back for more than a week. We've covered West Ocean needs with two ships from Sydney, but we could not think of any show of strength further north without leaving ourselves totally exposed on the West Coast. One submarine is due back from blue-water patrol in the West Ocean within the week.'

`Where is the squadron?'

`Two ships are off the Indian sub-continent. The third slipped Hong Kong yesterday.'

`Then she's still in the East South China Sea?'

Bluing nodded.`All three will rendezvous in the Andaman Sea in about four days. Then they'll take the long way home. South by Sumatra.'

`And the Indonesian Navy?'

Bluing shoved the question in my direction. `An unknown quantity at this point because of the German acquisitions, sir. We don't know how operational they are, but there has been some significant rearming. We couldn't get anything significant beyond the Torres Strait quickly enough to keep Papuan waters clear of an expeditionary force. But as far as we can tell, most of the naval tonnage is in central or western waters. Though that doesn't mean it's not a threat further east.'

Gall showed some puzzlement. I think to all around the table it looked very much as though PNG was headed for a Timorese-style showdown, though not all the cards seemed to be in the right place. But more serious was that Australia could not stand by idly while Indonesia lauched an offensive against a joint neighbour. I could see it was worrying him, and it was probably having the same effect on the other military members of the committee. On the bureaucrats, I wasn't too sure.

185

'And this bloody fiasco we've just been involved in with them? Have you any idea what that's about?'

'No, sir,' I said. 'And the worry is that it gives us no answer to the Alumina Queen affair.'

Gall closed his eyes and shook his head in utter frustration. `Do we wish to test them?' he asked.

`Make a point?' said Bluing. 'Make it clear that an international sealane is international? We'll get nowhere keeping our gloves on. The opportunity is right there.' He hadn't required much prompting from me before the meeting to grasp the idea.

`Which is?'

`The ship directly to the north of the archipelago. *Magnet*. The senior ship of the squadron.'

If Gall was capable of a smile it crept onto his face right then. `This will need a Cabinet clearance. Keep her clear of any territorial waters until we have it.'

Seventeen

Through the simulation I watched the LCTs make their way in real time in twos and threes across and around the two southern arms of Sulawesi. Some came down the west side, threading their way past Selayar and crossing the Bone Gulf. There they joined the stream coming down the east coast, where the navigation of the waters east of Tukang Besi was relatively easier. Others filtering down from the Moluccas and points further east made their way separately.

The congregation was purposely haphazard. Orders had been simple. Rendezvous with a fleet tanker lying to the east of Tukang Besi, fill tanks and reserves, and take a cautious course across to Ambon and then on to the final anchorage. Maintain a course at least ten miles from the coast off each reference point. Radio and other silence to be maintained. Final orders on final landfall.

Excerpted from Rusman Soekendro, LetJen (ret'd),
No Game At All: *Memoirs of a Strategist*

The *ibu* had clearly taken some pains with lunch. The front door had been wedged open, and a small boy was erecting several folding chairs on the front patio, in the shade of the roof. Inside, a large table, to one side of the parlour, bore several large covered bowls. A platter of fruit sat at the far end. Plates, glasses and cutlery were nearest to the entrance. There was the smell of wood smoke in the air, and the Australian saw a charcoal brazier in the garden, loaded with small skewers of meat. The fire sizzled as drops of fat fell on the hot embers.

They had walked back from the village alone, having taken what they thought was their farewell, and thanking Haji Umar for inviting them to see the display. But they'd no sooner arrived than several of the older men who had been present, Haji Umar included, also trooped up the front path. Greetings were renewed.

'It is important to maintain good relations with the people who have lived in this valley far longer than I have,' said the Javan. He spoke quickly to Haji

Umar, and the old man, in response, offered a short prayer, hands held open in front of him, palms up. 'Please,' said the Javan, and indicated the loaded table. The *ibu*, all smiles, was removing the covers. The small boy brought in another platter loaded with the grilled skewers of meat, now covered with a rich peanut sauce.

'This is *sate kambing*,' said the Javan. 'Well, really it is *sate domba*, because there are few goats around here. But we don't generally call it that.'

The Australian laughed. 'A loser from one of the fights?'

'Oh no. This was a lamb slaughtered this morning. The rams are too tough.'

The woman had filled her plate, and waited until she saw Haji Umar similarly loaded, then took a chair next to him. The white knitted hat on his head was very finely crocheted, and she knew what it signified. After a few words she asked, 'When did you go on the *haj*?'

'*Dua tahun lalu*,' said the Haji, two years ago. He stripped some sate off a skewer. 'The oranges have been good to me.'

'Oranges?' she asked.

'Yes,' he said. 'The oranges provide the money for the pilgrimage to Mecca.' He curled his fist and pointed across the valley with his thumb. 'There. That is my orange grove.'

The woman looked and saw a neat stand of citrus trees. She looked around at the gathering, and saw where a couple of the other men also wore the white hats. Haji Umar saw her doing it. 'Yes, oranges,' he said. 'From rice and sheep,' and he held up a skewer, 'we live. To fulfill our devotion to Allah we grow oranges. Only they pay the millions of rupiah we need for the *haj*. I have been three times. *Allah akbar*.' God is great.

***

Magnet did not keep her course for a rendezvous with *Mowbullan* and *Ord* off Phuket. Two signals changed it all. The first was quite straightforward. '*Return to Fremantle with all speed. You will set your course for the Makassar Strait and will follow the sealane until you are south of Lombok. International chart markings for the sealane apply. Be aware that your passage may be contested. You will use force only in the need for self-defence. Repeat. For self-defence only. Acknowledge.*'

The second came as a result of Bluing and Dixon having to decide what to do with me. I had some definite ideas about this, and did not intend to get shunted back to Jakarta to watch it develop from a desk. *Open Seas* was the empty shell it always had been, and there was nothing I could do about it. But it was now urgent that I find out more about the Red Fleet, because if the closure had anything to do with PNG those thirty-seven ships had to be on the move. I spent an hour with Intelligence, but had to put up with listening to Edmonds whingeing for most of it about the monsoon coming in and satellite surveillance being of little use.

A more practical solution had me back in the air on a Mach 2 military flight over PNG to Manila, and a long-range helicopter hop to *Magnet*'s rear deck, which was now in the South China Sea. I felt that the Makassar Strait held the secret, and Dixon and Bluing had finally agreed to let me test the idea. So the second signal warned Leach I was coming. At least he had a grin on his face as I crawled out of the cockpit.

But so did most of the crew over the next day, tensions and expectations growing. This was the closest *Magnet* had ever come to battle-ready action-stations in her history, but she'd been training hard and the chance of a coming scrap was catalyst to a wide range of emotions in the crew. It put an enormous strain on Norman Leach. 'They expect me to get them through without a scratch.' He had no smile now, just an ever-increasing seriousness as the ship made her way south.

The funnelling of *Magnet* into the Makassar Strait squeezed the growing tension higher. The coast of Kalimantan to the west had been visible on the longer-range radar sweep for almost a day but it was when the northern arm of Sulawesi appeared on the screen to the east that the sense of the sealane began. To Indonesia, *Magnet* was now acting illegally. To a man, the crew wondered what the reaction would be.

It was probably a routine military transport flight from Manado to Surabaya via Balikpapan that first spotted us. Norman reasoned that a maritime patrol would be flying north-south. This plane had come out of the east, and without any deviation continued westwards. But within half an hour, two interceptors came streaking across the sky from the south - someone had scrambled the Makassarese 5 Squadron. They circled *Magnet* for ten minutes, and then one returned in the direction from which it had come. The second maintained a high-level watch, criss-crossing *Magnet*'s course.

Slightly to the north of Palu, the first sea-level contact was made. A fast patrol craft was observed leaving the same bay from which I'd made the first *Open Seas* trip, and setting course directly for *Magnet*. She made no attempt at interception but took up position a mile off *Magnet* to port, whippet to the greyhound. Lightly armed, she was no threat.

Several hours later and about one hundred nautical miles NW of Makassar the radar operator reported the first serious contact. 'Probably a frigate, sir. From the southwest.' Either on patrol or diverted from a course between the two naval yards of Surabaya and Makassar, there was little doubt she'd intercept us. Perhaps I'd even seen her on another screen some nights before. Norman switched on the broadcast system. 'This is where it begins. There are to be no mistakes. This is what you have trained for, and you will do your duty just as it is expected. I depend on you. Good luck.'

The frigate came within visual range half an hour later, running hard on a line that would cross *Magnet*'s starboard bow. Norman decided to stay on the bridge with the Officer-of-the-Watch and asked me to stay with him. To go to the Ops Centre at this point was to take a very pessimistic position. Signal lights ordering Magnet to heave to started flashing as she drew closer. 'No changes in course or speed, OOW.'

'Aye aye, sir.'

'Radio contact, sir. A message coming across. Channel's open.'

Norman picked up the microphone.

'Identify yourself, foreign ship,' said a voice. 'You are illegal entry Indonesian waters. You will stop, please.'

'This is a vessel of the Royal Australian Navy. We are transiting the Makassar Strait in accordance with the International Rules of the Sea. You are in danger of obstructing my passage. Remove yourself from my course. The Australian Government will not be liable for any damage suffered as a consequence of your actions in international waters. Out.'

It was a watershed in Norman's emotions, and a calm settled across his face. Positions had been declared. 'Watch him like a hawk, OOW. Let's not misinterpret bad seamanship as aggressiveness.'

'No, sir. Will you change course if necessary, sir?'

'Only if he plays the fool. And then only on my command.'

'Yes, sir.'

The Indonesian frigate showed no immediate intention of altering course, bow wave curling up in a great sweep of blue-black and white. There was considerable activity on her decks, where crew appeared to be running for their stations. Gun barrels which had been pointing to all points of the compass slowly began to notch down and forward.

I could see her clearly now. Not the one I had seen before. 'A junior ship, Norman. Not much of a threat, I think.'

'Good to know.'

But a junior ship bound directly on a collision course could still do a lot of damage. Did the other captain not realize it? Port or starboard? Would she go? Combined speeds were narrowing the gap at more than fifty knots and any contact at such speed would instantly be disastrous.

And in the same instant Norman had the insight I did. `Standard evasive action, OOW. *Now!*' A wedge of silence seemed to drive all other noises from the bridge and *Magnet* heeled to the sudden thrust of her rudder. Even as Norman gave his own command to go to starboard I'd known the Indonesian would turn to port, putting herself impossibly in our path, a course of destruction for us both. And she went to port even as I was thinking it. A silly blocking manoeuvre, made without any understanding of mass and momentum. Stand and deliver! A junior ship indeed. But in international waters we'd had no choice. Port had not been an option.

It was still going to be close. The heel brought *Magnet* directly across the other's bow, and the two ships were still closing almost as fast as before. Now it was just a question of whether we'd turned in time. At least it seemed that the other captain's reflexes were sufficiently quick for him to try and correct his blunder.

From the bridge, the sea between the two ships disappeared as the Indonesian vessel's waterline seemed to push all the water aside and climb over our bow. *Magnet* was still heeling, dropping herself towards the Indonesian ship, leaning over it. All movement on deck had stopped as the other crew watched, horrified, at the two thousand tons of steel falling onto them, careening over them. But it was the confluence of the two massive bow waves that fell on them, deflected by *Magnet*'s hull in its acute angle of heel. The Indonesian frigate's deck ran with water, her maindeck crew knocked flat.

There was no more than fifty feet between the two vessels' rails as we charged past. The screaming blast of *Magnet*'s horn must have penetrated every cavity of the Indonesian ship. Some of her upperdeck crew fell over in surprise. Norman had kept his eyes away from any sight of the officers on the other bridge, but now lifted them from the deckrail that I'd expected to see twist into impossible shapes, and settled them on the sea ahead.

`Thank you, OOW. Take your finger off. Return to our previous heading.'

The Officer-of-the-Watch grinned a little sheepishly. The foghorn had been his idea.

As the ship came back onto an even keel, Norman stepped out onto the flying bridge. The Indonesian frigate had cut her speed and was wearing around in a turn. But even though *Magnet*'s engines were no more than a low rumble, there was no chance she'd be caught by the smaller ship. But there was the question of face. Would the other captain feel that he'd been humiliated enough that he'd want to send a sterner message? `Captain to Ops Room. Watch for active weapons systems. Defensive measures only.' He hadn't needed to say it, as they'd probably been waiting for an Indonesian bow to climb out of the radarscope.

But it seemed that calm was to settle for a while, the Indonesian frigate settling on a position astern. The belch from her funnel indicated that it was taking full power to keep her within touch, but over the following hour she gradually dropped back.

As a visitor to the ship, I had no active role, and could not step into the shoes of one of the senior officers. It was Norman's crew, and for the sake of operational effectiveness I had to stay out of the way. It was an unspoken rule, even though I had the run of the ship. I was thankful I'd already got to know him during the ASEAN manoeuvres, as it reduced other tensions that could quite easily have arisen. Strangers on board could be a menace. So I'd stayed in a back corner of the bridge, watching and listening. But then I reminded Norman why I was here.

He grinned at me. 'Hadn't forgotten, Trevor. Captain to Ops Room. Watch for a trace of a large number of ships anchored to the northwest of Makassar.' Then he peered up through the bridge windows. 'What's happened to our aerial escort, OOW?'

'Disappeared after we kissed the frigate, sir.'

Norman raised his eyebrows at the imagery. 'Calm before the storm, I imagine. They'll soon be back in force. I have a feeling that our next encounter will not be so easy. Will they get here before dark? You have the bridge, OOW. Captain will be in the Ops Room.'

'Yes, sir.'

There was a period of peace, but the inevitable radar warning came, and the thunder of a low flying interceptor squadron rumbled through the bridge windows. Five aircraft flashed across the bows and arced into a soaring climb. The ascent had a fateful cast. Deceleration with increasing altitude, followed by death by gravity. At this point I couldn't read the intent. Would gravity bring death? Had it really been a killing run, I thought they'd have kept well down on the horizon. Norman had left me a command channel headset and I listened to the sounds of the Ops Room. 'Right, Number One. Let's give them a warning. Weapons lock on all five. I hope they'll think about it.'

They did not think about it for long. 'We are active target, Captain, bearing one-four-two.'

'How many?'

'Just one so far, sir. The leader it would appear.'

'One SAM only, armed please.'

'Armed, sir.'

But these warplanes were like marauding gulls in a feeding frenzy, and they did drop low, criss-crossing the sky at and just above the horizon. Apparently, they found sign of an exposed underbelly.

'Missile inbound, sir!'

'I was afraid of that. Aerial countermeasures please.'

And shortly after the blast of the chaff launcher, the missile exploded in midair.

Even though two other missiles attempted a penetration, Norman kept the SAM in its tube, and only the thunder of the chaff launcher continued to fill an evening sky. And finally full darkness saw the gulls return to their roost. The night skies grew silent, the radar screens less phosphorescent, *Magnet* dropped south past Makassar and approached the northern fringe of the Flores Sea, the Lombok Strait the tantalizing freedom beyond. The rumble of her turbines was the purring of a great cat.

'The eye of the hurricane, Trevor.'

We both knew it. Magnet was still to be tested, the afternoon's activities little more than a stretch. We had still not left the main naval base astern, Surabaya lying a few hundred miles to the southwest. The Indonesian frigate had been bound from there, and now *Magnet* was shortening the distance to a greater interception force. The waters were becoming more dangerous, not less, and there would not be the cover of darkness that had sent inexperienced night fighters back to Makassar. I was invited into the Ops Room, and while we scanned the radar log, dinner was brought and consumed. No sign of the Red Fleet, but we hadn't eliminated the possibility that it was still there, now perhaps shielded in a different anchorage.

Norman moved around the closed space of the Ops Room talking to each of his staff. Unlike the ships of old, where an encounter was fought from the bridge, modern warfare had changed that concept. The bridge was now little more than a steering and navigational platform. The Ops Room had become the cerebrum. But the captain's were its hemispheres, his staff its motor nervous system. This staff did all it could to ensure that the conscious process of command was uninterrupted. But the captain was its identity. And he was Australian. And that was why *Magnet* was here to the north of the Flores Sea. And, I thought, later tonight, or early tomorrow morning, perhaps at the bottom of it. The net would be closing. How big would the mesh be? Would *Magnet* be able to sunder the fabric?

Time to move. 'I have to go, Norman.'

'Yes. I think you do.'

We had to go in very low, below any radar band that might pick us up. It was going to take time to do what we had to do, and on our run back to the ship we'd be completely exposed, arse to land, open to anything they wanted to put up it. The pilot knew my thoughts. 'No worry at all, sir. Fifty feet.'

And at that height you could see every ripple, though the speed made it all a blur, and there was no time for sightseeing. I had about three hours of flying time, after which *Magnet* would be so far south that we might not make it. So we island-hopped toward the coast, watching for active radar, but not able to use ours. My eyes grew used to the nightglasses strapped to my helmet, my sight far more technicolour than my imagination ever made it.

We made Pulau Pasir in forty minutes, and then I knew I had a problem on my hands. For there was a single ship at anchor, a Kondor minesweeper by the look of it, no lights, no life. And nothing else. And if we hadn't met them steaming north, which there had been no reason to do, then they'd gone south and we were going to have to fly too close to Makassar for comfort to make the final check. A few more minutes in the vicinity told me we hadn't missed anything, so we turned south.

We came down over the salt pans and shrimp ponds almost directly into the naval base at rooftop height. One look was all we were going to get and we'd have about ten seconds in which to make it. The pilot had seen the layout before we'd left *Magnet*, and went even lower once the main pool opened before us, empty down the middle, leaving me to inspect the landward wharf where the main installations were.

Not a bloody thing. And on the other just a clapped-out patrol craft.

`Get us out of here fast.'

`My own thoughts, sir.'

But the flight back wasn't simple, still trying to watch the main channel south, and the back bearing for anything that a rudely-awakened port defence might want to send our way. There hadn't even been small arms fire while we were in the pool. The pilot caught a whisper of radar at one point, but there wasn't enough for anyone to have plotted a course, and as the sea's curvature and successive headlands dropped Makassar from sight behind us I thought there was a chance we might make it. Assuming we could find *Magnet*.

In the end we came upon her from the south, up her course, having used the coastline as much as we could, running parallel to the sealane and watching for any profile or phosphorescence that would speak to a major maritime movement. But the fleet was long gone, and we saw nothing but the occasional *pinisi*, either at anchor off a beach or on a slow course north. So we turned farther out to sea until we had *Magnet*'s path under us and went north ourselves. We found her in ten minutes.

`They won't let us go.' Apparently there had been some radio traffic from Canberra, where a very irate Indonesian Ambassador had been stopped from putting his pyjamas on. But it was what Norman said then that caught me.

`They mentioned *Magnet* by name?'

`Yes.'

`Then they've clearly been watching you all the time, probably since the manoeuvres. You didn't declare your identity this afternoon, and though it's probable they radioed your number back to Navy HQ, I don't think it would have made the Ambassador's desk in Canberra today.'

Norman was doubtful.

`Think it through, Norman. *Magnet* is the flagship of the West Ocean Fleet. Indonesian Naval Intelligence would watch you like a hawk wherever you went. Whatever you did, you'd have Canberra's full weight behind you. And you're worth two of any ship of theirs.'

`What are you saying?' But then I could see the same certainty forming in his mind.

`They closed the sealanes because of you. Either they wanted to keep you north, or else they were sure you'd make a run for it.'

`They want to sink us.'

`My oath, yes. They want you on the bottom.'

And that put a very different perspective on the game.

And now the eye was long gone. The hurricane was gathering in the dark, clouds of steel and shuttered flame simmering towards a boil. It would come soon. The archipelago seemed alive with the charge, flashes of lightning shooting across distant skies as if releasing an electrical imbalance from an approaching fleet.

`Radar contact forty miles SSW, Captain.' Certainty. There hadn't been any doubt. The gulls were back in the air.

Norman picked up the microphone. `This is the Captain. The skirmishes of yesterday were just that. The real trouble is now approaching from the west, and the air cover has found us. Within the hour it is likely that we shall be fully engaged. Please make your personal preparations now. You have trained with me for years for a moment like this. I put my faith in your having learnt all the lessons we have been through together. I will do my best to meet a like faith. I pray that we will breakfast together in the morning. God be with you.' Then, `Number One, the signal to Canberra. Nothing else. They know where we are.'

Magnet was running hard. Her Achilles heel was her position, still too far northeast of Bali to escape the tongue of naval defence lapping eastwards from Java. She was going to run into a wall. She could not leave the sealane to find refuge and escape in the myriad sea alleys to the east. A deviation of yards into Indonesian waters would bring lawful retribution. At least, in their current frame of mind. *Magnet*'s single defence was the open sea ahead. But it was hundreds of miles and a day away. Beyond the gathering wall.

`Several ships, sir.' The First Officer's words were imbued with a solemnity befitting a priest.

`Cheer up, Number One. Good odds, I'd say. You saw them in the Natuna's. What marks did you give them for strategy?'

`There wasn't much. We knew that beforehand.'

`And what do you think they're going to do now?'

The intermittent contact that the helicopter-borne radar gave us showed three frigates in line astern on an interception of our course. They would have no trouble beating *Magnet* to the killing ground. Much would depend on how they worked together to saturate that ground with gunfire and missiles.

`If they've any sense, sir, they'll stay to the west. They'll close with us by steaming southeast on parallel courses a few miles apart. Any closer together and they risk hitting each other. And we couldn't miss. If one crosses our course to come at us from the east he puts himself at risk from his own side.'

`Submarines?'

`If there's one there, she'll take the east.'

Norman nodded. `Yes, I think so too. She'd be our main problem. They'd want to run us right onto her. The frigates'll stay in their own waters to make sure we don't scatter them. It's going to be a hard run right through the middle, pure and simple. Get the helicopter down there looking for her.'

`Do you think there is one?' I stuck my nose in briefly.

`If we're meant to go to the bottom and this has been planned that far in advance, I'd say the *demonstration* we were given of engine trouble in the Natuna's was just that. *Cakra* is probably out there ahead of us somewhere.' Then he looked at me. `Sly bastard.'

`Just checking.' But I couldn't keep the grin off my face.

Sub or no sub, no doubt remained about what lay ahead. Or what *Magnet* had to do. Each moment would be an opportunity. There was little point in dwelling on what the odds were that we would get through it alive, or on a moment of self-pity for a tomorrow that might not come. It was now pure duty in front of us. Time seemed increasingly linear at such moments.

`At what point do we return fire, Captain?'

Norman spoke generally to the men hidden behind flame hoods at the different stations around him. `We will only return fire when our opponents present themselves to us within the sealane. As long as they stay outside it we will not touch them. If we wish to return their fire, therefore, we shall have to entice them to forget their own rules. But until they do so, you will operate solely in defence. I hope that is understood.' There was a general acknowledgement of his command.

`Make sure there is not an instant's lag in the surface picture. I want to know *the second* they are in *our* waters.' All present noted the extra emphasis on *our* and there was no doubt it gave them a slight measure of relief. They could sense an attack taking shape in their captain's mind. His words seemed less bleak.

But there was really no attack, just defence. It would be a simple question of how long *Magnet* could withstand the weight of electronically-guided hardware that would be thrown at her. Her countermeasures had to cause sufficient havoc among Indonesian instrumentation that much of the hardware missed. It might come down to some simple gunnery in the end.

`Pour some more coffee, Number One. Don't want you nodding off at a critical moment.'

`I'll go to the bridge, Norman. I'm in your way here.'

There was method in my madness. The Ops Room would soon become a place of utter concentration where any word from me could break it drastically. If I was to contribute anything, it needed to be from where I could think alone, away from instruments. I had to be able to think about Subagio. So I found my small corner of the bridge where the more natural rhythms of Officer-of-the-Watch and helmsman took away the Ops Room oppression.

For this was Subagio, I was certain of that. It had taken on more and more of his style. Strategic planning, oil and cold killing. He'd been laughing at me every time I'd met him, I was sure of it, probably because of what was going on under my nose. He probably had tried to kill me through a *KOPASSUS* contact, but then I'd finessed him completely, giving myself a visibility that could not be cut off with a bullet. That would have brought all sorts of unwanted attention.

So what was the game? I didn't think I was wrong in what I'd told Dixon and Bluing. An armada off on a secret task, an expeditionary force to PNG. But was there a broader why? I could only think of the succession theory, a senior Minister laying the groundwork for control of the increasingly massive unrest from ongoing economic problems and grinding poverty. But I still couldn't see how access to PNG offered the opportunities millions would require to nip civil unrest in the rapidly-opening bud. And one couldn't only do it with ships. There had to be an equivalent ground force.

I thought the decision to send a junior frigate northeast to patrol the Makassar Strait had been quickly done, without actual intent to stop *Magnet* there. A smaller vessel, she would not have matched us in a duel. And it was unlikely that Jakarta expected *Magnet* to answer immediately with fire. No, she'd been a spotter, with a captain given to foolish heroics.

But it would be the heavyweights that were now on an interception course. About ten thousand tonnes of heavily armed and armoured warships, a total displacement against which *Magnet* would be no match. It would be only skill and speed that would get her through. And I could imagine Subagio's words ringing in the Eastern Fleet Commander's ears, for it would be him bringing that death. `You're the crab, *Laksamana* Wartono. I've given you claws big enough to crush him. Do it. You'll face a firing squad if he gets away.'

The danger for *Magnet* was inversely proportional to the distance that the Indonesian squadron decided to close. At sixty miles we had ample warning of missile attacks. At fifteen miles we were out of accurate range of any heavy gun. Between the two missile attacks were more serious. Below fifteen miles gunnery became a serious threat. *Magnet* would face both forms of attack. And might have to deal with a submarine, though the helicopter crew had not yet found one.

But Norman was thinking ahead. `Weapons Officer, we'll give any submarine something to think about. Rear-deck depth charge crew should be ready for intermittent drops on command. Think of it as an acoustic threat. It's the one thing we *can* throw at them without fear of hitting them. It may keep a submarine at some distance.'

I was watching the assembling trap on a surface picture screen on the bridge, driven by the compiler in the Ops Room. The ships had deployed as the First Officer had thought, and the screen showed no other ships closing. That would be the danger of decreasing speed. That there were other warships on the way. Norman could not afford to hang back, and I heard him call the Engineering Officer. `Can we get any more speed?' Speed would be a problem for the Indonesian gunners.

`We're running at rated maximum, sir. If we wish to sustain speed for a long period, I'd advise against anything higher.'

`And for a shorter period?'

`You might get a knot or two extra, sir. Hull speed.'

`When I call down, take her as high as you can. There is absolutely no point to sparing the machinery.'

'Understood, sir.'

The surface picture blinked, and, suddenly, the sealane was added. *Magnet* looked like a ghost ship heading into a rainbow carnage.

'Follow your eastern line, Number One. Let's see if we can draw them in.'

For the next two hours *Magnet* ran south at almost thirty knots. She hugged the eastern fringe of the sealane, making it look as though it were a normal course. The Indonesian ships were still in territorial waters, beyond the western limit.

The first incoming missile was picked up almost simultaneously with an aerial radar contact. The interceptors were coming back. But this wasn't the Makassarese squadron. This one was coming from Java, probably night-trained, and Norman saw the opportunity opening to him. 'Weapons Officer, any aircraft over the international corridor using active radar may be shot down. Standard countermeasures for the sea-to-sea missiles.'

The interceptor squadron may not have been expecting such an instantaneous response. But they made the mistake of running towards *Magnet* directly along her course from the south and that put them into Norman's own killing ground. Countering missiles were streaking from *Magnet* the instant her fire control crew received confirmation that *Magnet* had been made an active target. The instant reversal of roles from hunter to hunted brought disarray as the fighters split into the night. The missiles followed. Fire traced the night as two planes exploded.

But *Magnet* was now fighting for her own life. Scorching flame from the countermeasure defences marked the launch of decoys. The skies flashed with the explosion of two air-to-sea missiles among centroid chaff, and a brilliant tower of flame that stretched into the overhead cloud of the horizon marked the rocket destruction of the first incoming heavy missile from the Indonesian fleet.

The planes regrouped into two smaller flights, and took successive runs at *Magnet*. Her own rules of engagement allowed only the gradual whittling down of this force, and they became more canny, using the horizon to better advantage. Yet the next half hour saw three more planes gone, and only a single aircraft missile strike. The rocket had slipped through a chink in *Magnet'*s electronic armour, slicing into the bow plating just below the deck, leaving a jagged hole. Norman sent a party forward to report on the damage.

'The bow's sound, sir. It was the chain locker that took it. Starboard anchor's gone.'

'Thank you, Chief. We won't be needing it.'

It became clear that the Indonesians were launching their sea-to-sea missiles one at a time, waiting to see the outcome of each launch before deciding on another, and this made *Magnet'*s defence far easier than expected. However, each frigate probably carried up to eight long-range missiles capable of severely crippling or killing us. The game could go on for a long time.

`Time,' said Norman, ` for a diversion. Fire first depth charge. And change course to two-two-oh. Let's have them on the nose.'

Magnet was now within thirty miles of the Indonesian squadron and her course change would have her heading directly for it. It should make them wonder. And did *they* know precisely where any of their submarines was? There certainly wasn't one anywhere near where *Magnet*'s depth charge had gone down, and the helicopter sonar crew still did not have a fix.

Norman decided to try and split the squadron. Its course to the south east had brought it quite close to the edge of the sealane, and the lead ship would be on its boundary within half an hour. Perhaps she could be catalysed into imprudence.

He rang the engine room. `Whatever you can give me. Now.'

Within half a minute there was an increase in frequency of the vibrations running through the frigate. There was a slight lift to her bow as her counter sank into the deeper trough astern. Not visible in the night, it was evident underfoot, and I leant slightly forward.

`Log reading?' Norman asked.

`Thirty-one knots, sir'

Well, it was something. Perhaps more would come slowly. But, at hull speed, *Magnet* would be burning fuel at an incredible rate to sustain it.

`Another depth charge please.'

I stepped onto the flying bridge to watch the phosphorescence as the sea lifted above the explosion.

I had a quandary of my own. There was a good chance I'd go to the bottom before *Magnet* if the Flores Sea claimed her, and I had no doubt that the casualty bill would be high even if she survived. But I had some unfinished business to attend to, the small matter of the Red Fleet, and I was wondering how the hell I was going to be able to get back to land and keep ahead of a plan that seemed intended to bottle us up completely until the endgame was played.

It took about thirty minutes to consider what I had to do, and then about ten to decide on the how. But while much of the how would be decided elsewhere, with a very large element of luck thrown in, part of it involved a coded signal to the Embassy.

Not surprised to hear, finally, that there was a submarine in the water against him, Norman *was* surprised to hear of the submarine's change of course before any other. He'd said he felt sure it would be the last card played against him. But he had faith in his helicopter crew, and the passive sonar trace showed it moving directly west towards the squadron. In five minutes it would be in the sealane. A bonus where none had been sought.

Magnet's log had crept up to thirty-two knots, and the thrumming vibrations from her engine room were charging through the ship. The contracting positions of the ships on the surface picture proved that she was throwing herself into gunnery range, but her course reduced the profile being presented to the gunners and the rapidly changing range might reduce the immediate chance of a direct hit. But it was only a matter of time.

`First light of dawn, sir,' said the Officer-of-the-Watch, beside me on the bridge.

Norman had no window to look through. But I was surprised to see a touch of dawn in the sky to the east. The night was almost gone. I'd not expected it to end.

`The lead frigate is changing course, sir.'

It became clear that the Indonesian Commander did not like what *Magnet* was doing. He must have expected her to maintain a southerly course, and now instead of sailing past him it looked as if she was going to pass astern. It forced a course change.

Would it be soon enough? The squadron was very close and ought to have been almost visible in the aquamarine dawn, but I couldn't see it. I didn't think that would last long. It was the turn of the guns.

`Time to enter sealane?'

`One and five minutes respectively for the submarine and the lead ship, sir.' God, it was going to be close.

`Hard aport. New course one-three-five.' Right at the submarine.

But I wasn't given time to dwell further on Norman's words. The first shells screamed overhead to plunge into the sea astern.

`Submarine now, sir.'

`Fire torpedoes one and two. Second pair in one minute. And advise the helicopter crew.'

The first hit landed on the rear deck. It blasted most of the depth charges out of their racks, and brought a sympathetic explosion of one or more of the devices in the air over the rear-deck crew. I doubted we'd find any trace of them. *Magnet* shook to the impact.

`Damage check engine room please.'

`Second pair of torpedoes away, sir.'

`Lead vessel's entry time?'

`Crossing in thirty seconds, sir.'

`One Harpoon. And continuous fire main gun. On my command.'

`Fire.'

The command had almost been whispered. But the streak of the Harpoon's launch and the instant thunder of the main gun gave lie to its weight. The gun continued to pump in an aortic rhythm as shells were lifted automatically from the deep magazine.

Magnet detected an Indonesian missile launch, but a malfunctioning trigger in the countermeasures system left her wide open and the missile was still accelerating when it slammed into the aft superstructure. Only *Magnet*'s course and speed prevented the impact from happening further forward. The explosion opened the ship to the engine room, the funnel and upperdeck aft of the main gun obliterated, and *Magnet* shuddered with the blast and then staggered as power ran down. Her momentum kept her moving forward, but it would not be long before she lay to only whatever revolutions the damaged turbines could still put out. I wondered whether there was still a crew to operate them.

But Norman hadn't stopped thinking. `Another Harpoon please. Same target. Now.'

And then I had the lead Indonesian ship full in my optics, having followed the gunflashes back into the dawning sea. I saw the gunshell explosion at the base of the radar tower, probably cutting both defence and forward fire control systems, and I thought she lay even more exposed than did *Magnet*. But then that was irrelevant, as our missile hit the hull directly amidships. The force of the impact and the simultaneous explosion flashed forward into the ship, and then upwards, as the far side of the hull contained the blast. Everyone on the bridge must have been incinerated as it melted under them.

But I was just contemplating the consequences of that inferno when the second Harpoon struck. The frigate's weakened frames gave way completely to the new assault, and in less than a minute she folded slowly across the breadth of her keel. Her bow rose in the air to meet the stern as she went under, the water a vicious maelstrom around her.

Ten knots was the most a severely disabled *Magnet* was going to give. The surface picture showed the disappearance of the lead ship, but I gave it scant attention. It was the two remaining ships that worried me. How would they react to their loss?

`Torpedoes approaching target, sir.'

It had almost been easy to forget about the submarine, torpedoes now finding a homing contact in deceptively calm waters. She'd not even been a menace. But she had to be dead in the water or else *Magnet* was finished. She could not outrun a submarine in this state. I looked out over her shattered bow, still not believing I'd lived through the dawn on *Magnet*'s bridge.

But better still, far to the east, I saw the sea climb in majestic geysers, liquid Ionic columns. The rising sun caught the shattered droplets and cast immobile spectra, but their intensity faded as the water spread and then drifted away in clouds devoid of their violent birth. In their place I saw *Magnet*'s helicopter, a drunken dragonfly of a craft, fluttering its way across the foaming sea. Its crew had been essential to the killing of the submarine, the *coup de grâce* of a laterally-aimed torpedo, but there was now nowhere for it to land in the wreckage of the rear deck. It took station to port, keeping to *Magnet*'s speed, waiting for an opportunity to lift another torpedo and head back into the fray, or to ditch in a final act of defiance as its fuel ran out.

I closed my eyes for a moment, thinking that there was now a better chance that we'd escape, though it had taken a great deal of death to buy that chance.

Norman's voice came quietly back over the headset. `Position of the remaining two ships, Number One?'

I did what the First Officer would be doing and turned to check the plot. They were still outside the sealane, safe from *Magnet*, untouchable. But her ten knots placed *Magnet* easily within their grasp, could do little but goad them into retribution. We'd be pounded into the sea. It was no escape.

But death doesn't necessarily come the way it is expected, nor to those who've lost hope, and I was untouched by the searing mayhem of the shell that obliterated the rear firewall of the Ops Room. I became more optimistic, too, that most of the others had survived, hearing the spluttering figures under their flame hoods through the command line, still glued to whatever console had escaped the blast.

But the First Officer's shout broke it all, `Captain Gregory, sir!' and I went stumbling back into the wreckage. Daylight filtered through the smoke, fire evident at some positions, ignored by a ship's Ops Staff trained to work till the last utter moment. A fire-crew arrived behind me.

It was Norman who was no longer there. At least, not his head in its fire-retarding cowl. An incandescent metal shard had bounced off something in its path and sliced cleanly through his neck. The body had slumped to the floor and was pumping life itself all over the First Officer's feet. One arm had flown up, as if to shield the absent eyes, but presenting only the gold bars on the shoulder boards in final salute.

The head, a foot away, peered at the deck.

Eighteen

Initially, Amin felt a deep concern for the electronics. Each corvette now carried sophisticated weapons systems, and he was unsure of the reliability of the fire-control mechanisms. But, as the reports came in from each corvette commander, he was surprised to find that there were hardly any problems to resolve. And there was little trouble from his Bugis seamen, adapting well to their positions and responding quickly to orders. His nightly coded signals to me, essential input to our calculations, recognized the well-trained fighting force that was growing out of the daily intensive exercises practised as the fleet worked its way to its rendezvous with the LCTs.

And I could read into these transmissions the extension of himself that the fleet represented to Amin. Later, when I saw him, he said that there was a sensory aspect, reinforced through the electromagnetic linkages between the ships, that increased his own energy level. It was as if he were bleeding power from a much larger being. Each ship was a finger-tip, to be put on the chart precisely where he wanted it. So at that point he took them ESE across the Flores Sea, picking up the occasional trace of the LCTs as they too slid southwards. The monsoon built in intensity.

Excerpted from Rusman Soekendro, LetJen (ret'd),
No Game At All: Memoirs of a Strategist

The village guests were gone. They were still on the patio, glasses of tea long drunk. The feeling was one of peace, and the woman saw that they were being deliberately taken along a path which would bring them to whatever state of grace the Javan intended. She turned to look at him, beginning to smile as she did so, and found that he had anticipated her. He was looking at her, an intense expression on his face, one which suggested he was recalling certain events. 'In fact, and with no lack of respect to your husband, you were the greater worry.'

The continuation of the discussion that had ended the day before, as if that moment were only seconds ago, suggested to her that time, in this place, was anything but linear.

The Australian snorted. 'Another subroutine? Called Webb?'

'No,' the Javan replied. 'We understood completely that Mrs Gregory had been given certain responsibilities.' He paused. 'Again, meaning no disrespect, *your* activities tended to intrude into our plans like sudden spikes of electricity, or shocks. You,' he said to the woman, 'were, after all, the daughter of your father. And the *Jenderal* had known your father well, had spent many hours arguing policy with him.'

'I had forgotten it at the time,' said the woman. 'It only came back to me later.'

The Australian smiled grimly. "I remember that. It came as quite a surprise.'

'It must have done,' said the Javan. 'In fact, they had both, on one occasion, argued through what the *Jenderal* later decided had to be done. At that time more the why, than the means, because then neither considered it to be feasible. It was just an idea, a romance.'

'It did, in the end, lose its romance,' said the Australian.

'Of course it did,' said the Javan. 'Stark reality carries with it very little of that nature.'

***

Jack had not expected to see me. The Government immediately released its version of the violence in the Flores Sea to the Indonesian media, and he'd imagined I'd be the first on the plane after the official expulsion, *persona non grata* until eternity. He was quite shocked when I slipped in through his back door.

But neither had I expected to see Jack. The moments after Norman's death passed like years in my mind, the drawn out agony of the loss of a friend, and there was the high probability of a second shell coming in after the first, now that they'd got the range. I was in the awkward position of being the senior officer on board a ship where I had no right of command. But I could not deny the responsibility the First Officer had earned, whatever the note in his first cry to me, and I made him see me step back from any gesture of taking over. Besides, I had a different fish to fry, worked out in the moments before we found the submarine.

Norman's death did not buy us peace. The firefight continued, though the feared accuracy was not there, perhaps because of the smokescreen we laid, perhaps because with their lead ship gone they were less watchful of their own positions and hesitantly followed. It was their mistake, because it put them where Norman had wanted them all along, and it allowed *Magnet*'s crew to vent ice-cold anger over the loss of its captain. The First Officer placed three Harpoons very carefully in the maelstrom of shellfire thundering from the west, causing serious damage to at least one of the pursuers. At that point they wore away from us, and left *Magnet* to limp south in the unearthly silence of limpid seas.

The helicopter bore away from *Magnet*, ahead of the blanket of smoke that trailed her, not all from canisters filled in some ordnance depot in Sydney. It was a calculated risk, one hurriedly discussed with the First Officer, who had a long butcher's bill taking most of his attention, and worries about renewed engagements before reaching open seas, the rest. I was in his way, but I had to make it clear that the potential loss of his smaller helicopter was a price necessary to get me back onto the trail I had to follow. I made him privy to the final conclusion Norman and I had come to, why they'd sent the hounds of hell to kill him, and that finally persuaded him to give me the one piece of untouched hardware. Like its larger brother, it had been in the submarine hunt, sitting off during the final fury, and we managed to bring it onto a small part of the ruptured foredeck to top up the fuel.

It was still early morning, trouble really, because it meant I had to move during daylight, but Bali was visible to the west, where a foreigner could move fairly easily, and a hub for travel elsewhere. So I'd shed my uniform and found some clothes that wouldn't differentiate me from a Sydney pub-crawler intent on trawling the main street of Kuta. And then I was back in the cockpit for the second time in twelve hours.

I fell out of it somewhere to the east of Singaraja. Only into reasonably shallow water at low speed, but enough to raise a welt on my back from the impact. The hunt for a deserted beach had been fast, too many with small settlements back among the palms, but this was the north coast, away from the more densely populated areas of the tourist-driven south, and we found what I needed just as I started to get desperate. I waded ashore, untying my thongs from around my neck, and wandered up into the vegetation in the direction of the coast road. The morning heat had me partially dry within fifteen minutes, and within another ten I was picked up by the morning bus to Denpasar.

'It sounds as though we just fought the Battle of the River Plate off the coast of Lombok.'

By the time he got over his surprise that I'd come in on the afternoon flight to Makassar, we'd sunk the first beer and were into the second.

'It was just that, except we ran the blockade. One frigate against three of theirs. And a submarine. Canberra decided to contest the closure of the sealanes. The ship got through, but seriously damaged. And she sank the sub and a frigate.'

`And a few planes, I think.' he grinned at my apparent sole focus on the sea. `A regular dingo's breakfast.' But he knew it was no joke and turned serious. `Anything to do with what you were after last time?'

`That's my worry. *Magnet* passed within miles of where I'd seen the greatest concentration of upgraded hardware in the southern hemisphere. But it wasn't there, and it was the regulars from Surabaya that they sent after her. I have to find out where the other ships have gone.'

`And why.'

`Exactly.'

`And what do you want me to do? You didn't come here for a warm bed.'

`I hoped you'd let me have Ahmed for a day. I need him to go back up the coast.'

He thought for a moment.` Wait a minute,' and he went to the back door and called out. A young man came to the door, and I heard Jack tell him to go and find Ahmed and bring him back tonight. The young man disappeared. Jack brought back two more beers.

`Does Jakarta know what you're up to?'

`The Embassy hasn't heard from me since I left *Magnet*. I can't afford to let them know - they may want me out before I cause diplomatic havoc. But I do have to get some sort of signal out to Canberra, and it has to be untraceable. Once someone in Jakarta twigs to the fact I'm still around, it's probable that they'll go to some lengths to find me.'

`Concoct me a signal. I'll code it into my buyer's report.'

I must have looked blank for a moment.

`It's a good time to buy cocoa right now. Farmers want to unload it so that they can purchase seed and fertilizer for the rice crop. We're buying nearly every day. I send out an electronic report every day or so. Head office hedges against some of the risk. Messages are coming in and out all the time. I can hide yours inside.'

That was the only relief of the day. Because even before he'd opened the first beer I'd asked *Have you heard from Anne?* No, he'd replied. `Cocoa. Well, I'll think of something.'

It was a full twenty-four hours before Ahmed reappeared at Jack's back door for the second time in two days. He settled into one of the rattan chairs on the verandah, his bare splayed feet caressing the worn floor tiles. `*Selamat malam, tuan.*' As the day before, his greeting was warm, product of a shared past adventure.

He began to describe his activities, starting with the course he had taken back up the coast. It had been a quiet night with nothing other than the occasional fishing boat on the water. I hadn't gone with him because we had decided that he would do better by himself, so he hadn't had to avoid the lights strung on the fishing platforms, and a following tide brought him quickly to Pulau Pasir. It was instantly clear to him that the anchorages we'd visited before were now empty. He had only found one ship at an anchorage away from the groups we had closed on. After he was sure that there was no-one on board he had made a quick reconnaisance himself. `Mati,' he said, dead, implying that the ship had no life left.

He then described his visits to some of the fishing platforms, made casually but with care, cigarettes shared, fish examined, questions slowly getting round to the warships, answers noted.`Pulang minggu lalu, tuan,' he said, left for home last week. `Semua pada malam yang sama.' All on the same night.

I wondered if he'd made a mistake. `You're absolutely sure? Not at different times?' For all the ships to have weighed anchor simultaneously spoke of crew training beyond normal practice. And they'd been gone longer than I'd thought.

`Saya tentu, tuan,' I'm sure.

`I'm thinking that home is just an assumption, given that the ships had come from somewhere,' said Jack. He asked Ahmed a couple of questions, did anyone know where home was, where the crews had come from?

Ahmed grinned his pleasure. He seemed to have anticipated the need for this information, and described the extra labour that the navy had to hire to set up the anchorage and service the ships at anchor. Some of the men had come from one of the offshore islands where a brother lived, and he'd turned up there shortly after dawn and had shared breakfast with his brother and his family. He'd stayed most of the morning and in the course of time one or two of the visitors who came to his brother's house turned out to have been temporary workers. They'd run a victualling service to the ships. A lot of rice and dry goods. Enough food for many weeks. Even talk of roti, bread.

`And the crews?' Jack was getting a little impatient.

Ahmed bobbed his head. From Java. At least the officers and senior ratings were. Some sort of sealift vessel had shown up at the anchorages late one afternoon with all of them on board. Many ordinary seamen turned out to be from Sulawesi. It seemed that several months ago the navy had gone on a rush recruiting drive in some of the sea communities over on the eastern arm of the southern province. It had been an area impoverished by drought and poor fishing, and a series of disasters had lost them most of their traditional commercial tonnage. An agreement had been made with the regent of that area, the bupati, to conscript some of the experienced seamen into crews. No-one had demurred at silence being a requirement for badly-needed employment. The seamen had come in on another lift, from a training camp somewhere up the coast.

And the ships had gone south. It had taken them a couple of days to shake down into operating crews while still at anchor. On the third day, they had started the engines and run some final tests. They'd weighed anchor and set off, in line astern, having put well out from land first. They'd gone as they'd come. Silently. And at night. Therefore, they must have gone home.

And that's the problem, I thought. They had no home.

Sleep would not come. I lay staring at the silhouette of the mosquito net against the slowly revolving ceiling fan. Jack and I had stayed talking for an hour after Ahmed went. I'd thanked him for his efforts, and he'd left with the quiet slap of his bare feet against the garden path.

I'd not hidden anything from Jack. There was no reason to, and I owed him something for Ahmed's help. I talked openly about twenty-four harrowing hours and the death of Norman Leach, one death among many. Jack listened to my turmoil. At the end I'd said `There's something missing, of course. The fleet is cover. Protection. There still has to be another group of vessels out there to carry the primary threat. The East German tank-landing ships wouldn't be enough. I saw what appeared to be the obvious choice that time when I was picked up by the Army. Landing craft, new. I think they were probably ferrocement. They didn't have the hard-chined look of a typical steel hull.'

Jack looked thoughtful. `We've used one of those now and again to bring a load of cocoa across from the south-east province. Tried again a week or so ago, as a matter of fact, but was told that it was unavailable and that we'd have to go back to trucking it across on the ferry. I think perhaps I'll make a couple of phone calls in the morning. They're built near here.'

The fan slapped the night air. Beyond the immediate concern lay the deeper one, Anne. I thought wryly of the stereotyped Aussie male, unerringly rational in his thoughts, unfeelingly stable in his emotions, giving a damn about very little. For the first time in my life I was far from all three. A phone call had gone unanswered. Where was she?

`I think I have someone for you to talk to.' Jack was eating his way through a pile of freshly peeled pomelo. The large grapefruit-like segments were heaped in a pink mound on a plate in the centre of the table. A jug of fresh Torajan coffee steamed into the early rays of the sun.

My mouth was full, so I raised my eyebrows.

`I was on the phone to my local agent before you surfaced. When I mentioned that I thought it increasingly strange that we couldn't get the vessels we'd been using, he said that it was happening across the island. That it was now known that some thirty had been withdrawn from Sulawesi alone.'

`Thirty? How many have been built?' I suddenly had a hollow feeling in my belly. This sounded like an extension of the nightmare.

`That's what I don't know. But my agent said that the principal builder and licensee is PT Pinisi Semen. It's a state-owned enterprise right next to the naval yard here.'

`Licensee?'

`Yeah. Apparently the design is an American one, and the local builder makes them under licence. There's an American engineer on site to watch that the specs are followed. He's the one I think you should talk to.'

`Can you drop me there?'

`As soon as our secretary confirms that he's there. But you can't go barging in there as the missing attaché from Jakarta - alarm bells would be ringing within minutes. The place is run by civil servants. You'd better be a cocoa merchant. Start thinking and talking like one.'

`Grows on trees, doesn't it?'

`Right. On small ones, generally in the shade of bigger ones. But you'd be better off talking about some mythical expansion of our direct buying program from isolated communities around the coast. You've got to have a reason for wanting something as particular as this. Perhaps say the company brought you in as a consulting specialist in marine transportation. Not really far from the truth is it?' Jack grinned. `I think I've seen this American around town. He looks a surly number. You'll want to be careful with him.'

I nodded, recognizing the truth in his words. I couldn't afford to make an elemental mistake and blow my cover so soon in the game. I poured myself a cup of the coffee and buried my nose in its fragrance.

It was ten o'clock before a confirmation came back from the shipbuilders that the American engineer had arrived. Jack took me into the company office with him, dressed in new clothes, and introduced me to his associates. Touring, but an expert in marine transportation. Thought it was a good idea to review the company's own transportation policy with him. Taking a quick look at the economics. You never know, it could even save us money.

211

A couple of the associates were happy to talk of their work. It was evident that cocoa had become increasingly important, but there were many problems, not the least of which was collecting the crop for international shipment. There was a fermentation and maturation process as the cocoa bean dried. Moulds were a problem. Local transportation was a critical need in the runup to the monsoon rains. The government was complimented for having thought of building craft that could run right up to the beach in isolated areas. But it seemed that the government needed the same craft for a while. They'd had to go back to traditional shipping for transportation. The warehouse was filling at half the rate of before. But it was out of their hands.

Jack ran me down to the seafront, and we were waved through the gates without any difficult questions. He found the engineering office and dropped me outside. `I won't stay. Better that only you be identified personally with this if it should ever get out. I will explain my end away only if I need to.'

`Thanks.'

`Good luck.' He backed his landcruiser around and set off towards the gates. With him he had my first message. A futures contract for thirty-seven tonnes of cocoa in Dixon's name. Bought by his agent Chant. If he couldn't work that one out when the confirmation was phoned through to him, I might just as well take up monastic song myself.

Immediately inside the door of the office was a model of the landing craft I'd seen before. I was looking at it when a slim, middle-aged Indonesian came through one of the interior doors.

`*Selamat siang. Tuan* Trevor?'

I nodded. Jack had reversed my names once again.

`My name is Yusuf. I'm the Associate Engineer here. This,' he pointed at the model, `is what PT Pinisi Semen is famous for. Well, actually, it's the only ship we build at the moment, though we are trying to diversify. We are negotiating through our American partner to obtain the rights to another design.'

`Also ferrocement?'

`Yes, *tuan*. We can only build in ferrocement. Steel shipbuilding has to be done elsewhere.' Yusuf stood looking at the model for a moment then collected himself. `*Maaf, tuan*. Please excuse me. Sometimes my soul wanders into that little ship. It embodies so much of the past few years of my life.'

`You've built many of them.'

`Yes, *tuan*. Almost twenty have come out of this yard. We launched the first one a little over three years ago. We've put in a second construction slip, and can complete a vessel in an average of two months. We rotate construction crews between the two slips so that no crew lies idle. When the steel core has been laid for one vessel, the crew moves to the next slip, where the concrete and interior work has been completed and the vessel has been launched. Then they start all over again.'

`It sounds very efficient. You install the engine before launch?'

`Not now, *tuan*. We did in the first ones, but then Jakarta decided to speed up delivery time. The engine is installed at the wharf. It saves a few days of slip time.'

`And you say you've built about twenty of them?'

`Yes, *tuan*.'

`I thought somebody had said to me recently that there were quite a few more than that operating around Sulawesi.'

Yusuf looked chagrined. `Ah, *tuan*, the Government decided that we should not have a monopoly on these vessels anymore. We now train others in the building techniques, and they go and build the same elsewhere. I ...'

An inner office door burst open and a large, pallid-faced man came out. `Are you lookin' for me? The name's Slater. Yusuf, you go and do somethin' useful. You must be Trevor. What d'you want?'

I nodded at the model. `Yusuf was just describing the building program to me.'

`Hell, I can do that. Yusuf get your skinny ass down to the slip. Don't need two of us standing around. Come on in to the office. Got a chair you can sit on.' He swung around and went back into his office.

Yusuf excused himself politely and went out through the main door. I looked at Slater's retreating back for a moment and then followed. The stale smell of sweat went ahead of me.

`Greatest little vessel to be built in ferrocement.' Slater was talking even before he sat down. `Shallow draught, functional. Carries a shit-load of anything, anywhere you want to take it.'

`Seaworthy? Has it been tested in rough weather?'

`Hell, it's basically a concrete bathtub. Wouldn't get you through a typhoon. But why're you asking?' His yellow-toothed leer sprang across the desk.

Would Jack's story hold? I wondered. It would be better to stick to it. `We're considering buying a couple outright to avoid the leasing problems we've been having in the coastal cocoa trade. Transportation is our biggest problem.'

Slater nodded shrewdly. `Lots of money in coastal commodity trading. Lumber'd pay it off quicker, but you'd be greasing palms from here to Manado. We can't sell you one, of course. Not this year, anyway. Nor can anyone else. Jakarta's got first call. I reckon there's two a month been coming off beaches around Sulawesi - you don't need to build them on slips like we do here. From at least five builders.'

`But why would Jakarta want them?'

Slater cackled. `You tell me.' He leant forward over the desk in conspiratorial friendliness. `I seen what's happened when they've left the yard. Anything from here slips in next door.' He cocked a thumb over his shoulder. `Navy gives them a look over before they're classed seaworthy.'

I shrugged. `Seems reasonable.'

His face became even more hyena-like. `Fairies tell me the crews are theirs.'

I worked my way through his assertion. `Naval ratings?'

`That's what I said.'

`Just yours or everyone's?'

`The whole bunch, mister.'

`Just a program to ensure that they are operated as designed?' It would not be unreasonable to want to train new operators on the job.

`Fuck off. Why create excuses for them? They want to keep the vessels under their control.'

`And who is `they'?'

`Their toy-boat navy, who'd you think?' This came with a blast of foul breath, dumped on the desk in an explosion of frustration. Slater was clearly an unhappy man.

`Does it matter to you?'

`Shit, I couldn't give a damn.' His body actions suggested something quite different. But he went on. `Mister, I been here three years now, and two more months sees me outa here. Back to the good old US of A. They can all fuckin' sink for all I care.' He slammed back in his chair, nodding his head as if he'd made the decision that they would.

I pitied Yusuf, who'd had to put up with this for so long. `Perhaps the Indonesians look at it differently. Anything functional in this country can generate considerable wealth. Perhaps the navy needs to boost its operating budget.'

Slater leered at me again. `So what? The whole military's a conglomerate. Sealift Command is into big business. That's what all this is about.' And he poked a thumb over his shoulder at the construction outside. `So I don't think you'll be getting your LCTs any while soon.'

I'd considered asking Slater to show me around the slips where construction was still going on, but the combination of his overweening attitude and halitosis was finally too much. I left his office and walked towards the slip, without saying where I was going. If he saw me and wished to follow, so be it. I betted that I'd not see him again.

Yusuf was in the first slip talking with some of the construction team. The hull was a spider's-web of reinforcing rod, and welded mesh was being tied to the metal frame. There were already several layers tied on, and some men were trimming ties on one area of the hull where it was ready for the mortar mixture that would give it its solid form. This was still the steelworking crew, however, and there was no sign of any plasterers getting ready for their task.

Yusuf noticed me standing at the side of the slip and came over. `Almost ready for the next stage, *tuan*. Can I add anything to what *pak* Slater said?' His voice was bereft of any ingenuousness.

`No. But you were going to say something just as *pak* Slater came in. What was it?'

Yusuf thought a moment. `Probably just something about our training program.'

`Is the navy directly involved?'

`In the training?'

`No. In the commissioning of the vessels, and their subsequent use.'

`Why, yes, *tuan*. PT Pinisi is owned by the navy. Didn't you know?'

`No, *pak* Slater didn't tell me. He was more interested in conspiratorial rumours.'

Yusuf laughed. `Yes, our American friend is most happy when he's creating trouble. I learned his ways long ago.'

I realized that my pity for Yusuf was misplaced. The man had apparently overcome whatever unpleasantness his working association with Slater had brought. There was no subservience in him.

`So if the navy owns PT Pinisi, it also holds the licence on any other copy built elsewhere in the country.'

Yusuf looked at me with large eyes. `Ah, *tuan*.' He sounded reproachful, as if wondering why I was asking such questions. `The navy owns all the others. They are built on sub-contract. As long as the design fee is paid, *pak* Slater and his American company are satisfied. Of course, *pak* Slater would have to spend a lot of time travelling the coast to be sure just how many have been built and to be sure that the right number of fees have been paid. But *pak* Slater does not like to travel, and we are but a poor country. Why should Indonesia do his work for him?'

There was a hint of guile in his last comments and I saw that Slater had been sidelined by this man in front of me. Or rather that Slater had sidelined himself by his attitudes and approach. The Indonesians had no intention of going all the way to meet the spirit of the agreement if it meant doing Slater's job for him. And because money was involved, even less so.

`Do you know, *pak* Yusuf, how many licence fees the navy really owes the Americans?' It was a roundabout way of asking how many boats had been built, but seemed better suited to the sense of intrigue that spanned the couple of feet between us.

Yusuf looked at me askance again. But then he gave a slight smile. `Perhaps sixty, *tuan*. But then perhaps more.'

`But if the vessels are no longer in local waters the Americans will never find out, will they?'

`Precisely, *tuan*. Though why that information should interest the *tuan* I do not know.'

`Just wondering, *pak* Yusuf, why I can't get hold of a couple for my company. It just seems to me that they were really built for another purpose. If they were for trade I should have no difficulty.'

He shrugged non-commitally. `I'm sorry I can't help you, *tuan*.'

`And there's probably no point in talking to anyone in the navy itself.' I made it a statement.

`The man is no longer around, *tuan*.'

`You mean that there was a navy agent here overseeing all this?' I waved a hand in the general direction of the construction work.

`Unofficially, *tuan*. But he has been around less in the last six months or so. He had some other vessels to repair.'

A light came on in my mind. `Naval vessels here in Makassar?' I tried to stay relaxed.

Yussuf nodded. `The navy has been very busy here lately. There was much activity just up the coast. This officer was responsible there. He had to borrow our work crews on occasion for some of the steel work.'

`Perhaps if I go around to the naval yard they can put me in touch with him?'

`Perhaps, *tuan*. But as I said, I believe he has gone.'

`Could you give me his name, *pak* Yusuf, just in case I can find him?' But I knew what was coming before I asked the question.

`It will be a useless exercise, *tuan*. But he is from this region so they may put you in contact with him. A very clever man. A *Letnan Kolonel*. His name is Aminuddin.'

I was too preoccupied with my thoughts to pay attention to anything else. I heard a noise in the kitchen, and called out. `The pigeons have flown the bloody coop.' I leant on Jack's dining room table looking at the large chart of the Flores Sea I'd left there before going into town. 'I believed in the one but couldn't find the other. They are both part and parcel of the same bloody scheme. It's obvious, and I knew it had to be there, but I couldn't see it.'

Arms stole around my neck and that wonderful familiar scent of floral perfume filled my senses. 'Which pigeons, honey?'

I sagged back against her in relief, though, still perhaps doubting it was her, peered back over my shoulder. 'Where the bloody hell have you been?'

Anne laughed. 'Such a touching welcome. How long ago did you send that signal to your Embassy?'

I turned, and took her into my arms. 'Let's see.' I used my fingers to count against her back. 'A frigate, a sub and a helicopter ago. Three days? Four?' I couldn't seem to remember. 'What it actually said was: *Under attack, cast web, durian season in Makassar.*'

'Really? How did Celia work that out, then?'

'By the smell, I'd think.'

'But durians aren't fishy.'

'Let's leave it there, shall we? I needed you here, Celia knows me well enough to read between lines, and told you something you'd *eventually* understand. I couldn't have you rushing out and buying a first-class ticket to Makassar on Garuda.'

'But I went to Balikpapan.'

'And what did you find there?'

'I think everyone had gone underground. Nobody where they were supposed to be, anyway.'

'An active cell.'

'I think so.'

I said: 'The first time I came out here I saw a landing craft putting out from the naval dockyard. It didn't make any particular impression other than I remember thinking that it looked recently built.'

'Then I saw some again off the coast down in the south-east when *KOPASSUS* picked me up. Training exercises. An old man told me how the navy kept requisitioning the craft whenever they wanted them. I looked but didn't listen. Or think. Only when I started tracking the East German fleet did I start to worry.'

'Now, I find that the officer who masterminded the rapid refit of those ships was also overseeing the LCT building program. Under these conditions, it's almost inconceivable that one man could do both. But the LCT program started a few years ago. It's running itself now, so he was able to put all his energy into refitting the corvettes. And he could call on his workcrews from the LCTs to do some of the steelwork.'

`You got all this from the Yank?' Jack looked sheepishly at Anne. 'Sorry.'

I explained to Anne what I'd done during the morning. "A compatriot of yours, beyond hope of social redemption, I think, and only possessed of some subconscious understanding that there's something going on around him. No, it was his counterpart engineer. I got him alone, later, down at the slip, where they're putting one of these things together. He didn't say much, but what he did say left me no doubt. And what clinches it is the fact that the officer is the one that confronted me on the beach west of Raha. I knew he was in a position of authority, but I little guessed then that he was also the driving force. He and I had a little talk during the ASEAN exercises. Aminuddin.' I rolled the name around with my tongue.

`Where is he now?'

`That's what I'd give anything to know. Not only do I suspect that he's slipped port with the ships, I also think that he's got several dozen LCTs in line astern.'

`So what is it?' Jack finally looked shaken.

`An invasion force. Papua New Guinea. I think they want the rest of the archipelago.'

Nineteen

And we knew now there'd be three expeditionary forces, Topan, the storm, to Petir's lightning, and Elang, the hawk that came in after. Amin would have command of Elang. On the Jenderal's orders I would stay to run the system from Roti.

Excerpted from Rusman Soekendro, LetJen (ret'd),
No Game At All: *Memoirs of a Strategist*

In what way specifically did I worry you?' the woman asked.

'What would you guess to be the reason?' returned the Javan, perhaps wishing to avoid offering an affront.

She thought she knew very clearly, but as she wasn't prepared, at this moment, to state it baldly, she thought an initial dissemblance might be useful. 'My knowledge of the culture, the language, even the history?'

The Javan smiled, suggesting he knew very well that she was waiting for his admittance of the reason. But he could be equally crafty. 'Yes, of course, all of those. But...... anything else?'

'Well,' she said, knowing there was no escape, 'my studies, then.'

'Ah,' said the Javan, as if he were surprised, 'those.' He offered a brief laugh. 'It would be hard to compare any of your other understanding of our people,' and he moved a finger in a small circle, to emphasize the smaller Indonesia, and the Javanese, rather than wider cultural vista of the archipelago, 'wouldn't it, with what you wrote in your thesis?'

The woman smiled, but said nothing. After all, it was the Javan's view that was important, not hers. She had dealt adequately with the latter in what she'd written.

'You were your father's daughter,' he said. 'But even he had never showed your insight into the implications of Islamic militancy on Java's political evolution. *You*,' he emphasized, 'absorbed Islam almost from birth. He saw it from the perspective of a western scholar. There is a huge difference.'

***

The transition from night- to morning-garden was not yet complete. Colours were still emerging from the tones of grey, the faint rays of the morning sun just flickering through the humid air and stroking whatever lay in their path. As this one, a dawn-garden was always muted, and soft, whereas a full morning-garden carried the harshness of the direct strength of that sun.

'In the West we want to put labels on everything,' Anne said. 'We see a label as giving something substance. Though too often we're lazy and we forget to define the label. The consequence is that multiple perceptions give rise to multiple meanings.' She poked some fruit about on her plate. ' "Taliban", for instance. To nearly all Americans, "Taliban" means a Muslim sect slightly more extreme than most, conservative, rigid, but with the hatred for the West they see in all Muslims. Taliban actually means "student", and more specifically, students of a fundamentalist vision of Islam taught in Pakistani religious schools. Nearly all the precepts held by the Taliban are in direct opposition to the teachings of the Quran. The Taliban's downfall may be to protect Al Qaeda from what it sees as religious persecution from Christian America. Like all Muslims they don't separate religion from politics. Had they given up Osama bin Laden as the conspiring murderer he was, rather than shielded him as a holy warrior, they'd be in power in perhaps more than Afghanistan today.'

Jack's marmalade cat, relict of many holy wars of its own, lay on the patio in the early sun, trying to undo some of the damage inflicted on an already shredded ear. He was totally absorbed in the repetitive motions of licking a paw and dragging it over his head.

'Does America see itself as a Christian state?' asked Jack. He stuck a toe out to poke the cat, provoking a playful swipe but a vengeful claw. 'Hell,' he swore. 'What did you do that for?'

I laughed. 'Just putting you in your place. Feed me or leave me alone.'

'Only semi-secular, perhaps,' said Anne, moving on to some toast. 'The Christian Right supporters of the Republicans certainly don't separate church from state, and most Republican policy bows to their tune. Hawkish on the Middle East, and clear the West Bank for the second coming.'

'Say that again?' said Jack, still rubbing his toe.

'Much of the money flowing into Israel to support its struggle against the Palestinian intifada is coming from the Christian Right, not American Jews.'

Jack's mouth dropped in surprise. 'That's not only semi-circular, it's bloody opaque,' he said. 'I'd never have thought it. What do the Israelis say about it?'

'They laugh it off. Why should they care? Jesus did start out as a Jew, after all.'

I thought we'd moved off the more important subject. 'And Balikpapan?'

'The first time I spent the whole day with my University friend, exploring the fundamentalist strains beginning to show up in Indonesian Islam. Especially outside Java. Much of it is driven by poverty - the Christian West is rich, the Muslim world is poor, a very black and white vision. The problem is that Indonesian male youth craves for all the trappings of an affluent adolescence, and it is easy for spiritual messages to get lost in market rhetoric. When you realize that there are about fifty million of them in a population four times that size, you begin to understand the magnitude of the problem.'

'And the second?' I asked.

Anne didn't respond immediately Then 'I don't like what I see. Radical madrassas, particularly.'

'When I first came it was a quieter Islam,' Jack said. 'Then the Saudis began pouring money in to finance the construction of mosques. Indonesia is now practically an Islamic state. But I don't think the broad religious message has kept up with all the massive social changes.'

'Islam is a more personal form of worship than Christianity. Perhaps that makes it harder to transmit the Quran in a modern idiom.' Anne saw me studying her. 'What are you thinking about?'

'I'm thinking about a profusion of local splinter groups, all quite un-Islamic if what you say is true, yet the Government is turning a blind eye to the anti-Christian rhetoric. Why? It's not as if there aren't any Christians in the upper echelons of Government.'

'They keep very quiet,' said Anne. 'And they are a small minority. For what my two cents are worth, there is a vision in a certain section of Government which requires a broad radicalization of Indonesian Islam in order to move forward in the regional power structure. Suharto unknowingly started this when he became leader of the non-aligned movement - Indonesia became more visible as the largest Muslim population in the world. But that only went so far, and it was only when his power slipped that he had to add the main Muslim party to his power base.'

'This still isn't enough.' I was thinking about my immediate problem. 'Yes, there's a lot in what you say. But this business of roping northern Australia into some sort of Islamic superstate. That's a lot of nonsense. The place is bloody inhospitable and full of snakes. No, I admit I've been lulled by *Open Seas* into thinking we had a new partnership. That was wrong. But was it a diversion? That's what I don't know. There certainly is a large amount of hardware unaccounted for and I'm bloody well going to find it. I think it's going east. Papua New Guinea is nothing in anybody's Islamic vision, so I think religion has nothing to do with it.'

Anne gave a slight shrug. 'Quite apart from what the West believes, it would be very difficult for something like Al Qaeda to go to ground here. Almost all Indonesian cultures are very sensitive to outsiders, and rumours of a strange presence move very quickly.' She saw me about to add a comment. 'But, that doesn't mean the thread of an idea couldn't take hold and the same reaction not be evident. The Bali bombing showed that.'

'So what was *Open Seas*?' I asked. 'Or perhaps the question is: What was the Alumina Queen? Were they one and the same? Or did one get built on the shape of the other?'

'Trevor, honey,' said Anne, in a thoughtful tone which I thought was likely the harbinger of an unpleasant insight, 'what else have you been involved in of late?'

'Me? Well, the Natunas. If you don't count either Muna or *Magnet*, of course.'

'Mmm. What if almost all of those were not isolated events, but an orchestrated strategy?'

'That's a bit daft, isn't it? I landed on things in Muna quite by chance. The Natunas, well those were ASEAN wargames. We were just there as observers. *Magnet?* Yes, I grant you there was an element of cunning in that. *Open Seas?* Not sure about that. It's the one that bothers me.' But I remembered saying *what if?* to Harry Grant, and thought that I couldn't even have come close to that outcome. 'Are you saying someone's probably a lot more interested in my present whereabouts than I believe they are?'

'I'd say you're probably the Aussie wild card right now. So we'd better make sure you continue to stay that way. My second visit to Balikpapan is unimportant.'

'To me, perhaps. To your people, perhaps not.'

'That's why I'm going'.

Jack was growing unhappier by the minute. "It makes you want to drink beer for breakfast.'

I could hear the rain hammering the fuselage as the plane descended through the clouds. Lateral gusts buffeted it, increasing the general unease apparent in the passengers. An identical plane had flipped on attempting to land in the rain at the same airport some time before, but even if the passengers didn't remember the event they were still unnerved by the penetrating and frequent sound of warning hooters perfectly audible through the open cockpit door. The windshield wipers were ridiculously ineffective under the torrents that lashed the plane's nose.

Anne's hand gripped my arm. I kept my vision fixed on the grey light that seeped through the cockpit windows. It flickered as the density of the clouds changed, the only slightly soothing aspect of the descent. I kept my mind elsewhere, on the task in hand, to block out the broader panic that was building around me. One elderly woman began to moan to herself, in counterpoint to the drone of turbines.

A sudden vicious lurch dumped the plane out of the base of the cloud, bringing several screams and one stream of vomit. Unexpectedly, there were some flashes of sunlight as the plane passed under one of the very few clear patches of sky, and then it flew back into a torrential downpour, though now there was some forward visibility and the altitude was low enough for whitecaps to be visible on the sea beneath.

In response to the warning gong a stewardess, white-faced with her own fear and belted into her seat, grabbed the telephone set on the wall above her head and started to gabble the landing instructions into it, but they were inaudible in the main cabin. The plane banked suddenly as the pilot made a corrective action, and went into a steeper descent, shuddering against the outside forces. Then it seemed to swoop forward, and I caught a flash of the landing guide lights, now a blazing red, through the cockpit window. The touchdown was almost anticlimactic, though would have raised some complaints under better flying conditions.

Anne let out a sigh of relief. I let my mind come slowly back to the present. The repetitive thump of the landing gear on irregularities in the runway wormed its way into my thoughts as if heralding the new course of action that we'd just begun.

Jack had left us at the airport for the mid-morning flight. Given that we had little chance of finding out much more in Makassar, and an unknown chance of finding out the fleet's destination. I'd decided on a quick run through the major ports further to the east, finishing up with a cross-border hop from West Papua into Papua New Guinea, ahead of the invasion force itself. Then I'd get down to Canberra and into whatever roasting was coming. I didn't look beyond that. I left Jack my second message for Dixon. *Expect to contact seller Flores or further east. Believe final harvest substantially bigger. Could be extra sixty tonnes in simultaneous delivery. All illicit, repeat illicit. No eyes. Short contracts carry extra penalty. Chant.* If Dixon couldn't work out that there were sixty LCTs somewhere near thirty-seven other ships, time critically short, he'd need help better help than Edmonds to do it for him.

'I'm coming with you,' Anne had said. I'd looked at her and nodded. I'd wanted her in Makassar for her insights, and it was no time to pretend I was better at this game than she was. She also had a direct link to very high places, and I thought that might carry extra importance when the time came.

Ambon has a particularly unpleasant reputation in modern Indonesian history as a repository for political prisoners. Far from Jakarta, and before jet travel, people languished unseen for decades, the solitude of distance and less-than-pleasant living conditions the punishment for errant behaviour during the political minefields of the 60s. I sensed it now, in a much more modern context, where religious intolerance was creating different solitudes. But mine was also a solitude of ignorance, born of a break in the marshalling of knowledge from the past months. No longer was information accumulating at the rate it had before.

During my in-flight abstraction I'd pondered two things. If my guess was right, there had to be some significant troop movements underway. That meant staff officers also travelling in numbers. The other was how to find out where the fleet was headed. I could do that in one of two ways. Try to follow it, or backtrack from where I thought it might be headed. Given that I'd lost the trail in Makassar, finding it again could prove difficult. But after I'd told Jack about PNG, a quick look at a map of the area where I was heading only held a single possibility for its destination. If it wasn't there, or nearby, my whole hypothesis was wrong. So Ambon was my waypoint.

The run-down of the turbines brought me out of my trance. Once the crush to disembark had eased, I pulled our bags out of the overhead locker and we followed the last few passengers into the arrival hall. We avoided the press of excited spectators greeting the new arrivals and went directly to the taxi stand. Within a minute we'd made an arrangement with a taxi driver to take us around the local hotels until we found one to our liking.

After three hotels I was beginning to feel hungry. Each had been a typical small Indonesian provincial establishment, more guesthouse than hotel. We'd made enquiries as to rates and vacancies. All had a room available, and I'd asked to see each one. Desk boys had led us through corridors and patios to rooms in question, but I'd turned each one down, giving reasons that would not cause offence.

The taxi driver found us somewhere reasonably clean to eat, and we took a corner table, ordering food and drink from the menu painted on the wall.

'So,' said Anne. 'Is the hypothesis wrong?'

As I sipped my tea, I thought back to the hotels. 'We can't say that yet.' I'd based my analysis on expecting to find significant occupancy of each place. The best way to judge that was to see how many people were sitting around. Hardly any Indonesian hotel lacked a pair of easy chairs and a coffee table outside each room. Occupants would spend hours seated there, smoking and talking, and drinking the occasional coffee, rather than sit in a stuffy, cramped room hardly bigger than the beds it contained. 'This is where we should be able to spot what we're looking for. It's smaller than Makassar and still on route to where I think we need to be going. You can't get there directly - the flight schedules don't allow it.' It was a long bet, but there was none better that I could currently think of.

'All the occupants we've seen have been commercial travellers or medium-level civil servants,' said Anne. I nodded. There'd been none of the fitter, more prosperous-looking staff officers that would be following, or leading, a major troop shift halfway across the country. These men would stay in the type of hotel we'd visited, and the corridors would be full of the sense of their presence. We might even have the fortune to trip over a pair of highly polished shoes, even if the owner had stripped down to a singlet over his uniform trousers. But there'd been none. And there hadn't been one on the plane. Nor had there been a military transport on the airport apron.

We worked slowly through our lunch. 'Perhaps,' said Anne, 'the immediate flaw in the strategy is the time of day. Perhaps such officers, if they were in travel, would be elsewhere at present.'

I shrugged. 'I'm still worried about the broader assumptions. But let's say you're right. The hotels weren't full, so perhaps they'll arrive later. We've got little alternative anyway but to keep on looking.' Then a thought occurred to me. 'Hang on.' I went out and woke the taxi driver. 'How many flights a day come into Ambon?'

'Three, *tuan*.'

'What time is the last?'

'Five o'clock, *tuan*.'

I went back to our table. 'There are two more flights due. What do you say to another couple of hours of the same, and then head out to the airport to plane-watch?'

The driver tired of our seeming dislike of the rooms we saw over the following two hours. And as we did have to find somewhere to stay for the night we chose one that looked very much like most of the others we'd seen that day. I paid him off, and, as he drove away, we dumped our bags in our room and immediately went to the front desk to order a different taxi.

Within half an hour we were back at the airport. Groups of people were standing around in expectations of another arrival, but I saw no-one in uniform. There was no military transport of any sort in the parking lot.

By the time the last plane had landed and disgorged its passengers, I was feeling quite discouraged. But perhaps I'd been expecting too much. We watched the final few passengers leave the airport, and then took another taxi back into town.

Dinner that night was a quiet meal in a small sea-front *warung*, a palm-thatched, bamboo shelter at the top of a beach. Shrimp, fresh out of the sea and barbecued, sauteed green *kangkung* and steaming white rice. The only lights were the flickering mantles of a couple of hissing pressure lamps. The small boy who served us couldn't keep his eyes from Anne, more than once almost missing the table with the current delivery. 'You have a conquest,' I said.

'I'd noticed,' she said, and when he came back the next time, asked him some questions about his family and his school. That time he went away with a huge grin across his little face, though I thought he caught a cuff across the ear from an older sister, who looked as though she was chastising him for wasting time.

'So,' Anne said, 'you'd like a few of those?'

'More shrimp?' I asked, obtusely. 'No, I think we have enough.'

'No, honey. Those,' and she pointed at the little boy, kicking me under the table at the same moment.

I looked at her through the moving shadows cast by the lamps. An off-shore breeze sifted through the warung, rustling the palm thatch. She felt totally at home in this environment, and as I poured a little more beer in her glass I wanted to share with her every possible moment life would give me. I looked at the little boy. 'A couple of each, perhaps?' I said. 'But I don't know you well enough yet.'

'Trevor!' Anne laughed. 'You know every bit of me very well indeed.'

I shook my head. 'No. The outside bit is easy. I need to burrow deeper.'

She looked at me very seriously. 'Under my skin?'

'All the way to the middle.'

We made love that night very slowly, long minutes of touching and tasting. After, Anne snuggled against me, tongue playing with my neck. A hand rubbed my belly in long circular sweeps. 'A couple of each. I think I could manage that.'

I stroked her hair. 'When this is over.'

She was silent a moment. 'Yes. When this is over.'

She fell asleep before me, and I knew from her shivers and whimpers that she was somewhere where the time still wasn't right.

Over next morning's coffee we discussed the day ahead. I still believed in my theory and thought it fair to give us another chance, which meant delaying onward travel another twenty-four hours. I gave the desk-clerk our tickets and asked him to make the change.

As a result of Indonesian geomorphology, few coastlines have high cliffs directly against the shore. There was another taxi waiting outside the hotel, so I told the driver to take us somewhere where we could have a good view of the sea from a high place. But I was surprised when he stopped - he'd found a vantage point that was better than I'd expected. The old volcanic cone was irregular, and we were on a small tableland out to one side. I sat looking at the sea for a moment, and then pulled my binoculars out of my bag and walked along a seaward track. The hope that something would spring into view was as faint as that of my hunt of the day before, but it was better than sitting in the hotel waiting for the first incoming flight of the day to prod us into going to the airport. The rain had stopped the night before, and the air was fresh. The first riffles of the day's onshore breeze brushed my face as I started a visual traverse across the expanse below.

The heat haze had not yet built to the point where the horizon became indistinguishable. Small fishing canoes were visible at various distances from the shore, and a *rompon*, a large double-hulled fishing platform driven by a combination of sail and outboard motors, was making its way back into port after a night's work. A tramp steamer looked as though it would slice it in half as it approached from behind, but that was just the foreshortening effect of the lenses. There was a good mile between the two craft.

The closer waters showed nothing of interest. There wasn't even a regular naval patrol craft moored at the wharf. I looked toward more distant waters in the west. My theory required that my quarry be coming from there. But I had no more than twenty miles of visibility, and it was a miniscule arc in a very large sea.

And there was nothing. Or nothing that I recognized. I'd half hoped to see a pair of corvettes steaming for an anchorage in the bay below. But that was as ridiculous as hoping I'd find a *KOPASSUS* regiment bivouacked in an Ambon hotel. I started to worry about my grip on reality, wondering whether what was becoming an obsession was popping images in front of my eyes. For there was no corvette. But there was a landing ship. Not one I'd seen before, but a landing ship nonetheless. Anne must have noticed my pause. 'What is it? What can you see?'

'A landing ship. Big one. About twelve miles out.'

It was a long shape squat in the water, making very slow way diagonally across my field of view, with a probable landfall not far to the east of town. It was too far out to be able to distinguish much beyond its silhouette, but its bow carved a gentle delta in the smooth morning sea.

The new vessel, apparently a tank landing ship, was considerably bigger than my quarry, the LCTs. It was possible that it was heading for the port area, and if so, it would have to change course. But if it were heading further to the east, it would be arriving at an open beach.

I remained glue to my binoculars. 'Can you get the city map?'

I heard Anne head for the taxi, and then some seconds later: 'Here.'

The map showed no installations that far east, so it would pay to go and investigate. But that it would mean we'd miss the first arriving flight of the day. The tank lander, an LST, was heavily loaded. What was it carrying? Where was its destination? They were questions as important as any of the others, and of one in particular. Was this a military sealift that fortune wished me to pursue?

We had some time in hand, so went back to the hotel. As we ordered coffee, I realized that the presence of the tank lander was at least a hard fact that I could investigate. The other avenue was still a supposition, and it might not bear any fruit. But we did have an option. 'Can we split up for a couple of hours? You go out to the airport, and I'll catch up with you in a couple of hours? I need to satisfy my curiosity down at the shore.'

Anne nodded. 'Sure.'

'I'll be there for lunch.'

The decision made, I picked up yesterday's paper, left on our table. *'President unwell?'* ran the Indonesian headline. *'Not seen for days.'* Further down the page something else caught my attention. *'What are Australian intentions in Papua? Not only goats crossing our borders.'* The article went on to complain about Australian accusations of Indonesian inaccuracy in border delineation. *'We have never worried about the border before - we knew where it was. Why should Australia wish us to delineate it if not for the sole purpose of crossing it?'* They did it in Timor, the article stated, backhanding our own efforts to stabilize the region. *'They warn of border clashes, then provoke them.'* It was a bitter diatribe, but I was learning that our logic was not necessarily their's. Black and white are only two of the many shades of grey. I showed it to Anne. 'Is this part of the answer?'

'It's not the first time I've seen this reported,' she said. 'But it does look as though they're taking a harder line.'

Walking out of the lobby, I took a taxi for the harbour front. But there was no immediate evidence of the LST once I got there. I could see the arc of sea it must have crossed, if it had held the same course. A few canoes being tossed around on the developing chop were all that filled my field of view, so the glasses went back in my bag.

The town slowly trickled away into slum housing and small roadside businesses as the road ran further to the east. Handcarts and *bejaks* competed with heavier motorized traffic for the narrow right of way, and the driver started to make frequent use of his horn, to no noticeable effect. The sea was sometimes visible beyond household gardens and small coconut groves. An occasional lane ran down to the shore between groups of houses.

After a few minutes I told the driver to take the next lane. The town seemed as if it would never end, and there was the probability that we'd would overshoot what I was looking for. The car turned onto the dirt track dividing two small timber yards and bumped down towards the shore. The driver stopped before reaching the fringe of coconut palms, and I got out, bag in hand.

The glare off the sea was strong, and the heat was hardly mitigated by the breeze that was slowly building up. Storm clouds were forming massive crests, but there were still broad expanses of blue sky, and the rain would not come for a few hours yet. I walked onto sand that was already baking underfoot.

We hadn't passed it. The LST lay belching smoke about three hundred yards further to the east, and about half a mile from shore. She was still under way, a light wave curling from an ugly bow, but speed had been reduced to about half a knot. She had the look of a cripple, and a small launch was being slung over the port side.

I went back under the trees and sat in the shade, watching the launch speed towards the shore. The LST crawled slowly forward, and then settled to the anchor that rattled slowly into the water about two hundred yards out.

Her high sides prevented me from seeing what was on board. Her displacement suggested that it was a heavy cargo, which ruled out a transhipment of troops. I was puzzled by the choice of anchorage, given that there was no wharf or on-shore installation that could service the vessel, but if her condition turned out to be fact, and the ship really did have some sort of mechanical problem, it was possible that this was as much as the captain dared. One didn't drive a crippled vessel into the midst of other shipping. Her funnel continued to belch gouts of black smoke.

I watched for almost an hour. The shore party disappeared through the trees, and only a few faces moved about the ship. The tail being emitted by the funnel slowly decreased in thickness, and it appeared that she was to stay a while.

I found Anne sitting on a bench outside the arrivals hall, leafing through an Indonesian magazine. She gave me a smile when she saw me, and then a slight shake of her head. 'Nothing to report, boss.'

I bent over to give her upturned face a kiss. 'Me neither, really. The ship's at anchor, east of town.'

We tested the airport canteen's *gado-gado*, finding it a shadow of the Javanese version, and watched the second plane arrive, refuel and depart without leaving anyone of interest. Two young soldiers were among the passengers, but they had the manner of men on leave. They walked away from the airport, looking for cheaper transport on the main road outside, and I did not get close enough to them to read their insignia. But their berets were not the red ones that would tell me I was on the right track.

The afternoon passed slowly, the airport settling into a lull as porters and airline staff disappeared behind closed doors or stretched out on the few available chairs. We stayed in the small canteen, and I nursed a beer that very quickly became lukewarm. A pile of newspapers was delivered to the newstand outside, and I went out to get one.

'Food poisoning fells President.' The headline ran the width of the front page. *'Resting comfortably, full recovery expected soon.'* The medical bulletin was given military provenance, the Surgeon General in attendance. *'Bordering on obsession,'* ran a subordinate article. *'Australia rejects Indonesia's proposals.'* I read on, thinking it very unlikely that any Aussie broadsheet would carry this perspective. *'Aggression; impunity,'* were part of the interpretation. I remembered an earlier Indonesian Defence Minister describing the vanity of the UN: *It does not take blame.* In Timor, by extension, neither did we.

I replaced the unfinished beer with a coffee, and as I bought us a couple of rolls to go with it, the first crash of thunder of the day filled the airport building. The change in the weather seemed to bring people out of their sloth, recumbent forms starting to move, and the odd face peering out of an opened door. The first vehicle drove up and delivered passengers to the departure hall, and a porter scrambled to his feet to collect the luggage.

The weather slowly deteriorated over the next hour, and it began to look even worse than the day before. But airline staff continued to check in the departing passengers, and an air of expectation built gradually. The roof hummed to the torrent of water falling on it, downspouts spitting solid streams several feet beyond the building's perimeter.

The plane had already passed the terminal building on its touchdown run before anyone was aware of the sound of its arrival, but there was a general mutter of relief from those hoping to get out.

We had a good view of the arrivals hall from our corner of the canteen so decided to stay where we were, but even before the plane had reappeared from the end of the runway I heard the arrival of several vehicles on the far side of the hall. I stood to see better what the disturbance was. A military staff car with an escort of three landcruisers had pulled up outside the VIP lounge entrance, and two officers were making their way in, shielded from the rain by umbrellas held by adjutants. Guards took up position under the extended eaves.

I stepped back from the window, gesturing to Anne. 'Military,' I said. But coming or going? I thought coming, as the two officers did not look senior enough to warrant use of the VIP lounge nor an escort the size of the one outside in the rain. The sound of the plane's turbines cut through my thoughts, so I turned to watch its arrival on the terminal apron.

Even before the gangway had been wheeled to the forward door, a military welcoming party had formed at its base. It followed the gangway forward, every umbrella spouting rivulets of water onto each of its companions.

The forward door opened as the port turbine ran down. Several uniformed figures came down the gangway shielded by umbrellas held by attentive cabin staff. The party swelled to about a dozen, quickly making its way back to the VIP lounge.

So an arrival it was, but now I had a problem. I'd been expecting middle rankers, those that passed the orders on rather than gave them. High-ranking officers would not stay in hotels like mine, but high-rankers they had to be and it looked as though we'd lose the only possible lead we had. 'Can you watch from here?' I asked Anne. She nodded, so I gestured my intention and went out into the main arrivals area, slowly making my way across to a point where I was close to the VIP lounge door. I kept a thin screen of humanity in front of me until I found a pillar to give me partial cover. I'd only just got there when the lounge doors opened and an advance party came out walking to the staff car still in position outside. Umbrellas at the ready, the escort stiffened to attention as the emerging party came out in two groups.

There was nothing wrong with my hearing, but all sound went in a split second. That moment took me away from the grief of the Flores Sea, and the fat slug of a Yank who'd sat on his arse talking about military acquisition without recognizing it happening right at his door, and threw me back into the middle of the game, whatever it was, for some reason being played out right here and now. For while I first saw one of the officers in the first party with his back to me giving a series of orders to a second party paying close attention, the other two officers of the first party, one considerably younger than the other, were looking through and beyond me in the manner of most arrivals at an airport. I didn't have to see the red berets that mattered. *KOPASSUS.* I didn't need berets or caps for these two, young Lieutenant Soekendro and his mentor General Ars Bulyanto. These two *were* *KOPASSUS.*

Soekendro's eyes flickered over me as they'd flicker through any airport crowd, but just as I thought it impossible that he recognize me, my attention suddenly shifted back to the officer with his back to me. I recognized him more from his attitude than his form, and that shock did make me step back behind the pillar. Then he finished speaking and gave me a clear view of his profile. What was *he* doing wearing battledress? The face was one I was never likely to forget, and it changed all the dimensions of my hunt. For it was Subagio. Not an army man, but a navy one. And the one that had the answers I wanted.

The three of them climbed into the car and shot away with one of the escort vehicles in tow before I'd come to terms with the change in circumstances. And I now knew I had to focus on a man rather than a fleet. Or, perhaps, men. But what the hell was Subagio doing here?

The second party, by this time, was climbing into one of the escort vehicles, but a couple of orderlies passed me on their way into the baggage room. Nothing had yet appeared, and it looked as though the baggage handlers were working as slowly as they could, sheltered under the plane's wings. The orderlies began to make a fuss at the baggage desk, and one of them then went out to the plane accompanied by the desk clerk. Umbrellas came out again.

Perhaps this was the chance I needed. I walked over to the baggage desk where the one orderly still stood. `Will the baggage ever come in?' I asked in a very general way.

The orderly clearly wasn't sure if he'd heard what I said. `*Maaf, tuan?*'

`I wondered if the luggage was ever going to come in. I want to see if my bag is there.'

`I hope for the *tuan's* sake that it is. But these men are always slow. It may take another fifteen minutes yet.' The orderly didn't seem to mind talking.

`I came in yesterday, but my bag was not on the plane. I was promised it would arrive today.' The story sounded right.

The orderly accepted it. `That is too common, *tuan*. I hope it will be here. But this airline is not very efficient.' Then, `You came from Makassar?'

`Originally. Staying with friends there.'

`And you were coming here or going on?'

`Going on?'

`To Kupang, *tuan*.'

`No, my flight was just to Ambon.'

The orderly nodded in understanding. `Ah, just so, *tuan*. But this plane was going on to Kupang. And the weather there is even worse than here. So I must take my baggage off here.'

It seemed that there had been a change in some plans. `You were going to Kupang?'

`Ah no. Not me, *tuan*.' The orderly laughed politely. `I've never been off this island. No. It was my *Jenderal*. He was going to Kupang, but now must spend the night here. Perhaps the weather will clear in Kupang and he can go tomorrow. He is quite angry.'

I nodded in sympathetic understanding. `Yes, an important man would be. But I saw more than one *Jenderal* arrive. Does the other have the same problem?'

The orderly showed some surprise. `The *tuan* must be very observant. And yes, it is almost as the *tuan* says. But the other *Jenderal* is a *Laksamana*, and he too was going to Kupang. However, it is not the weather that brings him here. He has some other purpose to his journey, but it was unexpected and I don't know what it is. He brought many others with him.'

So it was obvious that the orderly's *Jenderal* was Bulyanto. It was Subagio that had brought the second party, for it had been him reeling off their orders. But they had both been going to Kupang.

The orderly had been paying more attention than me to the activity on the apron, for the baggage cart was now being wheeled towards the building and he moved away to join his mate who had come in looking very wet and indignant. There were knots of passengers in the baggage hall also waiting for their bags, though those less patient had engaged porters to do the waiting, and were themselves engaged elsewhere in animated conversations with those who had come to meet them. I had an idea and went over to one group of passengers.

`Excuse me, did you come from Makassar? I was expecting a friend to arrive on this flight. A tall foreigner with black hair. Perhaps you saw him.' I was given blank stares and a single response in the negative. I tried the approach twice more, but it caused more embarassment than anything. I could see the thought going through most minds. Stupid foreigner. And his friend is lost. But I finally elicited some sympathy. `No, I'm sorry. But many didn't get on this plane. It was overbooked in Makassar. The military had priority.' I nodded my thanks and moved away. So perhaps I'd been right in interpreting the orderly's remark as Subagio's entourage having been a last minute programme, a change of plans requiring some extra seats on the last flight. Not proven, but at least a possibility. I went back to the canteen, found Anne, and then requested a taxi to town.

But the feeling that I'd missed something very important still grew. We had the large-scale chart of the Flores Sea and the island chain to the south and east spread on the floor. Lombok ran into Sumba. Sumba into Sumbawa. Then Timor slightly undercutting the archipelago but running back up into the main axis. Kupang was on West Timor.

'That's where Subagio was heading,' I said, 'but he had to stop off here in Ambon on his way. Bulyanto was also bound there, with his young sidekick. That has to be significant. But it works against my main theory.'

'Why?' Anne was tracing some of the soundings, joining dots with her finger.

'This chart tells me that it all has to be heading east. It's like a funnel drawing a final fury onto the short history of Papua New Guinea. It's never been a secret that they wanted the whole archipelago.' And that was why finding the fleet was so important. How close I found it would be the key to everything. If I could find it. Just follow Subagio? 'I've seen or heard something that would answer my questions. But I don't know what it is, nor where I saw or heard it.'

'It'll come to you when it's ready to do so. Worrying about it won't help.'

But that wasn't enough. 'There's no time. If we haven't got it in the next forty-eight hours, I think it'll be too late.'

Twenty

The Jenderal took me round the installations the day I arrived. The first buildings were a little over three years old, begun at the same time as the LCT program. A sub-regional military camp, Jakarta had thought, ideal for training exercises, low cost, out of the way. Useful for local control, and back up if necessary for any action in East Timor, little more than a couple of hundred kilometres to the east.

Forward planning. One of three sites that had been set up across the country's southern arc. The Jenderal said it had not been clear then which would become the headquarters. There had been too many imponderables at the time, and the acquisition of the East German fleet had been less than probable. Essential but not a given by any means. It had taken consistent but very subtle pressure on the then Minister to convince him that the idea had been his, and that it was an idea beyond brilliance. Once his ego had been fed, the acquisition was a certainty. But there had been the occasional sleepless night.

And a training camp it had been. Groups of senior officers had passed through here, men thought to be reliable, and tested for allegiance. Not, as Jakarta thought, to the President, but to Indonesia. A country in trouble, being bled dry by civil unrest. It had taken years to identify the officers offended by this. It had taken great care to ensure that nothing was given away in those early days. The Jenderal smiled. There had been only one mistake. And he was buried deep somewhere out in the trees. A training accident.

So I came to understand the Jenderal and the Laksamana, two of my mentors (the Tionghoa, the third). True friends and partners in this leap into the future. Junior officers at the time of the Night of the Long Knives. Men who had thought that it was a simple road forward, once a few things were cleared up. But men who had became disenchanted with the trappings of corrupted power, the latter tacitly approved at the highest level.

They'd waited and watched. Waited for the right man to move towards the right position of power within the Government. Then they'd begun the slow process of association, the quiet motions of support for this Minister that eventually brought recognition. They gave him the honour, the power, the publicity, but they retained the strings. He knew it, but accepted it. And he'd not failed them. They'd not chosen someone who needed to be told what was to happen. He'd felt as they had, had wanted change. But now that he was close to power, there was to be an even greater surprise.

`There are still fools who hesitate, Soekendro. Afraid of the consequences of their actions should a President find out.' The Jenderal had smiled. `Little chance of that now. The real surprise will be when they find delivery was not for New Guinea but for somewhere else.' Discontent with ongoing Australian meddling in East Timor had remained the ruse. There were bound to be some leaks, so it had been a useful ploy. And when questions became more persistent, mention of Papua New Guinea had shut them up all together. The President knew this, of course. Secret knowledge was power.*

Excerpted from Rusman Soekendro, LetJen (ret'd),
No Game At All: Memoirs of a Strategist.

But I am not a Muslim,' she said.

'How do you know?' answered the Javan.

'Muslims are very clear in their understanding of their duties under God. They give themselves completely. I am agnostic.'

'Your writing showed you taking that position very clearly. Yet if I may presume, it was almost as if you were writing to convince yourself.'

The woman gave a wry smile. 'I am troubled by monotheistic religions where all the prophets were men. And almost everything I see shows me that men have benefitted hugely compared to women.'

The Javan looked sad. 'If Allah wills it, that may be one of the first corrections at the Day of Atonement,' he said. He turned to the Australian. 'Do you know that Islam speaks of the major jihad and the minor jihad? Given our joint history, you may be forgiven for thinking that you and I were engaged in the first. In fact, the major jihad is the struggle of the soul.'

For a few minutes the Australian had felt excluded from the deeply personal conversation between the Javan and his wife, and he was surprised at suddenly being included. 'At times they occurred simultaneously,' he said. 'I don't think I've struggled so much as during moments in battle.'

'Then that was because you did not make your peace previously with Allah,' said the Javan. 'Had you done so, you would have fought with a pure heart.'

The Australian was more prosaic. 'Would it have made any difference to the outcome?'

'We can never know,' said the Javan. 'But that is not the point.'

***

So I went back down to the bay early the next morning, leaving Anne to a leisurely breakfast, the taxi driving me into a morning very much like the previous one, scrubbed clean by the torrential rain through the evening and into the early night. We took a round-about hillside road steaming in the early morning sun, its gravel surface almost dry. Small gullies had opened across it, running diagonally and disappearing over the edge. The taxi bumped across them. A pair of fish eagles was testing the morning thermals before the long glide down to the water. I watched their spiralling ascent, and listened to their harsh calls, before focusing further out to sea, but there was nothing disturbing the sweep of calm water.

Unlike the placid morning view from the hillside, there was considerable human activity in the bay beyond the coconut grove. Two smaller vessels had moored directly to the crippled LST. The low rumble of their engines carried across the water, and cooling water discharged close to the stern. The new arrivals were riding so high in the water that they had to be empty. But there was one aspect to them that had my full attention. They were identical to those being built at Makassar, one of which I'd seen crossing the harbour mouth. As had been the craft that I'd seen on the beach near Raha, spewing their controlled violence onto the beach. The vessels that had been pulled out of the coastal trading system.

A section of the beach had been cordoned off, and military police were keeping casual observers well away from the site. There was considerable activity on the loaded vessel, and a launch was ferrying someone out to it. I used my glasses for a few seconds, but the face was not familiar. Today, no dark smoke billowed from the ship's funnel in uneven waves, coughed out as if by an unhealthy lung. She lay silent to the ministrations of her two smaller companions.

A naval vehicle pulled onto the beach and into the cordoned area, and I sensed who was in the vehicle even before the door opened. My binoculars confirmed the thought. Subagio climbed out, to stand looking at the ship, and then turned to an officer who had climbed out behind him, and apparently asked a question. The officer put a hand-radio to his mouth. A few moments brought a reply, and the officer passed it on. Subagio walked towards the water.

Within five minutes a launch had carried him out to the LST where he disappeared over the ship's side. Within a minute Subagio reappeared at the ship's upper deck, and stood looking over at the LCTs moored to her side. Then he turned and disappeared again.

It was clear a decision had been made. The pattern of movement on board the larger vessel changed, the focus of attention becoming the smaller craft. One of them was drawn into a position where her bow door abutted the side of the larger open ramp of the loaded vessel. A large work crew was assembled from the joint crews of all three vessels, and the transfer of materiel from the larger ship began.

I watched it for a while. But it was evident that it would take a full day to fill the two smaller craft, and that even then the job might not be finished. I saw Subagio cross into the smaller ship, disappear for five minutes and then reappear. The launch took him back towards the beach where he climbed straight into the vehicle that had brought him. It spun its wheels in the sand, and then disappeared beyond the trees.

The rain held off for the arrival of the last flight of the day, and we watched it land from a seat in the corner of the departure lounge. I'd chosen the seats with care, to be able to watch the exit from the VIP lounge but also be in a position from which we could board quickly once the flight was called. If anything was to undo it all now it would be to find ourselves sitting next to Subagio. I'd arranged seats right at the back.

The turnaround took well over half an hour, during which we worked out our boarding procedure. At the call to board there was a stir among the waiting passengers, a security guard appeared at the single exit door, and a young airline staffer also walked over. We picked up our bags, having made the decision to be right at the front of the queue. I wasn't sure quite how exposed we'd be to anyone in the VIP lounge once we left the terminal building, but at least there was no member of the party visible from where we stood.

We were about fifth and sixth out of the door, and kept ourselves close to the people in front as they walked the fifty metres across the apron to the waiting plane. A glance behind told me we had reasonable cover from the people following, but my height, and even Anne's, was a disadvantage. There wasn't much we could do about it.

As I turned to climb the steps into the plane, Anne already on the first step, I saw a knot of people emerging from the VIP lounge. The slow ascent of the gangway seemed to stretch itself out as each passenger was welcomed individually and the boarding pass checked. I kept my face averted, knowing that Anne was doing the same, but could do nothing more to hide myself. I was just at the edge of the doorway as the military party rounded the nose of the plane. The seconds it took to move slowly inside the plane seemed like an hour, the person in front of Anne taking an age to find where he'd put his boarding pass. I whispered to her to slip past him, put both passes into the hand of the surprised stewardess and shrugged at her as we made our way into the aisle. I found our seats in the last row of the plane, slipped my pack under the seat in front, and pulled a soft cap out of the side pocket. I'd debated putting it on before but kept it for possible moments of closer quarters. It changed the profile of whatever might have been noticed before.

The first two rows of seating had been reserved for the military, and as the last of the ordinary passengers sat down, an orderly appeared with a couple of briefcases in hand. He placed them in the first row and then disappeared. Other uniforms started to appear, but stood in the forward galley until the most senior officers had taken their seats. Subagio *and* Bulyanto. In my mind they were becoming a team. And I recalled what the orderly had said to me only a day before about his *Jenderal* as he moved away. `One of Indonesia's most famous soldiers.' But I knew that already, had known it that day the *undangan* dragged me to Bandung.

But what if they were *the* team? They hadn't given that sense on their arrival. It had been Subagio who had brought a team. But that could just have been my misinterpretation in the heat of the moment, all attention on Subagio. Bulyanto and his cohort had been walking apart. Bulyanto had not meant to stay in Ambon; Subagio clearly had needed to. But they had both planned to go to Kupang. The orderly had said so.

Was Bulyanto the other half of all this? Was he what it would take to motivate a ground force to the level necessary to see it through the type of hardships that would come in an expeditionary landing? It made sense. The monsoon was working towards full strength. It was the worst season to be going into the humid tropical rain forest of PNG. Impenetrable, if you were coming from the west across the land border. But if you were coming along the coast, and could be dropped onto any one of several hundred small open beaches, or be pushed inland up some of the larger rivers, it was a different story. A large force of elite troops would use those conditions to tremendous advantage. Trained to the heat and the wet, it would be a normal day's duty.

It was what I'd seen in Raha those weeks ago. Mock landings. *KOPASSUS*. Confident officers sitting on the beach drinking coffee, though admittedly not in the rain. Probably with no idea of where their skills might be applied, but certainly sure they could do anything that they were asked to do. And be given the resources to do it. A whole bloody shipbuilding program had been set up just for them - the ferrocement LCTs - cloaked under a coastal trading strategy.

The scale was beyond what I'd understood to that point. I'd originally seen a naval buildup, but even though I thought otherwise, that did not necessarily speak to anything other than a wish to patrol the seas. Perhaps to add weight to negotiations over who *really* had the rights to seabed riches. The Timor Gap would be a hot issue for years to come. But I'd seen a capacity for organization that no-one believed existed. Such a secret destabilization of the regional balance of naval power was so beyond what was felt possible that no-one *had* looked for it. Then there had been this other dimension. That the naval part was the mallet to the wedge. That the LCT programme was a parallel component which explained the naval development. It had to be PNG, didn't it?

And there was a confidence in Jakarta which had brought the first flexing of the muscle. Closure of the sealanes keeping the seas clear for whatever troop movements would come after. Perhaps an immediate challenge had not been expected. Perhaps the lesson which had been taught would rein in that confidence. But it was not a lesson without cost. And *Magnet* was certainly out of action for the foreseeable future. It tipped the naval balance of power even further. Australia had so few ships that the loss of one was extremely significant to her defence capacity.

It was this thought that made me really sit up. *Where* were the rest? Nowhere near where I was. Or they hadn't been when I'd left *Magnet*. The other two vessels of the West Ocean Fleet were up in the Andaman Sea, almost a week's sailing away. Perhaps the strike on *Magnet* had resulted in an immediate recall to Fremantle, but I didn't know. And even if it had, it still meant that a serious opposing force could not be put into the northern waters for several days. The Red Fleet could sail south, unopposed. Straight into the Top End.

'Oh my bloody oath!' I bit my tongue as it came out. Canberra had fallen into this trap without any inkling of the undercurrents. There'd been an eagerness to send a show to the ASEAN manoeuvres. And I'd recognized the closure of the sea-lane for what it was, a barring of *Magnet* from southern waters, though only later had I understood it as triggering the only Australian response possible. But I'd read it in terms of PNG and what Canberra would do in about another annexation, that much closer to home. But the bastards had been way ahead of us, had got the whole West Ocean Fleet swanning around South Asian waters while they were sailing hard for the east. But not as far east as PNG. And I'd read the headlines. *President ill. Not seen for days.* Not bloody ill, though. No, down and out, and here was the kick-start of a new regime. And not PNG after all.

'What?' Anne whispered, still in the mood of the covert operative. I heard a mutter and found my neighbour on the other side peering at me in concern, offering me an air-sickness bag. I wanted to shout with frustration in the the man's face, but instead assured him that I was well, *tidak sakit, pak*, not ill, well not really, but sick enough to defeat a flimsy bag. They'd calculated that we'd see it as PNG, had made sure we would by putting severe pressure on the border communities between West Papua and PNG, and had us committing our own Rapid Deployment Force as a countermeasure. There must have been howls of laughter in the planning rooms in whatever secret location this was put together, watching us fall for every move the instant they made it. For with our presence on the PNG border, the almost-certain incursion of joint Australian and PNG patrols across it into Irian, and *Magnet's* mangling of the Surabaya heavyweights, Indonesia could claim the right of self-defence and *launch a counter-strike.* It was the Top End, I was sure of it. They were hatching an invasion of far greater imagination than our restricted thinking would ever believe them capable. Right into Oz.

Had there been an understanding of what detaching the West Ocean Fleet meant to Australia's interim defence capability? Did we understand how angry Jakarta still was over Australian interference in Timor? Perhaps, in one or two minds, but not in terms of recognizing a new and paralyzing threat. It came back to Edmond's style of thinking. And Australia was currently at her most vulnerable. The loss of battle resources of the last few decades was only slowly being countered. There would be no significant enhancement of naval power at least until the end of the first decade of the new millennium. And that could now well be irrelevant, not being around today to keep at least thirty-seven secondhand warships out of the Timor Sea.

And Subagio. I startled him that day I first met him. I hadn't understood why, then, but I knew, now. He must, for an instant, have thought that somehow I'd rumbled him. When he'd understood that it was only concern over any future Alumina Queen which brought me to his office, there had been that inward laughter. Then, later, he'd delighted in continually interchanging *Operasi* and *Koperasi*. All along, it must have been *koperasi* with Australia on *Lautan Lepas* so that it could be *operasi* against her on something very much different. He'd wanted me fully employed, not looking elsewhere.

But it was only *koperasi* until the moment we were in place. Then the sea-lanes were closed, *Magnet* was forced to throw down the gauntlet, and we drove ourselves straight into *konfrontasi*. And I was wrong. They hadn't needed *Magnet* on the bottom. In the court of world opinion *against* Australia, given that we destroyed two ships of theirs, *Magnet* was a greater liability limping home.

And he'd wanted *me* angry, wanted *me* to crawl around to his office as soon as that headline appeared in the newspaper, calculating that shutting *Open Seas* in my face would catalyze the very reaction that it did. My rumbling the fact that it was an Indonesian operation was irrelevant, apart from understanding how well they'd reeled me in. I was his direct line to Bluing, and I did his work perfectly.

Twenty one

'What about the American factor?'

I had thought about this in detail, but, at the beginning, it was the area of greatest weakness of my analysis. It was ironic that the Americans were as much to blame for this. They were thoroughly unpredictable.

And then, gloriously, prediction had nothing to do with it. The hawks came into power, two towers became dust in a matter of seconds, foreign policy became dominated by the axis of evil, and they blinkered themselves over Iraq and North Korea.

Our strategy then required no more than China increasing her rhetoric on the use of force against Taiwan, after elections or any other irritant. It was almost certain that future Taiwanese governments would be increasingly pro-independence. From then on, American tunnel vision would be complete.

'Our reading of China must be exact, Jenderal. The Pacific Fleet must first be covering the dragon. Much of the Indian Ocean Fleet will be deployed in the Gulf, and while they may redeploy some ships, our timing will nullify any threat from that direction. Our lack of any nuclear capability means that North Korea will still rank higher on the scale of evil than us. That will force the Americans to hedge.'

'But is there any fallback should the Pacific Fleet decide to move?'

'The Pacific Ocean Fleet can be neutralized for a sufficient period by the strategic use of mines, Jenderal. But the monsoon is a key element.'

'What is your general assessment of the Americans?'

'I've weighted their intervention at twenty-five percent of the Australian defence, Jenderal. In terms of impact on outcome of our design, this can be decreased by a further five percent for each week of the dragon's fire. Unfortunately, the Australian defence improves by a greater margin for each period as they redeploy forward units and mobilize any ready reserves. It is the Australian weakness that is the most critical for our success, not the American strength. The latter will be neutralized politically.'

'And the effect of this on Australian morale?'

'The Australians have lived for too long under the assumption that others *would rush to their defence. This notion has been slow to evaporate, even though the man in the street hasn't believed it for twenty years. However, the morale factor is extremely significant. It is essential to make the populace as a whole believe that the Defence Force cannot do its job in the north. All simulations show clearly the importance of morale on effectiveness.'*

Excerpted from Rusman Soekendro, LetJen (ret'd),
No Game At All: Memoirs of a Strategist

What d'you think he's up to?' the Australian asked his wife, later that evening, when they had returned to the guesthouse.

'I'm not sure he's up to anything specific,' she said.

'Why do you say that?'

'I think he is a man who, were he a Buddhist, would say you and I are part of his karma, and important to his future state of existence. From an Islamic perspective, karma is complete devotion to God. Future existence is the afterlife. That, absolutely, is in God's hands.'

'Is he part of ours?'

'What do you think?'

'I think we're approaching two states of enlightenment. In the first we'll understand a hell of a lot which we didn't understand before. In the second, well, I'm not sure, but it does somehow connect to the future.'

'Are you worried?'

The Australian looked at her intently. 'Life has been very good to me - it brought me you. I just wonder whether you're on the edge of a state of disenchantment. Perhaps there is something far more important out there for you than living out a rural existence with me.'

The woman knew he was very serious. 'If there is, perhaps it will fit perfectly with what we have.'

'I bloody hope so,' he said, worried now as he hadn't been for twenty years. 'Oh I do bloody hope so.'

***

The weather in Kupang was as atrocious as it had been in Ambon, and I hoped it wasn't a sign that the gods were against us. Unlike Ambon, I had no strategy for Kupang, but Anne took over even before we disembarked, starting up a short conversation with the flight crew, keeping us out of sight of our fellow passengers a little longer. There were few of them still in the arrivals hall when we finally ran in through the rain. Of the military there was no sign. But there was one of those international phone-home calling systems that would have put Anne through to Pops in no time flat.

I convinced the Australian operator to go further up the line than Navy's front desk. Once through, I first had to convince Dixon that my commandeering the helicopter had been justified, and that *Magnet's* First Officer should not be further castigated for a decision the Navy had decided he'd taken without the appropriate authority. "You took it into Indonesian territory, Gregory. That required my say-so.' Whatever Canberra knew about it, *Magnet* would still be somewhere in the Indian Ocean, so I thought there was plenty of time for this to blow over, but I cursed the First Officer anyway. I thought it was a good job Dixon didn't know I'd done it twice.

'Yes, sir.' But by that time he was coming round to understanding what I was trying to say. And as I did so, another idea formed in my mind. I added it as a final suggestion.

He was silent for a moment. 'This is all going to create havoc. You'd better call me hourly - that'll be the easiest way to find out if I've got you what you want. If I can't, I want you out of there. Understand?'

'Yes, sir.' But I thought it unlikely it would take him long to know that at a pinch I was still more useful to him here than anywhere else.

`You want to take a spin?' It came out half question, half statement, and was yet to penetrate the mind at the other end of the line.

We'd stayed at the airport, our best bet for the moment, both in terms of logistics and communication. Anne did phone home, giving Pops the message, and suggesting an ex-student of his would be interested. We took advantage of yet another airport canteen, content that even a simple fried rice was able to escape the connotation of that derogatory Western appellation of fast food. And at the third call Dixon gave me a series of digits separated by a hyphen. 'Do you recall the tonnage in your last futures contract? Subtract it from both city and number'.

'Understood, sir.' We were both worried about the risks of an open line. Within a couple of minutes I was relieved to find I just had to make a local call.

`Yeah, I got all that, mate. Gregory did you say your name was? But we've stayed out of the air since that party in the Lombok Strait. Look, you'd better come around here. I need to think about it and then get in touch with our pilot. Can you make it about five?'

We arrived a little early, having left some extra time for the taxi to find the place. It hadn't been necessary. `*Orang Australi, tuan.* I drive sometimes.' The

245

driver's grin and broken English said that our host-to-be was not unknown in the town.

One of those well-worn, early-middle-aged faces opened the door.'Gregory? Come in.' A hand came out. 'Marty Hocking.' And to my other introduction, 'Anne? How are you? This is Jamie McAndrews, our pilot. No point in having to explain things twice. And Jamie's bored stiff.' He poked his colleague playfully in the manner of a close friend. 'Look, I've got the barbie fired up. Why don't you grab yourself a coldie and come out the back.'

The beer was bitterly cold and the first mouthful froze my tonsils. Both Hocking and McAndrews picked up refills from the cooler and led the way to the back patio where a makeshift barbecue fashioned from a large steel cultivator disc was piled with charcoal that already glowed red. A plate of steaks sat on a small table, covered with a cloth to keep the flies away.

'Right. Tell me again. Trev, isn't it? Looked you up once you'd rung off. Embassy staff list. Keep away from there as much as I can, but get to town about once a quarter.' Hocking grinned to show that he was his own man. 'But I don't mind you blokes visiting me. Another chance to fill the fridge.' Both he and McAndrews looked as though they enjoyed their beer, though McAndrews had Jack's cadaverous length and width, and a beak that would bury itself in the foam even before he'd taken a sip. As long as it didn't interfere with what I needed them to do, I didn't care.

I kept it simple, and left it as a statement of need rather than any suggestion that Canberra was involved. I had to have these two on my side, but they might not be so willing to accommodate me if it were put too forcefully.

'It follows on from *Magnet*. You know what I am. It's my responsibility to follow up a couple of leads that suggest that the whole thing is not yet over. It could mean more trouble for us. Australia, I mean. When I started looking at possibilities this place stood out like a sore thumb. But now I can't get the intelligence I need from Canberra. So I decided to do a bit of looking myself and need help to do it.'

'You *do* want to go up for a spin.' McAndrews looked at Hocking as he said it, but made it a flat statement. 'But where? We've not tested the air control blokes since *Magnet*. Didn't really need to, as we'd done a lot of our flying by then. But we'll not get off the ground without a good reason. The military watches us like a hawk.'

'What flying do you do?' It was time I knew more about what the frantic scramble in Canberra had identified in what was obviously some sort of field unit.

'You don't know?'

'Sorry. Canberra couldn't risk telling me over an open line.'

'Yeah. Good.' It came out that Hocking was the leader of an Australian mapping group that used aerial photography for generating photo-mosaic maps. 'The Indonesian government contracted the whole service, including plane and pilot, from our small outfit in Queensland. We're known for our coverage of severe terrain, so were a logical choice for a region not known for the comforts of home or reliable maintenance facilities. But I've got to tell you that all our activities are supervised by a military counterpart group. They have to vet all the photos before they go into the maps.

`As Jamie just asked, where?' said Hocking. 'Where d'you want to go? Anywhere particular in mind?'

`Perhaps you have the local knowledge I need. What I'd be looking for is anything that spells naval buildup. New jetties, fuel dumps, supply roads. Other small things that might not really stand out, but when looked at differently could change the interpretation. Have you flown all the coastal areas?'

Hocking nodded. `I'd say the major part. We don't really fly the coastline. Our flight lines are set up to cover the whole island terrain as efficiently as possible. The coastline comes together on the map as the photomosaic is generated.'

`Can you watch what you're photographing?' Anne asked.

He shrugged. `Most of the time you're watching your compass and flight plan. Right, Jamie?'

McAndrews nodded. `There's not much time for sightseeing. Once you set off down a flight-line, you're checking the instruments and watching the camera controls. Wait. Let me show you.'

Hocking went into the house, and reappeared with more beer and a large paper sheet, folded several times. He gave it to McAndrews, who opened it up and laid it flat on the ground.

`This is the first mosaic from a region halfway up the province.' We saw what looked like a collage of photos put through a photocopier sufficiently carefully that the resulting image joined them together. Small rivers and roads ran from one photo into another. McAndrews ran a finger along a series of photos, parallel to their lateral edge. `This was a single flight line which went beyond this particular montage. It gets too big to handle if you try and put it all on one piece of paper. You turn the plane around and come back on a parallel course, and that gives you this next set of images.' He indicated the adjoining strip of pictures.

Hocking was working industriously on the steaks `Don't want to overdo these. Here, grab a plate. And there's some salad in that cooler. Not Grade A Texan longhorn, Anne. Probably a good old Queensland Murray Grey.'

Anne smiled. 'I never was a cowgirl. Beef is beef to me.'

'I remember you seeing some Australian beef that you classified as prime,' I said.

Her smile broke into a laugh. 'Trevor has these tests he loves to put me through,' she said, and explained the visit to *Magnet*. 'I had to walk between two ranks of highly polished sailors. They were the beef.'

Hocking and McAndrews both laughed, and this gave Hocking the confidence to ask: 'Why is an American chasing through the islands with our Attaché?'

Anne gave me a sly look. 'He's found that two think better than one.'

I nodded wryly. 'Anne knows far more about Indonesia than I do.' I thought it didn't hurt to add: 'She's also in a position to feed back to her people whatever we find out.'

This raised eyebrows on both of them, and I could see the thoughts going through their minds. 'No,' I said. 'No spy. Just well connected to her embassy.'

After the meal, we drove out to his office where the assembled mosaics were kept. It took more than an hour to run quickly through the work that had already been done, and I had a slow, sinking feeling, as nothing appeared that was not already part of an established landscape.

It must have been evident on my face. `Don't despair, mate,' Hocking said.

But despair was precisely what I was feeling. `We've looked at all the areas you've flown. What haven't you flown yet?'

He considered the question. `Not a hell of a lot. We've just about done all the way to the eastern end of the province, where it joins up to East Timor. Something could be going on up there. Everyone knows that there's a lot of military close to east Timor. It'd be perfect cover.'

`That's not been the pattern. It would be too obvious.' I thought again. `When you're done here where next?'

`West Papua. We move the whole circus further east. But we'll not do much until the monsoon's over.'

That didn't suggest anything. The whole PNG idea was crossed right off. Then another thought came. `Has there been a part of the province that you've been told not to fly?'

Hocking looked at McAndrew thoughtfully. `Roti?'

He turned back to me, letting McAndrew chew on it. `Not been told directly, no. But the flight charts we've been given have very clear directions not to approach Roti. It's not unusual that there be an area off limits to non-military flights. And our terms of reference for the job were spelled out in a way that indirectly eliminated Roti Island.'

It was the word *island* that clanged the warning bells. *Roti* by itself hadn't done it. But it was the thought that had been plaguing me the night before, the something that I'd thought I'd missed.

`I think you've just done it.' I was thinking furiously. I looked at Anne. '*Roti. Bread.* I'd thought it had been something to do with the victualling of the fleet before it left Makassar. You weren't there when Ahmed told me what he'd found out. But it's where the crews knew where they were heading. It seems the sailing orders were not as secret as they should have been.' And I'd seen it on the chart, directly off the southwest tip of Timor, but hadn't made the connection. It had sat in my mind like a lost signpost waiting for the right clue. How long I might have wandered.

`I've got to get to a phone. No, an outside one.' Hocking had indicated the one on his desk. `I'm afraid you may not be going to Papua. Can Jamie find me a phone, while you work out how you're going to get me airborne?'

`Roti?'

I nodded. `Or its vicinity.' Then, `How many of you are there here in your outfit?'

`Four altogether.'

`Family?'

A shake of the head. `No. It's not the way we work. We're close enough to home to shuttle back and forth.'

`Through Bali?'

`If we go commercial, yes.'

`If not?'

`The company taxi, mate, the one you want to go up in.' And to my look of enquiry, `Sometimes there's some work just the other side of the Gap. In the Top End. We can't have Jamie sitting around on those wages.'

McAndrews grinned mirthlessly.

`Then you'd better make plans to get yourselves out to Bali. If I get the signal from Canberra, I don't want you here when the door gets kicked in.'

Hocking had little trouble in putting it together. `Jamie and you in the taxi. Me and the other blokes via Bali. I smell some compensation in the air.'

`I'll do what I can. But the odds are that it would have wound up this way anyway.'

`That serious, eh?'

I nodded again. `Make it tomorrow morning, Marty.'

`Fair enough. Thanks for the warning.'

Then I looked soberly at McAndrews, `I'm afraid you're shanghaied.'

There was a moment's silence. 'Trevor,' Anne said.

'Yes?' I looked into cool green eyes.

'Can I speak to you alone for a minute?'

I nodded, then looked at Hocking. He gestured to the house.

'I didn't hear me included in any of those plans,' Anne said, the instant we were inside.

'No,' I said, knowing this was coming the instant Hocking had made the separation in exit routes.

'Well,' she said, with a forced laugh, 'I can't stop you from sticking your head in the lion's den again. But you do know there's a limit to the number of times you can do it before it gets bitten off?' I could hear a note of anger coming into her voice.

'Then tell me what else to do,' I said. 'Is there any choice?'

'What about satellite coverage? Can't Canberra get that?'

'Dixon was less than optimistic. There's been complete cloud coverage of the archipelago for the last week.'

Anne shook her head in frustration. 'This won't end well. You're forcing a civilian pilot into a military role. He's not trained for it.'

'Yes he is. He takes aerial photos. Those are what we need, and the lower we're forced to fly the better.'

'If you find anything.'

'Yes. Grant you that. But we've got to try.'

She was silent a moment. 'I'm coming with you.'

I think my mouth dropped in surprise. 'No, you're not.'

She gave a grim little smile. 'You think I'm going back to Jakarta to sit on my little ass while you go off to war? I'm going to call someone very important, not Pops this time, just like you are. Then we're going flying. Once we get to wherever..... Darwin?........ well, then you can put me onto a flight for the US. We'll both have the information we need. What gets done about is then up to others. Right?'

I showed some puzzlement. 'I know the information I need. What is it you think you need?'

'Trevor. It's exactly the same. Don't you see? It's the interpretation that's important. Your guys will look at it as how much hardware's going south. My guys want confirmation of the full dimension of a holy war.'

'You've just said yourself that it'll be sticking our heads into the lion's den.'

'If you're going to do it, I want to do it with you. I'm not going to be someone's war widow.'

I scratched my chin for a few seconds, then wagged a finger at her. 'You've been keeping something from me.'

'What?! I haven't. We've been trying to see the fundamental reason behind this right from the beginning. That's what it is.'

I shook my head. 'I'm talking about that other dimension. I didn't know you thought it was a *little* ass.'

Understanding dawned in her eyes. 'You're not going to stop me from going?'

Another shake of the head. 'I think I'm going to need all the help I can get. No-one better than you.' Then, 'Is it a holy war?'

'It has all the markings. But we need the evidence.'

Twenty two

The Jenderal went on. `Well, I think that takes care of the last major concern. Apart from what we are intending to do, of course. The rest is in Allah's hands. Benar?'

And in that the Laksamana always laughed at him, argued long with him over how much actually would be in Allah's hands, and how much they'd have to take care of themselves. But as they were doing this for Allah, they both thought Him sufficiently beneficent not to be offended.

Excerpted from Rusman Soekendro, LetJen (ret'd),
No Game At All: *Memoirs of a Strategist*

They had remembered that moment when the small boy had served them in the restaurant, and they thought about having two of each. In the end they had two boys, sandwiched between two girls. Only the younger boy and girl were still at home. It was a matter of some concern to the Australian that his elder daughter might soon make him a grandfather. As this was just an issue of generational succession within matrimony his wife frequently calmed him down, reminding him that it would be a much greater disaster if one of his precocious sons were to get a young girlfriend pregnant.

When they had finally been able to get together, they gave themselves a year alone, first. This was necessary, they thought, because till then they hadn't spent any time together that had not been subject to severe external stresses. They never were sure that that year turned out to be normal, or the ones that came immediately after, because the fallout from the Red Fleet had lengthy repercussions on his career, and she had continued on her own professional road. On reflection she thought it hadn't mattered, because they had been wholly content together, and a young family was further cement between the bricks.

They were both still young and in good health, and it was perhaps the moment when the elder daughter announced her engagement which suddenly woke her to the fact that if still half her life was ahead of her, then she would have to find more to do than she was currently doing. It was perhaps the one thing that she had never shared with her husband, the little niggling worry that whatever she might end up doing would *not* fit perfectly with what they had.

***

The sound of the wire-cutters snapped through the air, even with a piece of cloth wrapped around the jaws. Changing tension rippled through the fence. I'd hoped to find a gap big enough to climb through, but there was nothing. But it was also isolated. Hopefully any hole I made would not be quickly found.

We'd rolled out of Hocking's vehicle as it had skirted the airfield on a perimeter track, and crawled well over a hundred yards to find the fence, keeping ourselves well hidden in the thigh-high grass. But the grass inside the fence had been mowed to within a couple of inches of the ground and we'd have to be at the plane well before dawn if we weren't to be found. It took five minutes to peel back enough of the fence for us to crawl through, and I set off bent double, parallel to the fence, Anne a pace behind.

The airport was quite small, but the non-commercial planes were parked in an area of the apron that was exposed. We reached a corner of the fence that doubled away from the apron and a look at the receding perimeter showed that it was no better than a shorter direct route. To the right of the line towards the planes was the airport control building where the tower glowed red under its security lights. Even though the airport was closed, the radar dish swooped around in the night air like a giant bat. The base of the tower looked like the first stop on our traverse across the open.

Then I stood still against the fence, movement at the terminal building showing me one of the security guards. I made a hand gesture to Anne, and felt her freeze against my back. But a couple of minutes suggested he was not an immediate threat, so I dropped to my knees and began a slow crawl through a night that I wished were far darker.

It took almost fifteen minutes to reach the back of the control tower, my senses tuned behind as much as ahead because I wanted to know the second Anne found the crawl difficult. We eventually made it without incident and lay in the shadow at its base, but it had been physically demanding and I could hear Anne's rapid breathing above my own. I gave us five minutes rest, and then, as I could hear no movement inside the building, pulled myself upright against the wall directly under the overhang of the tower's outward sloping windows. Jamie had said the plane was the second from the far end and though it was still too far to read any distinguishing marks I could see a Twin Otter where Jamie said it should be, about two hundred yards away. But each of those yards would bring exposure far greater than the crawl through the grass, every step would increase the chance of discovery, of a shouted challenge, of a confrontation that could end in little other

254

than some form of arrest. Was this where our luck would run out?

My watch said there was about half an hour to go before Jamie arrived so I waited for a while, Anne's head resting against my thigh, and her hand occasionally stroking my calf. I watched, but there seemed no set pattern to any security detail, and I hadn't caught any movement around the planes themselves. The occasional cigarette flared in the dark near the one commercial F-28 in front of the terminal building, and a slight scent of cloves drifted across the apron.

Then the sound of voices brought me out of a slight doze as I leant against the wall. Three figures came together at the end of the line of planes and began to walk towards the other end. It seemed that this was an occasional patrol, quite informal, and when it reached the end of the line it turned and walked back towards the terminal building, a hand sometimes reaching up to test an aircraft door. Once the patrol was over, the three split up and went their different ways. I saw where they went, and it showed me that at least one of them might see us.

But we couldn't wait now, so I whispered something to Anne, and walked slowly away from the building in a long arc, drawing around degree by degree towards the farthest plane. I kept mentally triangulating the position of the three guards, on the slim assumption that they would stay where they were. Anne kept well to my outside, further away still, silent. My feet made a slight noise that seemed enormous to my ears.

I was beginning to think I might have made it when a figure came around the outside of the end plane bent on doing up its flies. We hadn't been seen, but I was still moving, perhaps a little faster with the expectation of making it into cover, and now I was blown and there was nowhere to go but forward, with as much force as possible in the fist that went up into chin below the slowly gaping mouth, eyes swivelling to note the presence of a woman. Before the pain of that blow came back up my arm, I put the other fist into a softer stomach. The guard slowly started to sag at the knees so I clipped him on the ear to finish it and caught him as he fell forward. There was no resistance. I kept him up off the ground, and slung him over my shoulder, another problem presenting itself. What to do with him? He had to be kept hidden until the very last moment. Anne caught up with me, a startled look on her face, but read my nod of the head as a positive signal and slipped into the shadow under the nearest plane.

I felt in my pocket for the key Jamie had given me, slipped under the tail of the end plane and then into the shadow of the Twin Otter's wing. The key turned quietly in the doorlock, and I swung it open just enough to dump the guard on the floor and climb in after him. I gestured to Anne, saw her take a quick look around, and then she was climbing into the plane. I quickly locked the door.

The scuffle didn't seem to have raised an alarm, and it was so quiet in the plane, Anne a silent shadow behind me, that I heard nothing other than the ragged breathing of my victim. So I stopped listening and looked around the inside of the plane, a wall pocket yielding a short length of wire which I used to tie the wrists behind the man's back. In the compartment behind the rear seat I found a piece of cloth to use as a gag. Once my victim was secure I started to relax. Now we just had to wait for Jamie.

A rustling out on the left hand side and a slight movement of the plane nearly frightened the life out of me. Nothing was immediately visible through the window, and I hadn't heard anyone approaching. Then the noise was repeated on the right side. But shortly after, a key slipped into the door I'd locked, and Jamie's face appeared through the opening. As soon as he saw me he cracked into a grin. `Not sure that I really expected to find you here,' he whispered. He saw Anne back in the shadows, and raised a hand in silent greeting. He slung a large canvas bag onto the floor behind his seat, and saw the body of the guard. Jamie whistled silently and closed the door quietly behind him. `Now I know why I wasn't stopped. He's usually on guard at the duty entrance. Planning on taking him with us?'

`He goes out the door the second we're ready.' And, as an afterthought, `He's only knocked out.'

Jamie grinned again. `Didn't really think you'd killed him. You don't look the type.' Then he turned serious. `Now. This is going to be the shortest startup and takeoff in aviation history. Once I turn the switches we're committed. So you be ready at the door to dump your friend. Make sure the door's shut afterwards, and get back into your seat fast. O.K? I've already taken the tethers off so we're ready to go. I'll not be using any lights. This'll all be in the dark.'

I nodded. As he began his pre-start checks, I pulled the inert form to the door and grabbed the handle. As soon as Jamie applied power to the first engine I pushed the door open and lifted the unconscious form over the sill, grabbing both shoulders and lowering it as gently as I could to the ground, but the top half of the body flopped over onto the tarmac. The guard would wake up with another bruise on the face. I pulled the door shut and checked the handle.

The first engine caught as soon as I was back in my seat and at the same instant Jamie applied the power to the second engine. It caught more quickly, but he held the plane on the brake until he had the power he wanted, hand on the thrust levers in the centre of the cockpit roof.

I was keeping a watch out past Jamie's seat. The whining start of the first engine would have woken up anyone close by, and now that both engines were running security staff should be heading fast in our direction. As Jamie twisted the propeller pitch controls on the thrust levers, he simultaneously released the brake. The plane jumped forward. He gave it about twenty yards to be clear of the figure on the ground and then turned hard to port. At that point he slammed the thrust levers to full. `Right! Hold on.' He was now shouting over the noise vibrating through the airframe. `I'm using the apron. The taxiway is just long enough. Gives them less time to come after us. Belts both of you.'

But I'd already spotted several figures running towards the plane diagonally to the front of Jamie. The plane rapidly opened the angle, and one of the figures apparently realized that there was no easy way of stopping the plane. He dropped to a crouch.

`Anne! Get down! Jamie - watch it! I think we're under fire.'

`Shit,' muttered Jamie. `Just a few seconds more.'

I saw a muzzle-flash, and the bullet hit the airframe simultaneously, high behind Jamie's shoulder. Jamie jumped, then laughed. `Fired too soon,' he shouted.

The figure slipped out of my view but a couple more impacts were audible over the engine noise. I couldn't tell how close they were. 'Anne! Are you alright.'

'Yes,' she shouted.

The traffic control tower flashed past the right wing, and a pair of headlights shone into my peripheral vision as a vehicle shot from behind the control tower. But it was already losing ground and it fell behind us, effectively shielding the plane from any further fire from the apron.

`This should be it,' shouted Jamie. In the dark it was almost impossible to tell how far the plane was from the runway, and the headlights were fading rapidly. In the dull glow of the instruments I could see him pulling back on the yoke but the plane didn't respond immediately.

Then there was a slight lurch as the plane lifted and settled again. But a second hadn't passed before there was much stronger lift and the plane jumped into the air. He pushed the plane into a hard turn to port and it seemed to me that it must stall, but he held the turn for several seconds before coming back level. He made some adjustments to the thrust controls until he was comfortable. Then he glanced at me. `Two minutes and ten seconds. Not bad.'

I looked back over my shoulder. The pursuit vehicle was still visible as the plane pulled away on a tangential course but I didn't think there'd been any fire from it. As I got out of my seat to check on Anne, I patted him lightly on the shoulder. `Let me know if you want a job at sea. They're looking for someone who can land one of these things on a helideck.'

Jamie grinned. `Think I could land it, but even I couldn't get it off.'

`Wake up.'

I came to, momentarily disoriented, having slipped into sleep without realizing it, the long sleepless night and the drone of the plane's engines combining to defeat me. `Sorry, Jamie.' Anne was in deeper sleep beside me, but stirred as I moved. I gave her a kiss in return for her 'Hi, honey.' I crawled back into the co-pilot's seat

Jamie gestured to the lightening arch of the sky, hints of a sun coming up behind the clouds over the port tail, and glimpses beyond of a molten horizon. He pushed a map that he'd been holding on his thigh towards me. The altimeter showed a hundred and fifty feet. `Not far to your target area. We're here. ' He pointed at a spot on the map. 'I'll keep this altitude until we're nearer Roti. There's a good chance they still haven't picked us up on Kupang airport radar.'

I nodded. `Have you seen anything at all?'

`None of your lot. Just a couple of tuna boats.'

I pulled my binoculars out of my pack and began to look out over the nose, but the light was not strong enough yet to see features clearly at a distance. Below, a breeze was stirring the water, causing it to pick up paler grey tints. I saw another tuna boat heading on a reciprocal course back to Kupang. Someone looked up from the deck in surprise.

Finally the horizon ahead took on some form. The mountains on Roti appeared as low mounds under the broken but heavy cloud, a land mist still obscuring lower features. `About fifteen minutes,' said Jamie.

`Can you maintain this height? The lower we stay the less likely anyone is to see us coming.'

He thought for a moment. `We'll stay low on our way in from the coast and then take a long loop around the peak. That'll give us a chance to see the whole coast from a distance. I'll keep the same altitude relative to land, keeping us under the cloud, but it will mean that we'll climb higher. From there we can decide. If there is anyone unfriendly they may not react so quickly if we're inland.'

`There's a good chance they know we're coming even if the airport radar didn't pick us up. The airwaves must be hot by now.'

He wiggled his headset. `I'm listening. They've only just worked out which plane is missing. There's nothing about course.'

I turned my attention back to the forward view where the island was now looming large through the windscreen. Jamie adjusted the throttle and the plane climbed a little. Then he corrected course for an anti-clockwise circling of the peak, the mist lying like a white collar around the foot.

As the plane approached the shore the island spread sideways in a broadening stain against the sea. The deep tropical greens were just coming out of the blacks of the night, and the heights of land were taking on a fluorescence of their own as the first rays of the sun stabbing through gaps in the cloud split the morning dew into a billion spectra. A ray suddenly broke through into the cockpit, and a stab of light behind Jamie's head caught my eye. It was where the rifle shot had penetrated the airframe, much closer than I'd thought. I turned to look for others, seeing Anne looking sleepily out of her window, but none was visible. I didn't disturb Jamie's concentration with my thoughts.

`We're on the radar now. At least they think it's us. There's no other known flight in the area.'

I watched the shoreline as it curved away to the right. The occasional fishing craft crossed my field of vision but nothing larger. I worked my binoculars up the coastline until I was looking almost across the plane's nose. Nothing.

My stomach rumbled, and I said, jokingly, `No in-flight service?'

Jamie gestured to the bag he'd brought. `Couple of flasks of coffee and twenty-four hours worth of sarnies.'

I grinned. `Better than I'd hoped.' I reached back for a flask and mugs, and within seconds the cockpit was full of a rich aroma. Suddenly starving, I pulled a sandwich out for each of us, and saw Anne settle happily into hers. It was a moment of peace before a possible storm.

The shoreline shot away towards the southwest and then started a long arc back towards our flightline. The map over my knee suggested that it should then curve inwards even more into a large bay. I looked again towards the horizon, but the far point of the arc was not yet visible across the foot of the mountain. It would be another ten minutes before we were in range.

`They've lost us again. But there's a call gone out to watch for us. Nothing more.'

`No pursuit?'

Jamie shrugged. `There's nothing on the air force channel. I doubt whether they'd want to waste the cost of the fuel. They'll be thinking that we have to land somewhere. They'll get us then.'

The coastline came slowly into view as we crossed the foot of the mountain. It came up to meet us, a stretch of over-grazed, eroded grassland stabbed by the occasional pocket of deep green where a homestead lay. The crest flashed past about two hundred feet below and then the slope plummeted back down towards a small village, a flock of goats scattering in panic at the sudden noise of the plane's engines.

The far tip of the southwest coast was still invisible, but a stretch of mirrored light pointed to the position of the bay. Jamie corrected course to keep slightly to the east of the inner bay, and I raised my glasses again, but we were still too far for anything to be distinguishable.

As the arms of the bay swept away from us in an opening embrace, Jamie sat forward in his seat. He checked his instruments again and then looked through the windshield. `I'm picking up a directional signal close by.'

`An airstrip?'

`Yeah. But there isn't one marked.'

`Why would it be sending now?'

`They're expecting an incoming flight. Unless it's a very unlikely decoy.'

`Then there'll be radar here too.'

`Possibly. Depending on the airstrip, anything from a small mobile unit, to a fixed installation. We'll be almost dead centre on its screen unless we go lower. I'm going down.'

The altimeter unwound quickly as Jamie took the plane down below two hundred feet, the tree tops seeming to skim the underside as they flashed by. The perspective of the bay changed. I was about to scan it when Jamie made a quick adjustment to his directional sensor. `The angle's changing fast. We're very close. Look for a tower. It'll be to your right.'

I panned across from the plane's flight-line to beyond the starboard wing, but saw nothing. `No.'

Jamie shrugged. `Then a quick look is called for.' He put the plane into a hard right turn. The wing seemed to stand still against the trees as the plane turned on it. By the time he levelled out the bay had disappeared to his left.

I saw the strip and the plane at the same time. `Jesus, Jamie!'

He grinned. `A military transport. We probably gave its pilot the fright of his life.'

The transport had been on a converging course, hidden behind our starboard wing. It was no higher than four hundred feet and was now in a final approach. We had flashed across its flightline.

The strip opened like an enormous wound in the red tropical soil and I lost interest in the approaching plane. There were already two of them on a grassy apron at the far end of the strip. That fact, and the large number of camouflaged mounds of indeterminate shape, spoke of a significant movement of men or materiel, possibly both. Then we were past it, and heading in the wrong direction.

`Trev, I think we'd better get out of here bloody fast. Did you see enough?'

`The bay. It's got to be the bay.'

He repeated the earlier turn but on the opposite wing and the bay slowly opened again over the nose. `I'm going down to sea level over the shore. It'll make us harder to find. Whatever channel these blokes are chatting on is going to be red hot by now.' He fiddled with a separate panel between the two forward seats. `Hope they're all smiling.'

I didn't pay any attention to the last remark. I was looking at the water ahead, and it was making my blood run cold. The thought came into my head that it looked a little like the East Ocean Fleet Base at Sydney, for the water was a mass of grey steel and movement, and the shore was lined with landing craft, mouths open and being fed from piles of stores lying on the beach in front of each one. 'Anne! See it?' Columns of men moved like ants between the piles and the vessels, using the early morning cool to shift them on board. Farther out in the bay were the ships I was hunting, at separate anchors. Several small craft ran between them and the shore. Some of the corvettes had landing craft moored to their sides like suckling young, but the nourishment was going the other way. Rope slings hung from davits, lifting cases of all sizes on board the larger ships.

It took no more than fifteen seconds to see all this, and by that time the plane was well out from shore and approaching the main anchorage.

'Tighten your belt, Anne. You, too, Trev.'

Even as I moved to do so, without further warning Jamie put the plane into the hardest turn yet. All forward momentum went into a force that pinned me into my seat, the water visible directly below Jamie's side window and the horizon almost parallel to the windshield's main central strut. I heard Anne gasp. Again, he adjusted the small control panel at his side.

The turn seemed to last forever, and I counted what seemed like hours through the loss of blood to my brain. But it was less than twenty seconds, and Jamie had flattened out and was back on level course almost in an instant.

But he was intent on leaving the bay behind us as fast as he could. The left hand shore came at us with a rush, and the plane screamed up over the lip of coconut palms, faces below staring up at us in amazement, the trees no more than fifty feet beneath as we headed southeast across the island.

I was still puzzled by Jamie's manoeuvre, but we'd seen enough and the first priority was to get away and tell someone so. The biggest challenge was yet to come - several hundred miles of open water.

The first line of tracer shells stitched a seam in the air below my right hip. 'Go left, Jamie!' I had a stab of fear for Anne. Suddenly the water seemed a lifetime away, but someone had been wide awake.

He started an evasive manoeuvre, jinking to port and then dropping the nose almost to touch the trees. The tracer seemed to keep a parallel course, the lag between leaving the gun and reaching the plane fractionally behind the speed with which Jamie tried to get out of its path. Then it seemed to circle over us and drop towards the plane.

'Christ! They must be firing blind. We *have* to be out of line-of-sight by now.'

Jamie slammed hard to port as he spoke, but a shell got there first and came through the cabin in almost the identical spot to the lone rifle shot of earlier in the morning. Then my face was covered in blood, and I was gasping in the stream of air that came through the shattered starboard-side windscreen. My earlier stab of fear became a full-blown fright. 'Anne! You alright?' Jamie was struggling with the plane's controls, trying to get it back onto an even course. The plane was not behaving properly, though the engines hadn't changed their note. 'We've been hit, Trev. I think the rudder's damaged.'

I was out of my seat, hand on Jamie's shoulder, jumping back towards Anne, thinking the worst, when I felt the pumping ooze of blood under my hand. Even as I realized it, perhaps the pressure of my hand released the delayed reaction to damage caused by the passage of shell fragments. He arched in pain, struggling to keep his hands on the controls as he did. The plane staggered. 'Throttles, Trev, fast! On the roof over your head. Slowly up together. Yes, yes, those.'

I grabbed the thrust levers as I jumped back into my seat, copying what I'd seen Jamie do earlier, slowly moving them part of the way along the remaining end of the range towards 'maximum'. The engine note gained in power and the altimeter needle stopped falling. The trees seemed only inches away.

'Now, take the yoke and follow my movement. Pull back gently. OK. Hold it there. Ahh, my shoulder.' Jamie slumped back in his seat, his face ashen. 'Anne. You'd better grab the first-aid kit and patch something on me. It's behind my seat. No sudden movements. We're too close to the trees.'

It took Anne ten minutes to bind up the wounded arm. I had both hands hovering over the yoke, not sure of Jamie's continuing consciousness. Blood had steadily pumped from the wound in a venous stream and the bandage was impregnated with it by the time Anne had finished, but at last it seemed to staunch the major flow. 'Painkiller?' I asked.

He nodded. 'Yeah. It's throbbing like a bastard. Christ I'm thirsty.'

Anne wiped his face. 'I'll get you some coffee.' She looked at me, worried sick.

I shook my head in a negative, situation not good, then looked over at Jamie. How's our course and altitude?'

Jamie squinted at me with a sickly grin. 'Business first? We're OK on this heading for a while, but what happens next depends on what they send after us. We've got to stay down at sea level. Gauges don't show any fuel loss, so we should make Oz as long as we don't go in the drink.'

By the time he'd swallowed a couple of painkillers and half a mug of coffee, he looked as though he'd be out within five minutes. His head was swaying, and he was having trouble keeping his eyes open. 'Trev, you'd better keep most of that coffee for me. Sorry mate, but you've got to keep me going. Don't let me go out.

Too late for you to learn now.' The grin was a lopsided lear of agony.

`What are the radio frequencies for Darwin and Broome?

`Stay off the air for at least another hour. Just nurse it until we're closer to mid-point. Don't want to give too much away. Here, listen in on the airforce band. See if you can make out what's happening.' He slowly leant forward and set my headset. The pain was almost audible as he slumped back. `Christ, can't do much of that.'

I started talking loudly to him, realizing that I had no other means of keeping him awake. Every few minutes Anne leant over and gave him another sip of coffee. Each one brought some short measure of relief, but, finally, behind him I could see Anne indicate that the flask was not sufficient to last the whole trip. Then I heard something on the airforce band which made me forget to think ahead to the point when it ran out. It was clear that we'd been reported, but I couldn't tell what orders were being given.

I kept my hands lightly on the controls, following Jamie's jerky single-handed manoeuvres, and the plane continued to yaw gently from side to side. He was probably right about the rudder damage, as the yaw wasn't all due to him. Would it hold? What if the weather changed?

`What course did they take?'

The voice broke into my thoughts as if there was a third person in the cabin, and my surprise was almost total. Subagio on the air, there could be no doubt.

`We have no radar contact. The plane is either too low or has crashed. A gunner was awake and opened fire. We are certain the plane was hit.' It was not a voice that gave Subagio any rank, but I'd not heard it before.

`We cannot risk a pursuit. That more than anything would draw attention too close. We will pray that they drowned.'

`Agreed. Do we know who they were?'

`Not yet. All those associated with the plane have curiously vanished. Perhaps they were on board. We are still checking.'

`The affair itself is curious.'

`We are becoming paranoid.'

`Perhaps, but the pilot was a brave man. He stood on his wing tip in the middle of the fleet.'

`He did what?!'

`A circus trick. No more.'

A moment's silence. `I think not, my friend. But I'll let you know. Out.'

I looked over at the grim result of Jamie's suicidal stunt. The turn had certainly kept us in range long enough for some reactive gunnery practice. Then I recalled him adjusting the equipment aft of the centre console. I took a closer look and suddenly laughed out loud. Anne looked at me in surprise. Jamie peered at me groggily.

I pointed. `What's this?'

The grin in the ashen face was nothing short of sly. `Thought I'd tell you when we got there. It's the camera.'

`You're a miracle. Full of film?'

`Enough to cover the whole beach at Surfer's Paradise. Sheila in every frame.'

`And you got the fleet?'

`Build yourself a circular office, and you can paper the whole 360 degrees.'

`Get us there so that I can.'

`I'm doing my best, but I can't use the arm.'

Twenty three

It was a heavily overcast day, dark grey clouds close to the sea, but when it rained it would be in solid vertical sheets with no wind. The sea was a lake of oil, none of the fine chop of the dry-season coast.

Forces Petir and Topan were long gone, Topan already marauding in Bonaparte Gulf, and the minelayers lying off the coast of Papua for any further involvement. I was expecting the Jenderal in the command centre but it was the Laksamana and Amin that came in. Amin had to take Elang into even more dangerous waters. The Laksamana was in a fine mood, everything well on time.

`Are you prepared?'

`Yes, Laksamana. This is the day I've waited for. Few naval officers get the chance.' Amin had that detached look all men get before a battle.

But the Laksamana could also be bleak. `Today you sail. View it as just another day in serving your country, Aminuddin, even if much of our hope rides on you. Yours is the hardest task. I expect you not to fail.'

`Insh'Allah.' By the will of God, something he could say without implying disrespect. And then he stretched out his hand, something in it.

`What is that?'

`Left behind on board one night at the Makassar anchorage, Laksamana.'

`A flashlight?'

Amin nodded. `Just a flashlight. But I think the hand around it was something else. If you would care to examine the batteries, sir?'

The outermost one slipped into the Laksamana's hand as he uncapped the matt-black tube. He looked at it closely, and then his eyes raised to the Amin's face. `Australian? Does it prove anything?'

`The intruder caused my watch officer a serious injury. He was not Indonesian.'

And then the bleakness turned to stone. `I should have given you another chance to kill him. I would like to see him at the bottom of the Timor Sea.'

But Amin's face was a mask. `Perhaps events will transpire that way, Laksamana.'

`Insh'Allah.'

Excerpted from Rusman Soekendro, LetJen (ret'd),
No Game At All: *Memoirs of a Strategist*

What they now had was a vineyard and winery on thirty acres of the scarce red loams of Western Australia, bought with some of his retirement gratuity and some of her inheritance from her father. They had started it from scratch, seeing the challenge as something in which to use the excess energies of teenagers, as well as learning the business from its roots, as it were. They were in their fifth vintage, and spent many hours discussing the ongoing processes of styling their wines. On the road to becoming modestly profitable, it gave them huge enjoyment, though the boys continuing fascination with beer meant that, so far, only the elder daughter looked as though she might continue in the business with them. The younger daughter's fascination with music distracted her from understanding that *tasting notes* was a correct oenological term.

***

Within half an hour we knew Jamie would be unconscious before we got much further. I'd been putting more pressure on the yoke, learning the feel of the plane and watching its response. He either didn't notice or knew that I was going to have to help him with the Twin Otter for the rest of the trip. And that half hour had given me time enough to sort out the images in my mind, put into order the ships and movement in the bay, and come to the conclusion that I'd feared for the last forty-eight hours. This was a fleet going south, with only one possible destination. But if it were possible to worry more, then I was doing just that, for I thought some of it had already gone.

`Jamie. Give me a course for Darwin. And we'd better try the radio now. I need them to guide me in.'

He looked as though he'd never seen a day of sun in his life. `Sorry, Trev ... keep... coming and going. Heading ...150, but monsoon winds are ..... from the west and ... stronger during ... day. Should pick .. up ... ADF signal ... soon. This one...' he tapped a gauge with a weak left-hand finger. He turned a radio knob `Hello, Darwin. D..arwin. This ... this is.. mike...fox 423.Do you read?'

`Mike Fox 423, this is Darwin. Give course and destination.'

`Dar... Darwin, MF 423 ... course... 150, destination... Darwin.'

`423, you're strength one. Please say again.'

I pressed my transmit button. `Darwin, this is MF 423 inbound on course 150 degrees. We have some structural damage, and injured pilot.'

266

`MF 423, copied. Advise extent of damage and injuries. Will you make Darwin?'

`Darwin. Believe partial loss of rudder. Fuel appears enough to reach land. Pilot lost large amount of blood.'

`423, please advise reason for damage and injuries.' The voice suddenly became officious but I had no patience for a long explanation of the past hour's activities with an air traffic controller.

`Darwin. Urgent contact RAN HQ Canberra. Advise of your contact with Chant, repeat Chant. Message forest fire, repeat forest fire. Stay off air until you receive response. Treat this seriously, Darwin. MF 423 out.'

I glanced again at Jamie. He was completely unconscious, head lolling forward. 'He's not going to make it, Trevor.' Anne was devastated, helpless to do anything.

I sat quietly for a moment, wondering if Darwin would come back asking for more clarification. But the radio stayed silent so it seemed that someone had indeed treated my message seriously.

`Captain Gregory.'

The voice cut through the roar of the airblast from the broken window, audible through the headset, and I jerked out of my reverie. Subagio.

`Captain Gregory. Do you hear me?'

They must have been monitoring the aviation frequencies, for I'd not used the channel I'd heard Subagio on earlier. I said nothing, but waved urgently to Anne for her to put on the other headset.

`Captain Gregory. It doesn't really matter whether you answer me or not. I know you're listening. I wondered where you were. So you finally decided to go home. Pity you didn't take a commercial flight - you might have made it. Now that I know it's you I have to send someone after you. He'll be there very shortly. Live your last few moments remembering your mistakes. Die regretting them. You came very close to understanding everything. My wish to put you at the bottom of the Timor Sea was prophetic. *Selamat jalan*.'

The last two words were a mockery. Safe journey into hell, if Subagio really meant what he'd said. I wondered how long it would take for an Indonesian air force jet to reach us, if that was what Subagio had in mind. There probably wasn't any other option. And I wondered when he'd made that last wish. I looked at Anne's ashen face and shrugged. 'Sorry, love.'

I grabbed the chart that had slipped from Jamie's knee onto the console, checked the airspeed indicator, and made a rough calculation of how far we'd flown since leaving Roti behind. How many minutes would we have? Probably not many more than fifteen if there was a plane in Kupang or Dili, and those would be the nearest hardtop runways capable of sending a military jet. But I wouldn't know how many minutes it was if the pilot decided to shoot us out of the sky without any final warning.

Any further communication with Darwin was now out of the question. If I tried to pass on anything more, I'd be telling Subagio as well. As it stood, Subagio only knew what it was that I'd seen, and what I'd put into words in the last message. But he'd also know my urgency in getting home.

The plane was at a thousand feet and I decided to lose a little height in an effort to escape detection by any pursuer. It was a faint hope - they'd have plotted our position from my radio signal, and knew my course. But I took another look at the map, thinking that there was an alternative that might give us a few minutes grace. As the nose went down, I turned the plane slowly to starboard.

On our new course and at about five hundred feet I spent a few moments rechecking the gauges. They suggested that the tanks were slightly under half full. None of the instruments indicated that the engines had suffered any damage, both running smoothly, or as smoothly as I could tell, given the wind noise through the cockpit.

What *had* happened to Darwin? I'd been grateful that they'd listened to me and not kept me on the air, but now I was concerned. If they'd followed my instructions, they'd have been through to Canberra by now. Hadn't they been able to communicate with Dixon? Hadn't he understood my warning? God, if they'd failed in that, and within a few minutes I was blasted out of the sky, it would be all over. I put the nose down a little more. I felt more comfortable nearer the sea, and grinned to myself at the irony of it. But touching a wave top would be the end of us both.

Jamie groaned and stirred a little. `Ma says... to come on in, Trev. Don't... don't wait about outside.'

Anne jumped forward, full of hope. But his eyes were shut and he was hallucinating, struggling a little in his seat. She tried with one hand to give him a little more coffee, holding his head with the other, but he was too far gone. I kept my attention on the plane, its control a higher priority in the stakes for survival. But I had somehow to penetrate his broken thoughts. `Jamie, wake up. Stay here with me. We'll be near land soon. I need you to help me land this bastard.' Land was still quite a way away, but I knew I didn't have the skill to put the plane down. `Tell me what to do.'

He rolled in his seat. `It's only a ... a dead sheep, Trev. No .... good. Come on... Ma's waiting.'

God knew what images were floating across his mind, but he'd be better off left alone. Perhaps he'd come out of it later, if there were a later, so I peered out of my starboard window in the hope of seeing an empty sky, the only satisfaction left.

The plane droned on, hurling a stream of hot humid air into the cockpit. As the minutes ticked by, my thoughts went back over the past months. It hadn't been a bad time, and I'd made use of the opportunities given me. And there was Anne. I reached a hand back, and hers found it. 'You've been a wonderful dream, love. Thank you.' She *had* been a dream, now could only be a dream, the dream that had put everything into a new perspective, a reason for life beyond duty, a reason for becoming someone better. I knew that what I'd said to Jack was true, that I did love her. Knew that I'd been lucky to know what that meant before it was too late, even if it was too late now.

'Oh, no, Trevor. Don't talk like that. We'll make it. We have to.' Then she was behind my seat, arms around my neck, lips hard against my ear. 'Please...please get us there.'

But perhaps I was too gone in my own thoughts, the mind saying goodbye. Was there a way to say goodbye? To everyone? To life? Should there be a goodbye? Or should it be a big bang? Extant one moment, mincemeat the next. Mincemeat. Minced meat. Sharkbait more likely. Whether minced or not. I felt cold.

The bang when it came was a thunderclap between the eyes, a physical blow that was a stamp of blindness across the full stretch of the mind. I lost all sense of being, though I heard Anne shout in terror, and I remained aware that I was perfectly able to see. Probably carried your last visual memory with you to the grave. The light didn't actually go out after all.

Thought? Yes, I thought. I'm thinking. And gradually hearing. Whatever it was, it had been deafening, and it had been the momentary loss of hearing which had convinced me that I'd crossed the Rubicon, opened my own little door into the underworld. Even with my headset on. Headset? I felt it with my hand. Headset, yes. God, what had it been? The plane had jumped like a startled rabbit, I realized that now. But it was still on an even lateral keel. 'Trevor! Trevor!' I heard the shout behind me. My eyes flashed to the altimeter. Up a hundred feet and trying to climb. It was my hands. They'd jerked closer to my chest, pulling the yoke, making her climb. A horn was blowing hard. Warning? God, a stall!

I was conscious of Jamie flailing about in the other seat. `Drop the nose, drop the nose.' He was trying to grab the yoke with an arm that wouldn't work. The remaining arm had no force. I pushed away, realizing that he was trying to work against my own fright. The plane lunged a little, leaving my stomach behind. Then the horn cut out.

`Wha .. what happened?'

`Christ knows. There was a massive bang, and the next thing I knew that horn was blowing off.'

`Wo .. woke me up. Was I dozing? God, my ... my arm hurts.' The pain had come back into his face. `Thirsty.' His memory came back with a rush. `Ahh, shit. Mus .. must have lost some blood.' He was staring at his arm.

`I thought it was the end. The Indonesians are sending a plane after us. I don't know how much time we have left. Sorry, mate. Got you into something you don't deserve.'

`Half dead already. Little more won't hurt.' He seemed to perk up, and glanced at the compass. `Where're we heading?'

`Broome. Indonesians heard me say Darwin, so thought I'd try and hide. Thought it'd give us a little more time. Though God knows for what.'

He peered groggily at the instruments again. `Give her some more throttle. Ye.. yeah, that's right. Might as well b.. burn more fuel and drown a bit cl... closer to the old Oz.' There was a slight smile showing through the pain.

I hadn't thought much about airspeed; I'd just been trying to keep the plane going as it had before. `Do we have much speed in hand? Just nod yes or no.'

Nod.

`A lot?'

Shake.

`Right. Shake when I should stop.' I began the thrust changes again. After the second set, he shook his head slightly.

`Enough?'

Nod.

`Do I have to change the propeller pitch?'

Shake, and a whisper. `Trim's the wheel..... behind the console. M..move it forward a.. little. Fly slightly...... faster.'

When the nods and shakes were finished I looked at the airspeed indicator. Twenty knots more. It was evident in the engine noise and the vibrations coursing through the airframe. Twenty knots. Would it make any difference? I looked at Jamie and shrugged. He pointed down.

`Altitude?'

Nod.

`Down?'

Nod.

`Christ, Jamie. My feet are wet already. I don't know if I can fly this thing well enough to be that close to the water.'

`No choice.' It was again little more than a whisper in my headset.

I peered intently at the surface of the sea ahead. The sun was still behind us so there was no glare and the waves were high, in a long swell, but there were few whitecaps.

The shadow was a massive manta ray that leapt across the water past us, and I flinched back, aware that we were now imminently close to death. Immediate survival, if in my hands, meant careful control of the plane. No more stalls or dives. But the larger death seemed all around us now. I shook my head in despair, but, aware that Anne could see me, willed myself not to let anything more show.

Then there was a different sound. A rumbling that transmitted itself through my whole body. I turned instantly to the starboard engine, thinking that there was something wrong. But as I looked I saw a plane, climbing to gain altitude, thundering into the sky. A military jet; it had found us. My heart seemed to stop completely and it was colder than ever. It had been the plane's shadow that I'd seen, the shadow of certain death.

Jamie was slumped over again, eyes closed.

I looked around at Anne, seeing a dawning horror in her face. `Sorry, love. They've found us. This is it.'

It was no more than a whisper. But Jamie's head came up, and two endlessly deep broken eyes looked at me, speaking immeasurably of pain.

`Did what we could, mate.' He winked.

I looked up again, and saw the plane curving into a dive, arcing down towards the Otter's nose, perhaps a couple of miles away. Coming for the kill. Flying for it. In my mind, I could see the pilot's thumb on the firing button, waiting for the final laser lock before releasing the rocket. Or rockets. Would two hurt more than one?

Then the plane disappeared as it came straight at us, a pencil point of grey nowhere in a light sky. I smiled at knowing that death *would* be invisible. But would I see Leach there, I wondered? The other side? What odd final thoughts. Would Anne be with me? Why just Anne? Why not everyone, idiot?

'I love you, Trev. Remember, won't you?'

I was unable to speak, the anguish at the coming loss too great to allow words to form.

Then the sun opened in the sky ahead, a massively expanding fireball of orange and black. But it split apart into fragments and left the day as it was before, except for tumbling shards of burning metal streaming towards the sea. A trail of black smoke followed each one down. A shockwave from the explosion hit the Otter.

I sat stunned, unable to comprehend a sudden chance at a slightly longer life, that I wasn't already dead. I still felt ice cold. What could have caused a violent death meant for us to visit elsewhere?

`G'day 423. Off your port wing.' The voice came through my headset just as Anne let out a shout.

My head snapped around. Suspended beyond Jamie's lolling head was a second plane. It was having trouble matching our own slow crawl across the sea. The pilot had dropped his flaps. It flew slightly nose up, and weaved a little drunkenly in a sluggish airflow.

`D'you read me 423?'

I pressed my transmit button. Had I been dreaming long? Where had this plane come from, with RAAF markings blazoned on the fuselage?

`Yes. 423 receiving you loud and clear. Thought I'd already passed beyond. Sorry.'

`No worry at all, 423. Thought you'd heard me arrive a little while ago. But I'd already spotted your friend, so couldn't wait around. Can you give me your situation?'

So that had been the thunderclap. A sonic boom. The plane had probably passed within a few hundred metres but behind us and below the sun. There hadn't been the flickering leaping shadow of the Indonesian jet. He must have come in low, perhaps even underneath us.

`Pilot unconscious, and some damage aft. I can't tell you what. Hoping to get this thing to Broome.'

`Roger 423. Looks as though you've been in a little scrap. Do controls respond?'

`As much as I'm willing to test them. I'll tell you after I'm down.' But that sounded a little too smart, and better to set the record straight. `I'm not a licensed pilot.'

`Understood 423. Mr Chant, I hope?'

A surprise. `Yes.'

`Good. I'll stay with you until we close land. At some point something a little slower will join you. My job's to keep you safe. I'd say your ETA is about one hour. Good until then?'

`Should be. Thank you. Please advise Broome I'll need some help in.'

`Roger 423. Put her nose up a bit and approach the coast at about five thousand feet. Less turbulence, better visibility. Your heading should be 210. ADF functional?'

I wasn't sure, and better to say so. `I'm flying compass alone.'

`No worry, Mr Chant. Keep it on that course and they'll find you. I'll be watching. Out.' And the jet seemed to unfold and take hold of the space around it, blue flame shooting from the afterburner as it peeled away to port and climbed thundering into the sky.

Tears started pouring from my eyes, Anne's arms came back around my neck, and I suddenly felt less alone.

They did send a plane up to get us, a trainer, and he shepherded us across the rest of the Timor Sea into Broome, almost losing us twice. The first time was his own fault, not having done a proper visual inspection for damage, and putting me on my ear when the port aileron refused to work. I lost two of our four thousand feet in that one, only coming out of it because, in fear, the subconscious took over and undid the last thing I'd done, which brought the Otter groaning back onto the level. I was ice by that time, angry as hell, determined that I'd get down if I had to will the bloody thing onto the tarmac.

But the second time was me, beyond exhaustion, trying to keep all things straight in vision hammered for a couple of hours by the wind through the broken glass. The daft bastard a few hundred feet off to starboard stopped talking to me and I lost it completely, a massive attack of vertigo, and the runway climbed into the vertical, no longer an extension of the flight path. The white guidemarks became the welcome of a white wall of death, and the Otter staggered off to I didn't know where.

Anne shouted, but the instructor was slow to react. `What the Christ...? Wake up, wake up, man! HOLD THAT COURSE!!' That wasn't enough to get me out of it, but it gave me enough orientation in a less exhausted area of the brain to bring the anger screaming back. So I gave it to him and roasted his balls off, using that to cut out the hallucinations for the rest of the time it took me to get down. His fear then that I'd go off the end of the runway was very funny. I avoided it by twenty yards. Anne jumped forward, and I suddenly found my head buried against her, her arms tight around me, shouts of triumph filling the plane.

We were surrounded by a fire crew almost before the plane came to that final stop and I'd switched off the engines, hunting, from the sanctuary of Anne's embrace for the one control I'd never thought of needing. Then I sat slumped, energy drained, amazed at the silence, my face on fire from the continual wind exposure through the broken windscreen.

A ground crew had the door open from the outside and was in the cockpit before I'd thought what to do, the propellers still whistling through the hot monsoonal atmosphere. `Out please, sir. You, too, Miss.' They'd seen instantly Jamie's slumped form and assumed that I was able to move myself. But in the end, they had Jamie out before I could find it in my legs to move. `Sorry, Mr Chant,' someone said. `Assumed you were fit. Want a hand?'

273

But I lost them for a moment, thoughts now not focussed solely on survival but on the ships and movement I'd seen in the bay on Roti's southern coast. Subconsciously I'd been putting it into more order as the rest of me had been trying to get home. I was more convinced than ever that part of the fleet was already on its way, and that the remaining ships I'd seen would perhaps weigh anchor by nightfall. So would there be two, or perhaps three, expeditionary forces on our coast within thirty-six hours? The questions came roaring through the mist, and they came down simply to strategic objectives. I came back to the present. `Just a line to Canberra as fast as you can.'

Part III

FLOOD

Neil Thomas

Twenty four

The monsoon. Amazing how much hinged on water. Water to get us there, water to provide cover, water to see us through. The first was obvious. After all, it was the short roadway between the nations, the continuum between embarkation and landing.

The monsoon provided cover, isolating the Top End, increasing the problems of defence. It didn't make the offensive any easier, but this was a conflict that would be won on high-technology and high numbers rather than high-technology and low numbers. Compatible scales. This was what one had to remember.

There would be further moves to play on and with water. This wasn't a single leap forward where the objective was immediately won. This was the first step, with more to follow. Water is the essence of our nation, so many thousands of islands. We live it and breathe it. How could they understand it as we do? Perhaps they laughed at first, but not later.

I remember the thunder rumbling over the hills, promising the wettest day yet. The tall bamboo groves around the base soughed, a slight puzzling sound against the descant of the cicadas and the melody of the frogs. I looked out the window, not really seeing anything, but alive in every sense of my body, attuned to a greater life beyond this, almost an omnipotence in what I was doing. It was unbelievable, and I was a little afraid of it.

Excerpted from Rusman Soekendro, LetJen (ret'd),
No Game At All: Memoirs of a Strategist

The precepts of Sun Tzu and the revelations of Allah, blessed be His name, pose certain difficulties in interpretation,' said the Javan. 'Sun Tzu's writings come from the time of the Warring States, but there is no certainty that they were not deliberately ascribed to someone who lived in earlier Chinese times, in order to give them the weight of antiquity. Allah's commands were revealed to His prophet Mohammed, but they were not written down in his lifetime. The Quran is a compilation of revelations, but not in a chronological order . They have been grouped mainly according to theme. As a result, their interpretation requires the assistance of a guide.

The Australian, who knew his military history, said: 'The Warring States were far earlier than the beginnings of the Islamic empire.'

'Between about 450 and 220 before Yesus,' said the Javan.

'The Quran was written at least 900 years later,' said the woman. 'One would think there ought to be less confusion.'

The Javan bent his head in acknowledgement. The woman was noting the age-old polemic of abrogation in the Quranic verses, that of later revelations superceding earlier ones. The revelations had taken place over a twenty-two year period in relation to conditions and events facing the nascent Muslim community. But in the way they had been recorded they were neither chronological nor linear arguments on the subjects considered. Islam had, even since, debated which verse, in each case, had ultimate authority.

Sun Tzu, by contrast, was almost certainly a single author, with singular knowledge of war and command of strategy. It was just that he could not be properly placed within the professional generalships or strategists of those Warring States.

'But,' said the woman, 'if we are to understand the concept of holy war, then we must review jihad in the path of God from the earliest moments of Islam.'

A slight smile came to the Javan's face, and if it could be said that there was one moment which he had hoped for during this visit, then perhaps this was it. 'What concern you are the traditions, the *hadith*?'

'There are two traditions,' said the woman. 'The *hadith*, which collectively made up the habit and observance of Mohammed. And the oral account which conveyed the collective Hadith, or *sunna*, to the Muslim world. We cannot discuss holy war if we do not recognize that those early centuries of oral tradition made the imparting of Mohammed's personal *sunna* less than transparent.'

'Islamic scholarship has debated the issue ever since,' said the Javan.

'I think what Islamic scholars have debated is the degree of reward granted by God for self-sacrifice in war. I think they've paid less attention to whether war was the best path is achieving God's aims.'

'But Allah knows that Man is imperfect. Don't you think He can be beneficent in His accounting of individual purpose if His collective religious goal is achieved?'

'I think God must be horrified at the religiosity of man. Had He wanted achievement of His religious goal, the well-being of people in their devotion to Him, He would have revealed his Scripture to a woman.'

***

It was a trooper who found me, plate and beer-glass empty, and with my face down on the table beside it, just like any two-pot screamer. Hunger and thirst sated, I'd been thinking about Jamie and wondering whether one good deed carried any weight with whoever decided if another should live or die, but then it had all caught up with me and I'd gone into a world of dreams where a mocking Subagio ridiculed the bicycle I was riding and somehow managed to deflate the tyres from a distance of twenty feet. The nudge became a hard shake, and it was that which snapped me out of it, bringing me face-to-face with a neon beer sign and then turning me into the face of authority.

`Mr Gregory?'

I nodded at this, wondering how he knew my name. I looked around for Anne, sure she'd been at the table with me a moment ago. Saw her heading for the ladies'.

`You've led us a bit of dance, Mr Gregory. We've been looking all over Broome for you.'

Then I realized that perhaps a higher-order bill had to be paid, that perhaps Dixon had been shouting for me. The trooper seemed to confirm my thoughts. `You've started a bigger flap than last orders, sir. You're wanted somewhere fast.' And a mate of his came in through the door, between them getting me up and almost into their car in about five seconds flat, hardly leaving me time to pay the worried waiter. While I was building up the energy to protest, and say I wasn't alone, one of the troopers had a thought. 'Oh. Where's the lady?' Anne saved my reply, coming out of a bathroom hidden around some corner. 'Her?' the same trooper asked. I nodded. 'Come with us, miss.' Anne raised her eyebrows, but I shrugged. I was beyond resistance anyway, but I thought Dixon was probably behind it.

Neither one had much to say after that, but the airport was our destination and the flap was on there too, the thunder of a waiting jet clearly audible over the sound of the car. We'd hardly arrived when the door was wrenched open and I was hauled out by another trooper with a flightsuit in his arms. `Get that on, fast.' He was gentler with Anne. 'You, too, miss.'

By this time I was starting to resent the lack of communication. Perhaps one of them sensed it. `The plane's been waiting for you for two hours. We thought perhaps you were in the hospital somewhere, and spent too long looking for you there. Why didn't you leave word with anyone?' But he didn't give me time to answer. 'You've been holding up some very important people. So get a bloody move on.'

'Where am I going?'

'Ask the pilot. And we've had *them* on continual refuel for the last hour, ready for when we found you.' The noise of the twin jets almost drowned the disdain in the trooper's voice, and for the first time I realized that he hadn't said *plane's*, but *planes*. The implication was significant.

The flying suit was a surprisingly good fit, and I saw Anne snugly fitted into hers. I was coming fully awake now. Two planes, two everything. Then I was shoved by one of the troopers towards one of the jets just as the second trooper gently guided Anne towards the other. I waved in resignation. 'For God's sake, *move*, sir.' said the trooper.

I grabbed the helmet and slipped it on to have my hands free as I climbed the boarding ladder, the jet now thundering through my head. I sensed rather than felt the solid tread of someone follow me up. As I breasted the cockpit I saw the outline of the pilot against his instruments and he gave a wave over his shoulder. I clambered into my own seat and started to buckle in, and a separate hand connected the oxygen tube and headset, and checked the seatbelt. It tapped me lightly on the helmet, and then disappeared back down to ground. The cockpit glass came smoothly down over my head, bringing a complete change in sound as it sealed shut.

'Captain Gregory. I'm Andy Brockle, your pilot. I've strict instructions to get you to Cairns as fast as I can. My colleague will be flying on our wing. If you're not used to one of these jets this may cause you some discomfort. If you feel like throwing up, there's a bag to the right of your seat. Make sure you take your mask off first.'

His grin came over with his words, but he wasn't wasting any time and the jet was moving as soon as chock-release confirmation came over the headset. The plane was just off the end of the runway, and accelerated into an immediate takeoff as soon as it came onto the centre-line. The force crammed me hard back into my seat, and the lights of the city rotated through almost forty degrees against my lateral vision as the plane jumped into its climb. The cockpit noise was only partially shielded by the headset, but I could hear the pilot softly singing to himself as we gathered speed and altitude.

His voice came back. 'We've about an hour of almost Mach 2 flying to Cairns ahead of us, so will be going quite high. In Cairns, you're to make a transfer. They're already holding the plane for you, and I've confirmed you're on your way and that I'll get you there as fast as I can.'

I tried to avoid thinking about what that meant in flying terms - at the very least there would be an uncomfortably fast descent.

`And someone wants to have a private talk with you. Stand by.'

`Right, Andy. Thanks. Call me Trev.'

`Roger, Trev.'

`Any idea what the other plane is?'

`Just that it's a commercial flight north. Non-stop to somewhere. And you've got to be on it.'

`I'm getting to dislike planes.'

`Not this one, surely? Nothing like it. Look at the stars.'

And I could see them. We were well into the stratosphere and the arc of sky above us a blue-black, but some of the stars were probably just my own stress-induced retinal discharges. The noise of the jet was moderating to the level of an acetylene torch cutting off each ear but a separate whine of the turbines carried through the airframe into the structure of my seat, adding a subordinated counternote.

I heard the cut-out click of Brockle's mike, and spoke into my own. `Gregory here.'

Dixon's voice jumped right in. `About bloody time, Gregory. What the hell have you been doing? Those planes have been waiting for you for hours. They've been scouring the countryside for you.'

I could only offer an apology, and did so.

'I want to know, Gregory, why in blazes I've got the American National Security Adviser bleating in my ear about your kidnapping their top agent in Indonesia.'

I took a second to put my thoughts in order. 'We've been working together, sir. She was with me the last couple of days in Indonesia, and insisted on coming with me. She signalled Washington first.'

'I know she did. Washington said they asked you to wait for a specialist.'

I was on the verge of losing my temper. 'There was no time to wait, sir. Not for some bloody spook who didn't know what the hell was going on.'

Dixon kept silent a couple of seconds, and in the sigh that came I knew I was out of trouble. `I'll not mince words. You may be the key to a very tight game, so we'll be holding this flight in Cairns for your arrival. That should tell you how important it is. That, and the fact that we may have lost some oil platforms in the Timor Gap. You know who that is. We need you to get a message across, but I must tell you that you will not find it easy. Thank God you have an American with you - perhaps that will help. So far, there has been a large degree of scepticism amongst our friends, and they are close to being not friends any more. It is what you know and have seen that may tip the scale. I want the man who saw it all to tell them so.'

I thought that the friends were probably the Americans, even Anne's lot. If so, that meant that Dixon was going to hold a commercial intercontinental flight in Cairns, probably the Qantas ocean-hopper. So there was a big flap in Canberra. And *they*'d played an opening hand by apparently taking out the oil platforms. A diversion, I thought, from something more significant? But what?

`I think we'll be on the ground in an hour, sir.'

`You'll find me on the flight-deck.'

`Yes, sir.'

With that, Dixon was gone, and I was alone again in space, Brockle just a shape in the cockpit. Sleep came almost instantly, fed by the incessant drone around me.

But I came clawing out of the dream, one where the lift was screaming down the shaft having broken free from its mounting, one where I knew that that part wasn't real even if my stomach told me it was. Sweat was pouring from me by the time I understood where I was and what was happening.

`You might have warned me, Andy.'

The smile came through again. `Your snores told me you were happy, Trev. Thought I'd wake you gently.'

`Gently?'

`Sorry, Trev,' and then the seat really dropped away under me. For a while I was weightless as the plane described a parabolic arc out of its high-level trajectory. Then I felt the disc of the earth curling out and up towards me, its furthest extent lipping back. Brockle started to decelerate gently, pressure back in the seat, the sound through the airframe changing as the turbines slowed and airbrakes changed the airflow over the wings. But he didn't slow very much, and the final descent through the partial cloud layer into the night sky of the east coast was still a screaming turbulent ride into the humid lower monsoonal atmosphere.

`Five minutes, Trev.'

`Glad to hear it.'

`You'll be bored stiff on the next leg,' and I thought that after this I probably would be. But that would be alright. Wherever I was going, I'd get a chance to get some real sleep. It had been almost forty-eight hours since I'd last touched a bed.

A military police vehicle drew right up to the planes as soon as we came to a halt, Anne's plane still on our wing. The Qantas jumbo was not far away, and I could see that it too had its turbines running. 'Thanks, Andy.'

'Any time, Trev. Good luck.'

I practically fell out of the cockpit in my haste, and ran over to the second fighter to collect Anne. 'Wow!' she said as I bundled her into the vehicle. 'I think I'd like to do that full-time.'

Within seconds the vehicle had us at the stairs leading up into the jetway, and I pushed Anne up ahead of me. The purser was waiting at the plane's door. Behind him was a naval officer. 'First-class cabin, sir,' said the steward. 'Up the stairs.' Even before he finished speaking he was latching the door in place.

The naval officer stuck out a hand. 'Collins. Welcome. Ms Webb? You too. Admiral's on the flightdeck.'

We followed him up the stairway. The plane was already pushing back from the gate, and a cabin-steward came over to look at the reason for the delay. In our flying suits we must have looked like a pair of outback tourists, and I heard some muttering from a couple of the other passengers. I ran my hand across my chin, and felt some of Jamie's blood still crusted in my growing stubble. No, not quite tourists. But the steward was well schooled and showed no surprise. 'Strap yourselves in, please. I'll get you anything you need after take-off.' Anne looked across at me from her armchair. 'How are we doing on our air-miles, honey?'

'First class only gets you half the fighter bonus. Regular economy for the Timor Gap.'

I had an empty seat in front of me. Collins was sitting ahead of Anne, and he swivelled round as we picked up taxi speed. He was looking slightly puzzled, but I could read his mind like an open book. *Honey?*

'Just enough to get us up to Boston,' Anne said. 'You've just gotta meet Pops.'

All the pressures of the past days fell away from me then, and I broke into laughter. Collins suddenly looked cautious, but I thought perhaps he was just offended by my evident fraternization with an important NSA staffer. Then I heard 'Enjoying things, are you, Gregory?' and Dixon slipped into his seat ahead of me. I gave Anne a wink, not worried at all.

'Good evening, sir.'

Compared to our previous two flights, the take-off was elephantine, a lumbering climb off the runway. The nosewheel came thrumming up into its bay not far below our feet, and the turbines settled into their low-frequency drone. It took a few minutes for the selt-belt sign to be turned off, and I took those minutes to review very carefully what I was going to repeat to Dixon. The bare bones he'd had on the phone from Broome.

An aircraft cabin is no place to hold a meeting - no table and chairs, and too many eavesdroppers. But Dixon stood up and motioned Collins and me to join him. 'Ms Webb, I presume? I'm glad Gregory got you out safely, though I'm not convinced you couldn't have chosen a safer route.'

Anne got out of her seat. 'It wasn't his fault Admiral. I made it quite clear that independent visual corroboration would be required by my people if this was to be taken seriously.'

Dixon's eyebrows lifted a notch. 'They requested Gregory wait, if I understand correctly the message I received?'

'True, Admiral. But that would have added perhaps another day. Trevor thought it was too long.'

'I'm glad he did. I wasn't implying that he should have waited. From my point-of-view he acted correctly. And, if independent visual corroboration was indeed required, so did you. I made that quite clear in my response. This is largely an Australian matter. However, we have a treaty that binds us.' I hadn't appreciated how much the American imperative had rankled Dixon, but it was evident that it continued to do so. He turned to me: 'So? Any more thoughts?'

'Three, sir. Firstly, there are ships missing. I saw no minesweepers, and not all the corvettes were there. Secondly, it was still the Red Fleet. I saw no evidence of regular navy. Thirdly, the balance between troops and hardware in the LCTs was wrong. Too much hardware.'

'All meaning?'

'These are preparatory moves. There are others to come.'

'Collins?'

'We've thought for days the heavyweights in Surabaya were preparing for sea. That would answer one of the questions.'

Dixon nodded. 'I suppose what I really want to know is what type of war we'll have to deal with.'

'That's easy, Admiral,' said Anne. 'This is a holy war.'

For the first time ever I saw Dixon taken aback. "That wasn't quite what I meant, Ms Webb. What I meant was, will it be land or will it be sea?'

For the first time in weeks I had a chance to read a newspaper from end to end. Not that we didn't get them at the Embassy in Jakarta, nor that our Foreign Service didn't keep us up to speed on international developments. I'd been fully occupied these last weeks, and there hadn't been the luxury of time. Now, though, between a first-class meal, and the ultimate call from the body of rest required, I devoured the news. I liked none of it. The American occupation of Iraq had gone sour, and the frequency of North Korean missiles being shot into the Sea of Japan was increasing. China was largely ignoring North Korea succession and rattling its sabres over Taiwan. It was a scenario ripe for further destabilization and fortune-hunting.

Anne had already fallen asleep, but I saw her stir at one point and look over at me with a sleepy smile. I got up.

'Feeling better, sir?' The steward was stretched out on his own seat, finishing a quick dinner. He'd given me towel, razor and soap earlier.

I nodded. 'Thanks. A glass of wine if you have it. Here, not there.'

'Understood, sir.'

I felt an arm slip through mine, and turned. 'I thought you were asleep.'

She poked me gently with an elbow. 'I was. Just needed to stretch my legs.'

'Wine, then?'

'Mm.'

'Can you make that two?'

'Yes, sir. Something from the Margaret River?'

'As long as it's not the water.'

We stood there for a few minutes, finding some intimacy even though the steward was not far away. I looked into the glass. 'I've often thought of starting a vineyard. Got to do something after the navy.'

'You won't make crusty old Admiral?'

'A bit like him, you mean?' I said, nodding over Anne's shoulder.

'He's not crusty. I mean *really* crusty, in a bathchair.'

I laughed. 'No, love. They don't let you get like that anymore. Not *in* the Service, anyway. I could take a pension at fifty, start a new career.'

'How big a vineyard would we need? To live from, I mean.'

'Two of us and a few kids? About the size of an aircraft carrier's deck.'

'Do you always frame things nautically?'

'Only when I'm trying to impress a beautiful woman.'

'And haven't you been told size doesn't matter?'

'It does at sea, love. Gives you something to hold on to if you go overboard.'

Perhaps that was the last of the quiet waking moments. I didn't remember falling asleep, nor felt that I'd been out for hours. But we were into our descent into Los Angeles before I came to, a hand gently prodding a shoulder. I looked up to find Collins with a piece of paper in his hands. 'Signal for you. Sorry.'

I thought he was just apologizing for waking me, so took the sheet from him with no thoughts for its contents. I skimmed over the opening words, identifying Canberra as the point of origin. *Relayed from Broome. McAndrews died 0200. Treatment could not overcome effects of massive loss of blood from traumatic wound. Regrets.* It was a kick in the guts, and I felt that overwhelming sense of loss which soldiers feel for comrades killed on the battlefield when it is one for all and all for one. So Collins' *Sorry* was something else. I'm sorry, too, I thought. The war has just begun and I'm going to bloody well fight in it.

The US Immigration Service was waiting for us on the jetway, and took us out of public sight immediately. I'd hadn't given thought to it, but it was Anne they were particularly interested in, and it was very quickly clear that the red carpet treatment was courtesy of the National Security Adviser, who wanted Anne in Washington immediately. A plane was standing by, would she please get on it immediately? These gentlemen were to travel with her.

Anne turned to Dixon. 'I think I can get you there quicker than you expected, Admiral.'

Dixon nodded. 'Canberra advised me that there would be transport in LA, but I think we'll accept. Thank you.'

One of the US agents overheard him. 'Nossir. We've just given you your orders. You got no choice.'

Australian Admirals aren't used to orders from anyone other than Head of Navy. I saw Dixon coping hard to control his tongue. He gave the agent a cobalt Force 10 glare and turned again to Anne. 'Thank you, Ms Webb. As I said, we will accept.' Then he turned back to the agent. 'As you get older, you'll find choice comes before an order. But thank you for your advice.'

The agent clearly struggled to understand both the accent and the rebuff, but slowly went red. Anne looked over at me and rolled her eyes. 'Come on, Collins,' I said. 'Work to do. I need a uniform. We'd better signal Washington.' I turned to the agent. 'Can I do that from your plane? Where is it?'

The agent swallowed hard. 'Yessir,' he managed to get out. 'This way.'

Dixon gave me a sardonic look. 'I can look after myself, Gregory.'

'Yes, sir. I know that. I was just smoothing troubled waters.' No point in having a blue with minor officials. The real trouble was yet to come.

Even though they knew we were coming, and that it was a matter of some urgency, Pentagon security still had to compare us with pictures in some manual on *Odd Uniforms of the World* to be sure that we were bona fide Australians. Our Washington attaché had found me an old uniform of his, but even then he'd been bigger than I was, so it hung on me like a gorilla's rugby shirt on a chimp. At least it had me a Captain, and not Commodore as he now was. Anne was yet to see it, as we'd parted company on touchdown, phone call promised later.

We were ushered into a large conference room in the Naval Affairs wing, where a few souls had begun to congregate. After a rapid consultation, our ushers left us in the hands of a young officer. But he'd barely started to introduce himself, when a senior staffer came in, smart, crew-cut, tough. 'Gribbens,' he said. 'Admiral Dixon? Weren't sure when to expect you. Just give me a moment,' and before Dixon could reply, Gribbens had already turned to his junior and issued orders related to other business. This was a Pentagon that was distracted, pre-occupied. Gribbens reinforced it. 'Find a seat, gentlemen. Meeting is called to order. We've got Admiral Dixon from the Australian Navy with us this morning. Let's hear what he's got to say.' And he flopped back in his seat, mind clearly on other things.

Dixon looked briefly round the table, at the fifteen or so staff gathered. If he'd thought of a thorough introduction on the purpose of our visit, he must also have seen how quickly that might lose their interest. Most seemed out on Gribben's wavelength. 'Thank you, Admiral Gribbens. I won't say much now. I'd rather put certain evidence of the table. Suffice it to say that a new theatre of conflict has opened, resulting from the Flores Sea skirmish, and that the strike has already begun. You should already have the intelligence report from Canberra, and the photo files.'

Gribbens came back from wherever he was, and looked at one of his aides. 'Do we?'

The aide nodded. 'Ready for the screen now, sir.'

Gribbens raised his eyebrows in some combined air of surprise and approval. 'OK, Admiral. Seems we do.'

The signals to the initiated were that Dixon's temper was somewhere slightly below boil, but this wasn't anything anyone in the room was going to read. He turned to me. 'Captain Gregory, would you run through the photo files for us? Perhaps the pictures will tell the story better than I can.'

So I climbed to my feet, chimp in a gorilla's uniform. 'Yes, sir.'

I looked around at blank stares in the assembled faces in front of me, none of them suggesting they might have heard about a Flores Sea skirmish, but it was obvious what they were thinking, hell, it was the damn Chinese everyone should be worrying about, what are the Australians doing here? Even though Dixon wanted the photo story, I knew I'd have to lead into it. But, standing in front of this crowd, my eyes were still full of chaff, the sleep I'd achieved still not redressing the balance of the previous days. I'd circumnavigated half the globe, only partly in first class, and my body still ached. I had to treat them with care, though, for we needed them.

'In the South East Asian region there has been a massive transfer of weaponry, both from the West and the old Soviet empire, to technology-hungry Asian military. The most significant is that to China. I expect you know more about that than I do.'

Out of Cairns Dixon had subsequently grilled me thoroughly for a full hour on detail, what and how many ships I'd seen, how many leaving port, the course they were taking. And as I'd said, something was missing, these were preparatory moves. I'd guessed two or three expeditionary forces, but if they were out there now, then they had still to make their presence felt. I understood why they'd chosen the monsoon, the sky closed in and satellite observation extremely patchy, perhaps something they'd weighed more important than the conditions on the ground. But the Wet was late, so they had the benefit of the heavy cloud cover with no constraints yet as to surface movement.

And now I was trying to deal with the raw emotions woken during the past days, and didn't feel like being polite. But I had to present a polished argument. Their body language said these officers were professional doubters, except when it was something that affected them directly.

'Just a few words about Australia. A partner of yours in the ANZUS treaty, in annual Kangaroo joint exercises, and supporting you as a member of the coalition against terrorism and Iraq. But if you see us as only relevant to regional power shifts in which *you* have direct and immediate interest you will not understand what I am about to show you.'

There was a little scornful throat-clearing, and some squirming from Rear-Admiral Gribbens. His manner suggested that his country-cousins welcome had exactly the right tone. But I had Dixon clear in the corner of my eye, and he'd neither moved, nor shown any expression. I thought it likely he'd cast me a line if I went too far. Then, just as I was about to begin, another officer came in. As someone who out-ranked Gribbens, his arrival caused a stir, but he made a motion not to interrupt the proceedings, and found an empty chair.

I went on. 'The mirth in the West over the Indonesian purchase of some tens of thousands of tons of East German scrap steel is hardly louder than the roars of laughter in the halls of power of Southeast Asia. Non-operational, no trained crews, no effective armaments. I can hear the thoughts in your heads - *they'll never go to sea.*'

I projected a shot of a naval vessel onto a screen behind me, and checked that indeed it was one of Jamie's pictures. `Do you recognize this?' I gave them a few seconds. `Parchim corvette. Number 231. *Prenzlau.* Just prior to decommissioning from the GDR Navy in 1993. You can look it up in Jane's.' I went on to the next shot. `*Prenzlau* was renamed *Kapitan Patimura,* Number 371. Original armaments two 57mm guns with a 5-6km range, anti-submarine mortars, SAM quad launcher - a regular North Atlantic sub hunter-killer. Then mothballed off Surabaya.'

`This ship no longer exists. Nor do any of the fifteen others of her class. Not long ago, *Patimura* turned up at an anchorage near a secondary naval base at Makassar.' I projected a different shot. `New armaments on them all.' I turned and pointed to one ship. `Number 371, reborn, refitted, operational. A lethal sea-to-air and sea-to-sea missile platform with the latest hardware.'

But there was still doubt on the faces of my audience and I knew why. `I said operational. I didn't say how operational. Or which operation. Or by whom. That is where we come to this,' and with a periodicity of about five seconds I gave them all Jamie's shots, enlarged, enhanced. They could have papered this room, circular as it was. But there was no sheila in any frame.

`These were taken a within the last two days. I call it the Red Fleet. What you see is about one third of that fleet weighing anchor on the northern fringe of the Timor Sea for what we believe is a major offensive.' I left the last picture on the screen. `As in the others, you can see large numbers of LCTs and some larger LSTs. Close examination shows that these are fully loaded, complete with human and hardware cargo. In these photos, the ships lie three hundred miles due north of Australia's Top End. Within thirty-six hours of taking these photos, this force could land on any isolated northern cape.'

But the throat-clearing was still derisive. Dixon showed no emotion so I ploughed on. `Should there be any doubt as to the reason for mounting such an operation, perhaps you may recall your own analysts noting the absence of Indonesia's President from the public eye.' This was a gamble. I had no way of knowing whether any such analysis existed, but Collins had told me this was now recognized in Canberra as important. I thought it also likely to be known in Washington. `It is my contention that he is now either dead or deposed, and that this is a massive cover-up for the next transition of power.'

That, at least, sent the room quiet.

`Captain Gregory, would you mind tellin' me from where you got those pictures?' A senior naval officer long from the deck of any ship tapped his pencil on the table as he asked the question.

`No sir. I was on the plane that took them, just,' I looked at my watch and made a rapid calculation, `thirty-one hours ago.'

`You really mean this week?'

`Yes, sir.' Thouugh I'd also crossed the dateline, I was still certain.

Another voice interrupted. `And that show in the Flores Seas surely happened? It wasn't some Aussie grandstanding?'

Before I could answer, Dixon moved in his chair. He ignored Gribbens, his voice ice-cold, and if I was ill-fitted in this lent uniform and not what these men liked to see, there was no doubt that Vice-Admiral Dixon was all a sailor should be. The cobalt blue was arctic. `Gentlemen, I take exception to that. The action in the Flores Sea was a provocation intended to deny our rights of access to international sealanes. It was the aggressor's intention to sink our ship. The RAN has no time for shows.' Dixon looked stonily at Gribbens, not at the newcomer.

I continued. `Don't look at this from its relevance to the Chinese question. This is a brand new question arising from our neighbour's belief that Australia is indefensible. So let me give you some colour. I'll start by saying this: Perhaps Australia is indefensible. Is that a strange statement from a serving senior officer in that country's Defence Force? Could it be construed as treasonable? Not really. It's a position defined by a current reality, and I'll tell you why.'

`Part of the problem rests in our viewing Australia as one land mass, occupied and lived over as if it were fertile and comfortable everywhere. You *do* know it's not. It's a federation of very different colonial and modern mentalities superimposed on an environment which, over some eighty percent of the continent, is comparable to Death Valley.'

`So what we have is a concentration of some eighty percent of the population in the twenty percent of the continent that climatically is slightly less hostile, but requiring that the concept of its defence take in the whole one hundred percent. Why? Because it's ours and we love it, even if we don't live in it.'

`So what's the worry? Very simply that we see the defence of Australia as the defence of the continent. We don't want to share our island. Would we still be Australians if we had to live in only New South Wales? I don't know. But the fact of the matter is that most of us do, and we are.'

`Because of this, our defence policy places equal value on a square mile of the Great Sandy Desert as it does on a square mile of central Sydney. We cannot imagine a boundary drawn across the continent, and being forced to live on one side of it or the other. It is my interpretation of events that *this* is what Indonesia wishes.'

The newcomer finally spoke. `Admiral Dixon. Forgive my colleagues for perhaps some reasonable doubt, but some uncalled-for condescension. Thank you for your presentation. And I think we should commend Captain Gregory for what seems to me to be some insightful and perhaps dangerous work. Would you care to expand a little on your comments about Indonesia's President? Perhaps I can remind my colleagues first that it was a previous President, Habibie, who made the purchase of the East German Fleet. And that, as you say, your other recent naval action was a defence of the International Law of the Sea. In case they've forgotten.' There was some nascent anger here, too. An action not fought by the USN was too easily considered non-action.

`Captain Collins is our Intelligence Analyst for Indonesia,' said Dixon. 'I'll let him answer your question.' Perhaps still annoyed, he made no show of recognizing the newcomer.

'Yes, sir.' Collins looked as smart as Dixon. 'I'll be succinct. There have been several since Suharto, but each has inherited a mantle stained from Suharto's almost thirty years of absolute power. They also inherited all the suppressed dissent of those thirty years. Through successive transfers of power have come continuing revelations of past corruption and human-rights abuses. Most of the latter were attributed to the military. While increasingly open elections have satisfied the Indonesian people's initial demands for increased representation in government, the resulting governments have not been able to address or correct all the excesses of those thirty years.'

'During all this, the military went from being all-powerful, to being an unknown power broker. The central role played by the military during the Suharto years was evident in its territorial commands - these existed at four levels, and they resulted in military fingers resting on the pulse of every small hamlet across Indonesia's more than thirteen thousand islands. Naturally, the military found it difficult to keep them there when its knuckles were severely rapped over Timor, and its Commander-in-Chief was sacked. Answering to a civilian Minister of Defence was never something it had expected, and, perhaps subsequently, nor planned, ever to do.'

I took Collins' lead. 'It is clear that the military lost all confidence in the last President's political leadership. During implementation of some reforms over military involvement in Government, the military began to distance itself from the President and soon began to state openly that its primary duty was to the Indonesian people and not to politicians. Economic collapse has also highlighted the degree to which civilian leaders were involved in money politics.'

`As a country, Indonesia is ethnically extremely diverse. Through oppression, and Javanese colonization, Suharto's New Order managed to keep the cement relatively well in place. However, there are several regional movements moving toward autonomy as they see the lessening of the central fist held over them. The strongest of these is Acehnese, but the West Papuans are increasingly vocal.

Traditionally, the military considered the maintenance of unity and territorial integrity its role. Without a new Suharto, it is very unlikely that the military could hold the country together. Suharto himself prevented a reasoning, civil authority from replacing it. Anyone in the wings considering options as to a Presidential successor must see clearly that the latter has to create a unifying focus. What better than to distract attention offshore and offer perhaps a hundred million desperately poor Indonesians a mythically prosperous future in a rich new land? They've all heard of transmigration, the government's old resettlement plan, in the outer islands. They would not find it a hard leap of imagination. It would perhaps be more a matter of faith. They know of Australia's vastness, even if they don't know much about its aridity. But this is a people used to hardships, and surviving on almost nothing. Very large numbers of them would survive, do so in similar conditions in the eastern half of their own country.'

`The military has few options. This one provides it with the means to regain much of the power and prestige it feels it has lost in the last decade, and perhaps settle some scores from injustices believed meted out to it by more recent Presidents under other, quite different, and perhaps international, pressures. There is no other prize in the region of similar value. Forget East Timor or New Guinea. Neither is worth the trouble. I believe the next Suharto will rise out of the ashes of this fire,' I pointed behind me to the last frame showing the Red Fleet. `That, basically, is it.'

There was silence for a few moments, and then the officer who had asked me for an analysis stood up. Gribbens remained quiet, outranked. `Admiral Dixon, thank you for bringing Captain Gregory, and for what we have just been told. We do, of course, have a little homework to do. Perhaps I could ask you to wait in my office for a few minutes. Commander Stavitz here will show you the way. I'll be with you shortly.'

Dixon nodded his acquiescence, and we followed the aide. How long, I wondered, would we have to wait to see what USN Admiral-in-Chief William Gillinger pulled out of his hat.

Twenty five

The Laksamana transferred his command to the anchored Sudarso. It took him half an hour to transship, two aides bringing the charts and other plans for the operation. His pennant was raised to her masthead. A sister ship lay anchored a little to seaward. The Jenderal and I joined him in the wardroom for breakfast and the pre-departure briefing. The smell of grilled fish and freshly steamed rice hung over the table.

The Laksamana pulled a small fish apart with his fingers, picking the soft white flesh off the bones. `What was the word in Surabaya when you left, Salim?' The atmosphere around the table was informal, both captains chosen confidantes. They had slipped Surabaya less than thirty-six hours before and had kept their ears close to the ground until their departure.

`There is a groundswell of uncertainty, sir, though the Ministers have played the press well. What happened to the President is still being called a stroke. The ambiguity in that term is not lost on most people.'

The Laksamana laughed mirthlessly. `Ever our way. Confusion is such a useful tool. And of our Minister? What word of him?'

`His profile is becoming continually more evident, sir.' Yus spoke, his shoulder boards catching the early sun coming through a porthole, the reflection sparkling steadily against a wall. `More of the senior members of Cabinet are deferring to him on national issues. There are no apparent chinks yet.'

`They may yet come.' The Jenderal took a mouthful of his rice, the small dish of sambal into which he occasionally dipped his spoon sitting like a mine among the fleet of plates. `It depends now on the next few days, and what comes against us.'

The cutlery trembled as the rumble of the resting ship's engines transmitted itself through vibrations in the table. The meniscus on the water jug quivered. There was no other sound for a few minutes as we took our fill of the dishes before us. The Laksamana seemed lost in thought as he looked at the water jug. Then he glanced at Yus. `And the extra missiles?'

`On board, sir. My guidance systems officer should finish the last checks today.'

`Good.' He rinsed his fingers in the small bowl set to one side and dried them on a towel given to him by the steward. He took his untouched glass of tea and drank it all. It seemed to clear his mind as well as his palate. `Have the table emptied, Salim. We'll do the briefing now. As of noon today you will put both ships on Yellow Alert. From then on you must be prepared for anything.'*

Excerpted from Rusman Soekendro, LetJen (ret'd),
No Game At All: *Memoirs of a Strategist*

Then what is the argument?' asked the Javan. 'Are you saying He did not reveal his Scripture to the only person possible? Remember that Muslims acknowledge no other Prophet.'

'We must also remember the other revelations,' said the woman, 'the Jews, the Christians. The Quran explicitly recognizes the People of the Book as subjects of the One God. Muslims see themselves as descended from Abraham's son Ishmael - a branch of a single family. Yet in all the religious wars that have followed these revelations, each side has considered itself as God's sole authority on the battlefield. Where did they, where do they, find the right to think like that?'

'Is this why you call yourself agnostic? Because belief would put you in an untenable position?'

'I am agnostic only in the sense that I believe nothing can be known of the existence or the nature of God, not because I am non-committal.'

'Then you are not a believer.'

'Men wish to be feudal subjects,' she said. 'Belief is what they require, otherwise they wander in an existentialist fog. Women feel God and require no knowledge.'

***

What came out of that hat answered one of the questions, though not the one I'd been expecting. When he joined us, close to an hour later, Gillinger had a sheet of paper in his hand.

`Admiral Dixon, before I read you the contents of this signal, I think I should place our own position before you.'

Dixon nodded, unable to quibble.

Gillinger rested back in his seat, tilting his head, briefly looking at the ceiling. Then he looked down, bringing his chin almost to his chest.

'We are troubled by China. You know as well as I do that the secret to handling

China is to interpret her rhetoric against the broader body of known facts. I think we have done this well over the years, even though,' and he made a gesture suggesting a wider constituency, 'even though you'd think our politicians had often wanted to impress a harder, short-term vision.' He paused, marshalling thoughts. 'Taiwan is, of course, the main burr under China's saddle. So we relate what China says to what we believe is China's interpretation of our Taiwan policy. Sometimes we get it right, sometimes we get it wrong. However, in the main, we have been successful in limiting Chinese belligerence, even as we control our own. I think I can safely say, given there has been no catastrophic confrontation between us, relations with China have been ..... *normal.*' He grimaced slightly.

'Now, however, we find we cannot interpret Chinese rhetoric against that known scale. In fact, we are off it, and it worries us a more than a helluva lot. I must inform you that the Pacific Fleet has very specific orders to attend the waters between Taiwan and Japan, and most of the 5th Fleet that was in the Indian Ocean is being brought into western Pacific waters as a ready reserve.'

'Where are those ships now?' Dixon asked.

'The main group cleared the Sunda Strait six hours ago. Its intended passage,' and he had the grace to show some embarrassment, 'was communicated to Jakarta at practically the same moment Captain Gregory took his photographs.'

'There was no objection, of course.'

'None at all, Admiral Dixon. You proved very successfully that rights of transit of international sea-lanes could be defended. I suspect Jakarta was less interested in challenging *us.*'

Dixon barely nodded. 'I suppose there is little point in asking that you send a ship or two to support our West Ocean Fleet.'

Finally, Gillinger waved the signal. 'I have some bad news. Two commercial vessels have gone down in separate passages of the Torres Strait, both victims of an explosion and extensive fire damage. Does that tie into any of what you've been telling us?'

Of course it did, and he knew it, and I knew what I'd missed, both a number of ships and their purpose. For in that magic number thirty-seven had been nine minesweepers, less useful for conversion to more militant purposes but ideal as minelayers. The LSTs also had minelaying capabilities. Both types of vessel had been there at the Makassar anchorage, but, at that moment, of secondary interest. But there had been no sign of the minesweepers at Roti, and perhaps not all of the LSTs, and if their destination was indeed much farther to the east, then there had been no need for them to have made a transit of the bay which saw the rest head south. They'd probably used the cover of archipelagic waters all the way.

Gillinger read the response in Dixon's eyes. But he shook his head in further chagrin. 'Jakarta has just informed us that it has temporarily closed all sea-lanes, and, for defensive purposes, has mined them all. We would look a little foolish trying to disprove that claim.'

And that was very clever, because it shut the eastern Australian seaboard out of the equation for however long it took to clear the Strait, which depended on what we had at Cairns and how long it took that to get up there. Dixon read it immediately in Gillinger's face, a virtual marooning of the US Pacific and 5th Fleets in the China Seas and waters further north, a single mine explosion being hot political ammunition at a time when the cost of defending others' coastlines was becoming too expensive for voters in Kansas. I thought I was beginning to see more of my master gamer's results.

But Gillinger wasn't quite finished. 'Chinese mines, I'm afraid. We know Jakarta has bought them in large quantities.' He ran his eyes over the signal, again. 'Admiral Dixon. This will take a lot longer to assess than I'd originally thought, though I must say I see no immediate solution. I'll be meeting with the President and the National Security Advisor this afternoon. But it'll serve you little to wait in Washington. I'm sure I can reach you just as easily in Canberra.'

What Gillinger left unsaid was the larger issue of Asian destabilization, and how the ANZUS treaty and American obligations under it had to fit into that picture. It was my bet that fear of China had resulted in ANZUS, American obligations to Australia at any rate, being put aside for a while. The irony was that the treaty also obliged us to render assistance to American defence of *its* own interests.

So we went back to the Embassy, where I was able to shed my secondhand skin and get back into my flight-suit, cleaned and pressed, which would take me home.

But before we went, Dixon thought it important to leave our resident Commodore, who'd been with us at the Pentagon, ready for whatever might come. The Ambassador also came to Dixon's review.

'ANZUS is a treaty signed in different times. We and the Kiwis wanted confirmation of a shared defence against any new Japanese military threat. The US thinks we've both rested on our World War II laurels since then, and that we assume they'd rush in to save us. But the Kiwis are no longer in it. At the same time, we've made major reductions in our hardware and troops. The difficulty is that ANZUS does not cast US obligations in stone. Even without the Chinese complication, I have always questioned our own expectations, which have generally risen in contrast to what we've provided for our own defence.' He added a caveat 'Naval, at least.'

'What would it take to counter this threat effectively?' the Ambassador asked.

And this was where Dixon was out on a branch. 'More than I think we can deliver. For the ears of this room alone, and to add emphasis to the importance of the treaty.'

`But if they've no fixed commitment to the defence of either Australia or New Zealand?'

`It lets them off the hook, and I doubt that the moral issue will carry much weight.'

`That if both countries have assumed the US would come to their aid in the event of any hostilities, and have made their defence plans on that assumption, that the US is bound to render assistance?'

`Yes.'

`Not even a sporting chance, Admiral. Fear, yes - they can fear the Chinese. But they won't want any of their boys killed in Australia over a moral issue. Deaths cost votes.'

The helicopter swooped out of the black of the night, and dropped us at Logan Airfield as a hawk might drop its catch into the nest. A long black vehicle took us with hardly any sound at all into a Boston suburb. In front of a modest house, a townhouse, Anne said, men stood with wires in their ears and lumps under their armpits. 'It's not just Pops, then,' said Anne. 'I think my boss must be here.'

'Thought it was just the help,' I said, and received a sharp dig in the ribs for my pleasure. I then got several more from the men with wires, while they made sure I wasn't carrying, as they put it.

The small group waiting for us had itself staked out in relation to the two principals. I saw straight away that one had to be Pops, for he had a patrician slenderness that matched his daughter's lithe height, though he was older than I'd expected. He was dressed as one might expect a scholarly professor to dress - blazer, dark slacks and loafers. His tie hinted at ivy-league origins. His hair was perhaps unfashionably long for an American academic, but I doubted that he was often criticized for it. The second person was a woman of perhaps fifty, stern-eyed, severely dressed in a charcoal gray business suit, slacks not skirt, and she had a hand on Pops' arm as she made some telling point. He was nodding as he turned at the noise of our arrival, but everything else went from his mind as he saw Anne, and the woman's hand fell from his arm as if she were a bird with a broken wing. For a moment, he and Anne were alone in the room as they greeted in an embrace, then, with a sigh of release, he looked up and saw me. In a very brief instant I was critically examined, undoubtedly reviewed in light of the confidence he had in his daughter, before then probably being categorized as *must be better than he appears*. All I could do was march forward into the fray.

'I think I've heard from Mrs Coluchi about you,' he said, as he extended a hand. 'Seems you decided to abduct my daughter without waiting for help.'

I didn't know who Mrs Coluchi was, but about him I had no doubt. 'I had no time to wait, Dr Webb. And Anne insisted I abduct her.'

He slowly gave a smile. 'Yes. I imagine she did.' He didn't need to look at his daughter to know it was the truth. 'I forgive you, but you better get Mrs Coluchi's apologies directly,' and he turned towards the woman in black. 'Captain Gregory, Mrs Coluchi.'

Anne had beaten me to it, and was greeting the iron lady with a handshake, and then a peck on the cheek. Mrs Coluchi's inside knowledge put her outside the realm of new companion to Pops, and slowly I woke to the realization that this was Anne's boss, the National Security Adviser. 'Mrs Coluchi,' I said. 'How d'you do?'

She gave me a hard look. 'Not too bad, thanks, young man. If you were one of mine, though, you'd be in trouble.'

I knew how safe I was, so I said: 'No worries, Mrs Coluchi. It all went smoothly.'

She laughed at that. 'OK. I guess it must have, or you wouldn't be here. So, Anne,' and she turned, 'it's the real thing, is it?'

I wondered what my relationship with Anne had anything to do with such a formal gathering, but then she answered 'Yes, I'd bet on it.'

That seemed to settle it, so I turned to Pops to see what he thought. He was nodding in agreement. 'Twenty years. It's taken a long time.' Well, I thought, not that long, but perhaps when you have a daughter you start worrying about marrying her off from a very early age. I gave Anne a big smile. She returned it with a puzzled frown.

Somebody's assistant arrived with a tray of drinks, and distracted me for a moment. I selected what was obviously champagne, and suited to the occasion, then heard Pops say: 'I have to give him credit for it. The last time we met he made me the promise: *We will march one day, and you will remember our discussions.*'

The glass paused halfway, then I downed the lot in a gulp. It didn't all go the right way, so Anne had to ask 'Trevor, are you alright?' Mrs Coluchi looked at me as if her earlier thoughts were confirmed.

'Fine,' I said. 'Sorry. Glass slipped.' I mopped my chin with a handkerchief, and wondered where I was going to get the large whisky I needed. I'd almost flown blind right into a situation worse than the laser sights of the Indonesian fighter. After a couple of seconds, though, I was struggling not to laugh. I glanced at Pops, who was considering me with his own level gaze. 'Don't drink a lot of champagne in Australia,' I said. 'Not used to it.'

He clearly didn't believe a word of it, but he nodded slowly, then turned back to the iron lady. 'When I knew him, as a young Colonel, he was tough and energetic,' he said. 'He first approached me from the throng of young officers present at a reception to which I was invited. He asked some questions about my life and work, and implied that he'd like to meet me on quieter ground. Shortly after, I invited him to the house for lunch. It was the first of many extraordinary talks. And I shortly saw that Bulyanto was a visionary. As a Muslim, this implies a dedication to military purpose within the context of his faith. You must go back more than a thousand years to understand him. For me to explain this to you, I must digress a little.'

It was even harder not to laugh then, once I knew how utterly wrong I'd been. But I was suddenly fascinated in a way I hadn't been before. In that moment when he said *Bulyanto*, I felt scales drop from my eyes.

'Prior to Mohammed, the tribes of Arabia were constantly-warring kinship groups. Mohammed brought them unity, or rather his Islam did because it strengthened the concept of community along lines other than kinship. This community was the *ummah*, and all of Mohammed's efforts were dedicated to its survival and its ideals. It was a hard life for the Prophet, but he was, in the context of his time, amazingly successful.'

'Mohammed's death posed great problems for his successors. The first, Abu Bakr, spent most of his efforts in holding the *ummah* together - many of the tribes who had joined it tried to break away. The nature of traditional Arabian pacts was purely political, and were often considered to end on the death of one of the chiefs who had formed the alliance. The pacts were with Mohammed, not Abu Bakr. However, Abu Bakr, in two short years, quelled the uprisings. The result was the unification of Arabia.'

'He was succeeded immediately by a second Mohammedan companion, Umar. As the second deputy, or caliph, Umar had a different problem. What to do with the energies of a now-united people who were raiders and fighters? In order to keep the *ummah* whole, he decided that the answer was to launch raids on non-Muslim neighbours. The result of Umar's leadership, as that of Mohammed and Abu Bakr, is almost beyond believing. The Arabs tore into Syria, Egypt and Iraq. They defeated the Persian army. Within a few years they controlled Syria, Palestine and Egypt. Within a hundred there was an Islamic Empire across the range from what is now Spain as far as India.'

He paused. 'The General sees himself as another Umar.'

'Did he have a vision of how he was another Umar?' asked Mrs Coluchi, a little impatiently, perhaps because, as an ex-student of Pops, she knew all this history. Evidently, though, she hadn't been privy to the private lunches.

Pops gave a brittle smile. 'He used to say: *We owe the Dutch very little -*

centuries of servitude, and the ignominy of a Chinese-immigrant administration. But we owe them unity.'

'Unity?' asked Mrs Coluchi in surprise.

Pops nodded. 'Unity against all that. Independence was born from it, and Bulyanto saw conquest from it. Just as Arabian unity brought an Islamic Empire, so he saw Javanese unity bringing a different empire.'

'I trust he wasn't talking about becoming a replacement to the colonial Dutch,' said Mrs Coluchi, perhaps cognizant of how many of the non-Javanese peoples of Indonesia viewed the Javanese.

Pops shook his head. 'That was anathema to him. And he faced another difficulty. Islamic conquest in that first Empire was not religious conquest. It was plundering, pure and simple. Islam was never about conquest of Judaism and Christianity. They were accepted as equally valid monotheistic religions - their peoples were peoples of earlier revelations - and the Quran made that very clear. It is only later Islamic interpretation which has given religious connotation to the conquest.'

I was becoming distinctly uneasy during these present revelations, something working through my mind and coming to some sort of juncture with what Pops was saying. I'd never heard this history before, so it was not as if I were on track to some sort of scholarly resolution of a particularly difficult problem. What was surfacing was the argument I'd previously had with myself over how I'd been so neatly trapped by Subagio, and *Magnet* also. The idea that Indonesia was creating a position of just defence. 'East Timor,' I said to myself, quietly.

But it must have fallen into a moment of silence, and Pops hearing sharper than I'd given his age credit for. He turned his attention on me, a slight twinkle in his eyes. 'Yes, young man. East Timor. For in the eyes of the Javanese, East Timor took on sacred status. And if you are attacked in a sacred place, you may kill your aggressors. So says the Quran.'

'So it has nothing to do with international law,' I said.

'Java can be pragmatic about these things,' he said. 'Java knows that the West cannot see into Java's heart. It is easier, therefore, for Java to present its arguments as arguments in law. A just defence. However, the truth is that Java sees it as a religious struggle. First, the usurping Portuguese, catholics to a body. Secondly, the interfering Australians, protestants of many colours. The common thread, of course, is Christianity. Tell me,' he said, 'do Australians see themselves as modern-day Crusaders?'

I shook my head. 'No.'

'Avengers, then?'

'We like underdogs.'

He laughed, and turned to Mrs Coluchi. 'There you have it, Grace. Australia is for the underdogs. Java is for Islamic rights.'

Mrs Coluchi, Grace, was not amused. 'And Bulyanto?'

'Ah, yes. Our visionary. What would you say, Trevor?'

'The man's a killer. I felt it the day I first saw him.'

It fell flat into the room, and even though none of the hangers-on had said anything since we'd arrived, there was a moment's complete silence.

'You know him, then?'

'Not well, but I've met him.'

Pops nodded. 'The valid opinion of another soldier.'

I smiled thinly. 'Death in war is not visionary.'

'No. But its purpose may be. That is often hard for a military man to accept. It is where religion helps.'

'There's no chance you ever had lunch with Vice-Admiral Subagio?' I asked.

'No,' said Pops. 'But I know of him. A cut-throat, I believe.'

Grace Coluchi finally found something to amuse her. 'A visionary and a cut-throat. That's all I need.'

'But a Muslim cut-throat, Grace. Someone to fear more than a visionary, I think. If you can understand the vision, you may be able to foretell a lot. With a cut-throat you can do little more than follow the trail of blood.'

'I doubt we will yet for a while,' Grace Coluchi said. 'We're still busy. The President won't authorize the dispersal of any of our forces into a new theatre in the immediate future. I'm afraid,' she said, looking at me, 'you'll have to do it on your own for a while.' She grimaced, perhaps the closest she could come to a smile of sympathy. 'That message is already on its way to your Government.'

Grace Coluchi left shortly afterwards, and it turned out that all the others present, silent as they had been, were staff or sycophants of hers. She did not, at any time that night, live up to her name, eventually leaving abruptly, and with a terse goodnight. 'Grace does not like anything that smells of another religion,' said Pops, once we were only three. 'It complicates things for her.'

'Yet she hired you,' I said to Anne, who had come to stand by my side, arm in mine.

'She foresaw the need to,' Anne said. 'Pops instilled that in her.'

'Oh, I don't know,' said Pops. 'Poor Grace has a hard job. She is someone with her finger in a dyke full of the Christian Right. She daren't take it out.'

I laughed. 'In Australia a dyke is a dunny. Tough place to have your finger.'

Anne poked me. 'Trevor!'

'Sorry, love.'

'If a dunny is what I think it is,' said Pops, 'that's the first definition I've enjoyed all night. I'll have to remember it.'

'But she's left us with ours in a different one,' I said.

'It's not her fault alone,' said Pops. 'This Administration is now at the limit with the American people. The cost of the Middle East war is coming home to roost, and it has turned out far higher and messier than was originally promised. Expanding it on an even more distant front will be prohibitively expensive in the next Presidential elections. And Grace didn't say it, but there is far more worry about the Chinese in northeast Asia than Indonesians in the southeast. The Chinese are far more interested in manoeuvring over Taiwan than addressing the Korean threat. That sits badly here.'

'No chance of religious visions or Crusades,' I said. 'Must make the Christian Right very unhappy.' Black humour seemed to be climbing into my throat like bile.

Pops didn't seem to be very impressed. 'I can understand your disdain,' he said. 'But don't go away bitter. The Right is already very unhappy. Perhaps we will be less bellicose for a while.'

I saw Anne flinch slightly at the *go away*, and recognized myself that it was time to do so, anyway. 'I'm not bitter. Just wondering why we came all this way.'

'Probably because someone with vision saw it as worthwhile,' said Pops.

We gathered at the door.

'Anne says she expects to have children.'

Anne turned her face into the shoulder of his jacket, as if embarrassed.

I marvelled at Pops' equanimity, given what he must have viewed as my less-than-gracious comments to most of what had been said, and thought to myself how close they must be if she had already given him that news. 'I hope so,' I said, not sure why she should be embarrassed. 'I'd like to be their father, but I'm afraid I have other duties first. When this is over, perhaps.'

He nodded. 'If there's one thing I wish, it's that my wife had met you. The last day I saw her alive she wondered when Anne would marry. She died not knowing the most important thing in her life.'

I then realized that Anne had not been embarrassed at all. She was crying her heart out on her father's shoulder, knowing what it was he was going to say. His hand, when it stretched out to give farewell to mine, had strength, hope and sadness in its touch.

'You look tough and energetic,' he said. 'Are you a visionary?'

"That's a judgement of others,' I said. 'It's not something one can say about oneself. But no, I'm not much of a visionary.'

He smiled. 'But I think you have foresight.'

'Oh yes. But nowhere near enough.'

'None of us can have enough, Trevor, because then we'd be left without hindsight. But a little foresight is a tremendous thing. You'll need it, I'm thinking.'

'If I'm to do battle.'

'That's what I mean. But you're already at war in yourself. Good luck. And come back.'

I took a good look at him, surprised at his observation, and because I had no means of knowing if we'd ever meet again. 'It's been an honour. Goodbye, sir.'

Anne was still crying softly into his shoulder, and he gave her a squeeze in appreciation of all she was to him. 'Oh no. Just David, if you like. If I'm not there when the moment comes,' he added, 'you will already have my blessing.'

I took the proferred hand. 'Thank you.'

'Look after her well.'

We sat on the front step, wondering, at least I was, how to say goodbye. The long black limo sat there like a hearse, waiting to take me on a final bloody ride into purgatory. We held hands, like any lovers, and the seconds to takeoff counted down loudly like the old gong being struck for J. Arthur Rank. There wasn't anything to say, or any way to say it.

'Think of me as if going off on a cruise,' I said.

'Oh Trevor, how can I?' Her head was on my shoulder.

'You remember all those World War Two films,' I said. 'People standing on the dock. Bunting flying. Ship's horn blowing.'

'I've seen them. It's only now I can feel them.'

'Ah well, love. Perhaps it'll be an unholy war.'

'What do you mean?'

'Fun on both sides.'

'Trevor! People are going to die.'

'Sorry. But they do say that in moments of absolute terror, you reach a state of enlightenment you'll never feel again.'

'Stop it!'

'Oh, Christ. What can I say?'

'Nothing. So don't.'

'No. Sorry.'

The limo took me back to the helicopter. At least I suppose it did, because I remember nothing until I was in the air. I looked about, seeing space, hearing noise, and slowly the sense of where and when came back, I recalled who I was, and why I was there. I saw the helicopter for what it was, a means of deliverance, and suddenly I knew what it was I wanted to do.

I hadn't been lying in Washington. The northern half of Australia, and especially the Top End, is, to all intents and purposes, indefensible. Defence installations around the coast and inland are meant more to slow up anyone with real malodorous intent from getting to the meat down in the south-east. The cost of a significant defence is far too high for anyone willingly to gamble his or her political life on creating it, and that, with the complacency of the well-fed to take ANZUS as the be-all and end-all of defence treaties, was what led to the gradual wind-down of the naval hardware, paraded imperialistically around the Pacific and Indian Oceans until it wore out. When it came to replacing that hardware we were shocked at the price, with the result that the Royal Australian Navy is hardly regal.

The situation was little different for the air and ground forces, the majority of the north-western air-bases bare of long-term life support systems required for inhospitable climates, and most of the ground forces working hard to keep regimental headquarters where a stint on the beach didn't cook your brain in five minutes. Serious installations exist in Cairns and Darwin, but serious is a term relative to what you expect to come your way, and given that Kangaroo for years pitted the Defence Force against imaginary low-level foes with only mildly dangerous intent, serious could be taken as only slightly deranged. The inhabitants of Darwin were not pleased at Canberra's putting its main radar defences at Alice Springs, some thousand kilometres further south from Darwin and thus farther away from the Darwinians themselves than the latter were from Jakarta. Only in Western Australia did Canberra put a defence facility second to Sydney. In another place called Garden Island.

Dixon and I crawled off the long-haul flight to Canberra into what was a gathering storm to the north, what Bluing described as the monsoon within the monsoon. We had little more than an hour before an emergency meeting of the Defence Committee, time to give Bluing the gist of Washington and to listen to his frustrations. That storm was still only slowly filtering into the consciousness of the Government, highly publicized evacuations apart. It was as if the Wet brought a rusting of all process, especially the political imagination. Perhaps some of it was an unwillingness to recognize just how vulnerable the country really was, because once you acknowledged it you were liable for some decisions. Responsibility accrued with action. If you avoided it, the ultimate blame could fall elsewhere.

`Our decision to send a flying squadron to the ASEAN manoeuvres was a mistake.' Bluing said it with little conviction, and it sounded more like comments aimed at him from on high.

Dixon and I had debated this on the plane, a repeat of my earlier mental arguments when I'd shared a flight with master Soekendro. There was no doubt that it had marooned too much of Australia's naval capacity away from the immediate defence theatre. One of the three ships was now *hors de combat*, and the other two, while steaming hard for the Timor Gap, were still too far away to provide any support for at least forty-eight hours. A frigate and two submarines had comprised the interim complement in Fremantle, and these were now on their way north, but they'd mount little more than a running defence, full of holes, open to the sharks on their way in. Bluing's command was little better than a tin-pot admiral's in some Central American country, with rank but no boats even to fish from. But the manoeuvres and the gauntlet we had run had given us something valuable, an understanding of a foe who we hadn't known before. How high a price did one have to pay for information like that?

And what did we think of the Americans? On the one hand, so self-interested that it took the potential loss of an oilfield to motivate them. On the other, fully intent politically in keeping Taiwan an open sore, though the true festering was of Sino-American relations at the highest level. But the memory of Vietnam still lingered, when eyes had been opened and war shown to be empty of glory. And we couldn't blame them at all. Australian defence had been and was an Australian responsibility. It had been destroyed by politics, and it looked as though politics would continue to defeat it. Too little, too late. That's what the past ten years had been. A slow awakening to an independent future. One where you looked after yourself. If you could.

But they surprised me. `You're now Group Warfare Officer (West), Gregory. We are still deciding whether you will work from Canberra or Fremantle.'

305

That was Dixon, who must have done some signalling to Bluing from the plane while I caught up on some more of my lost sleep. I'd spent more than an hour giving him the Timor and Arafura seas from the charts in my head, and then my knowledge of Subagio and Indonesian Navy Command. But the key was my conviction that it would be Subagio himself on the water for this one. He would not delegate authority at a time when the regulars from Surabaya were coming to the game.

The appointment was beyond what I'd expected, sure as I had been that I was to be shunted to a desk somewhere in the corridors of Navy Command, under that idiot Edmond in Intelligence. That doom had been in my mind since Washington. But to be GWO put me right back into the fray, the next best thing to a shipboard command, though less technical than the Advanced Warfare Officer I'd been on the *Fraser*. An AWO provides instant interpretation and decision on the immediate field of action in which the ship is engaged, but GWO made me a strategist, better than a command, because with a command you had no guarantee of being in the right place at the right time. The more I thought about it, the more I understood that the gods were giving me a chance to pit my mind against Subagio, to play him at his own game. And the Western Fleet was the only one that could avert disaster, even though the truth was that we could hardly measure naval defences per mile of continental coastline in tons. So, with that feeble screen, even worse when measured in ships in service and on-station, I had to think of what we were going to do to stop Subagio from whatever he intended. But I also had to think of Subagio and Bulyanto as a team, brilliant men, with a lot at stake, who probably had separate courses of action leading to an ultimate joint goal. I couldn't separate them.

And I *was* coming late into the game, for the Red Fleet was already at sea, the lethal missile shield for its coveys of LCTs I'd thought it would be, and divided into different expeditionary forces which we did not yet all have pinpointed, the monsoon doing all the cloaking work it could. Wyndham still had me puzzled, a placement of some serious hardware in a very distant place, no immediate purpose, and which I thought already had our ground forces in fits of mirth, no need to go up there and take it from them. But I hadn't forgotten Soekendro, master gamer, and I thought that young genius probably had that landing very carefully calculated. My job was the sea, but understanding the broader picture was going to be the key to forward planning, and so anything that Soekendro came up with I was going to have to outdo.

`Right. That's it. I'll meet you in the Warfare Centre when I get back. That'll give you a couple of hours to work out what's missing.' Bluing's comment to Dixon brought me back to the present, back to the earth the appointment had me soaring away from, death just over the horizon.

`Just our fleet.'

`No jokes, Jim. I'm not in the mood.' And he walked out, leaving Dixon looking bleakly at the pictures on the wall. Ships that no longer were.

I gave up any thought of sleep, something Dixon had ordered out of some lame-brained idea that it would make me more useful. My anger was more likely to serve him better, so I found a uniform I could call my own, climbed into it, left the memory of the phone call in my hotel room and walked off some of the remaining stiffness on my way back to Headquarters. Dixon looked askance at me as I came in, short of sleep himself, and then muttered to the young officer at his side. `Brief him, Collins.'

From his build I made Collins a fast-bowler, or perhaps a footballer. He looked like a muscled greyhound. And, though a junior in the same Department, he was no Edmonds. He did what Edmonds had never been able to do and gave me all of the important facts in five minutes flat. He made me feel finally at home, someone on my own wavelength with whom to grapple whatever I threw at him.

Then a screen flickered and we had something quite different, but which made hardly any more sense than Wyndham, two ships bombarding the Larrakeyah Barracks in Darwin. It was a suicidal action, the one thing I knew was impossible, so I sensed another disaster waiting to happen, something more serious involving Darwin, but couldn't see how two warships in the approach roads to the port could make it happen.

`The patrol boats aren't there.' Collins gave me what I hadn't known, though should have guessed when Dixon gave me the original news on the Qantas flight. `They responded to the emergency call from the oil platforms on the Sahul Banks.' Did he see it as I saw it? A staged event? A diversion to forestall any confrontation in Darwin? Bloody Kangaroo, again.

So, finally we had something on the large screen that filled the end wall, an electronic map of the Top End, from Derby to Cape York. The small force which had attacked the oilrigs was being tracked, planes from one of the northern bare-bases underflying the monsoonal cover and giving intermittent radar feed to the ground station in Alice. Someone had decided red was to remain the colour for the marauders, and the small trapezium which represented this force, which seemed currently to be going nowhere, looked distressingly close to the coast.

Life was suddenly serious in a way it never had been, beer and skittles no more, and more than my reputation was on the line. Running through Eastern Indonesia I'd seen myself as a distant line of defence in some imaginary game. But once that last critical thought fell into place on the plane into Kupang, nothing was imaginary anymore and it became quite clear what was in front of us. And if anything brought a sense of dread, it wasn't that we had no ships and that the seas were empty, but that we suddenly had a foe grown up overnight, no cold war to give us twenty years to prepare, and that we were going to have to fight it any way we could. It was no thought to give Dixon, but I didn't even give us a whisker's chance in hell of doing it.

Twenty six

Death was a necessary price, and it came simply to the old man. Age and infirmity were no release from debt for the decade of nepotism and corruption which had plagued the land. It came swiftly, too, a thug's thrust of a kris, held momentarily against the skin, then pushed hard, straight to the heart. The kris made it ceremonial, more, even, than the killing of a sheep at the end of Lebaran.

For we who watched and waited while it was done, it was our killing even if it wasn't our arm. The snake-like curves of the kris, flowing from a jewel-rimmed hilt, slithered into the chest without a sound. Though the body was unconscious, it protested the penetration with a visible orgasmic shudder. Perhaps the heart beat once around the wafer-thin tempered steel, and then contracted in its own death, the final knell to the rest of the body of majesty dethroned.

But if he was unconscious through it, that final pain brought him awake enough to see shadows and a uniform. But it was the hilt that drew his attention, one long known, his favourite. Not a family heirloom, because his family had not had anything as fine as this, but the one he'd have worn had he come from a sultan's line. But as he hadn't, he'd bought it like he'd bought everything else. And it sat momentarily on his chest, then withdrew, bringing with it the devil's entrails, the rich red steaming snake of the blade. Then, perhaps in the sheer agony of that final knowledge of what had been done to him, he screamed.

One man watched the final moments with special care. When he was sure that death had come he nodded to the thug with the blade. It was replaced in its sheath, and the whole put in his outstretched hand. He, the Jenderal, had to show it to his Minister.

For the old man, there had to be seen to be a better ending. While it was time for him to go, the nation would be puzzled by a disappearance. So his corpse was regally attended according to the traditions of his religion, placed on a bier, where senior members of the government could be seen to be paying their last respects to a man who'd died of his age, and buried before the end of the day. The ceremonies were carried on national television.

Excerpted from Rusman Soekendro, LetJen (ret'd),

No Game At All: *Memoirs of a Strategist*

B ut, no, I am not concerned with Mohammed as the Prophet,' said the woman. 'He received the revelations, and gave them to his people. It was necessary for him to fight, because other Arabs saw Islam as a threat and wanted Mohammed and his people annihilated. So there was justification in war for the very survival of the Scriptures. Within those very few years, however, pre-Islamic traditions came to the fore and became the very rationale for the Islamization of the known world. It is with this that I have difficulty. This was not holy war, it was pure domination and plundering.' She remembered a phrase said to her many years before in another context. 'Unholy war.'

'What you're asking me to believe,' said the Javan, 'and which goes against every tenet of my faith, is that Woman, by her very nature, is a natural repository of God's scripture.' He was visibly shaken. 'This implies that Mohammed was an unnecessary vehicle.'

'No. In pre-Islamic Arabia woman was subjugated under man. It was a vicious society. There was no other path into Man's mind than through a man. No man other than Mohammed could have been Prophet. This is clearly recognized. He was the man for his time, and for His time also.'

'Then you are saying that Islam must change, and must undo much of what has driven it.'

'I'm saying that Islam must be honest unto itself, as I believe the majority of Muslims are. This world cannot go forward, cannot survive, if it is in a perpetual state of war. Any religion - Christianity, Islam, or any other - must grow out of its history. That, as a woman, is what I say God intended. That is the ultimate jihad.'

***

'But where the hell did those two corvettes come from?' I asked. Corvettes they were, and evidently sailed confidently because they made the approach roads without challenge and bombarded the Larrakeyah patrol boat base and naval barracks with the first rays of sun lifting over the back of the town. 'If they came straight in they'd have met the patrol boats going out, and that they didn't. So where did they come from?'

'There was a radar image of the western approach to the Clarence Strait which showed a vessel at 0415,' said Collins. 'It was assumed to be a coastal freighter which had just cleared the headland. The second vessel is timed at 0425. By the time anyone had any doubts, the first vessel was inside the roads. The bombardment started shortly after that.'

I grabbed a chart from a nearby table. `But did they leave Melville to port or to starboard? Christ, Collins. This is a shambles. They've been in our waters for several hours, where they weren't expected, and we can't trace their movements. We're almost blind up there.'

`They must have left Melville to port. I'd not take a dinghy through the Clarence Strait.' Collins was shaking his head at his own certainty.

`Tide tables? Do we have any tide tables?' I pulled up a reference list of the standard information I could access immediately through my own terminal. Tide tables, state port and date. I stuck in Darwin, today. What I saw was enough to make me want to be back in the Kimberley. `Admiral.'

It brought Dixon over from one of the priority phones.

`Van Diemen Gulf, sir. The highest tide of the year was at 0400 this morning. It's too much to be just a coincidence. The Clarence Strait was navigable.' And then the thought that made it obvious. `What else might they have brought with them? That far, at least.' I was remembering Raha and my *KOPASSUS* colonel

Dixon showed definite signs of wanting to be sick. `Darwin? Get on to Air Force. This isn't for Maritime Command. Explain the situation. I'll talk to the top.'

Collins was right in his assessment that it would have been a nail-biting piece of navigation even with tides as high as they were. The final achievement must have raised the sweat on their backs even more.

Joint Service Liaison was a few square yards of the Joint Warfare Centre. Navy had a man there, a slightly overweight middle-aged officer, and my call had gone through him. With the patrol boats gone there was no possibility of any naval involvement in Darwin, so I wanted to be where I thought news might be the freshest. Privately I thought Liaison a nebulous territory, and was glad that I hadn't ended up there myself. It would take many hours and at least one challenge to test where liaison would fall in the range from effective communication to hours spent playing cards. To a large degree, our superiors would decide which it was to be.

'We give them no more than an hour.' Perhaps the introductions were well past, and they had already found some common ground. They were sharing observations over coffee. Army was a woman of medium height, with short brown hair around an impish face. In uniform, and describing conditions in Larrakeyah, she evinced nothing of the imp.

Larrakeyah was a naval barracks, but she evidently saw anything being defended on land as Army territory. Perhaps there were some barrack-bound infantry. 'Not enough firepower.'

'You mean, the port facility and barracks,' Navy said.

'Oh, yes. The marauders are well armed.'

Air Force nodded. 'Too many other vessels in the offshore roads. Effective screen.' He spoke in short, sharp bursts, and seemed excruciatingly shy. Perhaps it came from being extremely tall and thin. I recalled Andy Brockle, and doubted that this man would have fitted in Brockle's cockpit. 'Our blokes would have to come at them from the sea. Likely to put half the missiles into the town. We'd be hanged.'

I think it was unspoken between us all that it was too soon to contemplate serious civilian casualties in an offensive that was only just taking shape. A sloppy attack, where any shoreward-fired missiles that missed a ship could hit the city, would be a political disaster as well as a human tragedy.

But the conversation went little further, so I went back to Collins and our own surface plot.

'They're making course for the south-west.'

It was the corvettes' first move since they'd entered the roads, and it made the next part of the outcome certain. We tracked them along the coast, and there they did become prey to the hunters from Katherine, a move that they themselves must have understood. So the commanders must have had specific orders, not to spare the ships and to sacrifice themselves. I had a clear image of Indonesian seamen rotating through the small musholla under the rear deck, making that final supplication to Allah before the rictus of a fiery death.

Air Force lost two planes in the five crucial hours it took them to pound the corvettes into the sea. Among all our electronic gadgets, a common television continually flickered, a helter-skelter of images, most too disjointed to merit continual attention. But one image stayed with us, the sort that presages disaster round the corner, so violent and colourful that you continue to watch: one of the two planes caught, for some reason, in a final attack, and it carried the leading vessel's radio-mast with it as it cartwheeled over the superstructure and exploded in mid-air beyond. As a still photo, it became the most-used media image of the whole conflict, a plane apparently standing on its nose, one wing gone, and in the first stages of its own immolation as the ship behind it too died.

But to sink them we had concentrated almost all our air power to the west of the waters that held my immediate interest. And still we hadn't heard back through Liaison from the command that had sent it there.

'It's Darwin, and maybe Katherine.' I had thought it at the time I'd looked north up a clear Stuart Highway, but had dismissed it as crazy.

Collins still looked doubtful, not convinced that it was to be this level of escalation. `Can't be.'

But he knew neither Subagio nor Bulyanto. `Those two corvettes were bait to our air defences just as the attack on the oil platforms took the patrol boats well away.' Simple stratagems if I was right but superbly effective. Looking hard at the coastal chart I thought we had probably given them what they wanted on a plate.

There had been incendiary missiles in the bombardment, and some must have been deliberately aimed over the heads of any barrack-bound infantry detachment. The city was on fire. '1942 all over again.' The comment echoed in the Warfare Centre more than once. And a voice on the phone said that the red berets of the *KOPASSUS* advance, the thrust to the heart, reached the city within three hours, timed against the corvettes' first attack. Even if they had been put ashore well before the first two corvettes began to navigate the Clarence Strait, it was, by any measure, a valiant run, inland from the Gulf. Then the voice went, the connection cut.

But it was when Katherine reported the direct attack against the airfield that I knew we'd been out-played, even if I'd had an inkling of it. This could not have been part of the Darwin advance, not enough time, so they'd chosen another route out of Van Diemen Gulf, tentacle of an octopus still not fully defined. And both of these must have been the first group out of Roti, lying hidden somewhere in cloud-shrouded waters until the tide reached its height and the Gulf took on a leniency not often shown.

` No longer can we believe that we are not facing the biggest threat to national security since 1942. We can safely assume that all our operational defences will be tested. What we still don't know is why, nor the extent of the how. Perhaps we can make inroads into both of those issues in the next couple of hours.'

The Defence Chief looked at the dozen and a half faces around the table. Introductions had been necessary, as there were a few not familiar to the regular meetings of the Combined Defence Committee. He had privately ordered an operational war footing, even though the polies were still debating the issue.

Dixon had brought both me and Collins, working men, and as the introductions went around the table it was clear that the other Services had thought likewise. That, at least, made me hope practical liaison would be possible, even if it took a while to convert the intelligence to action.

`Admiral Dixon, you have the floor. Ten minutes please.'

Dixon was done in nine. Brief it had to be at this point, not that there was much to say. His peers in the other Services followed. It was, all told, a dreadful half hour.

`Right. Your analysis Granby?' The Chairman nodded to one of two civilians at the table, who'd introduced himself as from the International Security Division of Foreign Affairs.

Granby said as much as I'd said at the Pentagon. 'But we still do not know whether there is a new Suharto.' `

'It's not an ex-President trying for a comeback?'

'Unlikely. None has the power base. And the connection with Habibie is coincidental - he may have bought the ships, but he no longer has power where it matters.'

I passed a note to Dixon, who, reading it, nodded.

`If I might speak, sir?'

The Chairman nodded. `Yes, Captain Gregory.'

`I believe that this started with an operational command in or around Roti. It was a small but complex operation. Given the volume of men and materiel that was gathered there, there must have been ongoing coordination within other units of the military.'

`Are you suggesting that we view Roti to be a target for a counterattack?' The Chairman sounded slightly hostile.

`No, sir. If you'll give me a moment. And it would be too late for that, even with our capability.' And Roti was, to a degree, a symbol, not a location. I had no wish anyway to feed a vision of heavy air strikes into tropical jungle. `Mr Granby indicated that there's a change in government in progress. That's a national movement. I believe the indications are that the naval operation to date was kept secret from the main body of the Indonesian Navy, and ABRI as a whole. It may be that this step has been an essential precursor to getting all of ABRI very quickly onside. The Flores Sea 'event' may have been part of the same. We should look at the overall threat very differently from what we are currently seeing. Once it's ABRI as a whole, Roti is irrelevant.'

'You're saying that this is not yet ABRI?' The Chairman looked around the table, perhaps looking for an echo of his thoughts.

'Yes, sir. At this moment, just a combined operation of a smaller naval clique and KOPASSUS.

'Granby?'

Granby looked uncomfortable, but perhaps glad he was not from Defence. 'Possible, Chairman. If this is a coup, it is the way it would have to start.'

The Defence Chief turned to me. `Captain Gregory, you seem to have set us a conundrum. And if the whole of ABRI turned its attention on us? How would you weight the problem then?'

`By at least a factor of two, sir.'

`And you think we have time to breathe before ABRI is upon us?'

`No sir. I think the rest of ABRI will now be wide awake.'

`Not one of our best meetings.' The lack of immediately possible Top End naval defence action had seemed to make time a luxury and we were walking back to Navy Command. Dixon was mentally reviewing the Chairman's wrap up. `I thought he was going to cut your balls off.'

I shrugged. `The trouble, sir, is that if this current force manages to take the edge off what little defence we have, we'd have no defence to anything else. I don't like hyperbole, and we're already facing their best. I thought a factor of two was enough.'

`Oh, so did I, so did I. It's really immaterial, as you say. Take a close look at Surabaya, Collins. We have some other fish to hunt.'

`I'd suggested that to Captain Edmonds already, sir.'

`Oh you had, had you? Thank God for that.'

I winked at Collins, who was looking nonplussed at Dixon's departing back.

This is too simple. I've missed something.'

I'd spent an hour looking at numbers and known course headings. From my original five and twenty blackbirds in a crimson pie, five corvettes, twenty LCTs, the total had reached nine corvettes and forty LCTs. Five and twenty to the west, four and twenty to the east. I'd called the groups *Ruby* and *Amethyst,* imagery that Collins questioned, but he had none better. Two corvettes from *Amethyst* had been spotted shepherding their twenty empty LCTs away from the waters of Van Diemens Gulf, just making the Dundas Strait exit under low cloud and on the ebb. The low-level data suggested I was seven corvettes and about another twenty LCTs short. Where were they? *What* were they? Another of the same? I needed a hawk in the sky to tell me.

`What do you think you've missed?' Collins was at my shoulder.

I'd gone back to a navigation chart, finding it an easier aid than a screen. `This is what we have. An apparent feint at Wyndham, perhaps partly intended to make us look away from Darwin, and then the advance on Darwin itself and Katherine bottled up. Serious targets, but this is the opening game. We know why, Granby said it at the meeting, and I've had my own guesses on the subject for quite a while.'

`So what is it they want? I've been trying to see a pattern, but I can't yet.' He peered dejectedly at the chart.

I replaced the chart with a topographic map of northern Australia. `Any pattern has to be based on what they've defined as military objectives. We know about *Amethyst* and *Ruby,* and that *Amethyst* took Darwin in the space of a few hours. *Ruby* seems to have been effort wasted at Wyndham. What do you see?'

`A region with widely dispersed population but economically important, a few large rivers, a heavily indented coastline.'

`Easy to penetrate, difficult to reach from anywhere. Let's say that there was another expeditionary force which we haven't yet spotted. Is there another obvious objective?'

`If the criteria are the same, either here to the west or much further to the east.'

`To the west, Pilbara. To the east, the York Peninsula. Which would you go for?'

He thought for a moment. `Pilbara.'

`Not much doubt, is there? Further still from east coast defences. Still a million miles from the southeast, but reaching down to where we are just as vulnerable as up here.'

`Where do you think Group Three is?'

I circled an index finger over the western fringe of the Timor Sea and gave it the name in my head. `*Opal?* Further west than the one we've found. Somewhere out here in the blue. Let's find it.' I reached for the Liaison phone.

What was obviously a disaster in Darwin, plus knowledge filtering through the northern defence arc of other possible incursions, I thought would bring the little military present across the Top End to a state of alert higher in reality than the order from the Defence Chief. The order had been given, but it was superfluous. It must have been clear to all that a die had been cast in a game beyond any which had been expected. Recent wargames were exercises to satisfy political demands, inputs to the ongoing alliances that were deemed essential to the country's defence, but nursery antics when it came to *this*.

The Wyndham force, *Ruby,* had come into Admiralty Gulf. *Opal* must have stayed well to the west of Seringapatam Reef, in about a thousand fathoms, for we only picked it up when making its crossing of the hundred-fathom line. It was very clearly heading for King Sound.

That news reached me within minutes of my having reached for the phone. `Sorry to say, this isn't in response to your request.' Our Navy man had obviously got over his own disgust. 'Air Force didn't go looking for them for *you*. They had them spotted already. The information hadn't reached us.'

A black mark for Liaison, I thought. `And numbers?'

`Estimated to be between twenty and twenty-five ships. Similar sized force as the one that hit Admiralty Gulf.'

`Thank you.'

`Right, Gregory. Any time. Air Force says the other request *is* being attended to.'

`There's *Opal*.' I nodded towards the screen where another red trapezium had appeared in response to my data entry. `That's the lot, I think. Everything we saw at Roti.'

Collins nodded. `If Air Force can't stop them they'll make landfall within six hours.' We both knew that neither the naval squadron northbound from Fremantle, nor the two ships returning across the Indian Ocean, could reach it before it hit the coast. But *Opal* was heading straight for an airfield, so could not expect an easy landing. What would they have planned for there that would give them an edge? At the moment I couldn't see it.

But there was the longer-term outlook to consider. `If we assume that the ships still have a strategic purpose after this first landing, we may still be able to interfere. *Amethyst* seems to be headed fast for Roti.'

`A second wave.'

`It has to be, though distance is a major factor. *Amethyst* is the only group that has any real chance of not being intercepted. Those patrol craft don't carry enough clout.' Only two of the three patrol boats had survived the run to the oilfield, one victim to a surprise low-level Indonesian marauder. The remaining two had been alerted not to return to Darwin, but it left them with no home base. And no-one was going to waste scarce resources on sinking empty LCTs.

Twenty seven

Elang was not intended to be the surprise that Topan and Petir had been. The immediate success of Petir had been essential, a strike into the soul of the Top End, Darwin and Katherine to be contained. Elang would be a broadening of that strike, under and into a weakening northwestern defence. Once Darwin and Katherine were ours, the Kimberly was a simpler, intermediate, target. Air defence there was and would be, but not the fury that could be expected to be launched from Katherine. Once Katherine was removed from the equation, Indonesian penetration forces were at much less risk of defeat.

Topan differed significantly from Petir in her cargo. For here it was more important that we deliver essential hardware. So only the troops to scare them out of Wyndham and prepare the column were necessary. Once air defence was dealt with, it would be easier and faster to deliver regiments by plane.

Excerpted from Rusman Soekendro, LetJen (ret'd),
No Game At All: *Memoirs of a Strategist*

How is it that women fight as soldiers?' asked the Javan. 'What brings them onto the battlefield?' Through her marriage, the woman had met many western military women - somehow *soldiers* did not seem to be sufficiently gender neutral - and had had time to understand what drove many of them, though she was loathe to think of it as a universal truth.

'I think modern military women have almost nothing in common with their historic or prehistoric forebears,' she said. 'The latter saw war as the very essence of survival, the former see it as a career path, and mainly in armies which have not been to war in their generation. A military career is advertised as something close to an extreme sport.'

'You are not told about the bullets?'

'I don't know,' she said. 'But as a woman I cannot help but think that a woman who wishes to fight like a man wishes to be recognized as one. And, to take it a step further, to be listened to as one.'

'If that is true, then it is the ultimate sacrifice. It is an abrogation of gender.'

She felt a moment of mischief. 'Perhaps the only instance where the accounting of a woman's individual contribution to His collective religious goal should not require beneficence.'

The Javan was shocked. 'Do you believe they do the right thing?'

The woman paused, recalling individuals and contexts. 'They are women of their time. But they should not need to do it.'

***

There are no words for the unspeakable, that hell-hot catastrophe of war. It is even harder to describe how we could actually deal with the menace we were facing. No chance, I said. Navies of the past relied on dreadnoughts and battleships, but time, technology and budgets gradually whittled these down to cruisers, destroyers and frigates, each time the vessels becoming smaller, more manoeuvrable and more lethal. Size counted only for aircraft carriers and we had none of those. But the Indonesians had gone one better. They had put the teeth of at least a frigate into their corvettes, smaller ships considerably, and had subdivided their land forces into units transportable in LCTs unimportant on a plane's radar screen when the larger corvettes were about. So when Parliament tried to deal with a foe it had not seriously foreseen, the rancour reached a level not even attained when an upset occurred in the championship game of Australian Rules football.

The House had been in a continuous uproar since the televised debate began, and we'd tuned in to it to see what our erstwhile masters had to say. The polies are able to sustain a level of abuse against anyone far longer than any football fan, but everyone wanted to hear what the Shadow Defence Minister would have to say, so the noise abated slightly as he climbed to his feet. `Mr Speaker. I demand to know how it is that this government has allowed the situation to degenerate so seriously. Perhaps the Honourable  Minister for Defence will answer that question for the House. I should like to quote from his very own Defence White Paper: `*The Australian Defence Force possesses significant capabilities to detect and monitor aircraft, ships and submarines in the sea and air approaches to our territory.'* It seems to me, Mr Speaker, that was what it didn't do. It seems to me, Mr Speaker, that its capabilities were less significant than the Honourable Gentleman believed.'

He went on. `Let me quote further from the same White Paper: `*The capability to detect and monitor any forces which may have been lodged on our territory is more limited.'* Mr Speaker, does that not suggest to the more intelligent members of this House, most of whom to the detriment of the current governance of the nation I believe are to be found within the membership of the Opposition, does that not suggest that we have absolutely bugger-all capacity to know WHAT THE HELL'S GOING ON?!' He sat down.

Not so much pissed off as in a mood for a rancorous exchange, even though the issue was a serious as any in forty years, the House exploded in greater jeers and cat-calls. The Defence Minister stood up slowly, seemingly not annoyed by the attack, but it took several minutes for enough order to be established for him to be heard. `Mr Speaker. My honourable friend is less than honest with his vitriol. He would lay whatever blame may attach to a defence deficiency to the government of the day. I'd like to point out, Mr Speaker, that his own party ministered to the defence needs of this country for a significant period. A significant period during which, Mr Speaker, defence spending was slashed and Service strengths were cut. My Prime Minister has laboured long and hard to turn this position around, and to build a modern Defence Force capable of defending what is after all ten percent of the land area of this planet. Let us not misrepresent intelligence.' Hoots of laughter went up from the Government benches.

`But, Mr Speaker, this is a very serious position, and I grant my honourable friend his right to be concerned. The Prime Minister has advised the House that we have come to a declaration of war with Indonesia. Unexpectedly, we find ourselves on the defensive. We do not yet understand what our aggressors intend to do with Darwin, and the significant population which we assume they are holding. Our response to them must be tempered by whatever we need to do to ensure the safety of Darwin's citizens. Once this is known, I assure my honourable friend that the House will be so advised.'

The Shadow Defence Minister stood up again. `Does the Government have a contingency plan for the rescue of these people?'

The Defence Minister shook his head. `Mr Speaker. My honourable friend obviously misunderstands defence. *His* cuts led to the position that we now find ourselves in. *His* party's was the contingency plan. We are now working to undo those mistakes. We cannot divulge our plan, because it may find its way to the ears of our enemy. But, let my friend rest assured that the safety of those people is of equal importance to the safety of the nation as a whole.' He sat down again and was seen to lean to the Prime Minister. But one of the closed-caption services for the hearing impaired picked the words right off his lips and exposed him to the nation. `One-all, I think. We won't do better than that today.'

The PM smiled for the House and was similarly betrayed. `I wish we knew what they intended to do with Darwin.'

`Your opposite number, sir, will wage quite a different war.'

I said it to Bluing, but it was Dixon who was running Naval Operations Command under Bluing's delegated authority. Bluing's job was to keep his masters informed and happy. He hated both ideas.

'Subagio.' Bluing spoke the name aloud as if tasting it. 'Where has he come from?'

Not privy to my earlier discussions with Bluing and Dixon, Collins took the question as it came. 'Ministerial protégé, sir. Strategic planning for several years. Ideal position from which to launch what he seems to have done. Made some right moves very early on and won the respect of some of the less pandering navy types. A serious officer who knows what a navy is for.'

'I want Subagio's mind opened up and spread on the Ops Table before us.' This was still Bluing. 'I want to know what he's going to do before he thinks about it. That's you, Gregory. You say a different war. I want to know how different, and why.'

'He won't fight this as you'll fight it, sir. He'll be on the water. He can't risk not to be. This will be very top-down. No democratic shipboard Operations Centre. No Warfare Officers giving the Captain insights into orders of battle, or tactical methods. Take out Subagio, and they'll have lost fifty percent of what they are. They're relying on a tremendous amount of luck.' But Subagio himself would have known that, and would not take foolish risks even if he were on the water.

'Luck almost lost the Brits the Falklands. In the end the Argentinians were just *un*lucky.' Dixon was pensive.

Bluing shook his head. 'Nothing sustained there that could have seen them through. Almost random action on the water. It was only the Argentine air force that came out of it with any sort of respect. And it made the most fatal mistake. Tried to kill the navy, not the troopships.'

'The difficulty, sir, is that we have almost neither.' I didn't say that the Indonesians had plenty of both, nor that we were able to do no more than the Argies themselves.

Bluing looked at me, searching for facetiousness. 'I won't hide my concern from you, Gregory. But we are going to do what we bloody well can to make sure whatever Subagio has in mind does not come to pass. You will look at what we have available in the area, and you will develop the strategies and tactics necessary to forestall him. His mind out on the table, remember? Make it clear, so that I can go to the Defence Chief with ammunition, not find myself continually on the defensive.'

'I already have Air Force looking for him, sir. Long-range sweep over the Indian Ocean.'

'That's a start.' He looked at Dixon as he got up from the table. 'Regular six-hourly reports, Jim. All positions, serviceability, weapons capabilities, fuel reserves. I've coerced two transports out of Seven squadron for supply flights west over the next forty-eight hours. Get on to them whatever we should have in Fremantle we don't already have. After that we're on our own.'

Dixon acknowledged the formal order. After Bluing left the room he looked back at me. `You'll stay here - we can't do this by radio link to Fremantle. So, a thumbnail sketch in a couple of hours. I want the noon signal to the West Fleet to include a summary assessment, and, ' looking at Collins, ` the latest we have on movements from Surabaya. Get on with it.' He left for the Warfare Room.

But I thought it would take a return call from Air Force to give us what we wanted on Surabaya, and that we'd have to wait for.

We lost the plane that found him, a long-range Orion that picked up at least two Ahmad Yani frigates and an auxiliary, but the intelligence had been uploaded to the satellite and we had it on the large surface plot even as the shattered fuselage hit the water. Death was becoming the price for any information.

But that little group was still a long way north, no suggestion that it was on a fast course to anywhere, meaning that Subagio was probably waiting for more reinforcements from Surabaya, perhaps the battle-hardened heavyweights that had seen one of their own melt in the Flores Sea and let Leach be brought home on his own bier. *Magnet* was still limping for Fremantle, not expected for another day.

Did that mean that it was unimportant that the landing in King Sound be a surprise? It was obvious that the immediate success of *Amethyst* had been essential, a strike into the soul of the Top End. Now that Darwin and Katherine were contained, the Kimberly was open to the taking. The air defence was fighting hard this minute to deny *Opal* that essential anchorage on a harsh coast, but not the fury that could have been expected to be launched from Katherine. The loss of Katherine left the Indonesian penetration forces at much less risk of repulse. It made me wonder again at the strategic purpose of *Ruby,* still, as far as I knew, anchored off Wyndham, troops perhaps ashore in the small town. *Opal* rendered it obsolete, Derby and Broome greater prizes, and the Great Northern Highway easily cut. Perhaps the landing hadn't need to be a surprise. This was a stark message in itself. It made dunny fodder out of the Defence White Paper.

We should have stopped them at Darwin, no doubt about it, but we'd been fooled in our complacency, and they'd made their own sacrifices to carry the larger scheme through. The work done in Makassar proved to be as effective as I'd feared, and it had become clear that we were to pay a high price in aircraft to stop the corvettes. Each expeditionary group had enough of them to make that certain.

And if we tried to do that, we'd be making the same mistake as the Argies. It was the LCTs that mattered.

And we had left our waters empty of ships. The cynic in me said they were empty anyway, even when there was an ensign on the jackstaff waving the Southern Cross in front of your eyes. Too much water, too few ships. And the ships we had steaming hard across the Indian Ocean, *Mowbullan* and *Ord*, would have to stop what was coming out of Surabaya, not play cat and mouse with fast corvettes among dangerous coastal shoals. Only aircraft could stop the latter, and the polies were currently putting more faith in the Rapid Deployment Force's ability to stop the invaders on the ground, for which they'd need air support. But the RDF was still being pulled out of PNG, where Indonesian foresight had caused us to put most of it, to control the mayhem of the border skirmishes. Even if the RDF didn't stop in Cairns to change its boots, it would not get to Port Hedland in time to stop *KOPASSUS* waltzing down Eighty Mile Beach.

Collins didn't have to work through that lacklustre Joint Liaison Group. Trinity, he called it. As Intelligence, he was cadging his information from elsewhere. He let me know that even as *Opal* fought for its foothold in King Sound, most of Indonesia's navy was converging on a still unidentified speck of water over the North Australian Basin.

I knew those waters, depths measured in miles rather than fathoms. In bad weather they were unfathomably black, soul-shivering waters that would lift a man off the deck with the whisper touch of foam, and then carry him straight down to a seabed as still and empty as the eternal night that ruled there. There, he had no future but to metamorphose into the other beings that came and fed, beings that looked upward for the manna that always fell, however occasionally. The calcium of his bones would move into solution, to drift away on whatever slight current brought breeze to the night.

To the north the Java Trench, deeper still by another mile, bubbles and groans. Tectonic movements bring surface phenomena of disastrous proportions, tidal waves that wash Indonesian coastal communities clean, laughing at the ephemeral nature of man who attempts to raise his house to heights thought of as safe. Six-foot stilts were nothing to a steel sea, which cuts them off as matchsticks at the same instant as the roaring wall comes in from above. And whoever survives, grieves for a while until the daily grind of peasant survival forces him back into the routine that dulls the loss. Until the next time.

I knew Subagio saw his destiny in these waters. While his squadrons fought to gain an anchorage off coastal Australia, and deliver the means to an end, his own thoughts would be growing closer and closer to his own encounter with us. Here,

324

he would fight the battle that *he* had to fight, the fleet action that would remove the final risk to an increased transfer of men and materiel across the Timor Gap. He had to fight it. Without it, Jakarta's leverage was thin, and the wave of elation that was needed to carry the country through a wrenching transfer of power would die a ripple on the beach of political history.

And in his battle group that slowly coalesced over the Java Trench were the heavyweights, ships mostly bought from western navies which considered them obsolete or unseaworthy, not built for the needs of modern warfare, too costly to maintain in expensive western dockyards. But what eastern yard, heavily subsidized by government and full of still cheap labour, could not turn these into operational ships, could not change outmoded weaponry, and restore some of the imperial glory that still echoed somewhere in their bilges? As long as there were trained and experienced men to operate them, they were the raw tools of war that they had always been. The Red Fleet taught us that.

But, by the hour, Bluing saw disaster in these waters. Still haunted by *Magnet*, and frustrated by the physical separation of his fleet between the eastern and western oceans, he looked upon the few ships that could put some teeth into the sea as little more than a gesture. Heroic action from his officers and sailors there might be, but the battle was being fought between Canberra and Jakarta. It was a policy battle, fought as independently separating trends over a period of decades, leaving each country with as different a set of military tools as could be imagined. Well, perhaps not quite. There was a much larger dragon stirring further to the north.

Apart from *Mowbullan* and *Ord,* on the homeward course that would bring them into range, we had only two modern warships available to the west coast: another Mount-class frigate, *Cornish*, and the new Lake-class submarine *Magenta*. Two old destroyer escorts from Fremantle were also steaming northwards, trailed by a lone 60s-built submarine, and an ageing destroyer and two frigates of Fleet Base East in Sydney which had not been sent north towards the Coral Sea were crossing the Great Australian Bight. But these last would probably not reach the Basin in time to be players in whatever action ensued. They were more likely to be guardians of blood-stained waters.

The northeasterly sweep of the NW coast I saw as my battlefront. I ranged from Exmouth to Darwin and out into the same deep dark waters that preoccupied Subagio and Bluing. But the coast was closing down, the tentacles of invasion wrapping themselves around every headland and into every bay. We couldn't keep them from the Kimberly. There was little to do about Darwin. That was already gone, and any action there was in the hands of whatever surface force the Defence Chief decided to send in. But whatever I did at sea might be the lever that still kept them from the Pilbara. And prevent subsequent waves of troops from crossing the

325

Timor Gap.

Collins put the latest intelligence data on the table. `At least five major ships, perhaps more.' His finger slid across the Java Trench. `Moving south, here.'

`The submarine?' It was an unknown I found irritating, but at least there weren't two. Leach had seen to that.

`We only know that *Nanggala* has not been seen for more than a week.'

`And *Mowbullan* and *Ord*?'

`Two hundred miles to the west. Current speed twenty-seven knots.' His finger slipped south. `*Cornish* is here, *Magenta* here.' The electronic screen updated the positions of the three Mount-class frigates, and the lone Lake-class submarine. `The two destroyer escorts are hugging the coast past Port Hedland, and should make contact with *Opal* by first light tomorrow.'

`I still don't like that idea. If we can't keep *Opal* out of King Sound, there'll be little to keep the convoy's watchers on a leash. The escorts carry no missiles. Those five corvettes will be deadly.' I thought there were six still unaccounted for, but Air Force said, no.

Collins nodded. `*Obregon* is close behind. That might make all the difference.' He had more faith in the older submarine than I did, but then I remembered her captain was Servage, an old Fremantle man whom I'd encountered occasionally. I corrected an earlier thought about no West Coast commanders. Unconventional, he'd made his vessel *our* war-gamers' nightmare. Perhaps he could cause the havoc we needed.

`At least she has missiles. But she's slow. She'll need a half-day to catch up.' I wished we had another Lake-class submarine instead of the old O-class *Obregon*, but the other Lake-class vessels were still in Adelaide, victims of serious design faults that had been partially corrected in *Magenta*. And the unions were still fighting our request that they work more than a seven and a half hour day. No, best forget about the Lake class. `Right. Let's talk to Dixon. It's time to see if he wants to think about calling this a Battle Group. *Mowbullan*'s captain is the most senior. He's met Subagio, so at least he'll understand what I'm saying. If they give the command to *Cornish*, there's no knowing what he may do on his own.'

Dixon did decide to call it Battle Group West, with the qualifier added in case the East Ocean Fleet was able to get through the minefields of the Torres Strait in time to be Battle Group East. He decided to send two fleet auxiliaries northbound from Fremantle with reserve fuel.

`Signal *Cornish* to rendezvous with *Mowbullan* and *Ord* as soon as possible, and for *Mowbullan* to develop his screen south of the Indonesian fleet. The destroyer escorts are to be the rearguard. I want no foolish grandstanding between any of the DEs and the Indonesian vessels. Only if the corvettes join the action

326

will the DEs engage. Otherwise we shall let them go. It's more than likely that they'll want to shepherd their LCTs home.' Once again no resources were to be wasted. ` We can only do one thing at a time. Let's make sure we do what is most important.' Dixon's asperity betrayed his lack of sleep. `Why isn't Subagio making faster time south?'

`He wants us in his waters, sir. Away from ours, away from his expeditionary forces.'

`Yes, well, we're not going to oblige.'

`The 15° parallel, sir. Southern edge of the Basin. 110°E is the best rendezvous point, and an easterly course will take the fleet towards the Kimberley. Subagio won't want that. And he'll have to come to find us.'

`Agreed. Advise *Mowbullan* and *Cornish*. *Magenta* should work to the north of the fleet.'

`Yes, sir.'

And so it took shape.

Twenty eight

The Jenderal waited at his Roti HQ until Elang's signal came in. He catnapped almost continually in his quarters, the combat soldier of old, sleeping instantly when the occasion warranted, keeping himself as mentally alert as he could for the coming action.

The Ops Room had a staff of five, enough to monitor progress across the Gap, and to feed my models with the latest data. I was always there, ready when the critical signals came in, watching the results of the updated simulation. Significant variance from predictions, if it occurred, was not something to leave in the hands of a technician. The critical parameters had to be identified, and corrective values tested.

`No departures from expectation, Jenderal. Darwin was the key. Petir was within all the values tested. So was Topan. The probability of success of the final strike remains high.'

The Jenderal swung around to his aide-de-camp. `As planned, Letnan. Takeoff at 0200 contingent on Elang's signal for a dawn drop.'

`The planes will be ready, Jenderal.'

`Green,' said the Jenderal, referring to the jump light, `is my favourite colour.'

And we'd trained hard for this for months, a large arid island east of Flores emptied of its sparse population, and made into a circular test-bed with a single well the only permitted source of water. Gradually the radius of the trail had been expanded, pushing the men's limits to withstand the true rigours of desert dehydration. More than one platoon had succumbed to poor planning in the use of the little food and water permitted, found unconscious by the next that came by, and airlifted out to the central base on receipt of the only allowed emergency signal. Barely recovered, they went back out again, learning by the recent mistake, able then to last perhaps a day more. By the time they'd finished they'd covered the desert run equivalent of three complete loops. The present journey, at the beginning of the Wet, would be a picnic.

Excerpted from Rusman Soekendro, LetJen (ret'd),
No Game At All: *Memoirs of a Strategist*

It was a sombre lunch. The Javan looked as though he'd been given too much to digest, and he ate in such a desultory fashion he hardly ate anything at all. The Australian had little to say, as his wife had taken the discussion to a level he recognized was far beyond his own understanding in religious philosophy, let alone in Islamic terms. It had been the one gray area between them, his inability to share her professional interests, and thus her intellect. He had dealt with it like a man, more or less ignoring it; she, as a woman, had accepted it as the single deficiency in their relationship.

The woman saw that she had pressed the Javan very hard. In one corner of her mind there formed an apology, for she was inherently gracious, above all with Indonesians, and he was their host. But throughout the rest of her there was this rolling ball, a massive weight of thought and feeling and knowledge which was carrying everything before it, and so she said to herself, *No apology. I am a woman of my time, and I should not need to do it.*

***

So we had no ships there, and it was Air Force that did all the work and took all of the punishment. The LCTs were too small for a long-distance attack, and gave no hard radar images anyway, so to avoid the Argie's mistake we had to leave the cover of the horizon behind and get in among the corvettes to kill the troops, because that required visual targeting. No picnic, and, in truth, murder of the worst sort for our pilots, because the corvettes picked them up as they came in over the horizon, or tried to go out over it, firing windows the size of the desert we were trying to defend. We had to split the planes between corvette and LCT, doing what we could in the minutes before King Sound became safe haven. And in the end we had confirmation only of two LCTs sunk and one corvette on fire, for the price of five planes lost. Derby spat fire over the radio for a couple more hours even though it was unable to do so elsewhere.

And there was still Wyndham. It worried me intensely, knowing, as I was beginning to, the quality of the mind doing the deeper thinking. If I thought of young Soekendro as no field soldier, he was Bulyanto's man, and Bulyanto was the one the Defence Chief feared, an Army man himself. So Soekendro would have taken all the information Bulyanto could feed him, and would have pumped it into those machines of his until he had something with a high probability of success. Wyndham wasn't a feint, I knew that, and it wasn't a mistake. Perhaps we were supposed to think that, and then forget the force that had landed there. The White Paper said it all. Once an invader touched the shore, there was little we could do to track him.

I knew that country, had travelled it often with Dad in the days when I'd had no school work. We hadn't gone often to Wyndham, but we'd gone south and east, travelling the back country, tracking the cattle against the background rise and fall of the vegetation which fed them, watching not just the annual rhythms but the seven and ten-yearly ones as well, the ones more important to long-term success as a grazier. There'd been floods and droughts, but we'd weathered them. This year there were no floods, just a late Wet, one building in the massive air streams on the edges of the Intertropical Convergence Zone, the boundary of the north and south monsoons. Floods might come later. But until they did the land was open. And while it was open it was a worry.

If they now had the Kimberley, which coming in through King Sound and bottling up Derby and Broome gave them, why waste resources at Wyndham? Resources that came ashore well ahead of *Opal* in King Sound. *Ruby* I'd called it, a stone that envelops you in its blood-red heart, but this was more a dingo, the canine barking in the distance but something you didn't necessarily worry about until you saw how close were the jaws that bit. And *Amethyst,* jaws far more fearsome, bit far away in Darwin. So it was easy to forget about Wyndham.

Because I was still worrying more about Subagio's intentions. Until his Surabaya heavyweights joined him it didn't make sense for him to push very far south. And nothing in the general experience of Indonesian military operations suggested they'd make foolish moves. If they made a southerly strike then it would be with a strategic goal in mind where the risk of high losses could be borne by a success elsewhere. Well, we would be no different. Subterfuge and Sun Tzu. But given that three expeditionary forces had already made land, the Indonesian Battle Group would strike either to keep the Australian force away from the returning corvettes and LCTs, or for a different purpose altogether. The Pilbara I'd said to Collins, but this could be nothing but a distant objective. But I had no better idea so I passed what seemed an insignificant suggestion on to Dixon.

`I think *Obregon* should follow *Opal*, sir. There's a good chance she can pick off a corvette or two on their return voyage. I'm assuming they won't stay at anchor in King Sound.'

`I don't like the idea of a bare backside, Gregory. But the Indonesian Battle Group is still well to the north of our ships?' He thought, then nodded. 'Signal *Obregon* her suggested station, and tell her captain that he's on his own until further notice. The destroyer escorts stay south of Battle Group West.'

I thought there were ten corvettes possibly still in Australian waters. But since the loss of the Orion less high-level intelligence was coming in. There was some fighter intelligence from Learmonth and Weipa, low-level pop-up scans that gave the odd piece of news but which did not allow much of a complete picture. However, we knew that *Amethyst* had left for home, empty LCTs bucking some monsoonal storms on the eastern edge of the Timor Sea.

And now I was blind across the whole Kimberly coastal arc, everything reduced to a guessing game. I could not begin to think what had happened to Dad - the Civil Defence was off the air, I presumed overrun by forces that it had not been designed to evade. Kangaroo had been the colossal waste of money I thought it was, war games that lulled everyone into a false sense of security.

`What would you do with ten ships, Rob?'

Collins was working on the other problem, that of trying to estimate how many more vessels might have slipped Surabaya and be making their way south. Intelligence reports with estimates of known serviceability, weapons capacity, trained crews, munitions purchases and movements, were scattered across his desk, and he was intent on some calculations of his own, ranking the levels of probability of further sailings.

`Phone Canberra and see whether they wanted to buy them cheap.'

I laughed . `Let's say you're Subagio. You've done what you wanted to do in the first strike. Get the troops across the gap. Now you have ten ships to spare. What would you do with them?'

`Assuming that they're not going back for more troops, which they might, I'd peel a few off and throw them into the fray.'

`Yes, it's fairly obvious isn't it? I'd assumed that they would go back with the LCTs. But let's say that they've got a critical mass of troops on the ground already, and might not send all the LCTs back. That frees up the corvettes. *That's* what he's waiting for, sitting up there over the Java Trench. Some are going to come in behind Battle Group West.' I picked up the direct line to Dixon.

`Sophistry.' Dixon wanted to find a chink, something that said his planning was better. But there was nothing here to make anything any easier, just something that brought a significantly higher probability of a rout to his small force.

`I suggest we don't wait for them to arrive, sir. *Mowbullan* should strike quickly at Subagio, and the destroyer escort screen should move south. We can catch the corvettes in our own pincer. *Obregon* should be almost right under them.' I was fairly sure that Subagio intended just to sweep the sea clean, which would be a fateful blow. The trouble was that the corvettes, smaller considerably than the destroyer escorts, were much more lethally armed. The escorts carried only guns. Size was irrelevant now. *Obregon* was a very important card, and the Battle Group had little chance of similarly sweeping the sea clean. A damaging strike, to keep the Indonesian fleet thinking, worried, was the only chance.

`Air cover from Learmonth?'

`Standing by for our call, sir.' Last chance for Trinity.

`Tell Battle Group West to go but leave the destroyer screen where it is. Give *Obregon* a while by herself. She may change the odds a little.'

But *Obregon* was still trailing the destroyer escorts on their northerly run. Capable of close to thirty knots, the escorts had no reason to hold themselves back for the slower submarine. So, over the next couple of hours she kept her northeasterly course up the coast, as the destroyer escorts peeled off to the north for their new rendezvous. I made the signal as clear as I could, what depended on him, so if Servage thought it would have been boring keeping station to the rear of Battle Group West and watching for possible flank action, he now had something much better. He was the hunter, and had been authorized to go looking for prey. But I pitied his officers. It was a tortuous coast, and they'd be making use of every piece of rocky cover that they could find. They'd have ulcers by the end of the first day.

So I left her ghosting the 20-fathom mark around the Baleine Bank. The Buccaneer Archipelago lay ahead, through which was the approach to King Sound and the current anchorage of *Opal*. While it was tempting to send *Obregon* in through Sunday Strait and create some havoc, Servage would have very little room for manoeuvre. And prudence was important to a submariner, so he was on his own after he reached the Strait. Five ships individually as deadly as him were, I thought and told him, still there at anchor, the sixth burned to a hulk by the air force. I hoped he took the time to have a good breakfast.

Twenty nine

The Minister kept his seat of power away from Jakarta. That is to say, where his confidential staff administered the rules of political engagement upon which he had decided. There was too much risk in the capital. And, given the upheaval that would follow the announcement of ascension to the yet-again rapidly cooling throne, Jakarta would be the worst place to be. Yet he had to be in Jakarta, if only to defuse the rumour mill, dropping out of sight the surest way of drawing attention to himself.

The Vice-President struggled because he didn't have the power he thought he had. But the Vice-President's struggle was the very thing that the man in the shadows wanted. There had to be someone who became the target for the dissatisfaction that boiled beneath the skins of the poverty-ridden masses in city and countryside alike. A weak Vice-President was ideal. Let him deal with a populace amok, with all of the bloodletting that very fearsome Malay word implied. If it happened, it was certain that millions would die.

Excerpted from Rusman Soekendro, LetJen (ret'd),
No Game At All: *Memoirs of a Strategist*

The weight of the Javan's depression did not immediately lift. The Australian thought that reverting to the link that existed between them as men might help to overcome what to him seemed to have been a cleaving of the Javan's beliefs as they pertained to women and God.

'When did the invasion become a reality, rather than a fictional war game?' he asked.

The Javan gathered himself, and came back from some infinitely-distant inner-self, where he had in fact been contemplating Woman under God, and focused first on the view beyond the window, and then on his companions. 'I prefer to think of a war scenario which in theory appears to contain all the elements of success not as fiction but as non-fiction.' But he was still grim, his struggle over devotion and meaning not yet put aside.

'Then let me put it like this,' said the Australian. 'If preparations were like the line of an exponential curve, of which the wargame would have been its flat beginning, when, in the geopolitics of the time, did that curve suddenly take off?'

'Yes, that is a very good analogy,' said the Javan, lightening a little. 'because it shows very clearly the continuity of the whole process. However, you must understand that there was an infinite variety of possible curves - not just a single one. The one you see in your mind is the one that became feasible. The remainder, because of incomplete exogenous and endogenous conditions, were infeasible.' He paused. 'In the geopolitics of the time, the invasion became a necessity when Australia interfered in East Timor. It became an operational reality as soon as we saw what the Americans would do in response to loss of the World Trade Centre.'

'You foresaw what they would do?'

'Perhaps that was a poor choice of words. It was already very clear to us that a fundamentally more conservative Administration was in place. This was a powder keg waiting to be lit by any perceived injustice to its religious values. But the loss of the World Trade Centre was an injustice several orders of magnitude greater than anything the Americans expected, and any society so wedded to television would be hard hit by those repeated images. Once they understood who the perpetrators were, the Christian Right had to avenge what it saw as a religious rape. It was a very short leap in foresight beyond Afghanistan to understand that war with Iraq was inevitable. We'd had everything ready for the moment when such a set of exogenous factors came together. So we took the fleet out of mothballs. You know the rest.'

***

The news from the travel industry that Jakarta had closed Ngurah Rai airport to commercial traffic, thus denying the delights of Bali to committed hedonists, penetrated the national consciousness perhaps faster than the announcement of hostilities made by Canberra. But, while Ngurah Rai really was the doorway, for thousands of Australian tourists weekly, to less-than-subtle temptations, it was also an airport of international standards, able to take the heaviest of wide-body jets. Its sea-jutting runway was an ideal launching point for anything the military cared to fly from it. With the news of the closure I knew that a squadron of F-16s, and probably another of F-4 Skyhawks, would already be flying sorties out to the south, directly down the 115° longitude. Very slowly, with utmost care, they'd push their noses over the top of the Subagio's Battle Group, looking for anything northbound. Anything at which they could fire a missile. And Ngurah Rai was so close to Subagio's back line that the planes could re-fuel and re-arm very quickly.

Almost on exactly the same longitude, but eight hundred miles to the south, Trinity said such sorties were being flown northwards by a Learmonth-based squadron of Hornets. Looking first for our ships, closing on their course from the east though staying well away from King Sound, the Hornets began pushing their envelope north towards the Java Trench. To circumvent the inverse relationship between range and weapons payload, Air Force put air-tankers into the sky, for airborne re-fuelling just before the devil's door.

Glaredon's signal was only just less than impertinent in acknowledging his air-cover. He suggested that his small Battle Group was the only component of the Australian defence, the sky empty since the rendezvous. Empty of the planes he wanted to see, anyway, for his signal said that the Indonesians got to him first, a lot of pop-up radar contacts from the north, look-see activities which had undoubtedly now laid his small force completely open. Each one was a scare, probably edging the fleet onto higher psychological levels of alert than the call to action stations had done, though nothing had yet come of them.

Though that had to end, and an attack eventually came at dusk still with nothing Australian in the air to stop it, two pairs of short radar contacts, and then nothing for a short while. Like the contacts before them, the bearings and range had been noted, and all the ships' electronics were focussing down those narrow beams, looking for anything incoming. It was the radar operator in *Ord* who spotted them, beads of light hardly visible, yet not part of the background clutter of the screen. Eight missiles rapidly approaching, but only four at *Ord*, the rest heading for *Cornish*.

It was as if I were back on *Magnet*, as I watched the defensive actions of both ships on my surface screen. Two missiles penetrated the defence screen and slammed into *Ord,* bringing explosion and fire instantaneously. This I knew almost immediately, one of several radio operators feeding me the data as it came in. Under ideal conditions fire-suppression systems operate instantaneously in damaged areas, but these were not ideal conditions, and we all knew that it was the fire that killed a ship, not the missile that preceded it.

It took a few minutes for anything solid to come back.`Casualties and damage report, sir.'

The signal was brief. *Hull damage at waterline. Taking on water. Fire in officers' quarters. Lieutenants Harrow and Spring seriously burned.*

A subsequent signal indicated that the waterline explosion had sprung plates below the impact area and it would take a while to see whether the pumps could hold the inflow.

But while the ship seemed physically crippled, my screens showed that her Operations Centre was still fully functional, even if I knew instinctively that everyone was waiting for that first telltale whiff of smoke. In the continual recompilation of the surface pictures transmitted from *Ord* was a better outline of the Indonesian Battle Group, where it was and how many ships it comprised. And finally there was something in the air, even if not the expected full air cover.

`Hornet flight has single radar contact one hundred nautical miles, bearing 340.'

The surface picture suggested that it was one of the ships they were looking for. Rob looked at me. `The forward picket.'

But even then there was a chance it wasn't. `Perhaps, but they have to look at the very least for a double contact. Glaredon can't be firing on a merchantman who hasn't heard that he's not supposed to be in these seas. Sorry, SO. Ask them to take another look.'

And it was that very risk that made this such a difficult task. Warnings had been broadcast to all ships in the area to keep clear of a 50,000 square mile patch of the East Indian Ocean. But merchantmen were notoriously independent, and, in truth, had not yet necessarily had the time to get out of the way. The bigger ships had responded immediately and their positions were known. But there could still be a smaller vessel within the warzone.

Ord's state of seaworthiness now limited further engagement. The radar contact was just outside her missile range, a distance that a sound ship could close quickly, but the captain had still to complete his damage assessment, so could not subject his ship to high-speed stresses.

But *Mowbullan* sat behind *Cornish* and *Ord* by only a few nautical miles, and Glaredon had watched and heard the missile attack on his own screens. *Cornish* was unscathed. So he brought himself up to *Cornish*, working to bring himself in range of *Ord's* target, and told *Ord* to hold her position until she was sure she was seaworthy.

It turned out that *Ord* was crippled beyond any doubt, and a newly rising sea became an extra concern. Not the minor swell of the frequent monsoonal thunderstorms that flew by, but the groaning heave of a larger depression that had settled into the same track. *Ord* had an engineering team over the side, working underwater with high-pressure riveters, but they could only manage jury-rigged repairs insufficient to withstand the stresses of even cruising speed in steep seas. She had to sit where she was, listening to other action and watching for any further strike.

Mowbullan ran as hard for the north as she could, Glaredon judging that the rapidly worsening conditions would bring a lessening in watchfulness of her foes, and that the moment was ripening for a strategic strike into the heart of the Indonesian fleet. *Cornish* kept station several miles to starboard, no doubt invisible to *Mowbullan* in the torrential rain, but undoubtedly a heart-warming speck on the radar screen. *Magenta* was somewhere below, not in a definable pattern with the surface fleet, but listening, and plotting from her towed arrays the spread of the

Indonesian fleet, hunting for opportunities. She would have *Mowbullan* and *Cornish* clearly identified, watching the distances narrow on her own surface picture compiler.

But the storm became a black hole, the sea a maelstrom at its maw, and the ships as if inevitably bound towards some final catastrophe. The flying conditions were as murderous, and the little air screen we had been able to put in place was now in shreds. Other data that came in suggested that two Indonesian jets had already been lost in massive turbulence, their simultaneous disappearance perhaps indicating that they had lost position and sliced each other apart. The range of the Australian pilots became severely limited, so weapons loads were cut back, allowing more flight time for search and identify missions.

Magenta found the southern picket of the Indonesian fleet several miles ahead of the main body. While it must have been tempting to remove the ship immediately from the scene, *Magenta*'s captain had orders to effect maximum surprise. So he went further north, so as not give the game away early, moving quietly around her, almost letting her leave him astern. Then he altered course to the west, moving tangentially, apparently on the track of larger game. And I thought about the Indonesian submarine. Was she in the field? Could he find *her*?

And Subagio? There was little doubt that he'd know we'd take advantage of the heavy weather. His picket at three of the fleet's cardinal points, smaller ships that had made the run in time from Surabaya, was his insurance against surprise surface attacks against the main fleet. Even if they picked up the submarine, which, with the ongoing problems of the Lake-class vessels was entirely possible, perhaps they'd have orders to leave her, not to lose tactical position in a difficult hunt in bad weather. So he'd probably be thinking that the weather could play him into our hands, and if I knew him well, he'd use that knowledge to do something we wouldn't expect.

In those endless moments when action was inaction, and all I could do was wait, I thought of life and the pain of war. Not the national pain, that festering sore to the economy, but individual pain, that of the poor bastard in the front line, paid to be there, but going because his mates were going, and he'd be thought a copper bastard if he stayed behind.

War culminates in twisted metal and broken bodies. I wondered whether the utter pain of a skin-destroying burn remained in the same tissue as a biochemical memory, and, that, when the morphine wore off, if it were that memory which triggered a linear recognition of time and the absolute horror of just a few hours before. Sickbays are places of agony, and very often just a waypoint before death. The signal said that Harrow and Spring, critically burnt, never made the journey back.

The surface pictures became etched in my mind, the known and probable positions of all the ships thought to be at sea. But I was cut off from the reality of it, a couple of thousand miles from the scene itself even if I was in instantaneous contact with the surface ships. The screens in front of me flickered as they were automatically updated from global positioning signals on our ships, and from what were now very infrequent radar contacts with the Indonesian vessels. But there was still the occasional reconnaissance, invaluable information coming from a plane's crew up there in the massive turbulence, using and looking through the storm, watching and waiting.

Looking at the main screen, I found it hard to believe that there was any possibility it would come down in the end to a broadside engagement. But could it be done in a single blow, or were there weeks of attrition ahead? Could the few ships we had use the storm as cover and catch the Indonesians unaware? It was increasingly improbable.

I went for a coffee and my mind wandered a little, retracing the journeys of the weeks past, coming to the intersection of my life with that of Jamie's for a few hours, and then the frustration of Washington. I found a corner of the rest area and sat lost in thought, images coming and going, hunting unconsciously for something that would give it form, present me with a path that would say this is what they're going to do. Anne was there somewhere, but too far away. Sometimes I found it hard to see her face, though I could hear her words, and occasionally feel her touch. But this was almost maudlin, not a state I could afford to be in now.

So, coffee finished, I put the cup down, and rested with my head back on my arms, eyes closed. Sleep came instantly, not looked for, but an inevitable result of the hours spent watching flickering screens and casting for new strategies. Images continued to fly, strange ones enhanced by the creativity of the subconscious, winged fathers, concrete flowers, abstract rockforms, iridescent water. A laughing Subagio, dressed like Nelson, clapped me on the shoulder, congratulated me on my ascension to leading seaman, highest rank in the Indonesian Navy, gave me a sailing ship twenty-five centimetres long of buffalo horn and told me to go to sea. I fell over the side on the first tack.

The hand that did clap me on the shoulder brought me out of the dream very slowly. `Sorry to wake you.' It was Rob, sounding exhausted. `Dixon wants you.'

I didn't see him for a moment, puzzled by something that had just flitted through my mind, the tail-end of the dream trying to say something to me. Then, still distracted. `Where is he?'

`At the main plot.'

`Thanks.'

Rob sank into the same chair as I left.

`You were looking for me, sir?'

`Any more ideas, Gregory?'

`Detach Magenta, sir. Strategic strike on Surabaya, or at least block the Lombok Strait.'

`Christ, Gregory. It's a little late for that.'

`Sir, we'll limit what they put to sea. An opening move in the next phase.'

`You think we have lost this one.'

`Not yet, sir.'

`Nor do bloody I!' Dixon's asperity was fully obvious. `If we detach Magenta, though, we bloody well will.'

`Its a feint, sir. Has been since he settled over the Java Trench. Subagio, I mean.' That had been the laugh in the dream, Subagio's foreknowledge that he had us all read, knew implicitly what we would do.

`What is he up to?'

`I don't know, sir. But he's about to do something. I can feel it.'

`I'm afraid you'd better do more than feel it.'

`That's what Admiral Bluing asked me to do, sir.'

`That sounded like a reprimand, Gregory.'

`No, sir. Just trying to work through some confused thoughts. I'm not doing it very well.'

`No.'

`We know, sir, that it has never made sense for Subagio to sit and wait for our fleet. In one sense he's far stronger, yet our desperation makes him vulnerable. And he's losing the Torres Strait advantage by the day. He can't afford to wait for more of our ships to come for him from the east.'

`What is he waiting for?'

`First, to see what it is we'll throw at him. Second, for the outcome of something else. Whatever else it is that they have planned here on land. This is a stratagem. We're supposed to focus on him.'

`Don't thump the table, Gregory. What do you suggest?'

`I already made my suggestion, sir. Detach Magenta. Block the Lombok Strait. Move Obregon up to cover the screen. We can't sink enough of this fleet to hold him up. And we'll lose some of our own in the process.'

`You suggest we back off completely?' It came out with a mocking laugh.

I traced the surface picture. `No, sir. Though it would be too late, anyway. I think *Mowbullan* may now be in the middle of them. But if there's no strategic advantage to putting them on the seabed, then we should get out with as few losses as possible.'

`Not the sort of analysis I expected of you, Gregory.'

`I'm sorry, sir.'

`I'd better talk to the Chief. Anything to do with the Lombok Strait will have to go to the Defence Committee.' Dixon moved away from the plot.

`Sir?'

`What?'

`Tell them to look again at Wyndham.'

Thirty

It was one of the few places in the world where the battlefront could be considered a tunnel. That was the way the Jenderal saw it, a line of objectives following the coast, deviations from that line, other than slight feints, running him into the solid walls of sea or sand. He intended to turn the Australians' reliance on the desert as their first line of defence, into the barrier preventing them from mounting any other. He thought that the desert would probably give him the few weeks of security he needed to get the rest of the job done; we almost had the sea already. And there really only remained a couple of strategic points on that two thousand kilometre stretch of coastline that were key to what had to come after. Once he had those, he'd face only local pockets of resistance from independent rifle companies seen optimistically by Canberra as core components of regional defence. He thought that particular notion quaint, ketinggalan zaman, left behind by the times.

His job was the airfields. But he had one of those already, Derby quickly sewn up once the town had been taken, much easier than Katherine. Learmonth, southwest of Port Headland, was the main concern, further west from Derby by almost a thousand kilometres and the thorn in the side for the Laksamana. So he had to sew Learmonth up too, initially to keep it too busy to put anything out over the waters further west, but also to eliminate the possibility of any sorties towards the northeast. He had his own plans for Derby.

The Jenderal and the Laksamana had thought long and hard about it. The odds that the Jenderal could finish it in one clean surgical slice were good, even I'd told him so, but something out of their collective sub-conscious military memory questioned over-confidence, and they decided to make completely sure. The final run on Perth demanded it.

So well before the Jenderal came out of the bleak sand horizon, four-fifths of Topan's firepower was already weighing anchor and preparing for a fast run around the coast. By this time, Amin should have had clear all the waters to the west of King Sound, leaving Topan with an unobstructed run past the Eighty-Mile Beach and Port Hedland, and down into the broad expanse of Exmouth Gulf, Learmonth the glottis at the curve of its throat.

Excerpted from Rusman Soekendro, LetJen (ret'd),
No Game At All: Memoirs of a Strategist

The Australian was not at all sure he knew all the rest. The history, yes - this was clear in his mind. But he was beginning to think that certain aspects which were, well, exogenous, to use the Javan's term, had in fact been endogenous. In this case, endogenous meant planned, and planning which had gone even farther than anybody could have guessed. 'Tell me about the Bali bombing.'

The Javan gave a wry smile. 'I wondered whether you'd mention it. Yes, that was a covert move we had to make. It was essential that Canberra adopt precisely the same posture as Washington on pre-emptive strikes against terrorism beyond its borders. Anything that Washington then did ensured that Australian forces would be committed to it. The war against Iraq meant the Persian Gulf, the Gulf meant warships, warships meant Navy. It was a simple results chain.'

'Then the Natuna manoeuvres were irrelevant.'

'No. They served a clear purpose. To come back to your analogy, we still did not know which curve we were on. We wanted a closer look at you. To gauge when we might put things in motion. Laksamana Subagio, in particular, wanted to leave a certain impression in Australian minds of Indonesian capacity.'

'But had other things not started when they did, those ships would have been back in Australian waters almost immediately.'

The Javan's smile broadened. 'Oh no. All of the straits through the archipelago would have been mined earlier than they were. Even had we not sunk a single ship, your three frigates would have been marooned to the north. We were prepared to incur Singapore's wrath by doing the same, in the name of regional security, to the Malacca Strait. As to the Torres Strait, well, you know what happened there.'

The Australian saw that unless extreme risk had been taken, the ships would have been forced right around the extreme east of Papua, followed by a circumnavigation of the Australian continent if they were to regain West Ocean waters. Sacrificing one ship ostensibly to clear a channel for the other two would not have guaranteed their safe passage. The point was moot, but he wondered what he would have done, had he been captain of one of the three ships, and forced to decide. More to the point, what would Canberra have decided?

***

As I had thought, *Mowbullan* was in the middle of the Indonesian fleet, or rather closing on one wing of it. There were two ships on the surface screen. The plot suggested that they were on a slow easterly course, the westerly contact having closed slightly in the past few minutes, and the one to the east then opening the gap. But the weather conditions remained bad and Glaredon needed a better contact than the intermittent ones he'd been getting before he risked a missile.

The radio officer patched me into the onboard command channel, listen only, a key to understanding what would bring change to the surface plot. I caught his Weapons Officer, intent on the various calculations necessary to define the launch window. `Coming to the point for Indo One now, sir. Mid-trajectory, active radar within thirty seconds of launch.'

`Then fire when ready.'

Even in the bad weather the whole ship would have heard the thunder of the launch. But within seconds I forgot any thought of the elements, the radio bleating the one fact I didn't want to hear. `*Emergency*! Missiles incoming! Bearings 068 and 311, sir! Range one five and one nine.'

So both Indonesian ships had him. There had always been that chance. Glaredon now faced the worst danger of all, halving his directional defences to deal with separate attacks. But he had *Cornish* and *Ord* in the squadron, so some defence could be shared.

`This is *Mowbullan!* Missiles incoming our bearings now 070 and 307. Range one four and one eight.'

Cornish: `Roger.'

`Chaff!'

`Active radar lock bearing 071. Range one two. We are active target, sir.'

`Roger. Standby decoy launchers range zero eight.'

`Missile Indo Two in five seconds. Fire!'

`Incoming missile now range one zero.'

`Second incoming?'

`Not gone active yet, sir. Bearing 302. Range one two.'

`AWO, advise *Cornish* second missile may be for them.'

`Yes, sir. This is *Mowbullan!*. Watch for active radar your bearing 305. Missile incoming your range one five.'

Cornish: `Roger.'

`Range zero eight on bearing 072.'

`Decoys, please.'

`Chaff!'

`Harpoon One, WEO?'

`Fifteen seconds to target, sir. Harpoon Two thirty-five.'

`Radar has Indo One chaff signature.'

`Incoming range zero six bearing 073.'

`Decoys!

`Indo Two changing course, bearing 320. Range two zero.'

`More chaff, please.'

`Active sonar on bearing 270. Noise signature Lake Class. *Magenta*, sir.'

`Roger.'

`She's trying for a firing solution on Indo Two.'

`Incoming range zero four bearing 074.'

`Officer-of-the-Watch! Hard to port. Full ahead!'

Bridge: `Hard to port. Full ahead it is, sir.'

`Decoys! Chaff!'

`Ready anti-missile gun at range zero two.'

`Gun at range zero two.'

`Incoming range zero three bearing 074.'

`Harpoon One target range, sir.'

`Roger.'

`Now range zero two, same bearing.'

`Missile two?'

`Bearing 290, range one zero. Definitely going for *Cornish*.'

`This is *Mowbullan!* Confirm you are under attack. Incoming missile our bearing 290, range one zero.'

Cornish: `Roger. We have the contact. Thank you.'

`Incoming missile bearing 074, range zero one.'

`Decoys! Chaff!'

`Sound the alarm, AWO.'

`*Missile strike! Hit the bloody deck!*'

There was very little that the weather did to affect the outcome. Of the four ships in the surface conflict, three received direct missile hits. One of the four was unable to escape the attentions of *Magenta*, cruising smoothly beneath the storm-wracked surface. Struck above and below the water at an interval of one minute, the torpedo finished the job begun by the Harpoon. The vessel sank within thirty seconds, probably taking all hands with her.

'*Cornish?*' asked Dixon.

A Naval Staff Officer of the Joint Warfare Centre was collating signals as they were received. 'Lost her helicopter hangar, sir. Ripped apart by the blast inside.' The helicopter in it was never found, he added later, probably lifted over the side in the explosion. Ironically the missile also took the rapid-fire gun that was pumping out thousands of shells per minute into its path, and which sat on top of the hangar. 'Twelve crew members killed, most probably from the downward force of the blast from the hangar into the ship.' But the engine-room was untouched, and she remained seaworthy, if scarred.

'*Mowbullan?*'

'Not touched, sir.'

But she had been witness to a massive firestorm, the incoming missile exploding within the innermost range of the ship's defences in the radar confusion of chaff, infra-red confusion of decoys, and the inertial effect of the 20 mm shells. Several of these must have hit the nose of the missile in rapid succession, destroying the active radar guidance system and triggering the explosive mechanism. The missile flared into a white-hot plasma that enveloped the rear deck, showered the vessel with liquid fire, and hit her with a massive sound wave.

But if *Mowbullan* had not been physically hit, the second Indonesian vessel had certainly suffered. 'Ship is stationary, sir. At least, there's no movement on the plot apart from a westerly drift. *Mowbullan* says there is neither radio nor radar coming from her.'

'Then all her antennae and fire-control masts are probably gone. Anyone going to take a look?'

'*Cornish* has advised *Mowbullan* she is sound, sir, so *Mowbullan* has asked her to sweep around the Indonesian vessel to the east.'

Dixon nodded. 'Yes. Glaredon still has some hunting to do.'

And Glaredon took *Mowbullan* north and east while there was still bad weather to work in.

The howl of a typhoon is a surface phenomenon. House-high ridges of steel-black water, trumpeting out of control across the earth's most dynamic interface, melt into the gentlest of swells not far below. There, with sea both above and below, the medium is more insidious, substituting catastrophic pressures for the cataclysmic imbalance between gas and liquid. The nature of vessels built to operate in this environment is as different from surface-ship design as the imagination can make them. Not a job for amateurs. *Magenta*, typhoon-free and hunting hard, was in a short loop, immediate quarry, immediate purpose. But strategy can change the loop, depriving the immediate seabed of more litter, the deep biology of another minor infusion of nutrients.

Magenta received her new instructions, my strategy, Defence Committee approved, shortly after laying that Indonesian frigate port-side down in three thousand metres of water. She became instantly a different weapon, her loop redefined, her unchanging hardware refocussed. So she added no more haemoglobin to the fringes of the Java Trench.

There were six hours to wait before she'd reach the approaches to the Lombok Strait. She was to take a slow passage into the Java Sea, looking for surface vessels making a reciprocal course to join Subagio. Not brilliant strategy, perhaps, but the only effective move in slowing Surabaya's spawning grey steel as fast as it could, and it would be far easier picking them out of the Strait than hunting for them over the Trench. At last I'd put something back in the mouth of the waters that had delivered death in that early morning to *Magnet*.

But if round Lombok my mind thought *quid pro quo*, there was no chance of that in the waters to the south. Where I thought the Indonesian fleet had been, not more than a few hours ago, Glaredon found nothing. *Mowbullan* had pursued a long arc to the northeast, thumping through seas that still would not abate. It became a long grind, crew remaining at action stations because of the ship's proximity to Indonesian air defences, and the thought that there was still an Indonesian submarine out there, unaccounted for. Finally at a loss, and because he had no immediate air support, Glaredon pulled back, and set course for a rendezvous with *Ord* and *Cornish*. It was time to regroup.

But Subagio had two ships fewer in his own Battle Group, and if he were on a southerly course, making all the speed he could through thundering seas, it was his first significant move since he'd come into the theatre. What had been a waiting game must now be something altogether quite different. So there was probably a rendezvous to keep, somewhere else to go.

Stress does strange things, and, in retrospect, I couldn't believe I'd forgotten. But other pressures had been in the forefront, and if I was thinking on the basis of personalities then Subagio and Bulyanto had been my quarry. Perhaps it was my ethereal presence over seas I was nowhere near, but the phrase came back into my mind and I spoke it aloud. `What in *Allah's* name is he doing here?' I startled Rob with it.

`My oath, Trev. What the hell are you talking about?'

`An old friend.'

The words had come out as if somehow that friend was close at hand, and knew I was part of what was being put into the seas ahead of him. *Aminuddin!* I suddenly knew he was there.

'What old friend? Have you been on the piss?'

But Rob knew I hadn't. Though neither could I explain why I knew *Letnan Kolonel* Aminuddin was out there. Rob didn't know him anyway, and there was no time to take him along a path that explained my Bugis pirate. Whom I knew would not be far from Subagio. But he'd not be given command of anything coming out of Surabaya, too many ripples at a time when it would be important for Subagio to hold the commanders of the heavyweights in his hand. But he'd not use Aminuddin there, anyway. I thought it more likely that Aminuddin was with the ships that had been in his care since the beginning. And then I bloody well knew where he was, that he was *Opal,* commanding that squadron so close to the Battle Group's rear screen, and that Servage in *Obregon* still had trouble on the seas right over his head, that no LCTs would be heading home from King Sound, and that the corvettes had a role as strategic as Subagio's Battle Group.

So finally the picture cleared, and I saw it all as *Opal* came up to the destroyer escort screen, just after Subagio began the evasion further north. At the first radar contact with the screen, *Opal* altered course to the west. At first almost stationary, the screen moved southeast to investigate. And if Aminuddin it was, it looked as though he had no intention of letting it get anywhere near him, and he made all speed to the southwest. Perhaps, until he knew what type of ships he was up against, he had no intention of engaging. So that chase took both groups out into the Indian Ocean. And *Obregon*'s signal, indicating that she was crippled and out of the fight until some serious welding had been done, took away any surprise we might have dealt them and made the final outcome desperately straightforward.

Gall called the meeting with the three Chiefs-of-Staff and principal aides late that night. As Bluing's GWO, I went with him. While the Defence Committee had been *their* day's work, Gall depended on his three direct associates for critical thought, and he preferred to do that away from the bureaucrats. He shut the door to his small conference room and pointed to the sandwiches and drinks tray that he'd had brought in. 'Help yourselves. This may go on a while.'

He sat distractedly for a few moments while we took what we wanted. Then he spoke to the Chiefs-of-Staff. 'It's time to worry, I'm afraid. Our current defence strategy has been blown open, which is no secret to any of you. We're at the nadir of our capacity since World War II, and none of our ready and rapid deployment capability is enough to cope with this. The small units we've put into the field must stay there unobserved for as long as they can, in the hope that we can find a key to turn things around. I must tell you that I'm not hopeful.'

The four senior men had been associates long enough for the atmosphere to be quite informal. 'Nothing from the Americans?' Townsworth had the whisky glass to his nose, savouring whatever he thought he could smell there.

Gall shook his head. 'The message is as it was when the PM talked to the President yesterday. Though he actually read him the ANZUS pact, describing it as Article III, parties consulting together.'

'And?'

'It was thrown right back in his face. Article II, continuous and effective self-help.'

'But Article IV? That it might have repercussions for them?'

'The President thought sending some of their boys down here to help might have greater repercussions still.'

'So it's Article X. Informal resignation. Without the year's notice.'

'It's just a piece of desert, and we should have thought of this sooner. The exact words of Seaton, the President's Deputy National Security Advisor, an hour ago.'

'Terse bastard.' Litner sneered a little.

'I think China has got under his skin. We're small beer under the circumstances.'

Bluing shrugged. 'We're hamstrung by Darwin, and may yet be further by Derby. There are few options open to us. Last stand at Alice?'

'Don't joke, Ted. That thought makes me ill. I never thought that this could gather so much momentum. It's a massive sore running right down the north-west, and we're bleeding to death.' The strain in Gall's voice was quite evident.

Townsworth put his glass down. 'I think we can hold them at the Pilbara.' The increase in troop movements across from the southeast had been discussed in full earlier that day. A paratroop regiment was expected to be in the field within a week, one company to be on the ground within a couple of days. 'For a while at least.' He acknowledged the question in the minds around the table. 'Oh, yes, perhaps in numbers and support we'll have superiority. But we'll strip a great deal of our eastern capability to do it. It'll take more than six months to get any of the main reserves up to battle standard. But if we put everything into holding them at the Pilbara we'll not have a lot left for elsewhere.'

Litner had been silent. 'By ourselves we can do little more than fight a running battle. And since New Zealand made herself a peace*keeper*, she has become a liability under the defence treaty - we need peace*makers*. Frankly, I can understand the Americans' dilemma. We're offering them something that could be as unfinishable as Vietnam. And the Indonesians are tough - perhaps better trained than the Vietnamese ever were. Our attrition rates will be very high.'

Gall shook his head. 'The Americans are quite right. ANZUS was about Japan, and *our* defence. Now they have China threatening not only to invade Taiwan, but also to put some military derivative of the Long March rocket into American West Coast communities. In other words, they are scared witless over their own.'

`Then it's a long war.' Though a statement, Litner clearly meant it as a question.

'If we have to fight it alone, yes,' said Townsworth.

`Speaking for Navy, we stand to lose the little we have if we take them bow on. I'm looking more at strategic strikes right now. Surabaya, for instance. It would leave their navy without any long-term operational capability. Blocking the Lombok Strait is a short-term measure, but crippling. Perhaps we retrench and fight at longer distance. Perhaps the whole movement in Jakarta will collapse and they'll go home.' But in this last Bluing was being flippant. They knew it and ignored it.

`Give them what they want for now until we're at a better advantage?' asked Gall.

Townsworth nodded in agreement with Bluing `No, just slow them down. So far we've had few people killed. None of us doubts our Services' sincerity in wanting to go out there and die in defence of the Nation, but none of us will rest easily if we cause more deaths than necessary because of only a short-term vision.'

`This sounds sickeningly like the Brisbane Line to me.'

`No,' said Townsworth. `Perhaps the Desert Line. We've made much of its defensive value, but in terms of its sheer inhospitableness and as a backstop to the defence of the coast. If we give them nothing to want to cross it for, it buys us time.'

`This won't fly politically.'

`Darwin may make it fly.'

`Oh Christ. This is treason.'

`Constructive reasoning, perhaps. Longer-term vision.'

`But they'll call it defeat.'

`History may not.'

But still I didn't hear them talk about Wyndham, and, knowing that my credibility at RAN, and continuing as GWO, meant that I first had to make my point to Dixon and Bluing, I kept my mouth shut when I should have opened it, whatever the cost.

In desperation I went looking for Rob.

'Can you find me your oppo in Army?'

He looked askance at me. 'Trinity not good enough?' But it wasn't a serious question, and I thought he also understood that I wasn't referring to any mirror image on an organizational chart. 'Give me a few minutes with the phone.'

I thought it would take longer, and went in search of a quiet corner, hoping that a few moments to myself might conjure up some insights. But I was too tense to slip into those first minutes of sleep, where stuff came at you like a landslide, and where, last, I'd been made leading seaman. In the end, I gave up and went looking for a coffee.

I took one back for Rob, who was still on the phone. 'Then, when he comes in have him call me. This is urgent.' He raised his eyebrows at me in silent question. I nodded. 'Repeat, urgent. Please remember.' He replaced the receiver. 'Can't guarantee that they will.'

I shrugged, still no closer to answering my own concern.

'But if I understand what it is you want, this is the bloke.' He passed a slip of paper. *John Smith*, it said.

'Seriously?' I asked.

'I've met him before. Not a codename, as far as I know.' He grinned. 'Even Army has original thoughts, from time to time.'

It took just ten minutes for the phone to ring, but catching me just at the point when my mind was moving on to other things.

'John, yes. Thank you for calling back.'

'Urgent, they said.'

'I think so. Do you remember Wyndham?'

'Wyndham? Of course. A small force came in there, what, about a week ago? We've rated it low priority for the moment - distance and lack of air support. You know.'

Was it really a week? I didn't know - I'd lost all track of time. 'I'm worried about it.'

'Navy worried about Wyndham? I thought I'd heard you were up to your eyeballs elsewhere.'

'We are. So is Air Force. That's why I'm calling you.'

'Er..Trevor, we're not exactly idle right now.'

'No, sorry. Hadn't meant to imply that. It's just that I am worried. I have a feeling that we, I mean Navy, are drawing too much attention. So much so, in fact, that no-one's looking at Wyndham.'

'Sort of offshore decoy?'

'Us? Perhaps a significant one.'

'Joint Service Liaison doesn't work very well, does it?'

'Trinity, we call it.'

He laughed. 'Won't tell you the label we thought of. You want to tell me why *you*, specifically, are worried about this? GWO, aren't you? I think I need to know.'

But he meant *me*, just another Navy man, with no right to do Army's thinking. 'All I can say, John, is that these people do nothing without a reason.' He'd laugh at me if I told him about Soekendro. But what about his mentor? Did he know the name? 'General Bulyanto. Special Forces. Through Wyndham.' It all came out in a rush. 'Don't ask me how. Or what they plan. But let me ask you something. How are you constructing your defence? Digging in around coastal communities for more shore landings?'

He was silent for a moment, perhaps wondering whether to hang up. Then, 'More or less. Not going to wander about in the bloody desert, anyway. But you're not convincing me of anything, you know.'

'No. I'm not, am I.'

But he still didn't hang up. ' Is it really the bloody desert you want me to look at?'

Then I thought of something. 'You know, if, in the next few hours, Trinity tells you that the naval action seems to be heading south, draw a straight line due east on your map from the point of latest maritime encounter. Draw another one due south from Wyndham. Try for some satellite reconnaissance at the point of intersection.'

'Look behind us, you mean?' His incredulity edged on scorn, but whether for me, or for the idea, I was not quite sure.

'I think that's what I mean.'

'Trevor, if I take this up the line, I'll be in a trench behind one of those coastal sand-dunes within the next twenty-four hours.'

'Yes. I know how it feels.'

Smith was right. There was no reason to look behind them. It was just as the Shadow Defence Minister said, when he quoted the Defence White Paper: *'The capability to detect and monitor any forces which may have been lodged on our territory is more limited.'* Trying to do so would, therefore, be a waste of time.

Perhaps had I said south-east, Smith might have drawn a more useful line.

353

'The trouble was,' said Smith, 'that when I drew a line of the type you suggested, all I found was the old Canning stock route. But there was nothing there, though we picked up clear traces of past traffic. Our satellite friends at Pine Gap, concentrating more on events to the far north, put it down to a late-season adventure group trying to get home before the Wet. That didn't sound to me like the numbers you were talking about.'

A large armed force came out of that desert a couple of hundred miles short of Canning's southern end.

During the summer, the Canning Stock Route is a blistering rock-and-dune-strewn twelve-hundred mile track that crawls across the deserts of west central Australia. Established to serve the cattle interests of the Kimberley early in the 20th century, it never became the economic axis that the planners had dreamed of, only the occasional herd of hardy barren-land cattle running its gauntlet, from well to well. It didn't occur to Australia, then, to consider it a military risk.

I hadn't either, though at the moment I'd gone to Rob for an Army contact, I'd already understood that if Subagio were going south, then Bulyanto was, too. Something about the region's isolation talked to strategies built on quiet and surprise, and as neither Air Force nor Army was yet yelling about large troop movements, there must, somewhere, have been something else. Subagio had evaded *Mowbullan*, had disappeared. What else couldn't we find?

'He must have taken the Talawana Track, swinging west past the salt flats of Lake Disappointment. It wasn't much in terms of distance from the desert's southern edge, but it brought him out where we would have been able to do very little.'

The desert run must have been punishing, testing men and machinery beyond normal limits. But I knew Bulyanto, knew it was Bulyanto, just like I knew where to find Aminuddin, and I'd no doubt that somewhere they had trained for this for months. We'd made it easy for them, seventy-five years earlier, by sinking water holes at regular intervals. But I thought it unlikely that they'd turned west just because Well 22 was now dry.

'He would have crossed the Great Northern Highway just south of Newman. Yesterday. You were too late.'

So Wyndham had been the key after all. Whatever he'd brought in *Ruby* he'd driven straight down the same road I'd driven before, but at Hall's Creek he'd kept going south, straight into the desert, not yet impassable in the early Wet. And we'd already lost Derby, so there was no way we'd have known. And if he'd backed *Ruby* up with an airborne regiment, we'd still not have pulled that picture out of the sky, the Jindalee and Pine Gap likely to have classed low-level flights anywhere other than in the East China Sea as a flock of Bali-bound albatross.

The Pilbara is one of the major sources of Australia's mineral wealth, home to mining companies that extract value from planetary amounts of rock. It's not a labour intensive effort, and the population of the Pilbara is quite low, centred in a few mining towns inland and the export facilities on the coast. But the Pilbara is an economic engine, driving a significant proportion of the raw finances of temperate Western Australia farther south, and adding daily to the value of the Australian Stock Exchange far to the east in Sydney. The Pilbara was a plum for the picking, and Townsworth's thought that we'd hold them there disappeared in the pipe-dream that it was.

Troop movements north from Perth and cross-continent from the Rapid Deployment Force were not yet complete. The analysts assumed that the Indonesian penetration force which had landed at Derby could only come down Eighty-Mile Beach, and there was already a defence post at Port Hedland with back-up air-cover from Learmonth. Forward spotters from Port Hedland, aboriginal scouts working their way slowly north, reported no movement. This hiatus suggested that no immediate move was likely, the invaders probably digging in for a longer, local occupation. Anything that came down Eighty-Mile Beach was asking for annihilation.

And Wyndham had been labelled a feint, that and the two corvettes drawing our attention from Darwin just long enough for us to lose Darwin completely. So the Defence Force strategists continued to believe it a feint, and made another mistake. For we'd continued to think that they would come from the sea, or follow the coast down from Derby. But they came far enough south, in a region where we would be very unlikely to spot them, and had the luxury of continuing to be able to choose their route.

So Bulyanto came out of the desert, through the Pilbara's back door, and just hours before Smith's call, launched his assault on Exmouth Gulf.

'He must have followed the headwaters of the Ashburton River down to Mount Vernon. It kept him away from all the main settlements, but the road then took him almost all the way to the Gulf.'

It was almost as if he'd taken all of the small mining towns across the Hamersley Range. 'Have you seen the nosedive in the Sydney All Ordinaries?' Rob said, shaking his head. 'They think the Pilbara's lost already. The copper bastards have lost a packet.'

I recalled Canberra's hopes of the independent rifle companies in the Pilbara, and thought that they'd have been able to do little more than phone us with the news.

But the demand, termed an instruction, came while Bulyanto was still somewhere in the desert. No further footage had been received from Darwin, and, though we were tired to the bone, none of the senior military minds was so foolish as to suggest that a dawn raid might recover all that had been lost. But Gall didn't tell the Cabinet that a crack team had made a partial penetration of the invader's defences to the north-east of Darwin; this news was considered to be for the PM's ears alone until there was something positive to report. The team reported that the defences were strong, and that any attempt to retake the city would be expensive in terms of civilian lives. One of the team had disappeared in the raid, a suggestion that their opposite numbers were no less capable of subversive action, nor unprepared for it.

A voice carried the instruction on a military waveband. `By the authority of the interim Ruling Military Council of Indonesia I transmit the following instruction. The city of Darwin is under Indonesian occupation. You will not attempt liberation. Any such attempt will result in retaliative action against other targets. The citizens of Darwin have not and will not be harmed. On acceptance of terms shortly to be transmitted to you by the Council, all those residents of northern Australia wishing to be relocated elsewhere will be free to leave. Their departure will be sanctioned by the use of mutually agreed-upon transportation only.'

Leaving us to ponder the military approach to what we faced left the polies in the Cabinet with time to focus elsewhere, and they finally understood that there had been a power shift of seismic proportions in Jakarta, and that a new President had to be in the wings. But who it was, and what he wanted, were still only shadows in the political analysts' minds, and many of them came tapping on our doors to ask questions. But it was hard to grapple with the political issues if there was no body politic with which to negotiate. And it seemed as if negotiation were still in the distant future.

`I doubt that my Minister's Cabinet brethren will unite sufficiently to give an impression of national political unity.' Gall was more pessimistic by the minute. The options open to the PM were disappearing fast, but hint of a policy collapse would render the country helpless, open to any propaganda weapon our foes decided to use. So in the end it decided to do nothing, officially refusing to acknowledge that any message had been received, or that any terms were to be forthcoming. News releases still focussed on the relatively minor incursion in the Top End, which the Government expected to be able to deal with shortly. There was no suggestion that the trouble might be more widespread, nor that other distant western-lying regions should be making any preparations for evacuation.

`Why should that be necessary? The Kimberley was the exception, and it has been taken care of. Our country's size and inhospitable interior continue to be the key to our defence, and Western Australia is safe.' The PM gave one of his thirty-second camera appearances.

But, in truth, the Government was paralysed, unable to provide vision, though able to recognize what might fast become a *fait accompli*. Its vision had been longer-term, bringing the country into Asia, recognizing the inevitability of new economic orders, even military ones, but not making immediate or massive policy shifts, apart from dropping the Queen. And so the money had come in dribs and drabs, restructuring and rearming at a rate that did little to offset the rate of attrition of the well-worn hardware upon which the current defence policy rested.

So there were the beginnings of panic. For no matter what Canberra said, Canberra was not Perth. And in Perth, everyone was far closer to where everything was unfolding. The first road-trains that had made the Hamersley Range had brought a stunned disbelief to the west. Here were people in trouble, people who'd suffered a disaster of unmanageable proportions. The morning papers, not as craven as the Cabinet, were full of it. And there was the same on the TV, from Alice. Everything north and west of the deserts was completely vulnerable.

None of the regular means of transportation was able to cope with the demand for a quick departure to the east. Air and rail terminals immediately clogged with those hoping for a space to open up where no space could open.

So Canberra's strategy of silence served little to prevent that panic. And I could understand what the upright citizens of Perth were thinking. When a people lost faith in a government, especially one that seemed only to serve an electorate on the far side of the continent, it did not listen to what the government told it. Stay calm? For what?

And if the panic had been calculated and timed, for I was sure it had, the placing of a pair of torpedoes into the massive hulls of heavily laden merchantmen in the approaches to Perth was Subagio's masterstroke. For it was a blow outside the very gates of the nation's new submarine base. But, to all intents and purposes, all but one of the submarines were still on the slips in Adelaide, not yet where they were needed, only *Magenta* still operational as my suggestion had put *Obregon* on the beach in Beagle Bay. The columns of black smoke from the burning ships were the final signal that it was Darwin all over again. And there were few illusions as to how soon the pubs there would re-open.

But I was sure that the captain of *Nanggala,* sister submarine to sunken *Cakra,* whose periscope must have inched above the waters due west of Perth, was no hedonist. *Nanggala* was no blue-water sloop, nor life aboard her that which many of the owners of the white-sailed vessels, which must have filled his vision, had probably led for years. He would have ignored them, minor disturbances in the grander scheme he was to complete.

357

It had been a long run south, and a cautious one, for we'd never heard him. Long-range maritime patrols regularly dropped hydrophones in these waters, listening for whatever might be out and down there. But I suspected that he'd done it all glued to the keel of a another large merchantman, except perhaps at night, snorting only when necessary, running silently for hours on end. She arrived in the waters off Perth undetected, a quiet black ghost.

But the daring strike right into the heart of the anchorage brought him risk several orders of magnitude higher. His torpedoes had a high-end range of fifteen miles, though distance was bought with lower speed, and the longer he stayed in those waters the greater the risk of detection by the seafloor defences of that submarine base down the coast. He would have come with a firing time based on the best estimates Subagio had, young Soekendro's estimates, of the developments in the land-based war. *Nanggala's* job was to create havoc. And with havoc, panic.

In the end, it was not hard. The western end of the Great Eastern Highway brought large amounts of cargo vessels into those waters. It was a matter of picking a couple that looked as though they'd burn hard and well. So *Nanggala* came in without raising a quiver on the electronic screens of our listening post a few miles to the south, though the launch of the torpedoes, and their active homing mechanisms, changed all that. There was some shock at the initial interpretation of flickering wavebands on the oscilloscopes, and then frustration at knowing that there was absolutely nothing that could be done to move whatever targets had been chosen. We did hear the submarine leave, so we sent a couple of fast surface craft after her. The dull crack of the torpedo impacts came through the hydrophones just as they were leaving port.

The surface picture to the north had remained confused for more than twenty-four hours. As the typhoon had slowly eroded all of the information systems feeding my screens, and there was still nothing new coming in, I'd left instructions to be called at any new knowledge on dispositions of either fleet, signed out of the Warfare Centre, and had walked back to my room.

I'd put Anne out of my mind as much as I could over the past days, but the knowledge that I'd hurt her remained a festering ulcer. But I couldn't see what else I could have done, any attempt of a warning a sure path for her into trouble, and certain to give me away. Nor could I have taken her with me on that mad dash across the eastern archipelago, not knowing really where I was going nor what I was going to have to do. No, rational thought said I'd done the right thing. But I felt her loss as a chasm in my soul.

`Sorry, sir. All phone connections with Jakarta have been cut. By them.' So that was that. No way of reaching her at all.

But sleep took a long time in coming, creeping unnoticed through all the thoughts of today, yesterday, and the days before that. It had been an escalating level of effort and commitment to the Service I'd never thought possible, from the first days when I went to Hong Kong and met Harry Grant. After that, everything seemed to have taken on a life of its own, carrying me along on a crest all my own. I was that casual Commander no more. I'd gone with it, enjoying the challenge of the puzzle that was being thrown in front of me. I'd come in on a game that I was not meant to find, one that fate had thrown me, a bone for a dog. At least I'd seen some of it for what it was, and had worked the rest out for myself. They'd almost got away with the whole thing - perhaps would have if it hadn't be for me. But any comfort I felt in that was a hollow victory.

When the dreams came, they were of all those faces, shouting and screaming at each other, anger, frustration, hate. And Anne was on the far side of the crowd, lost, unreachable, unattainable. She drifted further and further away until, finally, she disappeared altogether.

So I was asleep when Bulyanto took his force into Learmonth, a much shorter cross-country run than Canning, but the middle of the night.

'He sent only a token force in on the road, but sufficient to surprise the hell out of our sea-watching defences.' Smith continued on the phone. Before he'd started , he hadn't just told me to read the papers, so perhaps my less-than-early warning about Wyndham had been sufficient for him to adopt me into the kinship of Army's Intelligence circle. 'He got two artillery pieces within sufficient range to create havoc, though they proved not to be immune to some rapidly re-orientated defence. Unfortunately, that didn't matter. He knew he had to keep the planes on the ground, and he did that with his with his ground-to-air rockets. He made it an encircling movement, and timed it perfectly to coincide with the arrival of heavier weapons.'

It wouldn't have taken him long to find out that he was not fighting units of the Rapid Deployment Force, whom theory suggested would have given him an extremely hard time. This was a standard airbase defence group, good, but not bloodthirsty enough, ready for anything that might come at them from the airspace over the sea, but of little consequence to desert-hardened special forces with a partiality for long knives appearing out of nowhere. By dawn he had all of the main defence points taken, whatever remained of a hundred or more men under guard, and perhaps a rapid breakfast on the table in front of him.

But, after the defence finally crumbled the following noon, we learnt the real extent of the loss - apart from the base, several planes, only a few of the first flight managing to get out at the first whisper of the offensive, kept there to that point by the need to have at least a partial defence of this stretch of the coast. The few helicopters were already gone south, hunting for a secure fuel drop that might keep them near enough to the theatre perhaps to do something useful. And then the final blow, two ships coming up the gulf towards the base, running hard with the knowledge that all the planes that got out would also almost certainly have gone south. Ships that I knew could only have come from Wyndham, inside the screen that was trailing Aminuddin, well out into the Indian Ocean. A contingency for Bulyanto, if he'd needed it.

So Bulyanto the tiger finally showed his stripes, and was perhaps full of the heady knowledge of having secretly completed probably the greatest long-distance cross-continent strike in military history, victory of planning and hard preparation. And for him I knew it would be no time to stop.

Thirty one

The first transport would fly into Derby within hours of the Jenderal taking Learmonth, nothing expected to be in the water or air to stop it. It would bring the first wave of regular infantry from the large contingent on Timor. But the transport wouldn't stop there. Once the Jenderal confirmed that the runway at Learmonth was clear, it would make that final leg within a couple of hours. That would be the pattern of the next forty-eight hours, successive transports from Kupang, Denpasar and Surabaya concentrating core units of an army ten times the size of Australia's, at a point within hard striking distance of Perth. These were battle-ready battalions bled from regiments in the field from Sumatra to Papua. The advance south, behind the Jenderal's elite force, would begin within seventy-two hours of Learmonth's fall.

Excerpted from Rusman Soekendro, LetJen (ret'd),
No Game At All: Memoirs of a Strategist.

'Did Laksamana Subagio and Aminuddin expect to come out of it alive?' It was a question that had always haunted the Australian.

'I think that is the difference between the West and the East,' said the Javan. 'The West is always worried about how it will come out of something. The East, whether it is Muslim, Hindu or Buddhist, is far more concerned about how it will go into something. The result cannot be foretold.'

'I disagree. You defined your strategy on the precepts of Sun Tzu. He was quite clear about foretelling outcomes. He reduced war to its fundamental factors.'

'It is one thing to say that Sun Tsu was all-important to our planning. It is quite another to suggest we were arrogant enough to predict the outcome.'

For a moment, the Australian found himself confused. 'But you had a goal.'

'Yes,' said the Javan. 'We had a goal. But at question was whether our goal met with Allah's approval. Only He could know the outcome. To return to your analogy, we chose a curve. Allah would decide whether it was the right one. Our role was to provide Him with the opportunity. He would decide.'

'But that reduces war to a game of chance,' said the Australian.

'No!' said the Javan, finally offended. 'Allah is not chance. You are chance, I am chance. Allah is wisdom. Can you not see the difference?'

'I don't think I can,' said the Australian. 'I've always been taught to think for myself.'

'That has nothing to do with it,' said the Javan, completely frustrated. 'Thinking is one thing. Believing that those are your own thoughts is quite another.'

***

I knew that Aminuddin's decision, hardly a dilemma, was when to administer his *coup de grace,* the slaughter of the destroyer escorts shadowing the four corvettes in an apparently aimless drift west. The two escorts were at the disadvantage, pitted against a squadron that seemed determined to hold a pattern difficult to breach when all you had was gunnery. The Australian ships were old, ready for the scrapyard, a sister ship already having been paid off.

Little more than missile fodder for any larger fleet action, supporting-gun platforms to the larger destroyers, they were in an untenable situation. Supposed to be the rearguard screen to Battle Group West, they'd been manoeuvred away, had to go, the Battle Group now far to the north. *Opal* was the threat to the rear, but it had not behaved as I'd originally expected, had not gone for the first-raters. So Aminuddin did not want to go north. And now he was in some sort of holding pattern, gradually moving farther west into the open ocean, and reducing the threat of our air defences by every nautical mile. And we had to go with him, for he was one of the keys.

But I now knew he'd had no intention of going north. He had prised the coast open, the Wyndham ships safe inshore, and as long as he kept the escorts occupied I couldn't close it again. But neither would he just sit out there, because Subagio would have ordered him to put those ships on the bottom. So it was just a question of when. And, though I'd sent the strongest signal possible to the escorts' captains, warning of intent, I recognized that they were little short of helpless in an endgame.

Again the dream came, Subagio the laughing Admiral of the Fleet, and me his pilot, under orders to set a course into the midnight sun, due south, until the ice had us. He dumped me ashore, indistinguishable from the rest of the penguins in the new uniform of the Southern Archipelagic Navy and told me to recruit as many as I could for deckcrews. But the hand that brought me out of this one did so straight away, no half-hidden message testing the last vestiges of sleep, and took me into the opening move of that endgame.

'Captain Gregory, sir. *Opal* split five minutes ago at 0630.'

But it was 0330 in western ocean waters, the dead of night under a sweltering cloud-covered sky, a test of wakefulness of the men on the pre-dawn watch. The surface plot showed *Opal* split south and west, and over the ensuing half hour the southerly wing followed a curling arc that threatened to become a reciprocal course.

I stood at the plot, knowing that I could only see *Opal* before me because the destroyer escorts had also split, and surface radar feed was coming from two ships well beyond the horizon from each other. Rob came in, looking as though he'd managed only an hour of sleep. 'Trouble?'

'He's made his play.'

'Your Bugis pirate?'

'The same.'

We watched them for an hour, a separation of *Opal*'s wings of almost fifty miles, before a second dispersal, identical to the first, ships spreading themselves apart. 'That's it, then,' said Rob.

'I'd say in the next fifteen minutes,' and I doubted that the escorts' captains were any slower in understanding what faced them now. There was no possibility of their taking the initiative, because they faced a sea-change in modern naval warfare. The polies had decided that we should continue to go to sea with old guns, better than nothing, and had been pleased to train us to do so. There was a very strong sense in Navy that to command a destroyer escort in a battle theatre was to test the hypothesis that it was indeed the gun-control systems that had let down the *Sydney*. Though a much larger cruiser, she had disappeared with all hands in 1941 after a confrontation with *Kormoran*, a German raider. *Opal* carried the latest that could be bought off the shelf, and at no point in that drift westwards had allowed the escorts within reasonable gunnery range. The present raiders didn't need to do so - the menace was all with *them*, our ships little more than observation platforms, and to be left behind, certainly crippled, but destroyed if it could be done.

Though, in the end, I felt that I sat for days watching the surface picture, when Aminuddin's corvettes did enough damage to destroy the escort screen in a matter of hours, and was then lost running for the south, I understood what was flickering in technicolour before me, something I'd avoided thinking before. The corvettes made all the difference to Subagio's own safety, taking the critical mass of electronically-driven hardware and air defence over the top. And it wasn't just that *Opal* itself began that final run, but that *Ruby* was alive on the same coast. If the smaller *Amethyst* had managed to screen her LCTs from Katherine's fury days before, the losses to a major air strike against a concentrated Indonesian fleet now would be enormous. There was no longer an operational base on the whole upper arc of the west coast, the hope that Learmonth could be taken back from the Pilbara intruders, by a battalion moved up from Perth, being rapidly rethought and the force redeployed at Pearce. Pearce was in the heart of a more highly populated Western Australia and a base designed to conduct a sustained operation, unlike Derby or Learmonth. But it was now more a case of what Air Force could do rather than where it flew from, having lost close to its own critical mass of hardware. It had no longer any luxury of withstanding a high rate of attrition. It could nibble at the edges, but if a single massive counterstrike went wrong, the coast would be defenceless. Perth needed those defences, so perhaps the remainder of the coast would end up defenceless after all.

And that really was the crunch. For if the central deserts had been seen as a first line of defence to planners in Canberra, they'd seen the evacuation of coastal communities, Perth included, as unnecessary, and so had left that out of their planning. There were now a million and a half people perhaps likely to lose everything they'd ever had. No one had any idea of how many of Perth's residents were trying to escape, but any that went north would not get far. Bulyanto could not be more than a day away.

`He's practically invincible, sir.' But I was talking about Subagio.

`He'll run out of fuel and supplies this far south.' Dixon was still looking for the crack in the strategy.

`No. He'll have thought of that, Jim.' Bluing now had a measure of his man that put Subagio well above such simple errors.

But Dixon didn't really believe it either. `Then where will he stop?'

I knew where. `Perth, sir. And they won't need Surabaya after all.' And in not wanting to think about it before, I was feeling that I'd made a dreadful mistake. And it was possible that the defences would make no difference.

`What are you talking about, Gregory?'

`It's his new Fleet Base East. He wants the facilities at Fremantle. Garden Island. It doesn't matter if we flatten Surabaya after all.'

Dixon looked at me as if he thought I was hallucinating. ` Gregory. This is no joke.'

Bluing recognized the truth in the idea. `Fremantle doesn't yet have the supporting infrastructure of Surabaya, but I see what you're saying. It has tremendous longer-term strategic value to him.'

`He's the one with the ships, sir.' It was rather an artless statement, and I realized immediately that my irony had overstepped the mark. But, if Bluing heard it, his look suggested he was still thinking about Fremantle.

`Then we bloody well better make sure he doesn't get it.' Dixon was still angry. `If he gets Fremantle, we'll never keep him out of the Bight.'

Bluing shook his head. And it wasn't as if Dixon didn't know it too. `Gregory's right. He doesn't want the Bight. There's no better no-man's-land. He'll stop at Perth. That'll give them everything they want.'

`I wonder what the final message will be?' I thought I'd kept it to myself, but in my tiredness I'd voiced it aloud. None of the others wished even to contemplate the notion.

Rob's final analysis put Subagio's strength at between six and seven major ships. 'We know that the crippled Indonesian vessel left behind over the Java trench is one of the older, smaller frigates.'

'One of the pickets, then?' I asked

He nodded. 'But I think *Magenta* put something else on the bottom. She read the signature of a larger ship.'

'Then an Ahmad Yani, or one of the heavyweights we encountered in the Flores Sea.'

'Probably. As we know that both of the latter classes numbered nine in total, we can assume they have seven still at sea. We knew that they were all operational, so it is the sinkings that count.'

'Anything left in Surabaya?'

'Only a couple of really old ex-US vessels. *Magenta* found a third making transit of the Lombok Strait.'

I raised my eyebrows.

He smiled. 'But no longer.'

Well, it was a good piece of news when there was very little good news around. But the US ships were more than forty years old, and if that was all that was leaving Surabaya now, it meant that the important ships were already at sea, the old ships no more than an opportunity to earn a combat ribbon in a completed campaign.

But where was Subagio? I'd convinced myself that he'd been on board one of those vessels over the Java Trench. But perhaps that was just me, and he had been somewhere else, having already convinced other elements of the navy that they should commit to his game. Intelligence certainly hadn't given us eight major ships in that broth, though in the end we weren't certain what the total was.

But I knew he wanted Perth just, perhaps, as *KOPASSUS* had wanted Darwin.

365

Perhaps such separation of the Services made no sense, after all, they were part and parcel of the same invasion. But the two cities were the keys to victory, the milestones necessarily passed if the whole were to be achieved.

Rob shook his head at my question. 'The main fleet has to be somewhere here.' He sketched an area of the ocean to the southwest of the North West Cape. 'I imagine they were very quickly advised of the fall of Learmonth.'

I nodded. 'They'd have made all speed south as *Opal* took the screen out into the ocean.' And I hadn't forgotten Battle Group West, now down to just *Mowbullan* and *Ord*, *Cornish* no more than a partial asset, but they had continued hunting in empty seas, hampered by non-existent air surveillance. They were also moving south, any suggestion that the search continue cancelled in a last desperate attempt to put some teeth back into the waters off Perth. To do that meant that they had to overhaul Subagio, wherever he was.

But I recognized then that probable positions had been completely reversed. We had created a rear screen with the old destroyer escorts. Subagio had the luxury of both a forward screen, *Opal*, which would take on the air defences from Pearce, and a rear screen, *Ruby*, which would block any attack from the rear.

Trinity had done little to prove its worth. But it then passed on one piece of information which added to the foreknowledge of some difficult hours to come. 'Army believes a squadron of Indonesian Harriers has been moved forward to Learmonth.'

'Well,' said Rob, 'if it's true, it won't take them long to find our Battle Group.'

There was little I could add.

Navy did little to prevent the outcome. One cannot put patrol boats in the path of a fleet and expect the opposition to haul its colours. History had already seen the like, and Sir Richard Grenville paid the price.

But the few signals that came in, as the patrol boats attempted that heroic feat, clearly identified their immediate challenge as vessels smaller than frigates, the numbers 379 and 385 faintly visible under their maritime camouflage.

It had not been so long ago that I'd stood before a group of officers describing number 371. 'I wonder if one of them is Aminuddin's command?' For they could not have been from any group other than *Opal*. And I wondered, in that moment, if it were he that was my real nemesis, or whether he was just secondary, well behind Subagio.

Rob let the question go, used now, to my talking to myself.

'Glaredon will take his ships through your *Ruby*.' Dixon was tapping his notepad with a pencil. 'I want him up against the large ships, not wasting size and speed against terriers.'

We were, at last, getting satellite intelligence, and it confirmed what we'd guessed when blind. *Mowbullan* was within an hour of Subagio's rear screen, which was casually patrolling slightly southwest of Cape Inscription. But Dixon's hope was a faint one. We now knew that Subagio was over four hours ahead. If *Mowbullan* were to keep her course due south, then there was the probability that she or *Ord* would not escape *Ruby* unscathed. But even so, Subagio was making almost as good a speed as our Battle Group, so there was little immediate chance of that final, killing action.

I am active target of hostile aircraft, said *Mowbullan*'s signal, on my screen the instant it was transmitted. Perhaps the only omission was whether Glaredon's foe was singular or plural, but it confirmed Trinity's earlier message.

The news did not improve Dixon's mood. 'Aircraft operating from Learmonth. That neutralizes anything from Pearce.'

Not that Pearce was concentrating that far north. All air forces were now closely intent on Subagio's advance, more than a hundred miles to the south of *Ruby*. What the news really meant was that *Ruby* was now a greater threat than before.

'Order stands,' said Dixon, and committed Glaredon to a more difficult fight.

Dixon's order also confirmed what was becoming very clear to everyone, even Trinity. Air forces would be the final defence to the naval strike. Perhaps this should have been glaringly obvious from the very first moment, for distance and hull-speeds brought the perception of the naval chase to that of sea-turtles swimming against a tidal bore. But when you have committed yourself to a uniform, and all that uniform entails, it is hard to stand back and accept that a different service has acquired, by default, your responsibility. Perhaps Dixon saw it, but he also saw that there would be a political price to pay over either of the possible outcomes, so he could give neither Glaredon nor the thin forces from Fremantle any possible choice in the matter.

Conditions at Pearce must have become as desperate as they were on board any of the ships of our shrunken fleet. In contrast, the silence of the Warfare Centre, apart from the occasional updating of an order or a statement of significant change on the surface plot, seemed demeaning - ours felt a decreasingly useful function. The war had regressed to how the public saw it - death on a battlefield. And perhaps the public was much closer to the truth than it knew- there was no strategy left to make, no new ideas to grasp, and hardly any more resources that could be transferred from the east coast. We could only sit back and watch people die.

Pearce did what it could, both to back Fremantle against *Opal*, and to slow Subagio. But the main air-strike capability was housed across the continent in Queensland, so Pearce was unable to provide ground support at the level of counter-attack that the final moments of the naval strike required. Confidence initially borne by the foreknowledge that Australian technological capability had to be better than the Indonesians' own, it being generally assumed that smaller powers which bought technology off the shelf would be unable to operate it with the level of familiarity of our own forces, gradually eroded as the air strike against *Opal* lost momentum.

'They have far better decoy mechanisms and surface-to-air capability than I'd have thought possible,' said Litner, at one point. 'We do not have the upper hand.'

But I recalled seeing all the underdeck work that had been done, space made for all the materiel they'd need in what they had planned to do. All the derision that had gone into pronouncements of obsolescence had echoed momentarily in those munitions holds, and then died somewhere in the refurbished engine rooms. And I knew, but still seemed unable to convince others of the same, that neither Subagio nor Bulyanto would have led a military strike without being perfectly sure that those with responsibility for the use of the hardware would be able to perform at the level that same hardware demanded. *Aminuddin!* There had never been any lack of professionalism or confidence beneath the hate he'd borne for me. And *I* knew *he* was *Opal*.

So, slowly, planes were either lost or became ineffective in that final desperate effort to stop the southward race of the Indonesian fleet and the clear waters *Opal* was preparing for it. For it was clearly a race, Subagio's battle group steaming hard to complete that last hurdle, the most important one of them all because it was Perth and all that Perth meant that was critical. Without Perth it would be no more than a partial victory.

Rob was glued to his intelligence reports as they came in, a combination of satellite shots and damage estimates. 'One corvette sunk, perhaps another severely damaged - not all one way.' Then 'Do you want to know where Subagio is?' he asked.

'I know where he is. You told me so as soon as we got the first photo.'

'No. I mean which ship he's on.' He pointed to the cluster of ships streaming long wakes now permanently on a screen in front of him.The screen blinked intermittently and the ships moved. 'That's the *Sudarso*. Too small to see any Admiral's pennant, but she's had a continual forward and lateral shield,' he pointed to the other ships, 'ever since we picked them up. I'd bet she's the command vessel. It's the others that are taking the strikes.' Smoke was evident from a fore-deck fire on one of the outer ships.

'Admiral.' Dixon turned his head. 'Could you get Air Force to concentrate remaining forces on a single ship?'

He stared at me for a moment. 'Subagio?'

'We think so, sir.'

He moved quickly, a few steps over to one of his two other-service counterparts, and said something brief. Then he looked up. 'Position?'

Rob had already transferred the last exact numbers, accurate to within yards. But she was a moving target. 'Her course is east-by-south, 29 knots.'

Dixon's Air Force colleague looked over at us. 'You're asking us for an even higher payment.' It was slightly bitter, the way it was said, clearly castigating us for our own failures.

'Stuff it, Mac,' said Dixon. 'I'm the one asking. Not them.'

'Pennant number 353,' I said. 'Just in case you can get close enough to read it.' That brought a cobalt glare from Dixon, who had clearly heard my insubordination. But there was something else in those eyes, also. Cloud, perhaps, marking the death of a faith essential to his own being.

Opal proved finally that a number of small independent missile platforms could mount a defence as effective as the attack thrown at it. Our surface thrust petered out in increasing damage to the patrol boats, faster than the remaining corvettes though they were. It was again a statement of the end of the age of gunnery, even if there were now few guns on board - surface speed no longer guaranteed escape. A missile could follow your twists and turns until the bitter end. In this combat numbers counted, and *Opal* was still the superior force.

I wasn't sure how to find the words to tell Dixon, though he was as cognizant as I of how the fight had developed. Finally I said, '*Opal* has penetrated our final defence, sir.' It seemed less humiliating than *obliterated*.

He barely nodded. *And Subagio?* I heard him say to himself, not needing to ask me.

I did not need that unspoken question to recognize that this was now the critical moment. Critical in the sense of being on the edge of the final abyss, not of the many smaller precipices we had fallen from in the last few days. We calculated that eliminating Subagio would cause the collapse of the naval strike. Then we could turn our attention elsewhere. But it required the sinking of the *Sudarso* first.

But we also calculated an all-out assault on Pearce's defences, a tactic that would match Bulyanto's methods perfectly. As Townsworth was sure we'd hold them there, certainly troops enough on the ground to slow Bulyanto down, we felt we had been presented with the first opportunity to cut this southward flow.

369

It was Townsworth himself who muttered the first doubt. 'Nothing. I'd expected another Katherine. But there's nothing.'

Litner was fully absorbed in his own task. 'Just as well. Leaves us to get on with what matters.'

So I felt sure that if what we expected had not come to pass, then our own calculations were either wrong, or unnecessary.

It was the Indonesian Harrier squadron that fooled us. Most were of the opinion that it would support *Ruby* against Glaredon's two ships. But this was defensive naval thinking, and it became obvious that Learmonth had assumed an immediate strategic purpose far more important than any longer-term transfer of ownership of Fremantle's Garden Island.

It was Litner who was shaken. 'The main Indonesian fleet has air defence.'

Dixon stirred. 'Glaredon?' he said to me.

The surface plot showed a picture not unlike *Opal*'s encounter with the destroyer escorts. 'Busy with *Ruby*, sir.' But he knew that already. '*Ruby* is staying as far ahead of him as speed will allow. But his missile defences are being tested.' As were *Ruby*'s, and I thought it unlikely that *Ruby* would slow him down for long. But any delay made it that much harder to increase the surface pressure against Subagio. I had given Rob the coordinates, and the course changes as they happened.

Now, he said 'Three hours. Subagio will make Perth three hours ahead of Glaredon.'

And we all knew that if he did, then we'd have lost the race.

It was one of the ironies of the whole conflict that one attack we'd expected, on Pearce, didn't come. But it spoke to what we'd later understood - Learmonth was too important to lose. Bulyanto would have known that any air strike on Subagio's fleet was unsustainable, and, *Ruby* harrying Glaredon closer to Bulyanto himself, with no ships to support it. So it was essential to him to protect the Harrier's operational base. Perhaps, with Darwin in his back pocket, he also understood that the polies would be getting more nervous by the minute. He waited, and our air strike burnt itself out.

But it would be wrong to imply that we didn't throw everything we had into that fraught, final attempt. It was only the suicidal runs of pilots committed to the value of sacrifice as a catalyst to greater subsequent effort that brought the penetration that the air strike sought. If there can be any parallel drawn between sea and sky, then those moments were as tempestuous as the seas had been to *Mowbullan* a day or two before. Even with fighters working to cover the strike aircraft, Bulyanto's Harriers managed to draw enough of our teeth to ensure that penetration was heavily bought. Litner, later that day, reiterated what no-one had dared openly repeat. 'I wonder if any of our Defence-trained commercial pilots now understand the price of *their* treason?' We all knew that it was only the best that went.

There was no Australian grey-funnel welcome for Subagio when his own ships made that last horizon and saw the still smouldering hulks of two container vessels in the approach roads. He had left one of his own vessels in flames, and the *Sudarso* herself was damaged, but he made Perth within half an hour of Rob's best estimate, and fully two hours ahead of Glaredon's previous ETA.

Perhaps he hadn't been sure that the southern ocean didn't still pose a risk, and that a new threat might not come hard around Cape Leeuwin, or that there might not be another wave of desperate air defence. So he'd done what he must have planned to do since the beginning, or perhaps because that final air strike had annoyed him. Three hours before his arrival, well within the limits of the technology, he put several very large cruise missiles into the downtown heart of Perth. Those three hours, once we knew Perth had sustained those strikes, forced the drawing of Glaredon's teeth. He was ordered to remain well beyond short missile range.

Bluing got the first taste of his adversary's voice on the wavelengths that his colleagues had already used to communicate the first instruction over Darwin. `I, *Laksamana* Subagio, representing the Ruling Military Council of Indonesia, advise the Australian Government that I have today annexed western coastal waters. Effective immediately, no Australian naval vessel is permitted to pass north of Cape Leeuwin. All other vessels will respect a two-hundred mile maritime exclusion zone around that same cape. All Australian naval vessels in western waters will withdraw immediately. Should this order not be respected further retribution will be taken on the citizens of Perth.'

Canberra brought the few remaining planes east.

Thirty two

There were moments when I had imaginary discussions with the Jenderal, once I caught up with him in Perth. They would be tentative times, the terms and conditions of the accord settled but not yet completely fulfilled

`Selamat datang, Kapten.' The Jenderal has a sardonic gleam in his eye.

`I'm more grateful than I can say, Jenderal.'

He nods. `Anything new that I should worry about?'

`Not relevant to this immediate campaign, sir. There is something I'd like to review when you are less busy.'

His eyebrows climb a fraction of a millimetre. `Another idea?'

`Yes, sir.'

`I see.' He looks at me oddly. `I still find it curious, Soekendro, that you came to me with this when you did.' His gesture takes in half a continent.

`I explained at the time, sir. I had it as an idea in your war games course.'

`No, Kapten. It doesn't explain the timing.'

`My father has an extensive library, sir. I used to read a lot.'

`And who made the selections?'

`I must admit, sir, that my father had some ideas of his own as to what I should read.'

`An intelligent man, I think, your father.'

`He liked Soekarno, sir.'

`I wondered about that, Kapten. I thought perhaps there'd been a leak.'

My promotion to Kapten is the fastest fully-earned leap to that rank of any junior officer in ABRI's history. To my father's amazement his own retirement is postponed by a full five years. He hasn't the faintest idea precisely what his son has done, or where his son is, but in the turmoil roiling below ABRI's surface it is made clear to him that he is on the right side. He takes that message to heart very carefully.

Excerpted from Rusman Soekendro, LetJen (ret'd),
No Game At All: Memoirs of a Strategist

Then why should you even think of me as a lecturer?' asked the Australian.

'Because our students do not understand Western thought,' said the Javan.

'But you've just explained it to me, and I think I understand you. Why can't you do the same for them?'

'Oh, I've tried. They just don't believe me.'

The woman broke into laughter. 'After I don't know how many days, I think the only conclusion is that we are the three apices of a triangle. As far away from each other as we could possibly be.'

This unsettled the Australian, who still had not let go of the idea that something unpleasant was going to happen to his relationship with his wife.

She saw his confusion. 'I mean East, West, Woman,' she said pointing to each in turn. 'I don't mean Rusman, Trevor, Anne.'

The Javan saw the value in this description. 'Our purpose must be to maintain the triangle as close to isosceles as possible. Yes, Trevor? Allah will decide on the length of the sides.'

The Australian let out a huge gust of a breath. 'This is so far beyond me I am on the point of giving up. You, Rusman, are a bloody genius. I'm an ex-sailor. There's a hundred miles between us. Nautical miles at that. I think I'd rather just be friends.'

'Then you won't come and talk to my students?'

The Australian thought for a moment. 'Both Anne and I will come. You will make it clear we are the Western hypotenuse, man and woman. I'll make a dingo's breakfast of western military thought, Anne will do a bonzer job on Woman, generally.'

The Javan clapped his hands. 'The exam question will say: Think of Eastern and Western military thought as two great rivers. Is there a possible confluence? Or are they both doomed to spend themselves over the rocks of Woman?'

They had a good laugh at that, each with his or her particular, apical viewpoint.

***

'There will be a withdrawal of all Australians living to the west of a line drawn from Endeavour Hill on the south bank of the Victoria River in the north, through Lake Tobin in the Great Sandy Desert, to Eyre on the southern coast.'

I didn't recognize the urbane face. Standing before a lectern in the main reception chamber, its owner was reading a carefully prepared statement, and the television lights showed a slight sheen of perspiration on that face. Not, I thought, because the bastard was nervous.

'In recognition of the suffering brought in the past on the aboriginal population by the European settlers, and the common ties that we share with the former as the indigenous peoples of South-East Asia, this decree will not apply to anyone of aboriginal descent. We shall recognize them as our brothers in this struggle and extend to them the same rights received by our own people.'

It was a room I knew, with the slight mustiness of carpets and furniture long exposed to a humid climate hanging in the air, but it had not seen such ceremony for a long time.

'Our country is in transition. In a few short years we have seen a rapid succession of Presidents. We have mourned one or two of them, even as we recognized their inability to deal with the real problems confronting our people. We have seen them take shaky steps on the road poorly termed democracy. We have seen them wish to remove the military from its guiding role in government.'

It was not clear yet what it was we were watching, even if it had started with a decree. Canberra used the term *flux* to describe the picture in Indonesia, just as it was doing over conditions at the desert front, perhaps to avoid saying that any continuous change was still beyond its powers of description.

'Today we have taken the step that will give every Indonesian citizen the ability to work for a more prosperous tomorrow. By sharing these vast areas of an empty continent with people who really need them, and who have a greater right to be there than the remnants of an European colonial power, we bring a new dimension to our already great country.'

I thought that scholars of Indonesian history might find interesting similarities between the slur on European colonization and Java's own recent attempt at subjugating less powerful sub-national groups by sending them both Javanese bureaucrats and peasants.

'There have been certain destabilizing forces amongst us for some time, leeches on our economy who have used positions of respect to their own financial gain. This has created resentment. As of today, all shares held by these persons in whatever business will revert to the Government. Once these transactions are complete the shares will be offered for sale on the open market. We will purify the economy and put every Indonesian businessman on equal footing. It is time to spread the benefits.'

I wondered if some of his comments referred to Suharto and his old cronies. They'd buried him already, but I thought they'd probably purified the old man first, perhaps in his sleep, and God knows what they'd do, or already had done, to the family.

375

'Australia believes that it can be the victor in this, perhaps bolstered by what it also believes it has achieved in East Tomor. But no Indonesian can accept that the continuing presence of an occupying army on Indonesian soil is anything other than the expansionist vision of a deputy sheriff wishing to show itself eager to its American boss.'

There was some angry muttering in the room, but a hissed *'Quiet!'* from a very senior officer silenced it.

'Indonesia has suffered several other affronts. Senior military officers have been humiliated, inaccurately accused of human-rights abuses. Might we not also point a finger at Australia and her own record here?' He said the last as if it were enclosed in parentheses.

'Furthermore, she has invaded national waters at a time when we found it necessary to close archipelagic sea-lanes, and *after* the international community was so advised. And she has continually harassed Indonesian defence personnel on both the Timorese and Papuan borders.'

He paused. 'There comes a time when the well-meaning patience of any nation is exhausted. In our case, that moment is now. Indonesia has, therefore, exercised its right under Article 51 of the United Nations charter, to adopt in the same way as has Australia, but in response to attack *by* Australia, a security zone which will help prevent such threats in the future. We have moved unilaterally to establish this zone, in the belief that we would not receive consideration equal to Australia's at the Security Council. A few moments ago we defined the new boundaries of this zone, which approximate to the old ones of *Australi Barat*, Western Australia. Let this now be thought of as *Jawa Baru*, New Java.'

Then I understood the irony that had ignored Javanese expansionism in the historical record. These were Javanese officers, and this was all *for* Java. In the short term, at least.

'We have no doubt that the Australian government and general populace are witnesses to this transmission. Equally, we have no doubt that their self-righteous protestation also says that Indonesia will be made to look a fool over its move.'

The speaker again paused, perhaps to let us think about his last few words, or to make us wonder what was to come. 'It is important it be known that this is a civil protest and a civil movement. We of the military see ourselves as no more than the facilitator of an inevitable outcome in the relations between two nation-states. Were it not to happen now, it would have to happen later.' He was nodding as he said this, conferring the authority of diktat upon his statements.

'We have provided to all owners of passenger vessels, ferries, fishing boats and other craft, sailing directions to many of the coastal regions of *Jawa Baru* in order that they may carry as many settlers to these areas as they wish. It is our estimate that within the next three months, our security zone will see an influx of more than one hundred thousand immigrants.' He lifted his head and looked directly into the camera. 'We shall think of them as .... peacekeepers.'

I remembered thinking once that perhaps I could recognize chagrin on an Indonesian face. Now, at least, I recognized a smirk, though that was as much in the words as the speaker's expression, the latter perhaps very carefully schooled to let just a little of it show. Then, from his movement of the papers in his hand, I thought he'd come to the end of the speech. I thought it interesting that he had refrained from adding *and should Australia believe that she can prevent these hundreds of craft from landing, she should remember that she has just abdicated the waters in question.*

But he looked at the camera once more. 'During this period of national readjustment, the Presidential Office will be moved here. The Istana Merdeka will remain closed until further notice.'

And that answered the final question - why the news conference was being given at the Summer Palace in Bogor, an hour from Jakarta. The corridors of the Istana Merdeka, the national Palace, were probably still running with blood, a military house-cleaning. For the speaker wore the uniform of a major general, one of perhaps dozens in the Army, and, for the moment, the one either he himself or his peers had decided should be the public face of the transition.

'So now we know.' Gall was able to say little more.

'Well? What do we do?' Most eyes turned to the Defence Minister, who'd almost bleated this out.

'Until we can re-establish some sort of defence in the desert, they have us where they want us.' said Gall. 'Though we can't turn our back on Perth. We'd have no credibility with the rest of the country.'

'We have no bloody credibility now!' The Minister's anger was right on the surface, and as his eyes went from one Chief to another, they rested significantly longer on Bluing. The blame was attached to him.

Gall shrugged. 'It's important that we act as though we do. The question is whether they really expect us to give up Perth.'

He didn't mention Darwin, and I wondered whether that had suddenly become a price payable if we could recover Perth.

'Can we negotiate?' The Minister was shaking his head as he said it. 'We have no strengths in this conflict at all. Will the Americans come in at this stage?'

But it was Gall's turn to shake his head. 'They're so tied up over China they can't risk it.'

'You're not saying China won't let them?'

`No, I did not say that. But I believe that is the position. I do sometimes wonder at the coincidental timing.'

`That China has come in on this? That they're tying the Americans up *for* Indonesia?' The Minister's incredulity was shared by most of the room.

`Something like that.'

Peng's spite, I wondered, over the loss of the uranium? But it had to be more than that - his anger wasn't with the Americans.

`Then that really is it.' There were tears in the Minister's eyes. `Christ. I wish I understood how we got ourselves into this position. What happened to all the bloody bilateral relationships we built with these people?' But it was a cry of agony, not a request for information. It was clear his career would end when he told his Prime Minister that he would be responsible for the country possibly losing a quarter of its territory and perhaps half its wealth.

But the PM didn't blame the Defence Minister that night when he gave us more than the usual televised thirty seconds. The missile attack on Perth had been his watershed, for now we'd lost two cities, with all the implications for civilian security that implied. So he came empty-handed.

`Every nation is vulnerable to the predations of others. Over the past weeks we have suffered an assault of a nature this country has never known, far greater than the memories we still hold of the second World War. The men and women of our defence forces have paid a high price in an attempt to keep us free from what I must call this evil that has fallen upon us. Citizens of our far north are paying a high price in hardship and deprivation. All of these are costs that a nation incurs at a time like this.

`As your Prime Minister it ultimately befalls me to assess these costs, and to decide whether we should go on paying them. I have to decide whether there are other avenues open to us to turn this evil around. Your Government is exploring every possibility, and a protest of the highest order has been lodged with the Security Council of the United Nations. With the speed at which this body generally deliberates, I am not hopeful that this last will bring any immediate result. We need relief in days.'

`You may have thought that our defence was somehow assured through our agreements with other western powers. In particular, with the United States of America. I regret to say that we are unable to rely directly on such past agreements, due to the very unique nature of the assault made on parts of our country which are, quite frankly, inhospitable. By this I mean that our allies believe that there is no immediate defence. We cannot call on them to prove otherwise. I also need not remind you that there are some other serious rumblings further to the north which have pre-occupied our principal partner.'

`You should not interpret this to mean that your Government has been idle in providing for the defence of Australia. It was not so long ago that we undertook a public consultation on defence. We have done what we could with the resources available to us. Our country is immense. This particular conflict has taught us just how immense. We continue to strengthen our defences in those parts of the country of particular strategic importance. The vast majority of you will not be directly affected by this invasion. You will not lose your homes, nor be forced to relocate. You will, however, be indirectly affected. None of us will escape some of the consequences.'

`In the short term we shall probably lose effective control of the western arc, from Darwin to Perth. To those of you in south-western Australia who have not yet considered this seriously, I must tell you that you should make preparations to leave. This recommendation is for your own safety. I cannot foretell the final outcome of the next few weeks. However, I am not willing to expose you to the fate of the brave population of Darwin, which is unwilling captive to this invasion force. Your Government will give you what support it can in helping you in an immediate evacuation to the eastern side of our continent.'

`So I must finally say that this is a very bleak hour. Australia is already a very different country from what she was a few weeks ago. History has a tendency to teach lessons. I think the lesson in front of us now is that this world continually presents new challenges against which it is not always possible to be prepared. Perhaps we were not as prepared as we could have been. But perhaps this particular challenge was inevitable at some time in our history. Whatever the outcome, I wish you all godspeed. I hope tomorrow is better than today. Goodnight.'

So in three minutes he gave us what had been weighed in the costs and returns to actions designed to turn a tide no Aussie Canute could ever turn. He was less than honest in suggesting we'd probably lose control of the western arc, because we'd lost it already, and he'd left the poor bastards in the south-west to make their own evacuation plans. In the heat of the moment I didn't blame him too much, though I didn't give him much of a chance in the next election.

Neil Thomas

Thirty three

The announcement of the Australian adventure came as a great surprise to every Indonesian. Drawn as they had been for weeks towards the turmoil of civil unrest, the proclamation that Indonesia was about to take a vast slice of the Australian continent for her own brought a diversion as arresting as the delivery of free rice to every marketplace in the nation. The proclamation brought a promise of a new future for any and all those who wished to partake. It was the promise of sudden riches that everyone dreamed of, an alternative to the grinding poverty facing most of the 200 million souls that populated our ever more devastated islands. It was a way out. The promised land.

Land, to a person living in the confinement of most Javanese villages and towns, was a richness unattainable. There was none left, every square centimetre occupied, populations squeezed for the very air to breathe. So who did not understand, when offered alternative visions of two hectares of the sour swamps of Kalimantan or five of the rich wheatlands of western Australia, that Allah's blessing went with the latter? It required no thought.

Within two days the clamour for more information was deafening, and the streets of central Jakarta became packed with the most hopeful, thin bundles under thinner arms, ready to go. It was a gold rush, and everyone knew that those who got there first reaped the greatest benefit. The parkland around Monas, the national monument, became the itinerants' way-station, more packed every hour.

The announcement then came that the departure point would be Surabaya, and smaller ports farther east. The Government would supply buses to take the people there, but anyone who didn't get on a bus should get him or herself east as soon as possible. But just in case it was not possible to leave immediately, there was space enough in Australia for all and there were bound to be vessels leaving daily.

It was recognized as the greatest mass movement that Java would ever see. Java, because this was still for Java. If Java's attention was elsewhere, then the satellite islands became easier to address. So we had to keep Java occupied while putting down the Acehnese, the Papuans, the Minahasans and all the other ethnic groups who owed no real allegiance to Java and its modern sultanate.

The two long-term presidents since the independence of '45 had been Javanese, eschewing only the formality of the divine royal court in their rule, replacing it with an undivinable bureaucracy, and there was no love lost, no allegiance. So the army went in again. But only with Java occupied elsewhere.

Excerpted from Rusman Soekendro, LetJen (ret'd),
No Game At All: Memoirs of a Strategist

Rusman, tell me about Al Qaeda,' said the Australian. 'You've admitted that the Bali bombing was a military operation, and you haven't denied that the Alumina Queen might have been a ruse. You hanged me with my own rope during *Operasi Lautan Lepas*. I can see very little else to suggest Al Qaeda was ever operational in Indonesia.'

'There were exploratory tentacles, if you like, *pak* Trevor, in the early days of Afghanistan. Not directly from Al Qaeda, but from Pakistan. As we are the world's largest Muslim nation, certain elements in the Pakistani secret service saw it as natural that we'd be sympathetic to the cause. Our own secret service reacted with typical Javanese caution and relayed the message to a higher military echelon. It came very quickly to the *Jenderal*'s ears.'

The Australian almost whistled in surprise. 'Ohh. Handed to him on a plate, eh?'

'It was made very clear to the Pakistanis that no major sanctuary was on offer, but that some minor linkages were possible.'

'Anything else would have had the Americans down your necks in no time flat.'

The Javan bowed his head in acknowledgement.

'That fiction of an Al Qaeda presence puzzled all my contacts at the time. Especially Balikpapan.' said the woman. 'No-one could detect anything that resembled the cells that were supposedly responsible for the bombings, even the ones before Bali.'

'There were always a few *kegilaan*,' said the Javan, 'the half-mad who react out of infatuation with an idea. We left them alone - they were useful decoys. But, no, *ibu* Anne, the true cells were our cells. So your civil society contacts would necessarily have drawn a blank.'

'AQ,' said the Australian. 'I liked that.'

'No,' said the Javan, 'I'm sorry, *pak* Trevor. It wasn't a ruse. I have no idea what happened. We read the same letters and saw their potential. But we never expected you to come forward with what you proposed. *Laksamana* Subagio said you gave him the greatest surprise of his life.'

'No,' said the Australian, in disgust. 'That came a little later. When I sent him a rocket.'

***

`We will call it the Soekarno Line.' The broadcast ended.

I could see Gall choking on it, slumped back in his seat, knowing that history could call it nothing but defeat. He still could not accept that he'd been out-planned and out-thought. And he was to go with the Defence Minister on a humiliating trip, not even to Darwin but to Katherine, where we were to discuss demilitarization of the airbase if we wished to secure the release of the population. I think it was the vision of having to sit around a table with senior Indonesian officers that especially rankled, because Gall had been one of those who had promoted strength in bilateral ties as a means of ensuring defence.

The Soekarno Line, from Endeavour Hill to Eyre, was cunningly drawn, pointing directly at Darwin, but starting at a point slightly further south. It was an unequivocal statement - *we return Darwin to you, for it has served its purpose.* And the demilitarization was another poke in the eye - *as you did in East Timor so have we done unto you.* The Defence Committee was undecided whether longer term plans would see retrenchment to Amberley and other bases on the east coast, or whether Arnhem Land still had a future in defence against other possible moves. The old saw, the Ring of Fire, coined in reference to Indonesia's volcanic origins, was taking on a very different cast to stumbling defence planners.

The National Resettlement Committee was what they had decided to call themselves. It had a ring of Indonesian doubletalk about it, as if it had already achieved all its means, though there had been no doubletalk in any of the broadcasts, which had been a straightforward analysis of where they had us and what we would have to do. They saw themselves the victors in this, and gave themselves the right to call it what they liked. As they did the line. Soekarno. Someone whom old Suharto had tried firmly to put out of peoples' minds. It probably had no other significance than homage to the man who brought them independence, though it perhaps served to distance all this from Suharto's well-faded New Order.

Gall didn't like it at all. In fact he looked very sick. For I knew he still saw our capitulation as his treason.

In his position as part of a loyal opposition elected in peace-time, the Shadow Defence Minister was attaining a profile perhaps higher than he had ever expected. Each day the morning papers noted the relish with which he voiced what he considered to be the real concerns of the average Australian. But he then came to something rather different, again during a televised session of the House. 'Would the Government explain to the House why, when Pine Gap is labelled a *Joint Defence Facility*, and sits as close to the centre of this country as any navel-gazer could wish, ... why it is that Pine Gap is providing all possible intelligence on China to the US while leaving our own intelligence analysts in the dark over Indonesia?' He sat down.

One only needed an old black-and-white television, as the Defence Minister was now perpetually grey. 'My Honourable Colleague has, as usual, misconstrued comments made to the press by a dissatisfied public servant. This person has been reprimanded and placed in a position where he may do no harm to future security. And within the range of responsibilities attributed by the layman to Pine Gap, I do assure the House that unidentified flying objects, or UFOs as I believe they are called, remain well down on the list of priorities, and.......' the Minister had to pause for some derisive laughter, '....and that we share equally with the US in terms of the volume of intelligence processed by that installation.'

The Shadow Minister was seen to be losing his temper. 'But where was the intelligence when we needed it? Why didn't we guess that Indonesia would sail those German boats south? Don't they use the same radio waves up there that we do?'

The Minister was still standing. 'If I remember correctly, it was world opinion that put those vessels in the realm of scrap. Any transmission pertaining to the fleet picked up at Pine Gap would, naturally, have remained secret. But I don't think I am misinterpreting the facts that I do know when I say ....'

He was not allowed to finish. His opponent stood up once again. 'Hah, *facts......*! Mr Speaker, if it is so critical that we maintain as secret most of the operational issues relating to our conduct of this war, including our opponent's intent, would the Minister care to explain why it is that the facts of the considerable faults which our brand new Lake-Class submarines are experiencing, and which have rendered all but one so useless that the Navy refuses to accept them, I repeat, why it is that this information, which I should have thought was *Top* bloody secret, IS PLASTERED ALL OVER THAT THING THEY CALL THE WEB? Perhaps I could give the Minister the relevant address?'

It was *Mowbullan* that got the first whiff, a mutter on the bottom end of the scan, hardly anything different from some of the deeper sea noises. But her captain didn't doubt his sonar officer, who'd put it through the most exhaustive analysis he could devise. *Mowbullan's* trouble was the naval armistice, which had her under such tight control that any deviation from course, speed or friendly intent would immediately render the rest of it invalid, with who-knew-what consequences. After all, they still had Darwin and Perth. We caught the essence in a signal coded to a non-existent victualling yard. Not cocoa, but just as good. But it took Rob to tell Edmonds what he had under his nose, and to make him understand why none of the Indonesian surface ships was near.

Loops were loops, and *Magenta* had already been brought back out of the Flores Sea as quietly as she'd been taken in, a strike on Surabaya seen strategically then as pointless. We encrypted the signal and flicked the radiowaves across the Indian Ocean. It was the last idea, as GWO, I could put to Bluing. I made it my apology for any of the previous ones that hadn't been very good.

'I cannot commend any of our overall actions in the past days to a positive historical record,' Bluing said. 'But, of anyone, you've made a significant contribution to averting total disaster.'

I wasn't sure how he could rate what had happened as anything less than a total disaster, but thought it wise to keep quiet.

He considered the idea for a moment. 'I'll make my own assessment of the risk to the vessel and her crew. I may just be in the mood to ignore the fact that it goes completely against the agreement we've just made. The PM may not be told, Gregory. It'll be as simple as that.' But that was no more than an artifice, for it had also been my recommendation that *Magenta* be left off the list of vessels still in or close to the theatre.

I knew that her captain was even less of a hedonist than the one we were hunting. He was a submariner who lived for the depths, and he always worked his ship to its lethal limit. We tactical blokes nodded sagely even when we knew how close to the limits he went. It was faith from his crew that mattered, because he lived and breathed with them.

But this would be a different risk, and he'd have to put a lot of faith in us, knowing that he'd have to lock some watertight doors. His only response in another signal to the victuallers was that he'd probably have to come in for a new bow sonar.

And this would take extreme care from his pilot, who was going to have to steer as he'd never steered before, watching the screens that represented the three-dimensional space they'd shortly have to use very carefully indeed. But *Mowbullan* remained a key, for it was her sensors that were at work, replacing *Magenta's*, for the submarine had to remain hidden. Her final acknowledgement squeaked out as a millisecond radio burst berating the same victuallers for the substandard snags her galley was forced to serve up for breakfast. It was unlikely Jakarta would catch the irony in that.

But *Magenta* picked several signals out of the other communications loop that Canberra had devised. She left a small buoy at the surface, an electronic

Portuguese man-o'-war trailing its lethal tentacle well into the depths. Hidden in signals indistinguishable from the calls of the deep-roaming southern whales were the increasingly better-defined coordinates that *Magenta* needed, coordinates that defined the underwater shadow following *Mowbullan* and *Cornish. Nanggala*, the guardian set by her Javanese master, but a guardian now discovered.

We chose 0200 hours. A hidden engineering team on *Mowbullan* spent several hours rigging a couple of false bearings in the tunnel housing the propeller shaft. At 0130 they brought the bearings slowly to play around the shaft, itself well protected but the ideal medium to transmit noises of intense strength and pitch into the surrounding waters, a tuning fork of Cyclopean proportions, detectable at more than seventy-five miles, probably deafening at forty. *Mowbullan* literally squealed to a slow drift, *Cornish* dropping speed, but staying a mile to starboard.

Nanggala drew slowly closer, wasp to syrup, but finally kept station some ten miles to port, fifty metres down. If we'd done it right, she would have no reason to believe that there was any other vessel closer than the Cape of Good Hope. We gave the seas some life, signals from a buoy slipped over the side by *Cornish* an hour before echoing a pod of whales several miles further to the southeast.

The angle was 49° from the vertical. Any more and there was a real danger of missing. Any less and *Magenta* might be detected. This had to be clean and quick, no signals out from a stricken ship floating to the surface, and as long as *Magenta* remained undetected and *Mowbullan* and *Cornish* kept their stations there could be no certainty of the real reason for the loss.

I had no doubt that the silence was thunderous to *Magenta*'s crew, dropping more men-o'war in the miles before, waiting at maximum dive depth for our arrival, riding silently up the parabolic arc from two hundred fathoms, reading the continuous coordinates broadcast by *Mowbullan*, watching *Nanggala* drift into parallel station to us, finally seeing an image on a screen. A hologram of the German-built sub, West not East, growing, and then slowly the conning tower putting itself right in the way of the bow simulacrum at the bottom of the screen. *Magenta* was a bullet with three thousand tons behind her, but it was a single torpedo fired at very close range that was to fracture *Nanggala's* conning tower at the deck, splitting it vertically through the internal seals that kept the vessel dry, and rupturing the port ballast tanks.

We heard that *Nanggala* did not rear to the surface, magnificently wounded, to die a true submarine's death. The only surface evidence was a concussive bolt of air that would have curled up around *Magenta*'s hull as she passed overhead, bursting on the surface and observed in surprise on both *Mowbullan* and *Cornish*. *Nanngala* would have lost all buoyancy in that massive explosion.

Mowbullan's bearing problem was solved without any need for *Cornish* to come alongside, and the two ships continued a course northeast and beyond, to round the

Top End and eventually to take the Torres Strait into the Coral Sea. There, they would be in home waters. After that it was anyone's guess as to when they'd see this coast again. *Magenta* didn't even see it this time, but took the long way home, staying well out in deep water, watching and listening as she drove south, now the only submarine in these waters, safe.

If it became obvious to Subagio within days that he'd lost *Nanggala*, he'd know that none of the surface ships had touched her, for his on-board observers would have told him so. The minor bearing problem suffered by *Mowbullan* probably never came to his attention. He may never even have known that there'd been an Australian submarine involved late one night with filthy weather over the Java Trench, though another sinking in the Lombok Strait should have spelled it out for him. But even if he did he must have recognized his own weakness under the very water where he'd had the surface strength when it mattered. And now was not the time to hunt her. If she had come across *Nanggala*, then that was a loss to have to bear. Perhaps we managed to spoil the otherwise clean sense of victory he felt.

`We've lost almost half our seas.' A simple shake of the head in disgust seemed inadequate to Bluing, but it was more a recognition that he still didn't know how to deal emotionally with what he'd just said. The Naval post-mortem was simple. Ships enough only to respond to the low-level conflicts that the polies had felt it necessary ever to worry about.

There was still a dangerous sense of having turned that corner, that the decisions of the past years to add half a dozen frigates and a similar number of submarines made right the policy deficit of the more distant past, even if we had lost a war. Though if the present lesson wasn't enough to defeat that argument, then perhaps the corner was as far away as ever, for we'd come out of the engagement with fewer ships than when we went in. And Dixon was scathing about the submarines, the memory of the *Melbourne* perhaps still rankling. 'What an absolute shambles. Didn't I say that designing and building submarines is not something you can leave to amateurs?'

But it was the knowledge that the new ships could only ever replace a rapidly rusting fleet which was the main source of despair to all around the table. There'd be no net tonnage added to the navy's total displacement. Just some slightly higher quality steel, which, to begin with at least, wouldn't require repainting quite so often.

Dixon continued in his rancorous mood. `If you see it in a positive light it does mean that we've doubled our cover in the seas we have left.'

But I thought that might persuade the polies to make deeper cuts. Bluing voiced the strategic problem. 'We'll have to redraft naval defence strategy to prove that we will need that and more. And not because we have a hostile navy berthed at our own moorings. There is something much bigger and uglier out there that one day we'll have to deal with - Indonesia may just have made the Pacific very much easier for China.'

All present in the room were aware of the popular belief that it had been the navy's fault. It was very hard to find an argument to suggest that we could have done better even had all the ships been in home waters. That the invasion had come by sea made it our responsibility. But in the end there was the need for recognition of what someone else had said, that by and large it was just a bit of desert. It was clear that a different someone else wanted it more than recent history's tenants had expected, and the outcome was a fairly straightforward case of the contrasting political perspectives on the financing of different defence budgets.

`We won't get a penny more out of the Treasury now. Even if I agree that our job is not yet done, any extra financing will go directly to land and air defences. The Desert Line is perceived to be closer to the southeast than is Alice. We have suddenly become second-rate, and the principal job is someone else's.' Bluing was frank in his reading of the Cabinet mood. `For the moment, gentlemen, that is it.'

Most of our blokes wanted to go out and get roaring drunk, but I turned down Rob's invitation to a liquid supper. It was too facile a way to put immediate emotions behind me, marks burnt in by the strains of these short weeks' war, but then he'd not trodden the same path over the previous months, only coming into the fray at the end.

I walked out of the building and took a long and wandering path back to my quarters, now a small flat in a military residence. Crossing a park I watched two very small children being shepherded by their mother from swing to slide, unknowing and innocent of my cares. Their delight was in the moment, the thrill of releasing one's own tiny body into the hands of gravity, controlled only by the shear strength of the chain or the friction of the slide. The mother saw my concentration and flickered a smile at me, proud of her offspring and their momentary good behaviour. But I also saw through it, a uniform an eternal pheromone to some women, worth a smile.

I came out of the trance, smiled back, looking at the children as if they were mine and Anne's. At a moment like this it would be all one needed, to be able to find a different solace in the unquestioned love shown by a tiny hand in one's own. I found I wanted that touch very badly.

I prepared my own supper, a light meal made from the few things not gone bad that I 'd bought at some time over the past few days. My mind was still elsewhere, remembering but not really feeling what had happened, and there seemed to be no linear track to it all, just a continual jumble of recollected images, half mine, half my imagination, from the days spent watching the plot and living the urgency and fears of the crews at sea. I had no wish to have been there, and felt only a slight guilt at being alive when many others were dead, but it seemed an unclean ending to what I'd done. A glass in my hand seemed to prod some corner of my memory, and I recalled the image of the two fish in eternal pursuit incised in the bottom of the small dish I'd bought Anne. That was it, of course, no end at all, history continuing to be made in the ashes of today, tomorrow close on its heels.

But what would I do tomorrow? Not the endless reviews of naval policy and strategy that would occupy the days ahead, but tomorrow. Was this the pinnacle of my career, the time I would later see as golden, if bloody? Had the Service a future for me, or was I bound for a desk job now, no future at all? I'd get out if it were that. But perhaps for a few days at least I'd let my body command me, something I had not let it do, neither since Leach had died nor since I'd not said goodbye to Anne.

I had new knowledge now. That life can be too easily wasted in a sun-drenched complacency. I'd crossed my own Soekarno Line, which I'd found a bitter divide. I'd survived, but had found the crossing rough. And I was still at sea, would be for a while, until meaning came back. But that meaning would only come out of healing. And I thought - no, I knew - that there was one thing that would bring that healing, one thing worth doing. And that's what I'd do tomorrow.

Epilogue

What a blow we struck! What a new dawn the invasion offered our country!

Of all the elements the most important was the secret Memorandum of Understanding, bringing Indonesian recognition of Chinese claims to historic title over islands in the South China Seas in exchange for precisely-timed, full-scale Chinese manoeuvres against Taiwan. This was the tool which brought the initial bottling up of any thought of American participation in Australian defence. From the beginning it was a great risk, but victory demanded it.

And the justification, apart from our need for that land if our nation was to survive? Australian occupation of East Timor was a sore rankling at the very heart of Indonesian identity. Even a single independent state in our archipelagic chain of islands had the potential to destroy what the military and our greatest leaders strove to build for over decades. Before they assumed authority over East Timor under the cloak of UN authorization, Australia had continually interfered in our right of self-determination with its moaning over perceived violations of human rights, America's deputy sheriff in the South Pacific. So one had also to understand that Australian flat-footed forays into Asia, once Timor was under its belt, would not stop.

Maybe not grabbing more of our territory, on this or that UN pretext. But intrusions, ever-deepening intrusions into our way of doing things and our choosing of our own path to the future, these would only be a matter of time. Few Australians understood Asian ways, Asian values. Yet they were convinced that they knew best, that theirs was the model for all. It took little analysis to understand that, in our case, one could not rule two hundred million with the laxity with which they ruled their handful, especially when their claimed democratic principles had been underwritten by the easy affluence that came from a distribution of the region's resources disproportionately in their favour. What price China's billion?

But, even if we had not had just cause to react against Australia's presumptions, we did require Western Australia. We needed a New Java and its intended wave of transmigrants. So the means had to be engineered to achieve the social goals of the invasion, even if there were a good chance that the military methods failed to achieve everything we wanted. But, retaining the territory was not the be-all and end-all of our Minister's strategy. Boat people bring different dimensions to any struggle, though of course we could not know for certain, were we forced to retreat, whether Javanese Muslims would be offered the same consideration as Timorese Christians.

And there was an outflow, indeed a near exodus, to those vast 'open' spaces of New Java. So, whatever was to happen to those people, were Australia to consider not giving in, our Minister remained confident that Java would now be easy. And the rest of the country looked as though it wanted to climb on the same wagon. Opportunity was a great ethnic leveller, and he who offered it a hero.

But I knew that such 'success' would only be second-best. The ideal outcome was the only *outcome worth contemplating: New Java had to be taken in a bold stroke and then held with enough pioneers and military defence to render the costs of any response beyond consideration. Sun Tzu reflected on the importance of war to the state, but we expected the West to refuse to understand this. We expected righteous reaction and simplistic arguments such as the law against aggression, and convenient absent-mindedness about how often the West itself has honoured that law in the breach. Does not the imperative of a nation to survive stand outside mere manmade law?*

In a sense I failed Sun Tzu. Perhaps I thought the use of technology requiring more than the simple strength of a throwing arm rendered modern warfare different. I was sure he was wrong when he said that 'foreknowledge' could not be elicited from calculations. I thought that I had considered everything. Of course, I did not think that everything would go according to 'plan'. Indeed, I had planned for that, one might say. In a way there was no plan, but rather a continuously-linked set of changing possibilities for which there had to be contingent solutions.

It was inevitable that the Americans became the thorn. Even though our Chinese allies respected our MOU to the letter, it became clear to the Americans slightly sooner than I expected that it was again a case of Chinese sabre-rattling over Taiwan, even if they were the largest sabres America had ever seen. It would later be revealed that US Intelligence had found out – from Chinese courses or Indonesian sources, no one has yet been able to prove for certain – that it was only a case of China reminding Taiwan of what it could do. So the Americans realised that they had been duped, 'taken for a ride' one US Admiral said in his own memoirs 'by a cosy agreement'. No state could be allowed to get away with that. And so, the bald eagle turned its hawk-eye southwards.

There was never any question of the ANZUS response, whatever it turned out to be, undoing what the naval strike had achieved. By Allah's Grace, that went well! Amin, guided by the Laksamana, proved incontrovertibly that we had recognized Australia's weakest maritime moment. Our nation's pride in itself and its past was restored. Nothing would change that fact. But the American factor meant that

*New Java's right to exist, our people's right to feed themselves, would be denied.
When, even as the Jenderal was pacifying Learmonth, the news came of the first
ships of the US Pacific fleet in the China Sea taking a southerly course, I knew
then – we all knew – that we would be a nation under siege for some time to come.
And so it was that the Jenderal's last remark to me, before giving his green light
for take-off, contained a heavier irony than I, in my youth, understood at the time.
'Even so, 'kendro, this will take time.' His use of the diminutive, I now know, was
his way of showing kindness.*

Excerpted from Rusman Soekendro, LetJen (ret'd),
No Game At All: Memoirs of a Strategist

I t was early afternoon, and though the woman was looking forward once
again to that unique Sundanese sequence - wind, rain, silence, drum - the
three of them knew they had come to the end of this first visit. It had been
arrived at in a sense of mutual harmony, each still with his or her thoughts, but
with many of them aired, and some of them altered. The Australian was content
with the black and white of history, and while he had to cope with the fact that
he'd been a tool in the Indonesian armoury, it had not been complete news to him.
The Javan was content with the new beginning he had shaped between three
people; Allah in His wisdom would decide whether it had been shaped correctly
and how it would unfold. The woman, too, sensed a new beginning, but if it had
any shape at all, it was away from the agnosticism of her past; what that implied
for her future she had no idea at all, but she suddenly knew she was looking
forward to the road.

The Javan walked with them to the front gate, where a taxi waited to take them
to the train station. The *ibu* stood under the overhang of the roof, a large smile on
her ageless face, happy at the days they had spent under her care. *'Selamat jalan,'*
she called. Safe journey.

At the gate the Australian turned to the Javan. 'The *Jenderal*, Rusman, did he
understand what would happen to him?'

The Javan clapped his hands in delight at the Australian's continuing
preoccupation. 'Ah, *pak* Trevor. If I tell you everything now, what reason will you
have to come back?'

'Because you want me to talk to your students, that's why.'

'Oh no, *pak* Trevor. I mean to this house, to this valley.'

'I would do that out of friendship, Rusman. Not because I had more questions.'

The Javan was evidently touched. 'And you, *ibu* Anne. Will you come back?'

The woman looked around, and saw the thunderheads gathering above the tapestry of the valley. 'Yes, *pak* Rusman. I will always come back.' Wind, rain, silence, drum.

'*Selamat jalan,*' said the Javan. Safe journey.

'*Selamat tinggal,*' they responded. Stay safely.

Acknowledgement

Author's Notes on Sources and Navies:

This is a work of fiction, so the naval dispositions in this novel are imaginary. But the hardware facts are *very* close to the truth - the relative balance between the Indonesian and Australian navies within the decade is accurately reflected. My Australian class and ship names are my own, but they represent actual ships and naval strength at the time this conflict was fought - though I've chosen to go to sea with a slightly older fleet than the political context would suggest. However, there is risk attached to attempting to adhere to reality, quite apart from a reader's disbelief at my interpretation. One has only to consult the McIntosh & Prescott June 1999 report to Australia's Minister of Defence (was at http://www.navy.gov.au/8_archive/collinsrep/creport.htm) to know that I gave my Battle Group West more operational submarines (by one, *Magenta*) than Canberra could probably have sent to war. Perhaps the West Ocean Fleet actually has an extra, modern surface ship that I ignored.

Regional military capacity clearly worries Australia. Since 1994 there have been at least two reviews. The first shows how easy it is to fall behind on previous commitments to maintaining even just the *status quo*. Even if the current exercise were to result in a significant increase in resources being allocated to defence, a significant overall improvement in defence capability itself could take a decade or two. It requires little imagination to understand that both internal and external political forces could change drastically in such a period.

It must also be stated that this is a story as much about Indonesia. Emerging nations tend to be overlooked in terms of ability to take on 'emerged' democracies. Perhaps, here, I have been able to underline a fundamental difference in relative views of a future which, one day, I feel sure *will* have to be addressed. Whether I have foretold anything is irrelevant. Rather, there are issues of desperation that must lead one to ask whether regional dynamics will not, eventually, require something of the nature of the ultimate outcome of this book actually to happen.

I acknowledge several important catalysts to my imagination. Jane's

Fighting Ships of the World remains invaluable as an information source. The *Far East Economic Review* was a continuing source of up-to-date regional news (including Australian defence capabilities) essential to anyone with interest in the future directions of Asia. *The Jakarta Post* offered similar, more detailed, insights on Indonesia. Admiral Sandy Woodward and Patrick Robinson wrote *One Hundred Days*, the account of Woodward's command of the British Fleet during the battle for the Falklands. *Outback Australia*, Lonely Planet's Guide, by Ron Moon and others, was essential reading. It is the '94 Australian Defence White Paper which is 'quoted' by the Shadow Defence Minister. Many other reference sources, e.g. Cooksey, R.J. (1987), *Review of Australia's Defence Facilities*, were essential background reading.

East German Ships

Indonesia purchased (a unilateral decision by then Minister for Science and Technology Habibie) 16 Parchim-Class corvettes, 14 Frosch-Class landing ships and 9 Kondor minesweepers, terms used in this novel, in 1993 for $12 million. Initial expectations were that Indonesia would spend an additional $314 million in Germany for 'overhaul' prior to delivery, and a further $340 million in Indonesia on additional refits upon arrival. It is not known how much was spent in either Germany or Indonesia, or what overhauls have been done. Widely described (especially the corvettes) as obsolete, Jane's states: '....the [corvette] class is widely reported as being very active.'

Acknowledgements

Specific thanks go to Bill Thomas, RCNC (ret'd), Phil Thomas, Tim Babcock, Luc Spyckerelle, Dennis Goonting, Captain Roger Portch, BA (ret'd), and John Nurse for help and support. I thank various other friends for comments on the manuscript. To Eric Wright, my mentor from the Humber School of Writers, thank you for not rejecting the whole rough draft out-of-hand. Eddy Yanofsky, ex-Associate Director of Humber, was an essential catalyst. Thank you to Meghan Thomas for help on the cover and map.

To Craig Scott (in particular) and Jennifer Barclay I add my thanks for a complementary vision, which gave me the energy to undertake final revisions, and (to paraphrase Griffith's Sun Tzu), *[to] move when it was advantageous and create changes in the situation by dispersal and concentration of forces.*

For my wife, Ana.